★

Verging on panic, she focused on her driving, gripping the wheel even tighter. Despite her efforts, it became increasingly difficult to make even the smallest adjustments necessary to keep the car on the highway. The Bronco displayed a tendency to pull to the right and she had all she could do to keep from running into the concrete railing. She tried again to slow the vehicle, but the Bronco wouldn't respond. She stomped on the brake with her full weight. Nothing. She jerked the emergency brake. Nothing.

Clyde stared at the road, knuckles white from the strain, wrists stiff. She mustered all her strength, focused all her will on keeping the vehicle in its proper lane and headed straight.

Once off the ramp, she took a deep breath, but her relief was short lived. And premature.

★

MURDER
a la Carte

PRUDY TAYLOR BOARD

W☯RLDWIDE.

TORONTO • NEW YORK • LONDON
AMSTERDAM • PARIS • SYDNEY • HAMBURG
STOCKHOLM • ATHENS • TOKYO • MILAN
MADRID • WARSAW • BUDAPEST • AUCKLAND

For B. M. Foster

MURDER A LA CARTE

A Worldwide Mystery/August 2006

First published by ArcheBooks Publishing.

ISBN-13: 978-0-373-26573-2
ISBN-10:   0-373-26573-5

Printed in U.S.A.

Acknowledgments

My thanks to Enid Perll, a friend whose insights are profound; to the *Bloody Pens*—Chris, Dawn, Graeme, Jay, Joe, and Linda—for their Thursday night slashings and gashings of the work-in-progress; to Joanna Sinchuk of *Murder on the Beach Bookstore* for her unflagging support of mystery writers including this one; and to the production crew at WXEL-TV. The errors are mine; the success must be shared.

PROLOGUE

THE LAST RESORT

HE STRUGGLED AWAKE, disconcerted by the sensation that the bed was moving. He strained to see, but the dark was impenetrable. *Where was the window?* Rolling over onto his side, he pushed back the sheets and groped toward the nightstand to turn on the light, but recoiled when his hand struck something solid.

A wall. Rough. Gritty. Unfinished concrete.

He sat upright in bed. That wall hadn't been there when he'd gone to sleep. The air in the room was different, too. Stale. And cold. Much colder than when he'd fallen asleep.

Was this a dream? Was this a nightmare?

He touched his face. The familiar wrinkles and furrows were warm, solid, real. *You can't touch or feel in dreams,* he reasoned. Puzzled, he thrust aside the sheet. He turned away from the wall, and with arthritic joints complaining, he tried to get out of the king-sized bed, but collided with a barrier on the opposite side as well.

Another concrete wall.

Crawling on his hands and aching knees, in the void dense with darkness, he moved across the broad expanse of the spongy mattress to the foot of the bedstead.

Blocked again.

Panic pumped surges of adrenaline through his body. His heart throbbed and rushed. An icy sweat laced his brow and he shivered. He was trapped in a concrete vault barely large enough to encompass his bed.

But why? And where am I?

He struggled to remember. The fear made it difficult to think and reason, but he couldn't give up. Think. The night before he'd consumed a splendid dinner, prime rib, and in addition to three or four Scotches before and during dinner, he'd consumed several Drambuies after dinner. He'd gone to sleep in his room. He should have known he'd feel this bad in the morning.

Morning.

The concept of a new day aroused an incredibly poignant awareness of his life, which he now realized was not a limitless span of time. He had taken the concept so terribly for granted. He envisioned blazing sunshine. Blue skies. Imagined the fragrance of fresh, clean air. The taste of life and freedom.

What kind of cage or pen was this? And who would do this to him? He had enemies, but that was just business. Surely his foes weren't this inhuman.

He pummeled the abrasive surface of the wall with his fists, desperate to make a noise, to attract attention. His knuckles stung and bled. He sucked them to make them stop hurting, acutely aware of the taste of his own warm, salty blood.

Surely this was a joke. An expensive practical joke. A wave of relief followed by anger swept through him. He sank back against the pillows. That damned Sam! It had to be him. Such a prankster. Surely this was one of Sam's jokes. And they would laugh about it later. But not until he had chewed Sam's ass. This stunt pushed the limits, the envelope of friendship and—

A sound shattered the stillness: a hissing.

He pressed his back against the headboard of the bed. *Could there possibly be some kind of snake in this cage?* He held his breath for several moments and listened, concentrating intently, but he sensed no life force other than his own.

The air. There was a subtle change. Oily. *Could air be oily?*

His throat tightened and he clutched his chest. His eyes burned and watered. He grasped his throat with both hands as his esophagus began to spasm. *What was happening? Shit.*

Now he couldn't breathe.

His lungs burned and ached, praying for air. Images of his loved ones crowded his thoughts, but only briefly. As the need for air became desperate, bargains, deals, mediations, negotiations swam through his mind. *If God will let me live, I'll—*

A pain ripped across his chest. Gasping for the precious oxygen, he clawed at the cold, unrelenting wall with bloodied fingertips.

Got to get OUT!

Striations of pain flooded his body and the need for oxygen burgeoned so rapidly he could no longer think coherently. Like an animal, he raged and tried to scream for help, but didn't have sufficient air in his lungs to manage more than a croak. Although he fiercely battled to inhale, his lungs issued the final indignity, the final betrayal. They ceased to function, failing to draw in the air he so desperately needed. They were dead in his chest. Unmoving. Unresponsive in their final paralysis.

Barely conscious, he listened as his heartbeats, at first reverberating in his ears like a slow, deliberate jackhammer, slowed and faltered.

My God, he thought, *I'm dying…*

His brain succumbed to the nothingness. An eerie silence enveloped the chamber as his bodily functions shut down one by one.

Outside the Florida sun smiled, the warm waters of the Gulf of Mexico kissed the sandy beach and a new day began at Far Horizons.

ONE

"IF CLYDE COLBY can't hack the cooking show, buy out her contract and dump her." She'd recognized the voice on the phone immediately—the station owner in Philly talking to WTBR's general manager in Miami. A hundred and twenty-five miles and two and a half hours later, the words still scorched her ears.

Damn the bastard. She'd worked too hard, taken too much shit to give up now.

The rain thrummed on the roof of the Bronco, meshing with the static of the police scanner on the front seat next to her. She glanced out the window ignoring from habit the more routine 10 signals. "Ten-four. All okay. Ten-eighteen. In service." The Tamiami Trail between Miami and the turn-off to Rattlesnake Key was a narrow, antiquated ribbon of asphalt that grazed the edge of the Everglades, twisting through miles of uninhabited swamp—although civilization was eating away at the crusts of the Everglades much as if they were a delectable pizza pie.

Clyde sighed with relief when she drove off US 41 onto the causeway that led to Matecumbe Road, the main highway girding the perimeter of Rattlesnake Key. A small, discreet sign positioned between torturously entangled trunks of two Queen Palms bore the stylized logo of the Far Horizons Resort, assuring her she was headed toward her destination.

"Car One, what's your ten twenty? Come in, Car One," the voice on the scanner asked. *Uh oh,* she thought. *Lost your police chief, have you?*

Four or five miles down the road she reached the resort. Maneuvering past a parking lot crammed with BMWs, Mercedes Benzes, Bentleys, Lincolns and Cadillacs, she pulled in front of the entrance, stopping next to a Rattlesnake Key police car. Her instincts as a former police reporter kicked in. *Now why would a police car be here?* she wondered as she turned off the motor. Since there was only one cruiser, the problem couldn't be serious and she had a hunch she knew Car One's location.

A quick, stinging gust of rain drenched her as she stepped out of the Bronco even though she was partially shielded by the canopy over the resort's entrance. Shoving through the double glass doors, she sloshed across the tiled lobby floor, silently cursing her squeaking Nikes. Her favorite shoes and they were ruined. She brushed back damp, unruly chestnut curls that framed her heart-shaped face.

Shifting from one wet foot to the other as she waited in front of the registration desk, she banged the service bell. The sound jangled her nerves and the headache that had lurked behind her eyes all afternoon pounced with all the zest of heartburn after a particularly spicy gazpacho with jalapeno peppers.

"I'm sorry, we have no vacancies," a young, gruff male voice said to her right.

She whirled and choked back a gasp. Confronting her was a creature with the letters *"m a e t h"* scrawled in the putrescent flesh of his forehead. The creature looked at least seven feet tall, but she glanced down and saw that he wore cumbersome shoes with thick, built-up heels and a heavily padded, long-sleeved shirt and trousers. The face and clothes were covered in a plastic substance that glistened like wet clay.

"I'm Clyde Colby," she said, dumping her shoulder bag on the desk. "Of Gourmet Galley. The TV show. We're doing a shoot here." She scrounged through her leather Gucci purse looking for a Tylenol. "Who are you? Frankenstein?"

"Clyde?"

"Clyde," she said, silently cursing her mother for the millionth time.

The creature stepped behind the desk, punched several keys

on the computer terminal, and studied the screen with the bilious green letters. "Your reservation is for November one. That's tomorrow."

Her head ached. Her clothes were sopping and her patience was in its terminal stages. *Okay, you cretinous mud pack,* she thought, but smiled sweetly and said, "I know tomorrow is November first, but you're expecting me tonight." Rifling through the contents of her purse, she pulled out a fax bearing the return address and logo of Adkins & Lowry, a Miami public relations firm. She slapped down the letter, pointing to a paragraph, which read, "Your stay at Far Horizons has been confirmed with an arrival date of October 31."

"According to our records…" He splayed his big hands on the desk and she saw that the nails, although meticulously clean, were bitten. The cuticles were red and gnawed.

Clyde gritted her teeth, but smiled with as much charm as she could muster. "I'd like to see the manager. Please. Now," she added as the clod stared at her. Finally he nodded and left.

What a lout. Clyde studied the lobby as she waited for his return. One entire wall was coral rock with a huge fireplace. On the other walls were larger-than-life murals that depicted scenes from the Everglades: deer bending to drink from a creek, craning their graceful necks to avoid cypress knees that surged up from the water like wooden stalagmites and unaware of a bobcat perched on a tree branch above them, waiting to pounce; glassy-eyed alligators sunning themselves on the banks. Wicker rockers, chaises and Areca palms lent a flavor of the late 1940s and reminded her of a scene from the classic film noir *Key Largo. If Humphrey Bogart were here, he'd know what to do,* she thought. *Naw, Lauren Bacall. She'd get some action for sure.*

Clyde glanced outside beyond the tiled patio, beyond the sandy beach to the restless water beyond. The Gulf was grouchy today, choppy with rolling waves.

She paced restlessly past a piano bar in the dark corner, also bordered by potted Arecas. Despite everything that had happened, she could hardly wait to get into the kitchen and watch

Henri Doucette, the resort's chef. He had a recipe for Acapulco Lime Snapper that, while simple to prepare, reportedly rivaled anything James Beard had ever created.

Sniffing, she detected the odor of charcoal. Someone was cooking on a brazier and it reminded her of the week she'd spent in Haiti shortly before young Papa Doc fled to Paris. She'd been doing a piece on political unrest in the Caribbean for the *Herald*'s op-ed pages. Everywhere she'd traveled in Haiti the air had been rife with the scent of charcoal cooking fires.

A flurry of movement.

She half turned in time to see two tanned, muscular blonde men in their late twenties or early thirties step onto the patio. The men glanced around. Seeing no one, they vanished only to reappear a few seconds later. This time they carried an awkward burden wrapped in a white cloth. A design had been painted in bright red on the sides of the cloth. As they grew nearer, Clyde found it difficult to believe what she was seeing. It looked as though they carried a body.

Couldn't be, she chastised herself. *You need more rest.*

But as they passed, the cloth jerked back revealing a hand that bounced lifelessly in an eerie rhythm with the strides of the men who carried it. She'd seen her share of bodies, but she'd never conquered that first wave of shock.

From the corridor behind her, she heard men's voices and turned to see the clerk standing next to two men. The heavy-set man wore a police uniform. He was about five-ten with a paunch and black, graying hair. The other man was at least six four with a full head of bushy white hair. Their conversation was punctuated by laughter. The policeman balled his fist and pretended he was going to slug the older man on the chin. The older man ducked, but he was smiling.

She hurried across the lobby. "You," she said to the policeman, "come with me."

Irritated, he asked, "What do you want?"

She grabbed his sleeve. "Two men," she said. "They've got a body."

"What the hell are you talking about?"

The clerk who'd been waiting nearby for a break in their conversation, interrupted. He grasped the taller, white-haired man's arm and nodded toward where she stood. "Father, this is that TV person," he said. "She says we were to expect her tonight. Not tomorrow."

"Listen," she said to the cop, "Two men out there are carrying a body. I saw the blood."

After a pause that lasted two, perhaps three heartbeats, the policeman cocked an eyebrow. "Well, what about it, Horace? Are you doing something with a body?" The words were spoken in a serious tone, but the left corner of his rather full mouth twisted upward in a wry, half smile.

The older man looked puzzled, not worried. He stood quietly for a moment. Then the gelid blue eyes widened and a laugh worked its way up from deep in his stomach. "Yah," he said, pounding the policeman on the arm. "Come. Let me show you."

He walked toward the patio in strides so long she had trouble keeping up. "Todd," he called as he slid open the glass doors that led onto the patio. "Raymond. Stop. Come back. And be sure to bring the body."

By now she had caught up with him, as had the policeman and the clerk. The two blondes responded like soldiers, but wearing the uniform of the resort—khaki shorts and shirts bearing the Far Horizons logo. They about-faced and carried their bloody charge to where she stood.

"Show the lady the body," Horace ordered and they lowered the sheet and its contents onto the *Saltillo* patio tile. One of the men bent and pulled the sheet back. She stared into a mannequin's painted blue eyes.

"You see," Horace pointed to the corpse which looked like a department store dummy, "our body is very dead, but tonight he'll be the life of the party—the Halloween party, that is. He is the victim for our murder game. A surprise treat for our guests."

Clyde felt her face grow hot.

The policeman grinned. The two blondes stood expressionless, waiting for instructions. The clerk looked mildly triumphant. "Now Davy, what were you telling me about this lovely lady?"

The son smiled nervously as he explained who she was and how she thought she had a reservation for this night. Followed by his father, Davy went back inside the lobby and pushed through an old-fashioned wooden gate into the area behind the desk. "She has this letter." He pointed to the crumpled fax lying on the desk.

Beck glanced at the fax. His face grew taut with barely concealed irritation. "Find a room. Take care of it," he snapped. "Do your job." A condescending smile eased his stern features as he turned back to Clyde. "We can always find room for such a lovely guest," he said. "I am Horace Beck." He extended a tanned, leathery hand. "The owner." She gazed into ice blue eyes peering at her from beneath thick, frost-colored brows and a face with the appealing tan of a crusty Beef Wellington. "Unfortunately, we are full. Because of the special Halloween promotion," he added. "But we can certainly find something."

In contrast to his son, Beck was not in costume. He wore khaki slacks and a casual shirt with a pattern of large red hibiscus. His bearing was rigidly erect.

"Thank you," she said as Davy again consulted the computer.

Had she imagined it, she wondered, or had Horace Beck's blue eyes chilled ever so slightly when Davy told him she was with the media? She'd learned over the years that not everyone was thrilled by reporters and cameras. If that was the case with Beck, he was quick. He had collected himself in less time than it would take to shake salt on a rack of lamb.

"But father," Davy interjected, "the only room we have is," he paused and almost whispered, "room nineteen, next to room seventeen."

But the policeman had approached the desk and he and Beck were chatting and Beck seemed not to hear.

Davy splayed his hands nervously on the countertop. "I don't know if it's…suitable," he said lamely.

"For God's sake," Clyde said, her patience exhausted. "I'm soaking wet and I'm tired. It's suitable."

Davy glanced apprehensively at Beck who had walked to the front doors with the police chief. "I really shouldn't. Not without father's approval."

Clyde gritted her teeth and grabbed the registration card. She signed her name and under the blank left for the room number, she printed nineteen in huge numbers.

"Horace," the chief was saying, "Have fun at your party tonight. I'll catch ya later."

She couldn't resist. "Call your office," she said. "They don't know your ten-twenty. I picked it up on the police scanner as I drove in."

The chief, for she could tell by his uniform that he was indeed Car One, looked at her in surprise. "How do you know about ten signals?"

"In a past life, I was a police reporter for the *Miami Herald*."

He said nothing, but looked toward Beck who shrugged. The cop gave her a half-salute then turned on his heel and left. For a moment she felt lucky to be out of the news business. Getting quotes from cops had been a pain in the ass.

Horace Beck turned his full attention on her again. "Even though we didn't expect you until tomorrow, we're delighted you're here. We are always honored when lovely ladies grace our humble establishment."

Bullshit, Clyde thought. Aloud, she asked, "What about my crew? They'll arrive tomorrow. You are expecting them, aren't you?"

"We will check, Miss Colby," he answered coolly, and she suspected he was not accustomed to his charm being rebuffed. "Davy? Check the computer, please."

Davy nodded and returned to the computer. The keys clattered and he announced, "We have two rooms for them. In the annex."

"Good." Smiling pleasantly, Beck asked, "Perhaps you will indulge us and join our Halloween festivities this evening? Having a TV personality would add such luster to our little party."

More bullshit. Clyde shook her head. "Sorry. I'm bushed. And I had a long drive in the rain."

"But Miss Colby," the elder Beck persisted, "it would mean so much to our guests. You have quite a following on this coast. And you will see the good use to which we put your corpse." He smiled again.

She could almost hear the WTBR general manager's voice in her ear. *"Think public relations, Clyde. To get this show into America's living rooms, you're going to have to eat, sleep and drink promotion and public appearances."*

She said, "I don't have a costume."

"I'm sure Grace, my wife, can find you something."

When his father was out of earshot, Davy reached below the counter for a keycard and pushed the registration card back toward her. Once she had filled it out, he came from behind the desk to lead her down the hall. "I'll show you to your room. Staff's setting up for the party."

"What are you?" she asked again.

He straightened so that he towered above her. "The *golem.*" He paused in the corridor and pulled an oversized, old-fashioned metal key from his pocket. "Wait here a minute." Opening the door to what she could see was a supply closet, he disappeared a few moments then reappeared with towels over his arms. His hands were filled with bars of guest soap, shampoo and conditioner.

The *golem.* She'd heard of it, but couldn't remember what she'd heard. Had to be some kind of a monster.

Immediately adjacent to the closet, Davy paused in front of a door with a small metal plate engraved with the number seventeen. He moved on to the next door, to room nineteen, opened the door and ushered her inside, placed her luggage on the rack, put the towels and soap and other toiletries in the bathroom, checked the air conditioning, drew the draperies and moved to leave. She fumbled in her purse for a tip, but he shook his head.

"Not necessary," he assured her, closing the door carefully as he left.

The headache attacked. She retrieved the Tylenol container

from her purse and headed for the bathroom where she swallowed the tablet with a sip of water. Shrugging out of her wet clothes, she left them piled on the floor and toweled off before returning to the bedroom.

The luggage. She knew she really should put her clothes away and get organized. But the queen-sized bed was so inviting. She slipped beneath the covers, luxuriating in the feeling of the crisp, starched sheets against her bare skin. *For a moment,* she told herself. Only long enough for the medication to take hold.

The pain eased and she dozed, dreaming of bloody, dismembered bodies that turned into Barbie dolls wearing red thong bathing suits. It seemed only minutes later that she struggled awake, roused by a rapping on the door. She glanced blearily at her watch. More than an hour had passed.

Half awake, she scrounged through her bag for her robe, donned it and hurried to the door. The woman standing in the hall wore a dirndl skirt and ruffled drawstring blouse—the costume of a peasant. Her blonde hair was pulled back in thick braids. Blue-eyed and apple-cheeked, she looked as if she were her early to middle thirties, but Clyde guessed she was in her forties because of the fine lines around her eyes and mouth. She carried a garment bag.

"I'm Grace," she explained. "Mr. Beck said I should bring you this costume and make sure it's okay."

"Please, come in." Clyde unlatched the guard chain and stepped aside so she could enter.

The woman shook her head. "Oh, no. I'll just leave this." Her cheeks grew crimson and she lowered her gaze. Clyde realized the woman was either incredibly shy or frightened and that the color in her cheeks was not rouge, but natural. Clyde nodded and accepted the costume. "I'm sure it's fine."

After Grace left, Clyde realized she had called her husband Mr. Beck. Some marriage, Clyde thought. *Mister Beck,* she decided, *really cracked the whip.* And apparently he didn't have much use for his son either.

What kind of place was this anyway?

It took only moments to slip into the fishnet hose and the abbreviated French maid's costume with its miniskirt. The black uniform fit a bit too snugly. There's the *Drambuie mousse,* she mused patting her hips. And there's the *crepes suzette* from lunch last week. She patted an incipient double chin. Better use a darker foundation makeup to draw attention away from that area. When she'd finished her makeup, she studied herself in the mirror. Not too bad for thirty-five. Still, given the shelf life of TV anchors, it was just as well she'd moved out of news and into food. She thought of Julia Child, ninety years old and only now slowing down.

Party sounds beckoned as she walked down the narrow corridor a few minutes later. She followed the music onto the patio overlooking the Gulf of Mexico. The afternoon cloudbursts had cleared the atmosphere and the air was fresh. The Gulf was peaceful. In a party mood tonight, she thought. Japanese lanterns were strung around the perimeter of the patio, but their light was pale compared to the full moon. With Creedence Clearwater's version of *Bad Moon Rising* as a backdrop, the area was crowded with gyrating ghouls: red-mouthed vampires in black cloaks, werewolves wearing *faux* fur, the *golem,* even an outdated O. J. Simpson wearing a football costume and brandishing a long, shiny fake knife.

A tall, well-built Popeye in a sailor suit lounged against the railing almost directly across the terrace from her. His arms bulged with padded muscles and a can of spinach dangled from a rope around his neck. His sailor hat was tilted at a rakish angle. *Too bad I'm working,* she thought idly.

Popeye was deep in an animated conversation with the Emperor Nero. A laurel wreath crowned Nero's white hair and his pudgy body was sheathed in a toga. As she watched, a man wearing a periwig and a colonial costume with tiny square glasses perched on his nose joined them. Benjamin Franklin.

At the northern end of the patio, a white-uniformed chef stood behind a row of braziers on which he roasted chunks of meat on skewers. Next to him were tables on which a variety of appetizers had been artfully garnished with sea grape and croton leaves. The traditional entrees such as Rumaki were displayed, but there were also some interesting, innovative canapés. The ice sculpture in the shape of a Tarpon was impressive. She pushed her way through the crowd until she reached the food tables.

"Henri Doucette?" she asked.

He shook his head. "I'm Frode, his assistant," he answered, offering her one of the skewers. "Care to try the specialty of the island?"

"Love to." She took the skewer, carefully biting into one of the small chunks of white meat. Crispy and hot. Mild flavor. It tasted like chicken, but it wasn't. She gave up at last. "What is this?"

He grinned. "I should have warned you. It's rattlesnake."

"Not bad."

She sampled other appetizers—coconut fried jumbo shrimp, smoked mullet pate served with chopped chives—then sidled through the crowd to the bar festooned with plastic jack-o-lanterns and black cat silhouettes. She ordered a vodka tonic from the bartender who was dressed as Robin Hood. As she waited, Popeye crossed the patio to stand beside her.

"Got any Glenlivet, Sullivan?" he asked.

"For you, Sam? Sure." The bartender reached beneath the bar. "On the rocks?"

Sam nodded. "One rock. And Nero wants a Manhattan. Makers' Mark. Up." He turned to face her, leaning an elbow against the bar. "Recent arrival?"

Clyde sipped her drink. "Are you going to ask me what my sign is?"

"No." His bone structure was strong and prominent. His black hair was thick and slightly unmanageable. "What's your name?"

"Clyde Colby. Like the cheese."

"Clyde. That's an unusual name for a woman. But I like cheese."

She felt her face grow warm. "What's *your* name?"

He extended his hand. "Sam. Sam McKenzie. I have the local sailing school. Can I interest you in lessons?"

She shook his hand. Callused. "No, thanks."

"Why the look?" When she didn't answer, he said, "You just wrote me off. The right eyebrow. It nearly soared off your forehead and it said I failed the test."

She cleared her throat uneasily. "It's simply that most of the wind jockeys I've met are arrogant and pompous, but then I prefer the power of the horses. I like to get where I'm going." Then, thinking of her image and her less than adequate PR skills, she added lamely, "Of course, there are exceptions to every rule."

He laughed and blew on his fingers as if he had picked up a hot saucepan without a hot pad. "What do you do, Clyde Colby, when you're not putting down wind jockeys?"

She mustered the energy to brighten her smile and explained about the Gourmet Galley.

"Of course. You're quite the celebrity in South Florida. It's that costume. Otherwise I would have recognized you. I get a kick out of the way you *grill* the chefs. But it works. You get more inside information out of them than any other interviewer on TV. So you're going to be here a week?"

She nodded.

"Join us?" he said pleasantly, gesturing to the table where Nero waited. The cleft in his chin deepened when he smiled. "Nero and I like food and people who like food."

"Nero?"

"Arthur Pennington Dunn, the third. I've taken him sailing a few times and we've become friends. Although Nero is CEO of a Fortune 500 company, he's not much for parties so we've been chilling out together."

Without waiting for her answer, he took her hand and led her to their small round table at the edge of the patio. Benjamin Franklin had joined their table. Short, about five-four, with balding gray hair and a weak chin, he said his name was Greg Lanken and Sam whispered that he was CEO of Lanken Images, a major printing company with branches in ten states. An interesting man in his late fifties, she soon learned Lanken had traveled around the world and could tell wonderful stories of skiing in the Alps and tarpon fishing in the Bahamas where he'd barely escaped having his yacht hijacked. He'd spent six months living on a junk in Hong Kong, had spent several months in the Valley of the Kings in Egypt on an archeological dig, and could tell revoltingly fascinating tales of eating dogs.

Now that she knew Lanken was a printer, she realized his Benjamin Franklin costume was appropriate. "I've chartered the boat for a deep sea fishing trip tomorrow," he said. "There's plenty of room."

"Thanks for the invitation," Sam McKenzie responded quickly, "but I've got lessons scheduled. Now Nero here..."

"...would love to go," Nero agreed. "What time are you booked to leave?

"Six."

"Sounds good. I'll kick in on the cost," Nero offered, adjusting his toga, which was slipping off his shoulder.

"No way. It's all taken care of."

"Then I'm getting the next round of drinks and dinner tomorrow night."

Lanken said, "Miss Colby, you're included."

"No, thanks. I'm here to work." Finishing her drink, she rose. "Heavy day tomorrow."

Sam McKenzie shoved his chair back and rose, too. "I'll walk you to the lobby."

They made small talk as they walked down the corridor, but her mind was already on the next day. She was sorry she'd missed Doucette, but he was supposed to be available first thing in the morning. And she wondered which cinematographer Rod the Clod would send. She hoped it wasn't that preppie Mark Sawyer. She'd requested Andy Zabrinski, but Rod—

Her thoughts were interrupted as she realized they had reached the lobby and that Sam McKenzie was still talking. She shook his hand, but he wouldn't release hers.

"Are you sure I can't change your mind about sailing with me tomorrow?"

"No, thanks. I told you I have to work." She pulled her hand free.

"Then we'll have dinner tomorrow night. On my boat. And I'll cook. Now that's an offer you can't refuse."

"Why can't I?"

"Because if you do, you'll always be curious about the man who had the stones to offer to cook for you, the discerning cooking show host. Besides, you'll wonder how good a cook I really am."

"I don't even know you."

He straightened and stood as if at attention. "Name's Sam McKenzie. You already know that, of course. I'm forty-three, so if anything should happen between us, you won't be corrupting a minor. I was born in Cincinnati, Ohio and went to school there. Served my country as a Marine during Desert Storm and I was a stock broker in Baltimore before moving to Rattlesnake Key. Feel better?"

When she hesitated, he said, "Tell you what. I'll invite Penny to join us. As chaperone."

"It will have to be a very early evening."

"Great. I'll pick you and Penny up at seven."

"Do you always get your way?"

He leaned over and brushed her on the cheek, a light whisper of a kiss. "I try," he said.

She could feel his eyes on her as she walked down the corridor to her room.

Unlocking the door, she was delighted to see the maid had turned down her bed. She freed herself from the skintight costume, breathing a sigh of deliverance. She shrugged into her nightshirt, battling with herself over whether or not to eat the mint on her pillow. She lost.

Licking her fingers delicately, she slipped between the sheets and turned off the light, hoping this was not going to be one of those nights when she replayed every mistake and every pivotal scene of her life. She closed her eyes and tried to focus on the next day's shooting, but she kept seeing the expression on Josh's face.

When her ex-husband had dumped her eight years ago for a much younger check-out clerk from the local Publix, he'd accused her of being too cold and driven to be a good wife. He said he wanted a wife who was "a simpler, less complicated woman." And then, six months ago, the station manager had dumped Clyde from the six o'clock anchor slot. "You get too involved in your stories," he'd told her. "You care too much, take too long, lack objectivity."

He was right. She'd done exactly that. It had started in part because things at home had been so bad. Josh had been so controlling that she'd used her work as an escape, which had become a habit. It was the one place where she was more or less in charge of her own destiny. But those days were over and the cooking show…what a godsend. She'd loved food and its preparation since she'd been a little girl, and had helped her Dad in the kitchen. Cooking had been his hobby. As a circuit court judge, he'd needed a way to unwind and escape the images of the tragic people who populated his courtroom. The kitchen had been his sanctuary. How wonderful now to make a good living doing something she enjoyed.

The *golem*. Why couldn't she remember the golem?

She groaned and punched the pillow. She was not going to do this to herself. Not tonight. She breathed deeply, forcing herself to empty her mind, to relax until at last she dozed off.

THE MOON WAS LOW in the sky when the muted rumble of a motor somewhere close awakened her the first time. She groped for the travel alarm on the nightstand. The clock's luminous hands indicated 4:00 AM. The sound might have come from either the next room, room seventeen, or the parking lot. At least it didn't last long. Beginning with a grinding start-up burp, it segued into the rhythm of an oiled, smoothly running engine. The entire sequence lasted no more than a minute.

She'd just dozed off when she was aroused again by the same barely discernible rumble. Again it lasted no more than a few minutes, and again she looked at the clock. 4:19. Curious and more alert, she sat up and waited, but the sound did not repeat.

The next time she was awakened by thuds and bumps outside her window. *Now what?* Fumbling in the somber, semi-darkness, she clutched the clock. Six-thirty. The light filtering through the Venetian blinds was gray. She hated mornings. Her years on the news side had conditioned her to work afternoons and nights because that's when most news stories broke. Would she ever get used to the early hours?

She straggled from bed and stumbled to the window. Pulling back the draperies, Clyde peered through the slats of the Venetian blind. Two white-clad figures wheeled a stretcher out the double-doors leading from the darkened restaurant.

Rattlesnake Key Emergency Medical Services.

Ambulance attendants.

And their burden was clearly a body with a sheet pulled over the face. A body, not a department store dummy left over from the murder game. And no body bag. But then again, this was a small town. They probably didn't have to deal with many corpses.

As they rolled the gurney along the sidewalk in front of her room, one of the attendants tripped on the white sheet covering the corpse. The cloth fell away revealing the blue, lifeless features of Greg Lanken. He was as dead as Ben Franklin.

An hour or so later when Clyde was on her way to the Gulf for a quick swim, she overheard two waitresses talking. They were taking a smoke break on the terrace and standing on the other side of a Carissa hedge.

"Another guy bought the farm last night. Heart attack," the first waitress said.

"Another one? That's the second in six weeks. What's going on here? Is this an unhealthy place or what?"

"Beats me," the first waitress replied. "But if anybody else around here dies, I'm boogying on down the road."

"Yeah," the second girl said, "and you'll have to boogie fast to catch up with me."

The water was warm even though the breeze was a little brisk and the swells were gentle. It should have been a peaceful, relaxing moment, but it wasn't. Was something going on at Far Horizons?

TWO

An hour or so later, Clyde sat at one of the tiny wrought-iron, glass-topped tables on the terrace at Far Horizons resort. All traces of the Halloween party had been cleared away. She'd enjoyed a brisk swim and now the sun had risen and was gently toasting her shoulders. The sultry air felt good. She sipped her coffee and nibbled a fresh croissant lathered with butter and sea grape jelly that had been served in seashells.

Good presentation, she thought. The peach-colored linen napkins were starched and ironed. The napkin rings were made from coral and decorated with tiny coquina shells. A nice touch. And using shells as servers, another interesting idea. Even her father, a circuit court judge in Miami, would appreciate the table this resort laid. Big Clyde was a closet chef. He'd even had taken several courses at the *Cordon Bleu* in Paris. She'd lived with him after her parents' divorce and he had taught her to appreciate good food and attractive presentation as well.

Turquoise waves tipped with whitecaps surged toward the resort's pristine beach. To the right, a path meandered through the dunes following the shoreline. The breeze, laced with a hint of brine, played tag with stands of sea oats that fringed the dunes.

Beautiful. And she should have been happy as a clam in marinara sauce, but she couldn't erase the image of Greg Lanken's body from her mind. He'd seemed fine the night before. Full of life and enthusiasm. He should be fishing for tarpon at this very moment, not lying on a slab in a mortuary in Rattlesnake Key.

Heart attack? Probably. That's what the waitress had said. Wasn't that what killed most men his age? But why had Davy been so nervous when she'd asked what happened? Simple answer; a death at any resort was bad business. Even worse, this was the second death in six weeks. Of course, he didn't want to discuss it. Still, it was curious. Far Horizons wasn't that large a resort.

As she watched, Todd and Raymond raked the beach. Blond and deeply tanned, today they wore crisp white briefs bearing the Far Horizons blue and peach logo. A sea gull swooped low over the waves while a fat brown pelican perched on a piling at the resort's dock. The scene was peaceful until Todd picked up a shell from the beach and pitched it at the awkward bird, driving it away.

A sailboat skimming across the horizon reminded her of Sam McKenzie and their dinner date that evening. It would be interesting to see if his cooking skills matched his guts in offering to cook for her.

She glanced at her watch. 8:00 AM.

Her crew should be arriving from Miami within an hour or so. Time to get to work. She folded and placed the napkin on the table, stood, stretched and inhaled. The air was so clean. What a treat. But it was time to get to work.

On the way to her room, she paused in the lobby, scanning the huge room for possible sites to film. It looked so different in the morning light…cheerful, inviting. But the serenity was disturbed by the sound of angry voices and, as she watched, a blonde woman emerged from one of the offices. She was carrying an armful of fresh cut gladiolus blooms and she was crying. Clyde recognized Grace who began arranging the flowers in tall vases, which she placed on driftwood coffee tables, positioned in front of oversized leather sofas. As she approached, Grace looked up, and wiping her eyes, fixed a nervous smile on her face.

"Was the costume all right?"

"Perfect." She wanted to ask what was wrong and if she could help, but she sensed Grace would be uncomfortable if she pried. And besides, it wasn't any of her business.

"Did you have a nice time at the party?" Grace asked pleasantly, but then turned her head away and Clyde knew she didn't want to talk.

"Very nice," Clyde said as she continued toward the elevator. Her reporter's instinct kicked in and she stopped. "Are you all right?"

The already distressed woman took a deep shuddering breath. Her already pale skin grew even paler. "Oh, yes. Yes! I am fine. Everything is fine," she insisted as she forced a smile, then her eyes widened in concern. "Please. You must not mention this to Mr. Beck. He would be very displeased."

Clyde nodded slowly. "I won't say a word," she promised as Grace scurried away. *Beck should be upset,* she thought. Because his wife was obviously terrified and very unhappy. She passed the Surfriders cocktail lounge on her way to the elevator. *Open at 11:00 AM* read the gold leaf letters painted on the door.

On the far side of the fireplace near the entrance was the gift shop named Knicks and Knacks. Clyde wandered over and peered through the window. A gray-haired woman with a short, mannish haircut had the cash register open and was transferring cash and coins from a bank bag into the drawer.

The merchandise was typical. The shelves were crowded with out-of-town newspapers, magazines, paperbacks, notions, tanning lotions and sunscreen. One display case contained interesting coral and shell jewelry and the racks of swimsuits, beach coats and casual dresses warranted a closer look when she had time.

Back in her room, Clyde stripped off her bathing suit and donned slim-legged jeans and her favorite orange and blue University of Florida Gators tee shirt. Slipping her feet into comfortable moccasins, she pulled the case containing her laptop computer from the closet and placed it on the wicker table near the window overlooking the tennis courts. On the other chair, she stacked her supplies: extra disks, legal pads, 3 x 5 cards, chamber of commerce brochures on the resort and Rattlesnake Key.

Booting up the computer, she started to work. She couldn't

write the voiceovers until she'd talked with Doucette and knew what recipes he'd be preparing. However, while a lot would be ad-libbed live on camera, she wanted to get at least a rough draft of an opener and closer scripted.

Time passed quickly. When the telephone jangled, she jumped. Notes slid from her lap; papers scattered on the carpet. Hurrying across the room to the phone on the nightstand, she picked up the receiver.

"May I speak to Dade County's answer to Julia Child, please?" The welcome sound of Andy Zabrinski's voice resounded in her ear.

She felt an overwhelming sense of relief. "Zee man! So Rod the Clod came to his senses and sent the best man for the job. I was afraid he'd send that new guy, Mark Sawyer, just to spite me. Where are you?"

She and Andy had worked together for several years. They thought alike. And he was so damned bright that sometimes it scared her. He could make an overflowing trash can look like a piece of art. The other guy Rod had threatened to send was good, but he didn't have Andy's willingness to dive off the deep end— photographically speaking—to get a shot from a different angle or to try a new concept. Everything would go better now.

"In the lobby."

"Registered yet?"

"Habitation processing in progress."

"Enough already. I'll meet you there in half an hour. We'll check out the kitchen."

"By the way," Andy said, "Dade County's answer to Judge Wapner called me at the station and left a message for you."

"What did Dad want?

"Seems a certain tomcat, the one named Tyler. You know, one of the four that your father's babysitting while you're off playing Mizz Important TV Star…"

"Oh, shit. What did Tyler the Terrible do now?"

"Sprayed Big Clyde's briefcase. It was open. And had important papers in it. While Tyler is still alive and well, I'd worry about his future."

"Is this an FYI or am I expected to return home immediately to discipline Tyler?"

"Just an FYI although you might think of taking old Dad some very expensive single malt scotch as a peace offering. MacAllan would be appropriate."

"At thirty bucks a shot, I'd think so. You didn't explain that Tyler was actually expressing his approval of Dad, that Tyler was just staking out his territory?"

Andy cleared his throat. "No, when your father is in that frame of mind, I listen and agree. But I emphasize that something in the way of a reward or expensive gift of appreciation is definitely called for."

"Got it."

Replacing the receiver, she returned to the table and shut down the computer. She ran a brush through her hair, freshened her lipstick and plowed through the piles of papers and notes strewn around the room searching for the room key. She finally found it in her jacket pocket.

I've got to get a system so I don't spend two-thirds of my life looking for my keys and my purse. Now where's my damn billfold? She found it in the drawer of the bedside table where she'd stowed it the night before. Picking up a notebook from the table, she hurried from the room.

In the corridor, she closed her door just as a uniformed maid emerged from the adjacent room. The maid grabbed the handle of the laundry cart to wheel it down the hallway, almost running into Clyde.

"Watch it," Clyde snapped wishing immediately she could take back the harsh tone. But the feisty tone came naturally. She was the product of two different styles of child rearing and the real world. Her mother, a product of the 1950's, cautioned her to be pleasant and sweet, constantly reminding her men did not like outspoken girls. On the other hand, her father who'd brought her up after the divorce hadn't told her anything, but by his example cut through the crap of everyday life, dealing with things head-on. And then, of course, there was the reality of life in the media business.

Management—at least in the Miami market—was ninety-five percent male and treated women, despite the emphasis on political correctness, as if women weren't terribly bright and had to be led to the appropriate conclusions, had to be helped to think. She'd learned early on that if you didn't stand up and speak out for yourself, you were considered a mushroom—kept in the dark and drowned in bullshit for fertilizer.

The girl whirled quickly, concern registering on her pleasant face. "Oh, I'm so sorry. Did I hurt you?" The maid was slim, a little taller than Clyde, and her hair was a vivid red. She had a tiny, crescent-shaped scar on her chin. "Are you all right?"

"I'm fine. You surprised me." Clyde started toward the lobby then remembered the events of the early morning. "By the way," she said, turning slowly, "Have you heard whether or not Mr. Lanken's family has been notified? Are they coming down here?"

The girl's deep-set eyes looked troubled. She said, "Mr. Beck doesn't like the help talking about our guests and their business."

Clyde shrugged. "Thanks anyway." Bemused, she strode down the hall toward the lobby and her meeting with the chef and Andy, thinking about the conversation she'd had with Lanken the previous evening. He'd been so enthused about his vacation that he'd told her was a birthday present paid for by his twin sons. The sons were officers in the family printing business.

How sad for them, she thought. His death made her appreciate the upturn in her own fortunes even more. Never mind that she was under pressure, she had worked her way through the anger, hostility and damaged self-esteem resulting from the divorce and even from the demotion from six o'clock anchor. She still hated that airhead Mindy who'd sweet talked herself into the anchor spot. Mindy's professional background was limited to modeling eye makeup for a cosmetics manufacturer in New York, for God's sake. But she'd always wanted to be in TV and now she was.

Clyde had to give her credit. She learned fast. And it didn't hurt that the camera—any camera—loved Mindy's face. From any and every angle. But, Clyde smiled sweetly, Mindy had very fine skin. It would age quickly.

Clyde brightened when she spied Andy beneath the huge mounted silver tarpon that hung, centered, over the registration desk. His long, thinning light brown hair was parted in the middle and drawn back in a ponytail. A day's stubble dusted his cadaverous face. He wore jeans and a white shirt, sleeves rolled up, open at the neck revealing a chest of curly hair. A light meter and a St. Christopher's medal hung around his neck. When he saw her, a grin stretched his wide mouth almost the entire width of his face.

"Hi, Babe," he said, giving her a quick hug. "How ya doing?"

"What's new at the station?"

"You mean since yesterday?"

"Things were sort of edgy when I left. I wasn't sure for a while whether I'd still have a job after the way I left Rod the Clod's office."

"Hey, Kiddo, you're talent. We management types expect a modicum of temperament. However, you didn't have to call him an asshole." He shook his head.

"But I didn't," she protested. "I distinctly remember commenting that he was an outstandingly well-formed anal cavity. That's not the same thing at all."

He smiled, displaying even white teeth. The one front tooth had a slight nick. "What about telling him his ideas were bullshit?"

"Andy, I was definitely misquoted. I said most of his ideas were bovine defecation."

"Remember, Clyde," he gestured with his light meter, "Rod's the new kid on the block. The company didn't transfer him from our sister station to tell them everything's in great shape. He's got to prove himself. But here's a reassuring bit of office intelligence garnered from an impeccable source at the water cooler. They're designing a Web site for you. Even hired a hotshot Webmaster. There's going to be the cutest little animated Clyde cooking up her favorite dishes as a promotion. It'll feature a new recipe every week—which you have to provide. Now where's this wondrous kitchen?"

"Why didn't anybody say anything to me?"

"I told you. You're talent. They'll tell you when you need to know."

As if summoned, Horace Beck emerged from behind the key rack at the desk. "Miss Colby, Mr. Zabrinski," he addressed them. "I hope your accommodations are satisfactory."

Andy nodded. "Fine, Mr. Beck."

"I was sorry to have to put you in the annex, Mr. Zabrinski, but we are very full. The season begins early. What about your room, Ms. Colby?"

"Noisy."

The same expression of barely concealed irritation she'd seen earlier reappeared. "Noisy? What room you are in?"

"Nineteen."

The expression on his face darkened and Clyde decided she was glad she wasn't Davy.

"Davy put you near the auxiliary generator?" Beck was saying. "I cannot believe he did that. We use it to power our air conditioners when the weather's unusually warm and also if we lose power during a storm. We can solve that problem easily. Davy will move your luggage to the room we had reserved for you while we're in the kitchen with Henri."

Grace appeared and timidly tugged on her husband's jacket sleeve. He turned.

"Yes, what is it?"

Grace colored, but smiled. "Mr. Beck," she said, looking up at him from beneath white blonde lashes, "Did you want to talk to that salesman about new uniforms for the maids?"

"I thought you cancelled that appointment. We discussed it and decided now was not the time to buy new uniforms. And I am very busy. I was just talking with Ms. Colby and Mr. Zabrinski. We are about to go into the kitchen."

"Oh, I told him, but the salesman said he needed to talk to you. He said there was a sale." She looked at Andy and Clyde. "I'm sorry to interrupt." She glanced back at Beck and started to leave.

"Wait," he said as she turned to leave, apparently thinking she had been dismissed. "I will talk to him, but first I must arrange with Davy to change Ms. Colby's accommodations. Can you imagine? Davy put our special guest in one of the rooms near the generator. What was that boy thinking?"

"But we were full last night, Horace."

"No excuses. You're always making excuses for that boy. Now go tell the salesman I will be there in a few minutes." His voice was final. He turned back to Clyde. "I'll make arrangements with Davy to change your room. Go straight to the dining room. Tell the lady behind the cash register to take you to Henri in the kitchen."

Moments later as they entered the kitchen, Clyde paused, glanced around, took a deep, deep breath, exhaled and smiled. "I love kitchens."

Andy walked past her and stood a few steps ahead studying the room. "You better. You're going to be spending a lot of time in them."

Commercial kitchens were no-nonsense places. Utilitarian, ugly chambers where beauty resided in the end product—the food—not the process. However, she mused, there could be beauty in the efficiency and symmetry of a cook's crew that knew what it was doing.

She watched as Andy took the measure of this kitchen. It was a challenge to set up shots so that a kitchen looked interesting, but Andy was terrific. Sometimes, depending on the kitchen, he used mostly close, tight-in shots. Sometimes he photographed the pots and pans and stoves, the rows of metal tables, the hanging racks of spatulas and other kitchen utensils so that their forms and shiny, metallic hues and textures were appealing. This one would be tough because it was small and the natural light source, which was high and off the beach, would be difficult to control. She walked over to where he stood. "Wow. Look at that."

"What?"

"The stove." She pointed to what looked like a counter with coils under glass. "It's one of those electronic induction cook tops. Portable. Doucette must be trying it out. These things are hot in Europe, but slow catching on here."

"Why?"

"Why what? Why are they hot or slow catching on?"

"Hot."

Clyde smiled. "I've only read about them, but they're hot because they're not. They won't even turn on let alone heat up unless the proper pot is placed on them." She pointed. "Those coils form an electromagnetic field and that agitates iron molecules in the pots to create heat. So you have to have the proper pots, cast iron or steel, to generate heat. After a while, the heat from the pot warms the surface right next to it, but most of the surface remains cool." She studied the stove, reading the manufacturer's name. "Molteni. That makes sense."

"Why? It sounds Greek to me."

She laughed. "French. And it makes sense since Doucette is a very French chef who's never deserted his roots."

"How about his tubers?"

"Enough of the bad jokes already." She waited a beat or two and asked, "What do you think?"

He shushed her with a hand gesture and paced the perimeter of the room. When he was back at her side, he said, "We'll make it work. Not to worry. Do you know where you'd like to do the stand-up intro?"

She shook her head. "When you're through here, let's take a look at the terrace. Also there's that gorgeous coral fireplace in the lobby." As they conferred, a short, plump, dark-haired man with a thin, handlebar mustache approached. He looked exactly like the television version of the Belgian detective Hercules Poirot except that he wore a chef's cap and a wrap-around apron.

"I am Henri Doucette," he said with a very pronounced French accent. "And you are Mees Colby? *Oui?*"

"Oui," she responded.

"Shall we get to the work?"

She nodded. "Chef Doucette…"

"Henri, please," he interrupted.

She smiled. "Henri, this is Andy. His job is to make us both look good."

"For me," the chef said patting his ample middle disparagingly, "Mr. Andy, you have cut out your employment." Henri's chocolate brown eyes crinkled and the ends of his mustache twitched. He put his finger alongside his nose. "You know," he said, pretending to be serious, "I am a very, very famous chef. My friends tease, but I am in Larousse's *Gastronomique*."

"Larousse's *Gastronomique?* Henri, that's the culinary bible. I had no idea…"

"Just a leetle mention," he demonstrated by holding his thumb and forefinger about half an inch apart. "If you look under Doucette, you will see that it is another name for corn salad." He burst into laughter, a hearty sound that filled the kitchen. "So, with such a name, how could I not have been a chef?"

Andy looked puzzled.

Clyde relaxed. A chef with a sense of humor. What a treat. "Indeed, Henri, you were fated." She turned to Andy, "Henri was saying you have your work cut out for you," she explained.

Henri nodded.

"Nothing we can't handle," Andy said.

She couldn't resist asking how he liked the new stove and saw his eyes widen with surprise. "*Mais oui,* I like it, but…" He shrugged, "I don't know if I would like the entire kitchen dressed with the electronic stove. They have no—" he searched for the word, his eyebrows surging upward while he thought "—heart," he said after a pause. "I would miss, how you would say…the sight and sound of the flames kissing the sides of the pots."

Beck burst through the kitchen doors, impersonal and full of business. He immediately directed the conversation to the menu and after considerable discussion of possible dishes, Clyde felt comfortable with their choices. Henri agreed to a menu featuring Florida's tropical fruits. *Gasparilla Papaya Soup, Avocado en Gelee Salad, Acapulco Lime Snapper* and *Calabaza Flan* for dessert*. The preparation of the dishes

---

*Chef Henri's delicious recipes can be found in the Appendix to this novel.

would be dramatic and interesting to photograph. The meal would be the last segment of the show and shot in the Far Horizons dining room.

She turned to Andy. "Then if Henri agrees, we'll start shooting in the morning."

"*Mais oui*," Henri agreed, nodding enthusiastically to underscore his agreement. "The morning is fine."

"Yes, we can do that." Beck interjected his approval, Clyde felt sure, to establish the fact that it was his resort and he was in charge.

"Splendid, gentlemen," she said. "That will give me time to drive onto the mainland and do some research."

"Research?" Beck's thick white eyebrows rose so high they almost touched his hairline. "What research? I can tell you everything you need to know."

She smiled pleasantly. "I'm sure you mean to be helpful, Mr. Beck, and I appreciate it. But I won't tell you how to run a resort if you don't tell me how to do my job."

Behind her, she heard Andy groan.

Beck's face folded into a carefully created mask. His voice was chilly, but he merely responded with, "I see."

AFTER LUNCH, it was early afternoon before Clyde could get away. The sun was beginning its downward journey as she drove off the island. Once on Rattlesnake Key Causeway, which led to the mainland, her thoughts shifted from her destination to the previous conversation she'd had with Horace Beck. She was still curious why Horace had been so reluctant to appear on camera with her in the final segment.

Actually, reluctant was an understatement. "No, no," he'd told her. "No cameras." His frosty blue eyes and pursed lips radiated stubbornness. He wouldn't even discuss it.

When she was having dessert a little later—the Calabaza Flan, which Chef Doucette had insisted she try, Grace had joined her for a glass of iced tea. Grace mentioned almost immediately that the PR account exec in Miami had made a mistake, convincing Clyde that Grace was the family peacemaker.

"Mr. Beck's regular account executive at Adkins & Lowry was on vacation," she said, toying with her napkin. "Mr. Beck says his substitute was only supposed to take care of the print ads while he was gone. Mr. Beck understands the need for print ads, but he has never liked having people from the media here. Except for travel writers." She blushed. "Not you. I mean he doesn't dislike you."

Her discomfort was so obvious and so painful Clyde suffered for her as Grace took a sip of her tea before adding hurriedly, "It's nothing personal, Miss Colby. One time a reporter for a major newspaper interviewed him. He was so badly misquoted that he's avoided the media ever since. The new advertising man didn't know that when he committed the resort to doing your show. Mr. Beck says he was trying to make himself look good while his boss was out of town."

"Knowing that helps, Grace. I'll check everything with him to be sure he's happy." Clyde smiled. Grace's sweetness shone through the shyness. "But there is something you can do for me."

"What's that?" Grace had said, flushing again.

"Call me Clyde."

Grace nodded, but Clyde knew she was asking too much and regretted saying anything.

Later, Clyde realized Grace's comments still didn't explain why he was so adamant about not being on camera. Especially since she had offered to give him every question ahead of time so he could even write out his answers if he wished.

As she left the resort after going upstairs to change, she'd seen Grace again, this time at the far side of the terrace. Grace had been staring across the waters of the Gulf and weeping, her shoulders gently shaking. She had dried her tears when Clyde approached, but her red, swollen eyes had given her away.

"What's wrong, Grace? Is there something I can do to help?" Clyde had asked. "You're obviously very upset about something—this is the second time today…"

At first, Grace refused to answer, twisting her head from side to side. Her face had flamed scarlet to the roots of her white blonde hair. Even her body language, the way she leaned away from Clyde told of her panic at being caught in such an emotional state.

Looking away from the tortured woman, Clyde said, "This is one of the most splendid views in all of Florida. How fortunate you are to live here, to see this wonderful spectacle every single day of the year."

Grace had wept again, but not noisily. The tears had spilled quietly. "It is beautiful and I love it here. But..."

"Yes," Clyde probed gently.

Grace paused and when she continued, the words came in a rush as if she had wanted to say them aloud for a long time. "But it is not as beautiful as it used to be. Underneath there is much ugliness. If I didn't love Mr. Beck and Davy so much..."

"What do you mean?"

Grace's face blanched. She clasped her hands together in her lap so tightly the knuckles were white. "Please, Miss Colby. Please. Don't tell Mr. Beck I said anything. He gets furious when we discuss anything personal with outsiders. Please, promise you won't say anything."

"But you haven't told me anything," Clyde started. Then realizing how distraught the woman was, she agreed. "I promise, Grace. I won't mention what you said to anyone if you don't want me to."

"Oh, thank you. Thank you." Her gratitude was almost embarrassing.

Now as Clyde drove across the causeway, she wondered what was so ugly. Was it Beck? He appeared to be a dominating, condescending macho asshole, but ugly? In doing her research at the Miami Public Library while deciding which restaurants to feature on the show, she'd found an article about Far Horizons published in a travel magazine several years earlier.

In a sidebar, Beck had been profiled as a real comer in the resort business. In a few short years, despite the fact that his background was in engineering and that he'd made his first fortune by inventing a superior stabilizing system still used in all BMWs, he'd taken Far Horizons from a debt-ridden has-been

of a motel and turned it into a profitable, world-class resort. The
article also described his early years growing up in Argentina
and his move to the United States in 1974. Beck had been
quoted as raving about the beauty here and how deeply he
loved Rattlesnake Key and the resort.

What ugliness?

THREE

THE WHEELS OF THE BRONCO droned rhythmically as Clyde drove the two-lane concrete span that linked Rattlesnake Key to the mainland. The five-mile causeway had been built in the early 1930's and the lights were strongly influenced by the design of Colonial coach lights. The bridge's concrete side rails resembled the rungs of a staircase. And, in contrast to modern bridges and causeways, its sidewalks were at least five feet wide. It had been dubbed the "World's Most Fishingest Bridge" because so many locals dropped lines over its railing catching an impressive variety and quantity of fish.

Ahead, cars slowed and stopped. The drawbridge was stuck in the upright position, jaws agape like a monstrous, metallic maw. As Clyde coasted to a stop, she looked at her watch. One-thirty. She'd gotten a late start and now this. She hadn't scheduled any appointments, but she had planned on getting to the newspaper, the library and maybe the mall.

Clyde waited a few moments then turned off the motor so it wouldn't overheat and got out. A blonde head gleamed in the sun as a driver leaned out the window of a nondescript green Chevy four or five cars back. Was that Todd from Far Horizons? Squinting, she saw that it was and smiled, then waved. To her surprise, he ducked his head back in the car without acknowledging her greeting. *Screw him.* She was about to turn away a few seconds later when he stuck his head out the window and nodded.

The crazy idea that he was following her popped into her head, but Clyde immediately dismissed it as nonsense.

She wandered to the bridge's railing. The pale green waves

surged and subsided, surged and subsided. The movement was mesmerizing. She yawned and stretched. She was sleepy. Must be the combination of getting up so early and the salt air. She leaned back against the railing and stared at the sky.

White puffy clouds scudded by reminding her of how people scudded into and out of her life. One day they were there, the next day they were gone. Greg Lanken came to mind. Of course, most of them didn't die—they moved on. Sometimes there was a reason. Like Josh, her ex-husband.

She thought about the men she'd been involved with since her divorce. God, she had lousy taste. There'd been Ritchie, the up-and-coming attorney, a dynamo in bed, dynamic at parties, and ultimately a dud. He was delighted to be out with a television personality—because he figured it would help his career. Even her Dad had warned her about him. Then there'd been Carr, the actor: wavy blonde hair, gorgeous blue eyes, great physique, great dresser. Carr had lasted until she figured out he was also seeing his personal trainer, Bryce. She scrunched her face gazing up at the sun and enjoying its warmth despite the ever-looming danger of wrinkles that Jinks, the studio makeup guy, was always warning her about.

She liked the freedom of being divorced now, but the selection of men available for meaningful relationships that didn't necessarily lead to the altar had a lot in common with a supermarket shelf filled with dented cans.

The problem, she reasoned, was that she was a sucker for a handsome face. *Why? Why were looks so important?* Was it because she'd never felt attractive, never felt quite good enough and being on the arm of a good-looking, desirable man told the world she counted? *Counted?* As if math entered this equation. Character, Clyde, she reminded herself. Character is what counts. She'd have to remember that because Sam McKenzie, the sailing instructor, was another pretty face. Too bad, Sam. Your loss, Sam. She would not repeat her mistakes of the past. One dinner. A pleasant, properly chaperoned evening and that was that.

A grinding rasp cut the air. The driver in the green VW

Beetle ahead of her car cranked his engine as the drawbridge slowly, noisily descended, registering a complaint with each twist of the winch. She slid back into her car, switched on the ignition and looked at her watch. One-forty. Not too bad. If traffic moved briskly, she'd get everything done she'd planned.

Unfortunately, the traffic moved about as rapidly as a snail threatened with ending its existence as *escargot à la bourguignon.* It took her another half an hour to get off the causeway because an old Mustang had rear-ended a maroon Ford Crown Victoria. When the Crown Vic was struck, the force of the collision propelled it sideways so that it partially blocked both lanes. She had to drive with two wheels on the sidewalk to get past. Edging cautiously around the accident, she passed a green and white Everglades County Sheriff's patrol car and a tow truck creeping to the disabled vehicles.

Scratch the trip to the mall.

It was well after two when she finally drove past the Royal palms that lined the off-ramp, followed Main Street to Carson Avenue, turned left and then right onto Gulf Boulevard.

Palmetto Bay was a delightful old town, she thought, shifting her attention to her destination. She'd learned from her research that it was established as a military fort during the Seminole Indian Wars. Fort Carson had been renamed Palmetto Bay and deactivated for the last time following the War Between the States in 1868. She'd been here once or twice on get-away weekends so the town wasn't totally unfamiliar. As a native of Sarasota, there were few corners of the state she hadn't traveled and investigated.

Despite the sprawling growth encircling it on three sides, Palmetto Bay remained an enclave of the past, a good-sized city with a small-town mentality. The streets were lined with palms, and blossoming hibiscus, and homes that told the history of the town's growth. In the outer fringes of the town, the houses were newer and larger and had obviously been built in the 70's and 80's as the result of the influx of Northeasterners who flocked south after the completion of I-75. A few blocks closer to the heart of town, the houses were rectangular concrete boxes with lots of glass typical of modest homes in the 1950's. As she neared the downtown section, the homes showed the architectural influence of the Mediterranean villas so popular in the 1920's. In the center of the downtown area, most of the buildings were the old two-story frame Southern Colonial homes built at the turn of the century from durable heart-of-pine lumber.

Gulf Boulevard was the main drag. The joke around town was that if you ever got on Gulf, you couldn't get lost because sooner or later you passed anywhere you needed to go.

Driving down Lee Street, which intersected Gulf, she spotted the yellow brick Everglades County Courthouse with its Doric columns and wide granite steps, and then the Palmetto Bay Public Library, a modest frame, two-story bungalow on Hancock Street. She pulled into the parking lot, grabbed her purse and notebook and emerged into the sweltering heat of the afternoon sun as Todd drove by. This time she didn't wave.

A bell jangled as she entered the library. The air-conditioned interior was so chilly she shivered then looked around. At one time the library had obviously been someone's home. The enclosed porch where she waited was the reception area. A desk stood at a ninety-degree angle to the door. The black plastic nameplate on the desk read Lillian Albritton. And in smaller letters was printed the title Librarian.

As Clyde stood on the sisal rug waiting for assistance, a woman entered. Petite and imperious, she was dressed in a pale blue, raw silk shirtwaist dress. She wore her gray hair long and loose, drawn back on the one side with a barrette. An ice queen.

"May I help you?" Her blue eyes were friendly and her tone cordial belying the cool image she presented.

You've got to stop judging people by their appearance, Clyde scolded herself mentally. "Ms. Albritton?" The woman nodded. "Yes," Clyde continued, "yes, you can help me."

"Good." The librarian gestured to a wicker chair next to the desk. "Do you want a library card?"

"Oh, no, I'm just staying a few days. But I need to use your reference section. I'm staying at Far Horizons. We're doing a television show there and I want to learn more about Rattle-snake Key and the resort's history."

The librarian said pleasantly, "So you're staying at The Last Resort. A television show. How interesting." She paused thoughtfully. "I don't know how much help I can be," she said, toying with the heavy silver and turquoise ring she wore on her right hand. "We have very little information on Far Horizons. The owners stay very much to themselves. Seldom come to the mainland. I don't even think they buy any of their supplies here. But I can help with Rattlesnake Key." She led the way into what had been the living room.

The room was filled with shelves containing fiction and reference books, three exits and a staircase. Small placards over two of the three doors indicated the functions of the rooms beyond. On the right, the room was labeled "Children's" and inside Clyde could see small wooden tables and chairs. The walls were plastered with bright posters of Winnie the Pooh and Barney the Dinosaur. Three children were reading. One tow-headed, pigtailed tot was sprawled on the rug.

The staircase was adjacent and Lillian Albritton led her upstairs into a small room, which housed the historical collections. Carefully skirting a desk, file cabinets and shelves holding books of all shapes and sizes, new and old, some ragged and discolored, the librarian pulled out a cane-bottom straight-backed chair.

Clyde sat at the desk, plopped down her notebook and searched in her purse for her pen. Lillian opened a file drawer and removed a thick, legal-sized file folder, which she placed on the desk. It was crammed with newspaper clippings, brochures and booklets.

"This will get you started," she announced. "When you're finished with this, I'll get more. I'll be downstairs."

In the quiet room surrounded by the delightful aroma of old books, Clyde submerged herself in the past.

Rattlesnake Key had gotten its name because the island looked like a coiled snake with its rounded shape and winding canal supposedly dug by the Caloosa Indians. The tip of its tail was serrated as though it ended in rattles. A small island looked like the button or tip of the rattle.

Settled by Cuban fishermen in the 1880's, the island had later been the site of a castor bean plantation because castor oil was in demand both for medicinal and industrial purposes. The crop, she read in a newcomer's brochure printed by the Chamber of Commerce in 1921, was destroyed during a hurricane when a tidal surge bathed the plants in salt water. During another period in the island's history, farmers planted acres of vegetables—celery, green peppers, tomatoes and citrus—especially Key limes. *Check to see if vegetables used at Far Horizons are home grown,* she jotted in her notebook.

According to a yellowing newspaper clipping from the *Herald,* the resort business had originated in the 1880's when an early settler started a boarding house for vegetable brokers who came to the island to inspect and buy the crops. Once Thomas Edison began wintering in nearby Fort Myers, international attention focused on the area and soon an exclusive boys' school, founded and headquartered in Philadelphia, had been built on Rattlesnake Key. The boys wintered and roughed it on the island. A hotel was built to house visiting parents and the primitive island developed a *panache* that attracted even jaded European royals seeking adventure. A lighthouse had been constructed because there was so much boat traffic in the Gulf.

During World War II, the island was notorious because many German U-boats had been sighted in the waters off the lighthouse, which was, she read with surprise, still in operation. Supposedly pro-Nazi traitors had infiltrated the area drawn by the island's proximity to two Army Air Corps bases.

The sound of footsteps interrupted her reading and Clyde glanced up as Lillian Albritton returned. The librarian moaned. "Those stairs are going to be the death of me yet. Finding what you need?"

Clyde nodded. "Great stuff," she said gesturing toward the stacks of clippings. Putting down her ballpoint pen, she looked at her watch. "Four o'clock. I had no idea it was so late. Is the newspaper far from here?"

"A few blocks." As they walked down the stairs, Lillian in the lead, the librarian looked back over her shoulder and asked, "What television show are you filming on at Far Horizons?"

"A cooking show," Clyde responded. "Clyde Colby's Gourmet Galley. I'm Clyde." She knew that's what she was supposed to do, but it made her uncomfortable. She enjoyed the food, enjoyed the technical end of the business, and even delighted in meeting the chefs and watching them work, but the promotional part was pure misery.

She hated the candid photos people took because she knew she didn't photograph well in a spontaneous situation. She needed the studio with controlled lighting and a cameraman who knew her best angles. She was also on the tail end of a generation of women who'd been taught it was inappropriate to promote oneself. She had to fight her early training constantly haunted by the time her mother had informed her that well-bred women had their names in the newspaper only four times—when they were born, married, had children and died.

As they reached the bottom of the stairs, Lillian turned. "I thought you looked familiar," she said, a delighted smile curving her prim mouth. "I enjoy your show very much. We get *Broadcasting and Cable* magazine here and I read where you are hoping to start showing it nationally."

"Thank you," Clyde said. She groped in her purse for her car keys.

"I wonder, Miss Colby..." the librarian began, then hesitated.

Not an autograph, Clyde thought with dread. She'd been asked for an autograph a few weeks earlier and really screwed it up. She'd thought the young woman who asked was kidding and jokingly signed it, "Best wishes, Julia Child." The young woman was insulted and she had lost a viewer. Clyde vowed she wouldn't foul up this time.

She pasted a smile on her face. "You wonder what?"

The librarian's face flushed, but she forced the words. "Ah, I was wondering...if you'd...that is, I was wondering if you ever... Do you ever make public appearances doing cooking demonstrations?"

Clyde hesitated then said, "Of course, but I'll have to check my schedule with the station."

The librarian's eyes brightened. "We have an organization called the Palmetto Bay Marching and Chowder Society. It's pretty big. More than four hundred members. Our meeting is next Thursday."

Clyde made a mental note. In the future, she'd book some appearances before she arrived in a new town. Even better would be Rod the Clod freeing up a budget for a PR person to help her.

"Thursday," she said slowly. It would take more time to set up a demonstration than just do a talk as she was accustomed to doing.

"Tell us what you want to fix and we'll get the supplies," the librarian continued. "One of the members will work as a liaison to make sure you have everything you need."

"Where would you do this?"

"That's no problem," the librarian said. "One of our members is the fashion coordinator at Burdine's Department Store. They have the perfect setup for cooking demonstrations. They do them when they introduce new products or small appliances."

By this time, they had reached the door. As Lillian opened it for her, she made her final pitch. "It would be a wonderful treat for us." She extended her hand.

Despite her bravado, Clyde's stomach trembled with trepidation. She'd never done a live cooking demo. Part of her insisted it would be just like doing it in her kitchen. The hell it would. What if the recipes didn't turn out? What if she burned something? The ever-present threat reverberated in the forefront of her mind. *Dump her. Buy out her contract. The hell they would.*

"I'll do my best," she promised. "I'll check with the station tonight and let you know first thing tomorrow. Now where's the paper?"

Following the librarian's directions, a few minutes later she pulled into a driveway past a huge blue and white sign that read *Palmetto Bay Observer* in Courier typeface. She angle-parked in front of an awkward, two-story concrete building finished in sparklecrete. Consuming the entire block, the building had developed in stages. One wing had the 50's square, blockish look with the thick cubes of glass to admit light. Another section, obviously built in the late 70's or early 80's, had no windows and looked like a prison. Relieving the architectural schizophrenia was a hedge of brilliant purple bougainvillea.

Clyde pushed through the double glass doors and halted in the reception area. Behind the receptionist's empty desk, a display of bronze plaques from the Florida Press Association bore mute witness to the paper's quality. The awards the *Palmetto Bay Observer* had won for spot news, in-depth reporting, feature stories and photography as well as layout and graphics were impressive. Framed copies of the *Observer*'s front pages marking historic events—the end of World War II, Kennedy's Assassination, astronauts landing on the moon, Nixon's resignation—dominated the area.

A half-full coffee mug and a pile of unopened mail made it clear the receptionist was around somewhere. Clyde picked up a copy of the day's paper from a stack on a coffee table. Settling on the leather couch across from the desk, she searched for Greg Lanken's obituary. It was too soon, of course, but she got a nice feel for the newspaper. Foreign news dominated page one, but county and local news were also played including a feature on a lost pet recovered after an intensive search.

"Where's Marcy?" a male voice demanded from behind her shoulder.

"If you're talking to me, I don't have the vaguest notion." Clyde answered without looking around.

A tall, skinny man with a head full of bushy dark hair and wearing over-sized horn-rimmed glasses blustered into her view. She judged him to be in his late twenties.

"You're not Lesley," he accused.

"I know that," she said.

"From the back you look like her." He patted the pockets of

his corduroy jacket until he located a pack of cigarettes. He lit one, took a deep drag and sighed. "I'm quitting next week," he said, disregarding a no smoking sign posted on the wall.

"Since I'm not Lesley, I'll read the paper." Clyde slapped the paper in front of her face to blot him from view.

He laughed. "I'm Eli Nussbaum. Lesley is Marcy's best friend. Lesley's supposed to cover a special county commission meeting this evening. She wasn't in the newsroom so I assumed she'd be out here talking to Marcy."

Clyde put down the paper and stared at him. "Should I care?" Did it again. The guy was trying to be friendly.

Nussbaum raised his long, bony arms heavenward as if in despair. His sleeves were about an inch too short and his wrists shot forward. "Forget it. Can I help you?"

"Help me?"

"Yes. You came to the newspaper for something. You're sitting here waiting for somebody to help you."

"What do you do here?"

His intense face brightened. "I'm a reporter."

Clyde shrugged. "Maybe you can. I want to look at some files in your morgue."

He shook his head. "Sorry. The paper's policy doesn't permit the general public access to our morgue," he said. "We provide free copies of the paper to the library and they have them transferred to microfilm. Try there."

Clyde stood. He was tall, at least six five, and so skinny that he loomed over her like a five-tier wedding cake. She tilted her head back and stared straight into his eyes. "So much for professional courtesy."

"Professional courtesy?"

His blank expression was irritating. She rummaged through her shoulder bag, drew out her billfold and flipped it open. She held her press card up for his inspection.

"WTBR-TV out of Miami," he said, arching his neck like a hook so he could read it. "And you're Clyde Colby." His manner changed. A smile smoothed his sharp features. "I love your show. Follow me."

She followed him through a maze of portable partitions, narrow corridors and a newsroom crammed with reporters, desks, and computers and everywhere piles of newspapers, file folders, press releases and notes. In marked contrast to the reception area, the room was alive with ringing telephones, the underlying hum of many different conversations, the clatter of computer keys. A TV set was tuned to C-SPAN.

"Almost there," he said and finally, on the far side of the photo department, he ushered her into the newspaper's morgue. The librarian, busily cutting clippings from the day's paper, barely looked up.

"What do you want to see?" he asked, angling around the counter where huge rotating shelves stood in rows like beige pillars.

"Anything on Far Horizons."

"Far Horizons Resort?" Eli Nussbaum paused. A curious expression brightened his owlish, yellow brown eyes. "Far Horizons," he repeated.

"We're taping a show there."

Eli placed his elbows on the counter. He cocked one eyebrow and doing a rather tortured but identifiable Groucho Marx imitation, said, "Have I got a deal for you."

"I don't want a deal," Clyde said. "I want to see your files on Far Horizons." She was beginning to find coping with Nussbaum rather tedious, but remembered Rod the Clod's admonition to eat, sleep and think image. She didn't need to make an enemy of a print journalist.

"What I mean is I'd love to do a feature story on your show for our paper."

Clyde shrugged. Rodney Delmont would be so proud. One day in town and she was lined up to do a cooking demonstration and now a newspaper feature. Then caution prevailed. "What's the deal?"

"You TV types are as paranoid as we scribes have been led to believe," Eli responded. "You let me come out to Far Horizons to interview you and I will make available to you our morgue and my extensive knowledge of the area and incredible intellect. Deal?" He stuck a bony hand across the counter. "Tomorrow morning?"

"Why not do it here? And now? We start shooting the show tomorrow and I'm going to be really busy."

"Nope. It's gotta be on the scene. You've gotta get me into Far Horizons," he insisted. "That's part of the deal."

"Why do you need me to get you into—"

"Long story," he interrupted, and his expression made it clear he wasn't going to explain.

She shrugged. What did she have to lose? "Deal."

He motioned for her to come around the counter.

LATER THAT AFTERNOON Clyde found herself reluctant to return to Far Horizons. Horace had been friendly and pleasant, but she wasn't blind. The maid and the other employees seemed almost frightened of him. Even his wife and son treated him with inordinate respect. And what did Lillian Albritton mean about locals calling Far Horizons, *The Last Resort?* She should have asked Eli. There was the dearth of information in the *Observer*'s files. For a world-renowned resort, amazingly little had been written. At least locally.

She chastised herself. She was so uptight about the show it was making her crazy. She wasn't going to be at Far Horizons that long so what difference did all this stuff make to her even if it was true? For good measure, she chastised herself for chastising herself. Her mother, God bless Iris Medea Colby's conscientious soul, had so endowed her with the female essence of guilt she even felt guilty for feeling guilty.

At the resort, her room had been changed. Her clothing and equipment had been unpacked and everything had been neatly stowed away. She was now on the second floor with a stunning view of the Gulf of Mexico framed by lushly green, tremulous Royal palm trees. The room was larger, more luxurious. The pastel colors of the design scheme were sea foam green, delicate peach and ivory with gold as an accent. The draperies had a seashell pattern carried over into the fabric of the bedspread and the chaise, which was accented with peach and ivory throw pillows.

In addition to a table with a hanging light fixture, the room boasted a large television set with a wicker chaise positioned so she could watch in comfort. She stretched out on the chaise and clicked the remote, then rose restlessly. She was in no mood to watch television. She wandered onto the balcony and luxuriated in the panorama of surf, waving palms and white beach sprawled before her. Even that didn't relax her and Clyde grew impatient with herself.

Then she realized what was bothering her. The neatness was so precise, it made her uncomfortable. Even her notes and papers. Now why would anyone go to the trouble to straighten her papers, forming them in neat piles, aligning them with the corners of the desk?

Unless it had given someone an excuse to go through them.

Ridiculous.

There was nothing the least bit unusual or even interesting about the rough notes she'd drafted as a very preliminary working script for the show.

Absolutely ridiculous.

She'd even imagined Todd was following her. What was it Eli Nussbaum had said? Something about paranoid TV types. Was the shoe beginning to fit?

She forced herself to think about the evening ahead. Dressing carefully as the sun exploded into a huge orange orb that edged closer and closer to the precipice of night, she smiled. Dinner prepared by Sam McKenzie was sure to prove most intriguing.

Once downstairs, she decided to see if she could find Horace Beck. Part of her, the TV cooking show host, accepted as none of her business the fact that Beck was so determined to stay out of the limelight. However, she'd been a reporter longer than a cooking show host, and her reporter's curiosity wouldn't rest. She wanted to know why. It would definitely be to his advantage to have a presence in the community. Resorts and clubs as luxurious as The Breakers and Mar-A-Lago in Palm Beach, while certainly not accessible to the typical tourist, often opened their doors to charity benefits or community af-

fairs. It was known, she thought sarcastically, as generating
good will.

Davy, who was in the process of being relieved by the night
clerk, told her somewhat abruptly that he didn't know where
his father was, making it clear he didn't intend to find out for
her either. Miffed, she headed down the corridor to the patio.
But she paused by the door of his office. On a whim, she
pushed gently and was surprised when the door opened inward.
She glanced around. The office was empty. *What could it hurt?*

She entered Horace Beck's domain.

His desk was so neat she shuddered. The in/out box on the
corner of the desk contained a few letters and miscellaneous
papers, but they were as neatly stacked as the paper in an unopened ream from an office supply store. The pen/clock/
calendar set on his desk was so highly polished the gold shimmered even in the dim light from the hall. As she drew nearer,
she saw that it was in the shape of a three-pointed star wreathed
with laurel—the Mercedes Benz logo. *Interesting.*

The executive chair was positioned parallel to the heavy mahogany desk. The chair to the side was straight and carefully
lined up with the edge of the desk. It was also much lower than
Beck's and she smiled in recognition of the oldest management
trick in the world, tower over people and you could intimidate
them. Subtle, but effective.

A workbench stood against the wall to the right. A plain
wooden stool, looking out of place, was pushed beneath the
workbench. A fluorescent work light was affixed to the wall over
the bench, which was outfitted with a vise. Very utilitarian.

Dangling neatly from hooks mounted on the wall was
an array of tools—pliers, hammers, saws, different-sized
wrenches, screwdrivers, drills. Schematic drawings of a mech-
anized fishing rod pinpointing power sources and gears had
been neatly tacked at eye level and she judged from the various
components left in plain view on the workbench that he was
making progress on his current project. She was surprised because even though their meeting had been brief, she gained the
instant impression that Horace Beck was not a man who knew

how to relax. Somehow she couldn't envision him going fishing.

She turned her attention to the walls where framed glossy photos of classic Mercedes-Benzes and BMWs hung. Next to each was a schematic drawing of that particular auto's transmission and gear system. Clyde studied the photo of a beautiful powder blue and white model 380K, introduced in 1933 according to the caption. The engine was an eight-cylinder and it had a pointed radiator, she read. It was a two-door model and she was surprised to learn that as early as 1933, car designers had built the seats so that they bent forward to allow passengers to get into the back.

The office door was suddenly opened so forcefully it slammed against the wall. She wheeled around. Horace Beck was standing in the doorway. She could see that his face was red with anger even from where she stood.

"You—" he said, struggling to find words. "You. What are you doing in my private office? This is not open to the public. Out." Quickly he crossed the office and grabbed her by the upper arm, almost shoving her into the corridor.

Before she could explain, he had slammed the office door behind them. Reaching into his pocket, he produced a ring of keys and jammed one into the lock. The sound of the lock clicking into place seemed so loud to her it reverberated up and down the empty corridor.

"I was looking for you," she said awkwardly. "I just wanted to ask you—"

"Yes?" he hissed. "You wanted to ask me what?"

Desperately she searched for some reasonable explanation. "Uh, I wanted to know if I couldn't convince you to go on camera with your chef. When we do the final shots of the meal being served." She smiled and tried to look as guileless and innocent as she didn't feel. "You would photograph beautifully."

"Absolutely not," he said. "No." And then, he smiled and it was as if a charm switch had been turned on somewhere in his mind. "I understand you and Mr. Dunn are going to have dinner on Mr. McKenzie's boat this evening. I understand he is a very good amateur chef." Beck bowed from the waist. "I hope you find it most enjoyable."

Without another word, he turned and walked away from her toward the front desk. She waited a moment, and then followed him to the lobby where she sat down to wait for Penny and Sam. She rubbed her arm where he had grabbed her. His grip had been so tight she knew she'd have bruises.

What a strange encounter, she thought. Why had he gotten so angry? It wasn't as though she'd been going through his papers. She'd just been looking around. And what a temper he had. It was almost as if he were hiding something. *But what?* Then reality returned. She'd been nosing around in his private office. Of course, he was upset. He had every right to be.

FOUR

FROM THE DECK of the *Sanity,* the lights of Palmetto Bay glowed and shimmered like a cluster of tiny Christmas tree candles strewn haphazardly along the shore. The night was clear except for low-lying clouds on the horizon which banked and reflected the lights of the town. The air was brisk with a hint of brine. Sam McKenzie's 52-foot custom built Irwin sailboat, docked in the Rattlesnake Key Marina, rocked in response to the tide. The thought occurred to her that Sam McKenzie had money. He couldn't afford a boat like this on the money he made giving sailing lessons.

Sitting in the deck chair next to her, last night's Nero chuckled. She half-turned in her chair to study him. The lights of the dock glistened on his white hair. He wore a Rolex and a heavy gold class ring. MIT. Despite his girth, he moved with grace and was comfortable on board a boat. When you had the kind of money Arthur Pennington Dunn had, you were comfortable everywhere. Old Philadelphia money. Main Line, someone at the resort had said.

He'd asked her to call him Penny, which was what all his friends called him, and it pleased her to be counted as his friend. Throughout the evening, she'd tried to understand how he made his money, but the financial world was foreign to her and all she knew was that he invested in something called blind trusts involving real estate.

Below in the galley, Clyde heard pans clatter. Shifting in the deck chair, she grinned and sipped her Beaujolais. Sam McKenzie was blowing it. He'd scorched the Bernaise sauce, but the consistency and texture would have been just right. And the broccoli was so al dente it crunched. The filet mignon had been excellent, she'd give him that. He'd obviously put himself under a lot of pressure, and she wasn't sure why. If he wanted to date her, why not just take her out to dinner? Why did he feel he had to cook?

Penny picked up the carafe which rested on the deck near his feet. "More wine?"

"No." She covered her glass with her hand. "I'm fine."

"Sam's an excellent cook," Penny said, refilling his glass. Clyde laughed and he added, "No. He really is. I think you jinxed him."

"Clyde?" Sam called from the galley below.

"Yes?" She couldn't restrain a giggle.

"You and Penny come down here and laugh in my face where I can see you."

Treading carefully because the breeze had freshened and the waves were choppy, she maneuvered the companionway and descended into the cabin. His surroundings were orderly and free of clutter. From the entertainment center, the compact disc player tinged the atmosphere with the strains of Ravel's *Pavane for a Dead Princess*. Few personal items were displayed, but there was an old photo of a smiling, relaxed, much younger Sam standing in front of a university with his arm around a young woman and a little girl. Judging by the clothes and hair styles, Clyde assumed the photo had been taken in the late 1980's or early 1990's. She was stunned. Sam had told her he was single and she believed him. Sam was a grown man who could have had a life and a family, but he had struck her as such a loner she couldn't imagine his ever going home to a wife and family after work. Or going on family vacations or mowing the lawn. What had happened?

He had newspapers stacked neatly—*The Miami Herald, The Palmetto Bay Observer, The Wall Street Journal, Grant's Municipal Bond Observer*. The last two didn't surprise her because Penny had told her Sam had been a very successful stock broker. He hadn't told her why Sam had given up his career and she didn't ask. If she decided she was interested enough, she'd ask Sam.

Most of the books stowed on Sam's shelves had to do with boating. She scanned the titles—*The Boatman's Manual* and the thick, encyclopedic *Chapman Piloting*. He'd explained that the *Sanity* was an auxiliary, meaning she had motor power as well as sails. He'd also explained that meant he didn't qualify as an "arrogant wind jockey." There were also several of Charles Dickens' works. That was interesting. Dickens was one of her favorite authors.

"Dinner didn't turn out the way I planned," Sam said. The galley was next to the main salon in the cabin. He had the dishes in the sink where he was rinsing them. The sleeping quarters were aft.

As he reached below the double stainless steel sink for a dish towel, she said, "You get high marks for trying. Need help with the dishes?"

"No, no." He gestured toward the seat behind the table. "Sit down. I'll have these done in a minute."

Clyde slid into the seat. Penny sat at the other side of the table and leaned back into the pile of black and gray pillows. She studied Sam as he dried the silver. He was an okay guy. He was not ego ridden and he had a sense of humor. He also kept his own counsel otherwise he'd have explained about the woman and the child. She liked that, too. But why had an intelligent, attractive man left a successful career as a stock broker to hide out or submerge himself—whatever he was doing—in a backwater area like this?

"And I told her I'd eaten some wonderful meals with you here on board the *Sanity*," Penny was saying. "I vouched for you."

"Two thumbs up for the dessert," Clyde said. "I would never have thought of serving poached pears with a dollop of Chambord and cream drizzled over them."

Later, as they played Scrabble and she stewed over the difficulty of using a Q when she had no U, she told Sam and Penny how surprised she'd been that so little was written about Far Horizons.

"I'm not," Sam said. "Since the Becks took over in 1974, I'm told they've kept very much to themselves. A lot of businesses on the island advertise to draw locals—people from the mainland—especially in the summers when we have so few tourists. But Beck doesn't. Nor does he ever get involved in any local promotions. We have a pageant every February called the Sun Festival," he explained as he reached behind him to draw the curtains and shut out the glaring light from the dock. Closing the curtains lent an intimate atmosphere to the cabin where the soft interior lights gleamed off the teak walls.

"It's strictly a public relations gimmick designed to draw people to Palmetto Bay, but it has a royal ball honoring the Sunshine Queen and her court, a grand parade, flower shows…a lot of different events. The parade alone," he continued, taking a sip of Beaujolais, "draws at least a couple hundred thousand people so local businesses are usually standing in line to contribute money, time and personnel to make it a success. But not Beck." He slapped down an ED and added 40 points to his score by turning QUIET into QUIETED.

"But he must advertise," Clyde said, adding DIS to his word and remembering Beck's outburst earlier in the evening. "Penny, why did you choose Far Horizons for your vacation?"

Penny smiled and leaned back against the thick pillows. "I didn't." He frowned. "Right now would be the perfect time for a cigar. Too bad I gave them up."

"What do you mean you didn't choose?"

"My board chose it. This is the 25th year I've been chairman of my company's board of directors. The directors gave me this trip."

"They must think a lot of you," she responded, studying the rack of tiles in front of her on the table.

Penny laughed. "They think I'm a pain in the ass. Frankly, I'm amazed they paid for this trip. At the moment everyone on the board is bent out of shape because I won't go along with an outrageous scheme to invest a disproportionate amount of our liquid assets in a European theme park. Since I'm the majority stockholder, those young Turks can't do it without my approval. Let's talk about something more pleasant."

"I think I'll have a little more of that Beaujolais. It was a very good year. Anyone care to join me?" Sam asked.

"No thanks," Clyde said.

Penny shook his head and Sam rose and went to the counter. "Beck does not advertise locally," Sam said, pouring the dark liquid into his wine glass. "He advertises in travel magazines and various metropolitan dailies. Beck says he keeps a low profile locally because so many of his guests are high profile."

"I guess that's good business…" Clyde stared thoughtfully at the letters before her, willing them to make sense. ISDPODG. She felt a rush of elation. "Read 'em and weep, gentlemen." Using the E in Sam's word QUIETED, she built DISPOGED. "That's fifty points for using all seven tiles and since it's a triple word score, that's another forty-two points. A total of ninety-two points. And I've used all my tiles and there are no more in the bag. Gentlemen, I do believe you've been stewed, simmered and sautéed."

"Dispoged? There's no such word as dispoged." Sam shook his head. "I am very disappointed. I never thought you'd be the kind of person who would stoop to duplicity to win a Scrabble game."

"According to your bookshelf, you like Charles Dickens. Right?"

"What does that have to do with—"

"Right?"

"Right."

"One of my favorite quotes comes from *Martin Chuzzlewit*. Chapter eighteen to be precise. I like it because so often people try to almost force me to eat or drink things I don't want. The quote goes like this. 'Leave the bottle on the chimley-piece and don't ask me to take none, but let me put my lips to it when I am so dispoged.' Look it up if you don't believe me." She gestured toward the bookshelf. "As far as being duplicitous, I would suggest that if you can't play with the big girls, don't get in the game."

"You're not exactly a modest winner, Mizz Colby like the cheese," Sam said. "But it's not official until our scorekeeper says so." He turned to Penny.

Penny scribbled the figures on the score pad, added them and added them again. "She's right, Sam. She skunked us. She's got 492 to your 271 and my 202. I say let's call it an evening so I can get back to the resort and lick my wounds."

"Next time, Mizz Colby," Sam said as he swept the tiles into the striped canvas bag, "I'm not going to be such a gentleman. You got to choose this time because you were a guest. Next time, we'll play stud poker. That's my game."

Clyde rose and gathered their wineglasses. Taking them to the sink, she glanced over her shoulder. "You're going to get down and dirty? Fine with me. But I think you should know I am my father's only child, his pride and joy. And he taught me to play poker." The sound of running water as she rinsed the wineglasses drowned his reply. "I didn't hear what you said."

"I was talking to Penny, but I was wondering what else your father taught you," Sam said.

She noticed for the first time how shiny and wavy his black hair was in the cabin's overhead light. And the look in his eye made her glad she had worn her best Versace black pants suit and good pearls. The suit had cost a small fortune, but she had splurged, spending the dividend check from the trust fund her grandmother had set up for her.

This man, she mused, had his own quiet, elegance. Even dinner on his sailboat was properly done. He wore a pale green monogrammed silk shirt open at the neck and trim, tailored Armani slacks the color of cinnamon.

She felt a twinge of regret. It struck her there would be no next time. She was only here for a few days. Their paths would sever and chances were better than even she would never see him again. And then she felt a rush of relief. Not that theirs would ever become a true relationship. After all, loving meant trusting and opening yourself to betrayal and hurt and she had no intention of doing that again. She thought of Josh. His betrayal still hurt, but not as much as it had in the past. Even her dad, Big Clyde, the one man in the world she unconditionally adored, disappointed her now and then when he went on sporadic binges that nearly always erupted around the holidays. Good thing he'd been absolutely superb at his job.

"Listen up," Sam was saying. "Do you or do you not want a cup of coffee?"

No, she wanted to say, the reporter in me wants some answers. Who is the woman in the picture? And who is the child? And why are you here in Rattlesnake Key? Before she could respond, Penny interrupted.

Glancing at his watch, he said, "I've got a better idea, Sam. It's getting late for an old duffer. Why don't you take me back to Far Horizons and you can plot your revenge?"

"Revenge?"

"Absolutely. Miss Colby's victory casts a blight on the honor of men everywhere."

"You're not fooling me for a minute," Sam accused. "You've got a hot chess game waiting back at the inn."

"Guilty, but it's Bridge, not chess," Penny admitted. His face grew sad. "We'll miss Lanken. He made an excellent fourth. But Horace says he'll find someone to take his place. The only thing is it will probably be Westendorf, the police chief. He's a nice guy, but I never play my best when he's there. I feel guilty even though I haven't committed a crime."

"You're playing bridge with Horace Beck?" Clyde queried.

"Yes. He's quite good. That strikes you as unusual?"

While she scouted around for her purse, Sam disappeared into the cabin and emerged with her wrap. "He doesn't seem the type to indulge in anything as benign as Bridge," she said as Sam wrapped the sweater around her shoulders. "Rather like Attila the Hun playing Hearts."

Penny threw his head back and laughed. "That's a good one. I'll have to ask Horace if he plays Hearts. He may come across as a bit of a dictator, but he's a good businessman. I admire that."

"Spoken like a guest as opposed to a media type. However, he's been very pleasant to both me and the crew—even though he's made it clear he's far from thrilled to have us here," Clyde responded.

Penny was first off the boat, followed by Sam who helped her down. He led the way to his black Lexus parked at the marina. The drive back was brief even though the marina was at the northern end of the island and the resort at the southern. The Village of Rattlesnake Key was midway between the two on the eastern shore. Matecumbe, or Dead Man's Road, which Sam took delight in translating for her, followed the perimeter of the island except for those sections when the road veered inland because the shoreline was too low. They passed Sam's sailing school and that posed still another question. He obviously didn't need the money and, like Far Horizons, he didn't advertise and didn't seem to care whether or not he had students. What else did he have in common with the Horace Beck and the resort?

They were the only ones on the road until they reached the Village's city limits, passing on the right the sign announcing Rattlesnake Key was home to the Kiwanis, Elks, Moose, Jaycees and Rotary Clubs.

A four-faced clock surveyed the town from the tower of the Rattlesnake Key Savings and Loan. Although it was after ten o'clock, the streets were still busy. Stores were open: the tee shirt shops, the souvenir and curio stores, restaurants and sidewalk cafes. It was only the first week in November, but store windows already displayed Christmas wreaths and Santas.

A single light was on in the small one-story concrete building that housed both the Rattlesnake Key Police and Fire Departments, mute testimony to the lack of violent crime on the island. A lone police car was parked in front next to a fire truck that jutted out from a bay on the side.

A block further, they reached the heart of town, a circle dominated by a huge fountain decorated with coiled, concrete rattlesnakes arched as if poised to strike. Streets radiated from the fountain like the spokes of a wheel, bisected by Matecumbe Road. Sam stayed on the road and soon the lights of the town were behind them.

"I understand Rattlesnake Key got its name because it's shaped like a rattler." Clyde watched Sam's profile illuminated only by the dashboard lights as he drove too rapidly for her taste along the two-lane road.

"I've heard that," Sam answered after a pause. "But I've heard another story I like better. In the 1800's, this area was a sanctuary for pirates. One of them was a fellow called Gasparilla. When another pirate tried to move into his territory, he and his men dug a huge circle in the sand on the beach. Then they scoured the island collecting rattlesnakes to fill it. He would challenge his competition to walk through the pit. The few who took him up on his offer usually died of snakebite. Or maybe it was fear. Gasparilla, on the other hand, had been bitten a number of times and had built up a tolerance.

"Can't you see it now—the only light comes from the torches the half-naked pirates hold as they surround the victim lying prone on the sandy beach." Sam's voice took on a deep, melodramatic tone. "They watch, jeering as he writhes from the pain, gasping his last breath. Then they break out bottles of rum for a celebration."

"You've got a vivid imagination! I don't mind the taste of rattlesnake meat, but walking through a pit of hissing vipers is insane."

"It depends on the stakes, I'd say," Penny offered from the back seat.

Sam laughed. "No, Penny, it depends on the snakes!"

"You two are impossible." Clyde groaned.

Soon the Far Horizons sign came into view. Sam parked next to Rattlesnake Key's other patrol car. On the far side of the blue and white police car was parked a plain black sedan with municipal plates. "Guess the mayor and the police chief are comping it for dinner," Sam said casually.

Penny was quick to bid them good night and head off to find his bridge game. Clyde stood in the lobby with Sam, reluctant to have the evening end. "Tell you what, McKenzie," she said. "I can't challenge you to walk through a pit of rattlesnakes, but how about a drink in the bar?"

Sam whipped an invisible pirate's sword in through the air

then made a loud slurping noise. "Dueling drinks. Is that what you have in mind?"

Clyde glanced around the lobby where two young couples were sitting in front of the fireplace chatting. They looked toward where she and Sam stood and looked again as if recognizing her. "It depends on who's buying. But let's get out of here."

"How interesting," he said.

"What?"

"For a person so blatantly in the public eye, you do not enjoy the attention. You're even rather shy. I find that interesting."

"It's known as preserving one's privacy. And that's enough of your amateur armchair psychology. Do you want that drink or not?"

He nodded and took her arm. "I'm buying," he said. "That was a cheap shot. You are definitely entitled to your privacy so the vodka tonic is on me. Surfriders alright or do you want to literally get out of here?"

"Surfriders is fine, but I'd better stick to soda and lime. You can have whatever you want. You don't have to face a camera in the morning."

"You'd look terrific after three days without sleep…with a hangover…even in the middle of a snake pit."

She grinned. "You just may turn out to be okay." Then it kicked in, that sarcastic streak she had so much difficulty squelching. "Especially for a wind jockey."

"Ouch." He said. "Let's get that drink." He gripped her hand and led her toward the lounge.

They listened to the music of the Sundowners Trio in the Surfriders lounge, danced a lot and she had three sodas with lime wedges. Then a little after eleven, she regretfully called it an evening. As they stood in the lobby, he said, "I could walk you to your room."

"I can get there from here," she said. "My sense of direction isn't that bad."

"Your loss. I'll see you soon."

She started to walk down the corridor to her room, but turned as he swiveled on his heel to leave. "McKenzie," she called. "Thanks for dinner. It was delicious."

"It was so-so. I'll do better next time."

"McKenzie?"

"Yeah?"

"I have a question."

"Just one?"

"Enough already. I have to know something."

"And I want to be honest with you." He grinned. "This is not my first time, but I have led a sheltered life. If you'll be gentle with me, I'll be brave."

"McKenzie, be serious. I want to know why you insisted on cooking dinner. You could have taken me out to a restaurant."

"But you might not have accepted. And don't get your dander up, Colby, but it was a bet. I thought you were good looking and had decided to ask you out—even after that crack about wind jockeys, even before I knew you were a famous TV star. But Penny bet me I didn't have...uh...the male genitalia to cook for you."

She sighed. "I hope you won."

"Penny says I haven't won until I fix a meal without any culinary disasters."

"What did you bet? What were the stakes?"

"The snakes, er stakes, were high. And that is our secret, Penny's and mine. However, I think you can appreciate how important it is that we meet and eat once more."

FIVE

IT WAS STILL DARK OUTSIDE, but the brightly lit kitchen was an oasis crammed with cheer and frenzied activity. Never a morning person, Clyde understood the necessity of filming around the dining room's schedule and so she had set her alarm for three thirty. Now as she entered, she put her small makeup kit on one of the bus carts and headed for the coffee urn. She poured a cup, looked longingly at the cream carton, but took a swallow black and surveyed the kitchen.

Andy had his crew well-organized even though it was not quite four-thirty. Bernie, the red-haired, freckle-faced light tech, had lugged the five lights into the kitchen. Yawning, his eyes were still filled with sleep as he placed two 2K and one 4K zip lights so that they cast a semicircle of light around the stove where Henri Doucette worked. Then he positioned the 2K Fresnels he would use as key lights for Clyde and Henri Doucette.

Out of the range of the lights, Pete, the sound technician, adjusted the dials and knobs on the audio mixer. His pale face was unshaven and his nondescript brown hair was uncombed. Dark circles of fatigue meant he'd probably been out all night "cattin' around," as he called it. Clyde was always amazed at his success with women. He looked so woebegone she could only reason his conquests began by feeling sorry for him, although the scuttlebutt around the station among the interns and "gofers" was that he was overly endowed.

Andy locked the Betacam SB into the Steady Cam and ran

it as low as it would go on this updated version of the tripod. That was one of the many things she appreciated about him. He knew she liked to be filmed from a low angle shooting up because it made her look taller and slimmer, and she didn't have to remind him all the time. Many a promising career in television had been ruined by a hostile or even careless cinematographer.

Wearing a crisp, starched apron, Henri Doucette was clearly in command of his kitchen. His mustache looked freshly waxed; his eyes were animated and bright. His assistant chefs, Frode and Juan, would not appear on camera, but nonetheless played important roles for they bustled about the kitchen assembling ingredients, chopping fresh herbs, and dicing vegetables.

As she stood nearer to watch, Henri explained with obvious pride that his recipe for veal medallions with artichoke hearts had been featured on the *Great Chefs of Europe* television show while he was still a student at Cordon Bleu in Paris.

"Set up for a two-shot," Andy directed as he spotted at the far end of the kitchen with Henri. "It's going great, babe," he enthused, his ponytail bobbing as if to corroborate his assessment. Then he paused to study her. "I thought we decided you were going to wear that sleeveless blue dress we picked out. That and the pink, heart-shaped apron sent in by one of your fans from Orlando." He scratched his head.

She walked over to where he stood in front of a long metal table and shoved up her left sleeve revealing the ugly bruise. "Our host mistook me for the bad guy."

Andy's eyes narrowed and he straightened. "I'd better have a talk with that dude," he said quietly.

She put a hand on his arm. "It's okay. Really. You know I can fight my own battles, if need be."

"What happened?"

"Later. And I promise that if I need reinforcements, you'll be the first to know." She stepped back and struck a glamour pose, one hand on her hip, the other fluffing her hair. "Just perform your usual camera magic. Okay?"

"I don't like this, Clyde. Not one bit."

"Let it go. We won't be here much longer. Won't make that much difference, will it?" She'd substituted a tan and white striped A-line linen dress and a chocolate brown apron a fan from Tallahassee had sent. The outline of the state was embroidered in white. Tallahassee was indicated by a Seminole Indian and a red star in the upper quadrant. It was a neat gimmick. Her fans were great, but sometimes she got tired of wearing a different apron for each show. They'd sent enough aprons to last a year even if she did a daily show, but it was tedious trying to coordinate the apron with what she wore. However, surveys showed many viewers liked the kicker at the end of the show where she acknowledged by name and hometown the person who'd made the apron.

"The dress," she asked, when he didn't answer right away. "It works?"

"It's fine. So's the apron." He looked away from the eyepiece and squinted at her face. "You could use a little more blusher."

"I brought the makeup kit. Everything else okay? The script?" she asked as she walked over to the cart, put down her white china coffee mug and retrieved the blusher. It was round, a professional model's kit with her initials in gold, Old English letters. Carrying it made her feel as if she were pretending to be something she wasn't, but she used it because her dad had given it to her as a Christmas present. It was a symbol of his hard-earned, long-time-coming acceptance of the fact that she didn't want to go to law school and follow in his footsteps.

Andy broke into her reverie. "We've got some good area shots already in the can." He waited until she dabbed the blusher on her cheeks, made a thumbs up sign to signal his approval, then said, "Move in next to Henri. Where's the boom mike, Pete?

"Coming," Pete said as he reached into the trunklike case that contained the sound equipment and withdrew two Shore/Senheizek wireless microphones about half the size of spark plugs. "I'm using these, Andy. I think we'll get better quality in here."

"Just do it."

While Andy double-checked the light with his meter and brushed back a strand of Clyde's hair so that it didn't obscure her face, Pete clipped one mike to the neck of Henri's uniform so that it didn't show. Clyde took the other from his hand.

"I can do that," she said and snapped it beneath her collar. "Ready for a sound check?"

"Yeah." Kneeling on the floor in front of the large gray portable console, Pete donned headphones. They mussed his wavy, light brown hair. Adjusting the dials with short, stubby fingers as she counted to ten, he made a circle of approval with his thumb and forefinger. "Hey, Henri, can you count for me too? In English, so I know what you're saying."

"Enough, Pete," Andy said.

Doucette counted to ten in heavily accented English.

"Got it, boss. Cut and print."

"Enough, Pete. This is not the set of 'The Wizard of Oz.' Now, Clyde, let Mr. Doucette demonstrate to you how he sautés the onion. Sir, will you do that?" Andy looked through the camera eyepiece.

"But of course, Meester Andy. Come, Mees Colby." The chef gestured for her to stand next to him while he melted butter in a sauté pan. When the butter had melted, he spooned into it the onions, then the chopped tomatoes, green chilies and fresh parsley. He drizzled key lime juice over the mélange in the pan.

"Get in closer, Clyde," Andy instructed and she did as she was told, hovering over Doucette's shoulder. The sweet, tart scent of lime juice spiced the air, almost overwhelming the onion.

"Mr. Doucette, hold that pan very still," Andy moved in nearer. "I'm shooting a close-up," he said. At his direction, the lighting technician moved one of the lights and, while Frode blotted the beads of sweat on Henri's forehead with a napkin, Clyde reached into her dress pocket. She pulled out a compact and took a quick swipe at her forehead and nose with the powder puff. The heat from the lights wasn't as overwhelming as usual because it was so early in the morning and the air was cool. That made it almost worth getting up early, she thought. Almost.

The shoot went smoothly and they finished the Acapulco Key Lime snapper recipe by 6:00 AM when it was time for the chefs to prepare for breakfast, which they started serving at seven. While Henri Doucette seldom did breakfasts, the kitchen had to be free so he and his assistants pitched in to restore order, moving the kitchen equipment back into place while Andy and his crew removed the lights, cameras and sound mixer.

Once free, Clyde hurried upstairs, anxious to reach her room where she could change and scrub off the heavy makeup. Dawn, the maid, was coming down the hall toward her from the supply closet pushing the linen cart ahead of her.

Clyde still felt bad about the way she had snapped the previous morning. She nodded her head and smiled. "Hi," she said as the maid reached into her supply caddy and removed the glass cleaner.

"Good morning, Miss Colby," the girl responded, spritzing the mirror on the wall opposite the elevator then wiping it clean with a cloth. "Is your new room all right?" she asked over her shoulder.

"Fine," Clyde answered.

Once inside the room, Clyde managed a quick nap, did a little more research on the resort and felt very pleased with herself for being so productive so early in the morning. Just after nine she had changed into jeans and an over-sized pullover decorated with a cartoon of two cats wearing boxing gloves and sparring when she heard a knock on the door.

"Come in," she called.

Dawn stood on the threshold, her linen cart in the hall behind her. She held a bottle of wine and a floral arrangement dominated by a Bird of Paradise.

"They sent these up for you from downstairs," Dawn said. "If it's too early to clean your room, I can come back."

"No, no," Clyde said standing back from the door. "Now's fine. Come on in." Dawn entered and handed her the wine bottle. "I can't imagine who'd be sending me wine and flowers."

"I'll put the flowers on the table by the window for you." Dawn removed the small envelope staked in the prongs of the clear plastic cardholder and handed it to Clyde. "I love that shirt," Dawn said with a shy smile. "Do you have a cat?"

"Four. I am owned by four spoiled rotten beasts."

"I have two. Tabbies. My stepdad didn't think he liked cats when he first married my Mom. He said cats were too aloof and independent. Now he says he'd give anything for an aloof, independent pussycat. They're all over him."

"Thanks," Clyde said, gesturing toward the flowers. She studied the miniature white envelope. Must be from Sam. He was the only person who might send flowers who knew where she was.

She withdrew the cardboard square. On it was written, "Please accept my apologies for the misunderstanding of last evening." The script was small, almost Gothic. The letters were carefully formed. It was signed H. B.

Some misunderstanding, Clyde thought.

She reached for her purse for a tip, but Dawn shook her head. She was all business now. She had a routine and followed it, starting in the bedroom, stripping the bed and carrying the linens to the linen cart in the hallway and returning with fresh sheets and towels. Clyde admired her efficiency.

"How long have you worked for the Becks?"

Without interrupting the pace of her work, Dawn answered, "Since summer. I'm working this winter to make enough money to go back to school."

"Where?"

"Ringling Art School in Sarasota. If I can get a scholarship."

"And what are you studying?"

Now busily engaged in making the bed, Dawn glanced up at her. "Commercial art. I've always wanted to be an artist. But I'm not as interested in fine art, portraits, and landscapes. It's too hard to make a living."

Finished in the bedroom, she carried her supply caddy into the bath. Clyde was changing her shoes when she heard a crash and then an exclamation. Hurrying to the door, she looked in. Dawn was on her hands and knees wiping up blue liquid.

"Oh, I'm so sorry, Miss Colby. I dropped the glass cleaner. Mr. Beck will have a fit."

"Are you okay?"

"I'm fine, but what a mess. And Mr. Beck—"

"What about him?

"Oh, nothing. It's just that he keeps track of the cleaning supplies." She paused. "He's figured out the precise quantity of cleaning materials we should use and he budgets that amount. If we use too much, he docks our salaries. Grace says it's because he's an engineer and works with very precise measurements and figures. I like working for Grace, but…"

Handing her a cloth from her caddy, Clyde said, "Tell him I did it. Say I came into the bathroom while you were cleaning and knocked it over."

"Oh, I couldn't do that, Miss Colby. I couldn't lie. But thank you. He's not a bad boss, he's simply very detail minded. We joke about it. We don't think he ever sleeps. Nothing goes on around here that he doesn't know about."

"Protecting his investment, I guess," Clyde said, amused at the idea of Horace Beck washing dishes, vacuuming, emptying the trash. Actually, she could see him doing all of those things if necessary. And doing them with dignity. "So you want to be an artist? How interesting."

"That's what everyone says."

"But I mean it. I'd like to see—" She paused as the telephone rang.

It was Eli Nussbaum who called to tell her he was in the lobby waiting to do the interview. By the time she hung up, Dawn was gone.

If Dawn was serious, maybe there was a way Clyde or the station could help. An internship in production. Or if Dawn's grades were good enough, a scholarship of some kind. Maybe Iris had connections or knew someone on the Ringling Board. Her mother loved causes and it would keep her busy, give her something to do other than complain about Clyde's single state, which she considered socially unacceptable. As Clyde headed down the hall, she made a mental note to check on that.

In the lobby, she spotted the lanky reporter lounging against the counter. He wore a brown corduroy jacket over his faded jeans. He spied her and loped over, his face reflecting an alert, focused intelligence that contrasted to his puppylike, gawky movements.

"Miss Colby," he hailed.

She saw Davy lurking in the corridor outside the office door and realized this was the first time she'd seen him since the night of her arrival. Beck's son looked very different out of costume. Davy was probably in his middle twenties, a little shorter than his father but every bit as blond. His eyes, although as blue as Horace's, were not as direct. She waved and he nodded a jerky, uncomfortable gesture.

"At your disposal, Mr. Nussbaum," she said as she neared the counter.

"Eli, please." His right hand shot out. The sleeve of his jacket was too short and she thought it must be difficult for him to buy clothes that fit properly. Especially in such a small town. She thought, too, that when he got a few years older and a few pounds heavier, he'd be a good-looking man. His faded blue tennis shoes were ragged, but when he saw her appraising look, he said casually, "Ah, yes, but they're comfortable."

She missed the news business. Especially print journalists. They were so down to earth. No makeup kits and hair spray for them. "Clyde," she said shaking his hand. "Where do you want to do this interview? Shall we get some coffee?"

He shook his head and studied their surroundings. "Not the dining room. Just my luck I'll end up with wonderful tape recorded memories of clinking glassware and rattling silver."

"The terrace then?"

Eli agreed and followed as she led the way past the half-open office door where she could see Davy on the telephone. He spoke quietly, shielding the receiver with his right hand. He repeatedly sliced the air with his left. His eyes, as he looked at her, were wide, his blonde brows rising and falling as he spoke.

"This is way cool," Eli said as they sat at one of the little tables on the terrace. "I mean like awesome."

"You've never been here before?"

Eli shook his head. "Nope. Horace doesn't like the locals." He removed his reporter's notebook from his pocket, flipped it open and crossed his interminably long, denim-clad legs. "Now about that interview."

He reached into the pocket of his sports shirt and drew out a sheet of paper with typed notes on it. Referring to those notes, he double-checked the basic facts of her life—date and place of birth, parents, early career history, and so on.

She was impressed by the extent of his preparation. "You've certainly done your research," she commented.

He leaned forward, slipped in a cassette, clicked on the tape recorder, counted to ten and replayed to be sure it was operating properly. Before launching into the interview, he labeled the tape by dictating the date, time, place and name of interview subject. The basics taken care of, he asked her about her relationship to food, how important it was to her and what different roles food had played in her life.

She found herself telling him how she celebrated with food, fought boredom with food, treated her down times with food and even about learning to cook in the kitchen with her father when she was so small he had to bring in a stepstool so she could reach the counter. It wasn't long before she was forced to add that she was also impressed by the depth of his questions.

"Frankly," he said, "I don't intend to be stuck in Palmetto Bay the rest of my life. I have a plan. Two years from now, I intend to be working for the *Miami Herald*. Ultimately, I want to end up at the *Washington Post* covering some aspect of national politics."

"Big dreams, Eli. But I'm betting you make them come true."

"From your mouth to God's ear." He paused. "You worked for the *Miami Herald*," Eli said tentatively. "What was it like?"

Clyde leaned back and smiled. "It was great," she said, remembering. "Exciting to be around really good reporters and writers. And editors who made your work better. I'd recommend it highly, Eli."

He swallowed and his disproportionately large Adam's apple bobbed. He face grew flushed. "Would you…" he began and then stopped.

She sat up. "Would I what?"

"Would you, er, that is, would you recommend me? Could I use you as a reference?"

Clyde smiled. "I've still got some friends there. Put a batch of clips together for me to read and we'll see."

"Oh, my," he said quietly. "Oh, my. Thank you."

Time passed quickly. The shadows on the terrace grew longer and finally, he said, "One last question. Photographs?"

"Andy can take some, if you like," she offered, knowing Andy never traveled without his Pentax. She preferred having Andy take the stills. He knew her good side, best angles.

"Oh, no. Binky, that's my editor, will want our own photos. When will you be filming your show tomorrow?"

"Early."

"How early?"

"Four-thirty."

Eli winced. "Is that the only time we can get into the kitchen?"

"Get your beauty sleep early. We have to be out of the kitchen by six so they can prepare for breakfast. We're shooting around Doucette's schedule. Now how about lunch? My treat."

"I never turn down a free meal."

During lunch, they talked about Horace Beck and the electronic fishing rod he was developing, about how the butterfly ballot had damaged Florida's image, but mostly about the different ways the bombing of the World Trade Center had impacted the country. Afterward she walked with Eli to his car in the parking lot, a battered red VW Beetle. He removed his corduroy jacket and tossed it into the back seat.

"Now I owe you," he said, twirling an imaginary cigar and flexing his eyebrows in his imitation of Groucho Marx.

Was he coming on to her? God, she hoped not. She thought of him as a younger brother.

"You haven't lived until you've tasted my grandfather's

Kreplach and *Kugel,*" he was saying. 'You've got to meet my grandfather and come over to my place for dinner."

"Kreplach? Kugel?" she echoed. And grandfather, she thought with relief. A guy coming on to a woman did not invite her home to meet his grandfather.

"Kugel," he explained, "is a sweet casserole made with noodles and raisins and cinnamon. *Kreplach* are dumplings filled with chicken or meat and used in a soup."

"I know what they are. I've never had them," Clyde said. "But that would be wonderful. I love to try new dishes and I know so little about the Jewish cuisine."

"Not much to know," Eli interjected. "Most of it's pretty bad. Except for *Kugel* and *Kreplach*. Tomorrow night?"

"Works for me."

"Clyde," he said, then paused, half bending as he grasped the car's door handle. The door was rusted and dented; the red paint was oxidizing into a reddish orange.

"Yes?"

"You were a news reporter in Miami."

"I thought we'd been over that."

Again he paused, staring at her intently. "There's a lot going on here," he said finally. "Under the surface stuff. My editor thinks I'm mentally out to lunch, but I'm convinced something's wrong. There have been a series of deaths here. A printing executive was the latest."

"Yes, I know. Greg Lanken. I had drinks with him one evening."

"All the victims are wealthy businessmen. Since I've been with the *Observer,* there's been Lauren Sipowicz. He was CEO of a company that manufactured air conditioners. Fred Alberts. He was CFO of a national grocery chain. And Theo Simmons, chairman of the board of a conglomerate of department and hardware stores. Their deaths were recorded as heart attacks and the bodies were released almost immediately. There was no investigation, never a coroner's inquiry. Not even an autopsy. I've tried to get close to someone out here, but no luck. Beck recruits his employees from out of town, they're strangers and no one will talk to me. You could be the break I need."

She'd been very surprised by Greg Lanken's death, but she wasn't ready to attribute his death to anything other than natural causes. Still, if there had been more than one death under such unusual circumstances.

"Have you noticed anything out of the ordinary?" he asked.

She looked into his kind eyes. Framed by the horn-rimmed glasses, he looked rather like a raccoon. His earnestness was touching. She'd been like that once, determined to root out crime and wrongdoing and convinced she could make the world a better place. When she'd done an article on corruption in city hall, she'd learned firsthand of the reality of the clout of advertisers and the corruptive power of political influence. The mayor's family's appliance business did so much advertising with the station that the general manager delayed and watered down her story on municipal bond fraud until it had no impact.

"Not really," she said. "It's more a feeling than anything else."

"Maybe I'm wrong to ask you to get involved, but you're here. Nobody will think anything if you ask questions or look around. You're the host of a cooking show, not a nosy reporter."

She could hear old Dad: "Your job, Clyde," he'd say, "is to do an excellent cooking show so entertaining and informative it will be picked up for syndication. You're not covering the crime beat anymore, thank God. Let it go."

And she couldn't argue with that. But Eli had his right to a chance to try to make a difference. If there was something here and he uncovered it, that story might be his ticket to the *Miami Herald*. She'd gotten a lot of help when she was a rookie and felt an obligation to pass it along. She was curious, too. She had questions of her own.

"I'll do what I can," she said at last.

He grasped her hand. "Thanks, Clyde. I'll see you at four-thirty. AM." He crossed his arms over his chest as if he were lying in a coffin. "I may be more dead than alive since I don't regain consciousness until at least nine, but I'll be here."

She watched thoughtfully as he folded himself into the front seat and chugged away.

Still mulling over what Eli had told her, she returned to the lobby. She needed to find Andy and brief him about the newspaper photographer. He wasn't going to like it because he was hell on meeting deadlines and didn't like distractions. However, he wouldn't be as ticked if he knew in advance.

Striding through the lobby, she passed Surfriders and glanced inside. The cocktail lounge was deserted except for a man seated at the bar who looked a lot like Sam McKenzie talking to Sullivan, the bartender. Sullivan was slicing oranges, lemons and limes to use as garnish for drinks.

It *was* Sam.

She was sure now as she drew closer. Her first instinct was to barge in and say hello, but the men looked so engrossed in their conversation she paused. Their heads were close together and they spoke so softly she couldn't hear what they were saying. "Conspirators" was the word that rushed into her mind. But what were they plotting? The night before when they'd had drinks in the lounge, Sam and Sullivan had been friendly, but had given no indication they knew each other well. Then Sullivan spotted her and nodded. Sam whirled on the bar stool and extended his hand in invitation.

"Come in and have a drink with me," he said.

Only then did it register that he didn't have a drink. So why was he in the bar? "Don't you ever give sailing lessons?" she asked.

He jerked his hand back. "I was looking for you."

"For me? In here?"

"Bartenders always know what's going on and who's where. I have to go into town this afternoon to pick up some supplies and I thought maybe you'd like to ride along. We could have dinner—that I don't cook. And I could show you some of my favorite spots."

"Oh," she said. "I can't. I have to work tonight. On the script."

"Work?"

"That's right."

"Don't forget our bet."

"That bet's between you and Penny."

He leaned back against the bar railing. "You are making this very difficult," he said as she turned to walk out of the bar.

"I mean to," she said without looking back. "The show is very important to me and the station."

It was just as well they not see each other again, she decided riding up in the elevator. Their relationship had no future and she now had two jobs to do.

SIX

"CLYDE, REMEMBER THE TIME we got caught in that shootout between the police and that gang? The Black Gangster Disciples in Liberty City?" Andy asked, between bites of the spinach salad he had ordered for dinner that night. "I didn't think we'd come out of that alive and here we are, bouncing on the knees of luxury." Sitting across from her between Pete and Bernie, he gestured with a casual twist of his hand around them at the Far Horizons dining room.

Clyde followed the movement of his hand while she picked at her mahi-mahi fillet. It was served with a very delicate yet intriguing dill sauce and she made a mental note to ask Henri about the sauce. She nodded.

The dining room was luxurious in an understated way compatible with the feel of old Florida. The tables were made from cypress knees topped with beveled glass. Arrangements with baby's breath and rose buds decorated the tables. The draperies framing the floor-to-ceiling windows were made of a rich, forest green fabric in a pattern vivid with Royal Poinciana blossoms. The floor was of glistening terra-cotta tile. The walls were dressed with oil paintings depicting Florida scenes; a Seminole paddling a dugout through the Everglades, a panther lurking on the edge of a palmetto patch, a white egret flying over a meandering, curving river.

Two tall, blonde and muscular waiters wearing short tan jackets with the Far Horizons logo were weaving between tables clearing them, stripping linens, removing salt and pepper shakers and sugar bowls. At the moment, the dining room was almost empty and would soon close because it was nearly ten.

Only one other table was occupied, and to Clyde's mind, that didn't count because the diners were Horace Beck and three other men. Two of his guests she recognized because she'd seen them coming out of Beck's office the previous night. One man had worn the rattlesnake lapel pin. The other was the police chief. Now he was in a light blue business suit. *Off duty?*

"Do you ever miss our hard news days?" Clyde asked, picking up the thread of his conversation. "It was certainly exciting."

"More exciting than coping with Horace Beck and Monsieur Doucette? Surely you jest, Clyde," Andy said wryly. "Give up the delight of shooting a hot sauté pan or filming with steam-fogged lenses? Sacrifice the artistic integrity innate in spraying glycerin over dried-out casseroles to make them look fresh? The answer is yes, sometimes I miss it. But what we're doing isn't that bad either."

"Don't let him kid you," Bernie said. "He doesn't just spray the glycerin, he sniffs it. Gets off on it. Loves his new job." A fellow University of Florida alum, Bernie was another of Clyde's favorites. He was flexible. Got the job done. All in all, she liked the crew. The sound guy, Pete, could be a bit trying. He was a bit of a nerd with a dweebish sense of humor. He could also be temperamental and demanding, but when that happened, Andy usually stepped in and straightened him out.

Funny guy, Andy. Terrific sense of humor. Brilliant at camera work. A good leader who kept things together and moving, he also had ethical values unusual in the television business. He didn't eat meat—not because he didn't like it, but because it was against his principles. He echoed Mary Tyler Moore in explaining he could never eat anything with a face that could look back at him. He never pried into anyone else's personal life unless invited and never shared anything from his own. Sometimes she wondered if he was gay, not that it mattered.

Andy smiled at her. "Shouldn't we be talking about tomorrow? You ready for *avocado en gelee* at 4:30 AM?"

She shuddered. "You really think we can get that and the *calabaza flan* done in one shoot?"

"You in a hurry to go home, Princess?" Pete said, laughing

his high-pitched giggle that drove her bananas. "What's the matter? Not happy with your room?" Pete pointed his finger like a gun and shot her. His pseudo hip attitude was unbearable. "Princess got flowers from the Beck, guys." His small green eyes glinted.

"How did you find out about the flowers?"

"I was in your room today. Remember? You sent me up for your script notes."

"Yes, that's right. I did. I didn't ask you to snoop around though."

"Chill, Pete," Andy said.

He sat his chair back down on the floor with a thump and pouted like a petulant child. "I was just having fun."

"You're lucky you're good at your job, Pete." Andy paused and glanced toward the dining room door. "What's Sam McKenzie doing here so late?"

Clyde turned to see Sam on the threshold. He waved to her, but headed toward Beck's table on the far side of the room. He sat down next to Beck, but spoke to the police chief. The police chief rose abruptly, shoving his chair back. While Beck and Sam remained seated, he and the other men rose and left quickly.

"Wonder what that's all about?" Andy said.

"I wonder."

While she watched, Beck motioned to the waiter who handed him the check. Beck scrawled on it and handed it back. Beck rose. He clapped Sam on the shoulder then vanished through the side door leading to his office. Sam stood then slowly crossed the dining room toward her. His broad shoulders were bunched in a rust-colored cable-knit pullover. He wore navy blue slacks and tassel moccasins. But even while she was appraising his physical appearance, she realized Sam was concerned about something. At the same time, she realized the crew was watching her watch Sam and she colored.

"Clyde," Sam asked as he reached her table, "mind if I join you?"

"Pull up a chair," she said, gesturing to the next table. As

Sam drew a chair over and sat down, she said, "Sam, this is Andy Zabrinski, AKA Zee Man, the best cinematographer in the business. Bernie, lights. Pete, sound."

Andy shook Sam's hand. "Nice to meet you, Sam. Don't mean to rush off, but we'd better call it a night. Clyde doesn't have to be in the kitchen until four-thirty. We get there at three-thirty." He motioned to the lone waiter who was hovering, anxious for them to leave. Andy and Bernie pulled out their chairs, but Pete didn't budge.

Bernie was pleasant, but obviously ready to get back to the room. "Murphy Brown's on tonight," he said. "I can't miss it. Tonight the great unwashed masses of TV viewers find out who's the father of her baby."

Andy turned to the redhead who was taking a last gulp of water. "Bernie," he said patiently, "the whole world knows who the father of that baby is. That show aired years ago."

"Since I work in television, Andy, I only get to watch re-runs," Bernie explained. "See you in the morning."

Pete smiled. His wolf-like teeth glittered. "Sam McKenzie," he said. "So you're the guy giving our princess sailing lessons." Clyde gritted her teeth. Pete was obviously ready for a nice long chat with this new person. Under the table, she placed her high heel on his sneaker-clad foot. "What's our princess like on a date?" he was asking. "Is she fun?"

Flushing, she leaned slightly forward, placing more weight on his foot so that her high heel dug ever so slightly between his toes in the sneaker and into the tender flesh. He glanced at her in surprise, and then grimaced as she increased the pressure. "Oh, uh, I guess I'd better find something to do. Andy," he said as he pulled out his chair and rose, "you wanna run into Palmetto Bay and see what's going on?"

"Come on, Pete," Andy grabbed him by the sleeve of his windbreaker. "If you want to go to Palmetto Bay, that's okay with me, but I'm turning in. Just be sure you're in the kitchen on time."

Sam waited until the three were leaving, then said, "Buy you a drink."

"You handle rejection well," Clyde said. "I've already turned you down once today."

"One of the many secrets of my success," he said. He rose, pulled out her chair, put his hand under her elbow and steered her out of the dining room. The waiter locked the double glass doors behind them. The deadbolt slid into place with a thud.

"What was your conference with the police chief all about?" Clyde asked, pausing in the lobby. The lights were low and the atmosphere was relaxed and intimate. Lila, a petite blonde who—according to Penny—had been playing at the resort's piano bar for twenty years, was deep into a Barry Manilow medley. Two or three couples lounged in overstuffed, oversized loveseats.

"You're nosy, Miss Colby-like-the-cheese," he said, guiding her toward one of the seats.

"I've spent the majority of my career life in the news business. And that's the business of asking questions. Old habits die hard. Now tell me."

"Let's order first," Sam said.

Out of the corner of her eye, she saw that one of the couples had risen and started toward them. The woman held a napkin and a pen in her hand.

"Sam, let's go somewhere more private?"

Sam followed her gaze. "That's understandable. And I know just the place."

ONCE THEY WERE IN the Lexus, he pulled out of the parking lot and turned left toward Rattlesnake Bay. In the darkness of the car, she tried again. "What was all that about with Beck and those men? It looked as though you brought bad news."

Sam kept his eyes on the winding, two-lane macadam road as he answered. "The news *was* bad. Eli Nussbaum, the reporter who interviewed you this morning—"

A sick feeling gripped Clyde's stomach and she clutched her handbag for support. The green light from the instruments on the dashboard lent a pasty, eerie cast to Sam's face. She twisted in the front seat to face him, but it was too dark to see his expression. "What about Eli?"

Sam's voice was deep and controlled when he spoke. "He's in the hospital."

"The hospital? What happened?"

"Let's get a drink. Then I'll tell you everything I know." Sam wheeled into the parking lot of a rundown, wooden restaurant about six or seven miles down Matecumbe Road. A neon sign announced that this was The Rattler's Den.

"You do know all the better places," Clyde murmured.

"Hey, you wanted privacy. And the interior will surprise you."

He was right. It did. Inside, the lights were so low no one would have even recognized Madonna. He led her to a booth in the back and slid in next to her. Thumb-tacked to the booth's wall was a string. Three sets of rattlesnake rattles and a silver bell dangled from the end of the string. Sam lifted it and rang for service. But she couldn't wait.

"Why is Eli in the hospital?" She didn't know Eli well, but in a short time she'd grown fond of him, charmed by his whimsical sense of humor and impressed by his quick mind and drive.

Sam covered her hands with his. "He was beaten. Left for dead. And that's not the worst."

She jerked her hands back. "That's pretty damned bad."

"Whoever did it pinned a yellow star on his chest."

For a moment, she couldn't get her breath. "Those bastards," she said at last. The image of Eli beaten and hurt infuriated her. She bit her lip. Then a sobering idea occurred to her: What if the anti-Semitism was a ploy to draw attention from his investigation into the deaths at Far Horizons? And, if that inquiry had motivated his beating, did they know he'd talked to her about helping? Was it possible that her friendship with Eli could put her in some degree of jeopardy? Maybe she'd better get the .22 Dad had given her out of the Bronco. But she refused to worry. If there were danger, she'd deal with it when she had to. Consciously she put aside all anger and fear and focused. Now was the time to concentrate on asking questions. The right questions. That's what counted now.

"Where was he found?"

"In the parking lot behind the newspaper office."

"In Palmetto Bay?"

"No, the bureau here on Rattlesnake Key. The *Observer* has a bureau downtown. It took a while to ID him because Rattlesnake Key isn't his regular beat. People over here don't know him."

"When?"

"Just before I came to Far Horizons to tell Frank Westendorf. The police chief."

"That guy in the light blue suit."

"That's right," Sam replied. "The other fellow was Irwin Thompson, the mayor. The third was the medical examiner. Small-town politicians socialize."

The waitress, a plump, round-faced Florida cracker, came over as he spoke and slapped down a couple cardboard coasters with the Budweiser logo.

"Get you folks something?"

"The lady would like a vodka tonic," he said, but he said it with a question in his voice so that she could change the order if she wished. "I'll have scotch with one rock, Avis. Glenlivet, if you have it."

The waitress shook her head and her tight perm coils bounced. "Chivas."

"Fine," he said as she walked away.

"How bad is Eli hurt?" Clyde dreaded the answer.

"Too soon to say. Bad. He was still in the Emergency Room when I left."

"Any idea who did it?"

"This is Rattlesnake Key, not Miami, Clyde. They're just starting the investigation."

"Could we see him? I'd really like to see him."

"Tonight?" Sam glanced at his watch. "Not a chance. Wouldn't do any good anyway. He's unconscious. I'll take you in the morning after you're finished shooting."

"How did you find out about it?"

"I was at the hospital visiting a friend who'd had an attack of appendicitis when they brought Eli in."

The waitress slapped down their drinks and a check. "Getcha anything else, Sam?"

"Clyde?"

"I'm fine," she said, thinking of Eli, wishing he could be well and strong and sitting across from her with Sam, doing his stupid Groucho Marx routine.

"We're okay for the moment," Sam said, "but it's been a tough day. Keep us liquid."

"You betcha, hon," she said. She picked up the check and headed back to the far end of the bar where she flopped on a stool. Her rear end, clad in purple terrycloth shorts, slopped over the edge.

"This isn't a bar, it's an experience," Clyde said.

"Hey, it's private. Nobody knows you're here. And you must admit it has atmosphere."

"You've got that right."

Rattlesnake skins stretched on green felt backing and mounted on lacquered pine boards crowded the walls along with pictures of rugged-looking men, each holding a dead rattler.

"Make you a deal," he said. "If you kill a diamondback while you're here, I'll take your photo and see that you, too, are immortalized on the walls of the Rattler's Den." She didn't say anything. "Penny tells me you live in a lighthouse." He tried again.

"Yeah," she said thinking of the peace and isolation. And her cats. "It's wonderful. The first level is where I have the living room, my kitchen and the dining area. My bedroom is on the second level and the view is incredible. And the sounds. Every night I fall asleep to the sound of waves lapping against the shore. Mornings I wake up to hear birds singing. I get up and walk the beach. It's fresh and clean and quiet. Keeps me centered."

"I understand," he said quietly. "That's why I live on the *Sanity*. But a lighthouse? That's way cool, as the kids say."

"I inherited it from my grandmother. She inspired the term 'free spirit.' A lover, well-placed in the government, bought it for her in the 20's."

"He must have been very well-placed."

"He was. Mel was eccentric, but she had no time for losers."

"Like you?"

"That, McKenzie, is none of your damned business."

A couple drinks later, she felt a hundred percent better. Relaxed and calm. And friendlier. "Sam," she said, and without thinking, she reached across the table and took his hand. It was so much larger than hers that she wrapped her hand around his thumb.

"Yes," he said.

"Thank you."

"A service of the McKenzie Sailing School and Escort Service," he quipped, covering her hand with his, immediately adding, "Shit, Clyde, I didn't mean anything by that crack."

It destroyed the mood and she was glad. She wasn't upset by his joke about the escort service anyway. It was the sailing school. And the fact that she never saw him sailing. Or with students. It reminded her she needed to be on guard because Sam might not be what he seemed.

"No harm done," she said. "But I've got to get back. I'm sleepy and I've got to be in the kitchen so early."

"You're right," he agreed. "Besides, I wouldn't want to be responsible if you look bad on camera tomorrow morning."

As he drove back to Far Horizons, she yawned and relaxed. The next thing she knew, he was gently shaking her shoulder. Quickly, she sat erect. Embarrassed, she said, "I'm so sorry."

"You weren't kidding," he said. "You really are beat."

She nodded. "Long day."

"That's a relief. I thought it was me."

"There you go, fishing for compliments," she retorted. "Besides, it wasn't really a date."

He didn't insist on coming in with her, just kissed her on the cheek as he leaned across the front seat to open the door. "See you in the morning," he said. "Sleep well."

The lobby was deserted. She had almost reached the elevator when the desk clerk called her over and handed her a pink telephone message. Someone with the ridiculous name of Binky Beresford had called. He was the editor and publisher of the *Palmetto Bay Observer* and now she remembered Eli mentioning him. He wanted her to know that Kathleen Terpen was the paper's photographer and that she'd be at the resort in the morning to take pictures for Eli Nussbaum's feature, which he completed and faxed, to the mainland before he was attacked.

Later, when she was in her room getting ready for bed, she began putting things together and asking herself questions: How had Sam known Eli had been out to interview her? Had she told him? She didn't think so. If he knew that, how much more did he know? And what did he know? Did she really believe that business about a friend with appendicitis? And why had he been the one to inform the police chief? Why hadn't they just sent a patrol car?

The answer to the last one was simple now that she thought about it. Rattlesnake Key only had two cars and the chief had one of them. If the other car had been sent to Far Horizons, no one would have been left to patrol the rest of the island or to respond to calls. But the phones weren't out of order.

She would let Sam take her to see Eli in the morning. It would give her an opportunity to ask more questions. She slipped into her Gator tee shirt and crawled between the sheets. Setting the travel alarm clock on the nightstand for three-thirty, she turned off the light and began waging the nightly battle, the battle to slow her mind so she could sleep.

The one thing she must remember was that she couldn't trust Sam. She had to remember because she was attracted to him. And she couldn't let him use that attraction against her.

Not that he would.

Would he?

And why would he? What did she have that he wanted? She didn't know anything. At least not yet. Did she?

Damn.

She sat up in bed, reached for the remote control, turned on the television and channel surfed until she found an old black and white movie on the AMC channel. It was *Golden Earrings* circa 1945 and featured Ray Milland, wearing too much eye shadow, and Marlene Dietrich, with hands meticulously man-icured for a Gypsy. Together, they camped in the woods and occasionally battled Nazis.

She fell asleep with Dietrich's seductively guttural voice echoing in her ear.

SEVEN

NOVEMBER 3

A HEAVY FOG ROLLED in the next morning, and as Clyde dressed she mused that it accurately reflected her mood. She'd slept fitfully. Her dreams had been filled with six-sided stars, coiled rattlesnakes poised to strike and sleazy people huddling and murmuring. She drew near to hear what they said, but they melted and she found herself alone in the Far Horizons lobby. Now, as she stood ready to leave at 4:30 AM, hand poised on the doorknob, the telephone rang. Startled, she dropped her keycard, bent quickly to retrieve it and hurried to the phone.

"Clyde, we got a problem." Andy's voice sounded troubled.

"A problem?" She was still not completely awake. It was too early for room service and she hadn't had her morning coffee.

"Yeah, we can't shoot this until later so you might as well get some extra shut-eye."

"Why can't we shoot?"

"Beck just called. He's having some work done in the kitchen. Something about clogged grease traps and drains backing up." She could hear the frustration in Andy's voice. Deadlines were sacred to him and she knew he'd also be worried about going over budget. Once they were established, it wouldn't be as much of a problem, but the program's status was tenuous at the moment.

"Anything I can do to help?"

"Nope."

Awake now, her frustration matched his. "This is a heck of a time to repair the kitchen. Or whatever it is he's doing."

"He says the kitchen crew just discovered it when they went in to work a few minutes ago. The good news is that you can go back to bed."

Clyde slumped into the chair next to the nightstand. "What does this do to our schedule?"

"Puts us back a day. That's all. It's not so bad. Tell you what. There's nothing we can do until the sun's up when the light's better. Meet me in the lobby around eight-thirty. We can shoot the intro. Oh, yeah. Eli's photographer showed up right on time. You wanna talk to her?"

"No. And Eli wanted pictures in the kitchen. Rats. Just explain and apologize. Tell her we're shooting in the lobby at eight and see what she wants to do."

"Gotcha covered. Now go get your beauty sleep."

She tried. Taking off the linen A-line dress and apron she was wearing for the show, she scrubbed her face free of makeup and shimmied back under the covers. But sleep proved as elusive as the perfect soufflé. Around six, she gave up and wandered out to the tiny balcony where she sat, wrapped in a thick terry cloth robe, and stared across the gray horizon.

Ordinarily, she hated this time of day. It was too early to do anything. The air was wet and chill and the noise of the surf was like the quiet, low-pitched warning growl of a bone in a blender.

She thought of the day ahead, about Eli Nussbaum. She envisioned him in the hospital amid a tangle of tubes. What would today hold for Eli? A return to consciousness? The first steps on the road to recovery? Perhaps his injuries weren't as serious as Sam said they appeared. Head wounds bled profusely so perhaps they looked worse than they were. She hoped that was the case. He was so bright. A man of integrity who cared. The world needed people like Eli Nussbaum. A man with dreams. And the determination, intelligence and talent to achieve them.

He didn't deserve what had happened to him. If he'd been an Episcopalian or Baptist or Methodist, he'd probably be walking around happy and healthy now. Unless, of course, his attack had not been motivated by anti-Semitism. If it was the result of his investigation, what could he have found out? Would he have made notes?

She glanced at her watch. Nearly seven. The day stretched ahead. No, it loomed. The show. Focus on Clyde's Gourmet Galley.

Shrugging out of the robe, she took special pains with her makeup and her hair, which she twisted into a French braid. She and Andy had chosen an elegant black, halter-topped hostess gown with broad white satin lapels for the intro and kicker shots in the dining room. She loved the dress. It was from one of the trendiest boutiques in Bal Harbor. The station had worked a deal and her wardrobe was so gorgeous even Mindy, that blonde ditz, was livid with envy.

Funny, she thought a few minutes later as she walked through the lobby toward the fireplace where Andy, Pete and Bernie were setting up. Here she was early in the morning wearing a hostess gown, attracting furtive, curious glances from guests and staff and it didn't bother her at all. That would drive Sam crazy. He was sure he had her all figured out. But she had a secret. She'd done stand-ups in front of courtrooms in the Metro Dade Justice Center with people lined up on both sides of the halls watching. It hadn't bothered her because she'd been focused on the story, on what she was doing. Clyde Colby wasn't important, the story was what counted. Same principle here. It was only when she wasn't working that she became so uncomfortable.

"Looking good," Andy said as she neared them. "Even with all her Wall Street woes, Martha Stewart's eating her heart out."

She noticed that Pete's eyes were red today as he came over to the fireplace to hand her the tiny mike on its gator clip. Pete's nose was slightly swollen and she had a hunch he'd scored some blow after they'd parted company in the dining room. As long as it didn't interfere with his work, it was his business, but she hated drugs.

"I need a level, Princess," he said and she counted to ten. "Got it."

Bernie clapped her on the shoulder. "Move a little to the right, Clyde," he said. "Not that far, just a couple inches. If you hadn't moved, you'd have a staghorn fern growing out the top of your head."

The shoot took longer than Andy had planned. He'd nicknamed her "One Take Colby," but she hadn't lived up to it this morning. It also didn't help that about midway through Kathleen Terpen arrived loaded with 35mm camera equipment.

Kathleen was a woman in her mid-forties, a straw-haired blonde wearing a khaki shorts suit with a safari jacket. Nervous and quick, she moved in brisk, staccato steps.

"Heard anything about Eli?" Clyde asked.

Kathleen shook her head. "He's critical. When I left the newsroom, Binky was still at the hospital. The scuttlebutt around the paper is that there will be brain damage, but you never know. Can I get you to sit in that wicker chair over there? The one next to the piano bar? And Mister…"

"Andy."

"Mr. Andy, would you move in a little with the camera so I can get an action shot? It'll look like we're photographing the actual filming of the show."

Andy rolled his eyes, but did as she directed. Then it was back to the actual filming and although Kathleen was well-intentioned, she kept getting in the way. As a result, shots that would have taken thirty, forty-five minutes at most took nearly two hours. Andy was tolerant, though, and worked around her without complaint.

Usually, Clyde was able to compartmentalize, to block out her personal life and even the rest of the world when she worked. She had learned long ago to stay focused, to get the job done, but this morning Clyde kept thinking of her conversation with Eli at lunch the previous day. He'd obviously gone directly to the bureau to write his story after he left her. But then what? A simple feature story wouldn't have taken Eli that long to write. Where would he have gone? What had he learned? Anything? Nothing? Had he merely been found nosing around? She would help finish Eli's investigation. Whatever it was, whoever was involved. He had paid a tremendous price even if he walked out of the hospital a fully functional human being.

Once she'd made the decision, she was at peace and she was able to focus. Things went more smoothly, but it was still close to noon before Andy was satisfied with what he'd shot, and she was exhausted. Kathleen Terpen hung around, then she shook everybody's hand and took off, cameras and light meter dangling around her neck, rolls of film jammed in the pockets of her safari jacket.

And where was Sam? He'd said he would take her to the hospital. She was glad she hadn't started to depend on him. Her stomach growled and she realized she'd been so involved she hadn't had breakfast and it was lunchtime. No wonder she was hungry. Fine note for a food aficionado.

She asked, "Andy, you want to get some lunch?"

"Not now," he said, looking up from the camera. "I got a few loose ends. Can you give me half, three quarters of an hour?" She noticed for the first time that he looked tired, too. Dark lines fringed the warm brown eyes. The corners of those eyes drooped ever so slightly, giving him a perennial hang dog look. She must remember she wasn't the only one feeling the pressure of making this show work.

Her stomach growled again. "I don't think I can last a half hour. I might perish from malnutrition."

"You better go on ahead then. We can't have the star of the show perishing."

In her room, she changed into a tailored navy blue suit and spectator pumps, adding a white scarf and accessorizing it with a gold pin inspired by the Duchess of Windsor's famous leopard brooch. She would have been more comfortable in jeans and a pullover, but this coast of Florida was still very conservative and a visit to the hospital warranted proper attire.

Dawn had cleaned her room while they'd been filming in the lobby and had left her work on the table for Clyde to see. The portfolio, a huge leather binder, was so large she had to spread it open on the bed. The first sample was an ad for cat food. It featured three gray and white kittens and the mother cat, paws around one another like a barbershop quartet, singing the virtues of an imaginary brand of cat food. The next, obviously a class project, was a brochure for a widget. Dawn had designed a trifold brochure emblazoned with a logo dominated by a laughing widget with wings and wearing aviator's glasses.

The promise was there, she thought. Even with Clyde's limited knowledge of art, it was obvious Dawn Hicks had talent. The colors were strong, the lines were sure. The eye saw a different vision, not as different as to be truly great, but interesting. Clyde jotted a note to remind herself to talk to one of the guys in the production department about an internship for Dawn when she got back.

Downstairs again, she walked onto the terrace. The fickle, out-one-moment and gone-the-next sun had burned away the fog and, because the sky was still rather overcast, the beach and the waves had a greenish-gray tinge. Gusts of wind whipped through the tops of the palms whisking the fronds into frenzied dances. She chose her usual table on the edge of the terrace in the shade of a sea grape tree. Max, the hunky blonde waiter who'd served them the night before, appeared with a menu.

When she'd ordered, she wandered restlessly to the edge of the terrace to stare at the roiling waters of the Gulf. She'd decided to help Eli, but she didn't know where to begin. She wished she could trust Sam. She needed someone who knew the local territory. Maybe the newspaper editor? But he was not only a complete stranger who might think she'd fogged her lenses, he was apparently a friend of Sam's.

The waiter returned with her lunch, an enormous helping of conch salad served on a bed of shredded lettuce and garnished with kale and thin slices of green, red and yellow peppers. The salad was served with hot biscuits, butter molded into the shape of seashells and sea grape jelly. It was gorgeous and she savored every bite, carefully analyzing the ingredients. *What made it special,* she wondered thinking that part of what she loved about food reporting, *was its element of mystery.* In the body of the salad, she isolated the flavor of minced jalapeno pepper. That was different. But it was the marinade that intrigued her. She took a few drops on her spoon and rolled it on her tongue. The Key lime juice she recognized immediately, but there was a tantalizing secret ingredient here. She must ask Henri at the shoot in the morning.

She finished about two-thirds of the salad and pondered dessert. Ah, yes. The pink grapefruit sorbet.

She was spooning the last of the tangy ice when she spotted a stocky, white-haired man in a sweat suit jogging down the beach. Even from half a mile, she recognized Penny. Penny. She hadn't seen him since the night they'd had dinner on Sam's boat and that seemed like months ago. What a nice evening that had been. Penny. Maybe he could tell her something about Sam. Something she could check to make sure Sam was trustworthy. Or untrustworthy. At least she'd know. That is, if she ever heard from him again. He was late. And he hadn't called.

Penny bobbed up and down, heading away from Far Horizons. She'd have to catch up with him later. In the meantime, she'd drive to the hospital to see Eli. She was sipping the last of her iced tea when Horace Beck paused at her table. He wore khaki work pants and shirt and carried hedge clippers. His clothes were uncharacteristically wrinkled and marked with blotches of sweat.

"How was your lunch?"

"Delicious. I must talk to Henri about the marinade for the conch salad."

"I have been working with the gardeners," he said indicating his messy appearance. "We were trimming limbs from the Royal Poincianas in the parking lot. As I passed through, Davy said to tell you that you have a telephone call. You can take it on the house phone in the lobby." He drew out her chair as she rose.

She smiled. "Thank you."

In the lobby, she nodded at Davy who connected the call and she picked up the receiver.

"Clyde? Sam." His voice sounded tired and strained, but she

felt no sympathy, only irritation. "I'll pick you up in about half an hour."

"Don't bother," she said.

"I said I was going to take you to see Eli. I intend to do that. Sorry I'm late, but things came up. Half an hour."

"Some day we must have a chat about the way I feel about unreliable people."

"And we'll discuss how I feel about rude women."

"There had to be a telephone. You could have called."

"Thirty minutes," he said. He hung up in her ear.

"You clod," she said to the receiver. "I don't have time to stand around and wait for you, McKenzie." She stormed over to the desk. "Where's the hospital?" she demanded.

Davy looked at her, stepped back a pace in surprise, and then began to explain. Clyde wrote the directions on the back of an envelope, thanked him politely and headed out the lobby to the parking lot and her Bronco.

Roads were choked with tourists, but traffic on the causeway moved steadily and she made good time. Davy's directions were clear and she had no trouble locating the Glades County Hospital on Gulf Boulevard. Sprawling in two wings, the two-story hospital had been erected in the post–World War II construction boom. The rear of the building fronted on Gulf Boulevard.

When she turned off Gulf and drove into the parking lot, she was confused at first because she had to drive behind the hospital to find the entrance. She parked, got out and walked through the automatic sliding doors entering a small but immaculately clean reception area. The building was well-maintained. The paint was fresh although the bilious green was definitely institutional. The purchasing agent must have gotten a deal he couldn't turn down on the paint, she mused.

The pink-pinafore-clad auxiliary member at the desk told her Eli had not regained consciousness, that he was in a coma, but added that his vital signs had stabilized. "I'm afraid you can't see him," she said. "He's just been transferred out of ICU and he's not allowed visitors." The woman shook her head sadly, jarring her pinkish blonde hair, which she wore in a bee-hive. "Terrible thing."

"I see," Clyde said. "I'll go have a cup of coffee in the cafeteria."

The woman nodded as Clyde circumvented the reception desk, passed the banks of elevators and walked to the main corridor of the hospital. Doubling back, she took the elevator to the second floor and dodged through a hall crowded with nurses. It was almost shift change. Food carts and visitors impeded her path. She pulled her reporter's notebook out of her purse, stuck a pencil behind her ear and walked down the hall assuming the protective coloration of someone who belonged there, someone with a specific task to perform. Eli would expect her to get in. Professional challenge and all.

When she entered his room, a miasma of grief infused the dimly lit chamber. The shadows made it look crowded although she seemed to be the only one there. The air was layered with the scents of disinfectants, medicines and disease. It was as she had envisioned. The blinds were drawn and Eli laid motionless, eyes closed. His bed had thick white curtains drawn around two sides. The main illumination came from the subdued light over his bed. Tubes issued from his mouth, his nose. The needle from an intravenous drip was taped to his hand. The machine monitoring his vital signs bleeped and blinked. As she eased into the chair beside his bed, a sound drifted toward her from a darkened corner.

"You know my grandson?" an ancient voice rasped.

Startled, she peered into the darkness and saw an old man huddled in a chair. He looked almost tiny, but she couldn't tell whether that was because he was actually small or because he had folded in upon himself in the chair.

"Yes," she began. "I only met your grandson twice, but we were—" she hesitated. Could she really say they were friends? Fellow journalists? Perhaps. Acquaintance was too impersonal. After all, Eli had trusted her. He had asked for her help. And they talked. Really talked. Besides she genuinely liked him. She was his friend. "New friends," she said finally. "We were new friends."

Behind her the door cracked open admitting slants of shadows. A tall figure, framed in the light from the hallway, formed a dark specter.

"Eliahu," Sam said, nodding to acknowledge her presence. "I was sorry to hear about Eli. How is he doing?"

The old man pulled himself erect, compressing the pain he felt into every movement. She saw that he was much taller than she had thought. Tall and gaunt. Like Eli. He was dressed all in black and wearing a cable-knit cardigan for warmth. He took two steps toward the door. "Sam? That you?"

"Yes, Eliahu. And this is Miss Colby."

"Miss Colby?" His whispery voice quavered.

"Eliahu, what do the doctors say?"

Eli's grandfather tottered into the light veiling the bed. His thin gray hair was unkempt. "His vital signs are strong, his body is alive, but it is too soon to say whether he will live or, if he does, whether he will ever come back to us. His mind," the voice choked, "his mind may never recover."

"Oh shit," Sam said. "That bad."

A female voice announced over the intercom that visiting hours had ended. The old man shuffled over to his grandson lying so still and strangely shriveled beneath the light hospital cover. *"Sholft gezunt,"* he croaked. "Sleep well." He tucked the covers around Eli's chin and bent to kiss the pale forehead. She remembered Eli's hilariously bad imitation of Groucho Marx and wanted to cry.

"What are you going to do now, Eliahu?" Sam's voice broke the reverie. "Do you need a ride? Can we do anything?"

"Yes," Clyde added. "Anything at all." She was sad to think this was how she would meet Eli's grandfather, not over a meal of *Kreplach* and *Kugel* as they had planned. That would have been a good time. They would have laughed and the old gentleman would not be looking bereft as he did now.

Eliahu stared at Sam, misery shimmering in his dark eyes. "Now? I go home. I wait." He turned to her. "New friend? Good. My Eli needs friends."

"Mr. Nussbaum," she ventured, "could I come talk to you sometime? About Eli?"

"About Eli?"

Clyde was miserable. She didn't want to say anything in front of Sam, but if there was a chance that Eli had said something—anything—to his grandfather about the investigation, she had to try. "We were talking about Eli's writing career." She paused, searching for a reason both the grandfather and Sam would believe. It hit her. "I have some friends in Miami…"

"Eli's new friend," the old man said softly, "come any time."

In the hallway as he stumbled along sandwiched between her and Sam, Clyde realized once again how fragile he was and her heart ached for his grief. Knowing Eli, she was sure Eli would have cared for him regardless of where his career had taken him, would have loved the old man and made him feel cherished, important and needed. Who would do that now?

"Now, Sam, now is the time we need the *golem*," Eliahu said, twisting his thin lips into a rueful smile as they paused in the reception area.

Why, she wondered, did Eliahu need a movie monster? Because she had finally remembered where she had heard of it. *The Golem* was a movie—originally released in 1920. She'd seen it years ago in a film history class. She remembered it had starred Paul Wegener, one of her favorite German actors, but she didn't remember the plot.

Sam nodded and clasped the man's creepy hand with its veins that stood up like ropes against liver-spotted skin. "How will you get home, Eliahu?" Even as he spoke three elderly men rose from plum-colored chairs in the center of the area and gravitated toward them. Their shoulders were hunched and they reminded Clyde of three crows.

"My friends. They are here to see me home."

"Promise that if you need me, you will call." Sam pressed the wrinkled hand.

The old man bowed his head, patting Sam's hand with his free one before drawing away. "Thank you, Sam. I promise."

Sam shoved his hands in the pockets of his jeans and watched as the old man and his friends plodded slowly out of the hospital. He took a deep breath then turned to Clyde. "You don't take directions very well. We'll have to work on that." He put his hand on her elbow and started leading her toward the exit.

She balked like a stubborn mule. "You're not going to tell me what to do."

"Not now," he ordered. "I'm in no mood. I'm tired. That old man's heart is breaking. His grandson, my friend, is dying and we're not going to argue. We've got to talk. Let's go."

He was right, she admitted, but only to herself. It was neither the time nor the place for a stand-off. But that didn't mean he was going to play macho male and boss her around.

"Where?" she said finally. "And why should I go anywhere with you? I've had my fill of irresponsible men who say they're going to do something or be somewhere and then they show up hours later."

"I'm irresponsible? What about you? Taking ridiculous chances. A reporter you talked to yesterday is beaten nearly to death. Doesn't it occur to you that there's a possibility—however remote—that *you* might be in danger?"

"What do you care?"

Sam laughed and it wasn't a pleasant sound. "You know damned well I'm not irresponsible. I don't know about those other men, but I had a damned good reason for being late. I'm not at liberty to explain at the moment. But I haven't done one damned thing that would lead you to mistrust me." He led her through the doors into the hospital parking lot.

The sun was sliding beneath the horizon bathing the world in outrageously beautiful shades of maroon and orange and shocking pink. "And besides," he added, "you're upset because Eli got hurt and if I know you, you want to go off like Woodward and Bernstein and investigate. Be a TV cooking star. That's enough for anybody." He led her to his car.

Once she comprehended what he'd said, she was stunned and then so angry she couldn't think of a single thing to say. But her reporter's curiosity, as he had predicted, got the best of her. What did he think she was up to? What did he know?

Had Eli told him she was going to help? Had Eli talked to him about the deaths at Far Horizons?

It didn't matter. She wasn't going anywhere with him. Not until she'd talked to Penny. "I'm going back to the resort."

He ignored her, opening the car door on the passenger's side. The black Lexus gleamed in the descending rays of the sun. "Get in," he said impatiently. "And don't try to give me the business. You're through for the day. Andy told me."

She slammed the door shut. "I'm not going anywhere with you. And that's that."

He threw his hands in the air. "You know what the matter with you is? You're so damned leery of making a commitment, you're looking for reasons to run away. Yes, sir, I know about women like you."

He got into the car, slammed the door shut and drove out of the parking lot leaving her standing, flatfooted, wondering what the hell all that was about.

Clyde drove back across the causeway. It had been a total waste of time. She pounded the Bronco's steering wheel with a clenched fist. She'd learned nothing. She still didn't know whether she could trust him. Why couldn't he tell her why he was late? Was he a cop? An agent? A spy? She snorted. To hear him tell it, he was a retired stockbroker running a sailing school.

Sure he was. And she was the reincarnation of Princess Diana. She shook her head impatiently. Good thing this time she hadn't let herself get emotionally involved.

But she was forgetting something important. She was a police reporter. And where did a police reporter get her information? From the police, of course. Once across the Causeway, she headed for the Village of Rattlesnake Key and the police station. When she walked in a few minutes later, Chief Westendorf was seated at his desk doing paperwork. He looked mildly surprised to see her and put down his pen.

"Miss Colby." He rose from behind his desk, coming to stand by the wooden railing that barred visitors from the rest of the room. "Something I can do for you?"

She glanced around. The police station was small and old

fashioned. Westendorf's desk was in a far corner with a half-partition lending him a modicum of privacy. A signed photograph of President George Herbert Walker Bush hung on one wall and she thought about telling him he had a new leader or two since then, but decided against it. On the other wall, a bulletin board was cluttered with wanted posters including a list of the FBI's 10 Most Wanted. To the right, a plump, blonde secretary wearing a flowered dress that was a tad too tight sat at an old gray metal desk with a PC in front of her. She was talking on the telephone and it sounded like a personal call judging from the tone of her voice, but no one seemed to notice or care.

Another gray metal desk was decorated with outdated city inventory numbers on an adhesive sticker. The police officer who sat at that desk was the typical redneck—hefty with a soft gut, small eyes a little too close together. Blond hair and gray eyes. He had a cow's lick at the crown of his head and the hairs stood up almost like a spike hairdo. The desk plate read "Sgt. Stan Reeves."

"What are you doing in our neck of the woods, Miss Colby? It's a pleasure to see you, but aren't you a little out of your territory?" The chief interrupted her observations.

"I've spent so much time in police stations they feel like a second home, Chief. But this isn't a professional visit. I was wondering if you could tell me anything about the investigation into Eli Nussbaum's beating."

"Awful thing, Miss Colby. It really hurts me to think anybody in Rattlesnake Key could do such a terrible thing." He moved forward and held open the wooden gate. "Come on back. I'll fill you in best I can."

She edged through the gate and he gestured to the wooden barrel chair next to his desk. "Would you like some coffee?" When she shook her head, he said, "You're smart. It tastes like it was brewed with cow dung."

She smiled politely and sat down. "About Eli Nussbaum," she said. The legs of the metal chair she was sitting on were uneven and every time she shifted her weight, the chair made a grinding sound. Very unsettling. She wondered if it was deliberate.

"Of course, you have to remember we're a very small department, but we're checking Nussbaum's whereabouts. Now he saw you earlier the day of his assault. I believe he interviewed you. That right?"

She nodded.

"Did he seem worried about anything? Nervous? Frightened? Anything *you* can tell *us?*"

In her determination to get to the bottom of Eli's attack she hadn't thought that she might be questioned by police and she wasn't sure how much to tell him. Surely, as a lawman on Rattlesnake Key he was aware of the deaths at Far Horizons. She decided to tell the Chief a little bit to see if he would take the bait and reveal how much he knew.

"Well, he did say something about some strange deaths at Far Horizons. But he didn't go into any detail." Mentally, she crossed her fingers and apologized to Lillian. "He also said the locals call it The Last Resort, but it was almost a joke. And that's all he said. Other than that, we talked about the news business and my TV show."

"You sure that's all he said?"

"Why, yes, Chief."

"You'd tell me if there was anything else, wouldn't you? This is a serious crime, Miss Colby. I don't mind telling you we're all upset because things like this don't happen on Rattlesnake Key. Not on Frank Westendorf's watch. So anything you can remember might help. Even something that doesn't seem important to you." He chuckled. "Of course, you would. You're a friend of Nussbaum's. You want us to catch whoever did this to him."

"Do you have any leads at all? Any clues? Any suspects?"

He rose. "We're leaning toward the theory that it was a transient. Maybe somebody on drugs. Robbery."

"That's ridiculous." Clyde stood so quickly the chair tipped backward and she barely caught it. "Why would a robber pin the Star of David on his chest?"

"To throw us off the track, Miss Colby. Drug addicts are very clever people. But we are continuing our investigation."

"But what about the deaths he mentioned? And people referring to Far Horizons as the Last Resort?"

He opened the gate. "I'll certainly look into that. But I have to tell you that a lot of folks around here are jealous of Horace Beck, him being an outsider and so rich and all."

"You can't be serious. He's been here since 1974."

"Yes, ma'am, he has. But he's never mixed in with the townspeople. And he's a hard man to get to know. Sort of standoffish, if you know what I mean. And they resent that. I've been working on him to get more involved in local events, and I guess it won't hurt to tell you that I've heard the Last Resort comments, too. I've been doing my own investigation, but he's a mighty important man so I'm keeping it very low key. I'll appreciate your keeping that to yourself. Sort of off-the-record, so to speak. And if you find anything, you'll let me know. Right?"

"Of course, Chief."

A drug addict, she thought as she drove back to Far Horizons. She hoped the Chief abandoned that kick, but one thing was clear, he might be a nice man, but he wasn't much of a police chief. No wonder strange things happened on the island.

She parked and walked absentmindedly through the lobby, nodding to Davy. She wondered idly if he ever had time off and what it would be like to work for your father. God. She'd never work for Big Clyde. Clyde Charles Colby would have her in law school and then a courtroom in a heartbeat. But it would be corporate law. Something safe.

Men.

She decided she'd go to her room, change and go for a walk on the beach. She needed to clear her head. And although she hated exercise, it was a necessary evil and getting up at three-thirty meant she was having to eliminate her early morning run. If she didn't, she packed on the pounds. And one pound looked like ten on camera. Maybe she could work out in the resort gym. If only she didn't love food—

"Miss Colby?" Davy's voice interrupted her musings and she turned. He waved a letter in the air. "This came for you in today's mail."

She backtracked, returning to the front desk. "Thank you," she said, seizing the letter from his hand while barely missing a step. Couldn't be a bill. Or a fan letter. No one knew where she was.

In the elevator, Clyde glanced at the envelope. Rattlesnake Key postmark. No return address. She edged the flap with her fingernail and withdrew a sheet of plain white paper. She didn't recognize the erratic, back-slanted handwriting, but the signature caused her stomach to lurch. Eli. Even though she was alone in the elevator, she crammed the letter into her purse. Hurrying down the hall, Clyde waited until she was safely inside her room before she took out the note.

Dear Clyde,
I'm sorry I've gotten you into this because I think it's becoming dangerous. Someone is following me. I've seen the same car outside the newspaper offices and around town. I've got a gut feeling it has something to do with Kristallnacht because of something Mr. Beck said to my grandfather, but I don't know what. If something happens to me, don't—I repeat—don't go to the police. Stay out of it. Finish your show and leave Rattlesnake Key.

Be smart, Clyde, and pay attention to what I'm telling you. In the meantime, let's forget about dinner tonight. Someday we'll have that Kreplach and Kugel and I'll introduce you to my grandfather and he'll think you're the cat's pajamas—his favorite expression.
Your friend,
Eli

Her hands trembled as she began to comprehend the note's implications. She took a deep breath. Then another. She thought about her trip to the police department and wondered why Eli was so adamant that she not contact them. She replayed the conversation she'd had with Westendorf to make sure she hadn't given him any information he shouldn't have. Then she shook her head in despair. She didn't know what information he should or shouldn't have. But Eli must feel that someone in the police department couldn't be trusted. She decided it couldn't be Westendorf. He seemed like a regular guy, if not too sharp.

Despite Eli's warning, what had happened to him and his note only reinforced her decision. People were dying at Far Horizons. She would find out what was going on.

She re-read the letter. *Kristallnacht.* That was the first order of business. To find out what it was. Like the *golem,* the word was vaguely familiar. Too bad her computer didn't have a modem. It was deliberate—she hated e-mail. It was such an intrusion. She'd have to pay another visit to Lillian Albritton at the library. Lillian would help her figure out about *Kristallnacht.* And while she was at it, she'd ask the librarian what she'd meant when she'd called Far Horizons the Last Resort.

And maybe it was time to bring Andy into this. He'd been a big help when she'd covered the cop beat a couple years earlier.

No. Not if it was as dangerous as Eli thought.

And judging by what had happened to him, Eli knew what he was talking about.

Clyde had laid some groundwork with Chief Westendorf. If she uncovered any concrete evidence of what was going on, she'd take it to Westendorf. She'd be smart. She wouldn't take it to him in the police department, though, just in case there was somebody on the department she couldn't trust. No, she would call him and set up a meeting with just the two of them. Maybe she could find out why Eli didn't trust them.

EIGHT

CLYDE COULDN'T GET ELI and his note out of her mind. All during dinner that evening, she was distracted. She tried to make the usual, easy conversation with Andy, Bernie and Pete, but she couldn't stay focused on what they were saying. Thoughts of a television show, of what lens to use, of demographics, of news and accounting budgets—it all seemed so shallow and frivolous when a friend might be dying.

She kept replaying the dreadful scene in her mind—Eli lying motionless on that hospital bed hooked up to IV bags and machines that bleeped and green-lined, recording all the data that established Eli as a viable living being—pulse, blood pressure, fluids flowing into and out of his body, heartbeats. She wondered if Eli was aware of what was happening to his body and his life. Or was he, she hoped, somewhere resting, gathering strength for a return to full consciousness. And, by damn, she hoped he could remember the bastards who'd done this to him.

The grilled shark with dilled Hollandaise sauce she'd ordered seemed tasteless even though she knew it was properly prepared by Henri Doucette and undoubtedly delicious. The morsel grew larger and larger in her mouth and she could barely swallow. An hour from now she was sure she wouldn't be able to remember what she'd eaten. Furthermore, she had absolutely no appetite so it was a waste of time to even try.

She was reaching for the napkin in her lap when the expression on Andy's face changed. His mouth froze in a half-smile. His eyes became carefully noncommittal. She twisted in her chair and saw that Horace Beck was approaching followed by the wine steward who carried a bottle of wine in a bucket of crushed ice.

"May I join you?" Beck said pleasantly.

"Of course," she said.

He pulled a chair from a nearby table and squeezed in next to her. She hadn't spent any time with him other than the hour or so they'd spent discussing the show and the recipes Henri would feature.

"I have come to apologize," he said and the merest hint of an accent revealed a carefully controlled excitement. "The delay. I am so full of regret. Tomorrow will be back on the target."

His head was large, almost but not quite too large for his body. His eyes were the dominant feature of his face and tonight they exuded a restless energy. The whites were the same intensity as chalk so that his irises seemed bluer in contrast. Even as he spoke to her, he scanned the room, hesitating at each entrance. When he fixed those startling eyes on her, she felt impaled like a shrimp on a skewer. It was difficult to look away.

"I have spoken with Henri. He will be in the kitchen waiting in the morning at your preplanned time," Beck continued.

She looked toward Andy who was sitting very still, waiting, watching. She knew he hadn't forgotten the bruises on her arms.

"Will you and your crew share my wine? It is from my own private stock, a very splendid Riesling." He displayed the bottle, which bore the label of a German winery—*Weingut Dr. Bürklin-Wolf.* "Are you familiar with this winery?" When she shook her head, he responded, "Then you are in for a splendid surprise. *Weingut* was founded in 1597 by Bernhard Bürklin and is still managed by his descendants. They have a tradition of creating very, very good wines."

As he spoke, her attention was drawn to his mouth, vivid red, perfectly formed, but wide and framed by thick lines that emphasized the long, straight, white teeth.

"Thank you," she murmured, wondering why he was being so friendly.

As if in answer to her unspoken question, he said, "You must think we are terribly disorganized. First, there is the confusion about the date you are to arrive. And then the plumbing problem."

"Mistakes happen in any business," she said while he gestured to the sommelier who opened the bottle, poured a small portion into a glass, and paused while Beck breathed in the wine's bouquet before tasting it. He nodded and the wine steward filled everyone's glass. Andy put his hand over his glass, but looked at her as if to ask, *are you sure you want to do this?* She nodded her head ever so slightly and he lifted his hand so the steward could pour.

"Thank you, Fritz," Beck said and motioned to him. The steward returned to where Beck sat and bent down, awaiting instructions. Beck spoke quietly and Fritz nodded, almost snapping a salute as he left.

"I hope you will not mind. I have asked Grace to join us. She will be here shortly."

"That would be lovely." Clyde meant it.

After three glasses of the interesting wine, Beck relaxed. Soon he was joking with Andy, but she found his humor ponderous, almost too hearty. "The Nikon?" he was saying with a laugh. "Bah. Never a better lens made than Zeiss. Never a better camera made than the Hasselblad."

She was amazed when he dismissed Ansel Adams as lucky and praised Albert Renger-Patzsch, someone she'd never heard of, as perhaps the world's finest photographer. He talked to Bernie about lighting, citing fill lights and discussed—very knowledgeably—the superiority of handhelds as opposed to built-in light meters. Without skipping a beat, he segued into a discussion of food and shared one of his favorite stories about German food.

"My mother," he said, "made the finest *Rolladen* I've ever tasted. I can still remember her pounding and pounding the round steak until it was paper thin. Her secret was the slice of dill pickle in the middle of the roll."

Grace joined them a little later. She wore a pale blue chiffon cocktail dress. "I'm sorry. I know I'm so late," she said nervously. "But after dinner," she explained, directing her explanation toward Beck, "the women held a quick meeting to hear reports on this year's Oktoberfest. We did very well, Mr. Beck," she added softly. "We made a lot of money, more than last year." When Grace was carefully made up with foundation, blush, skillfully applied eye makeup, Clyde realized for the first time that she was a very pretty woman when she was out of her housekeeper's uniform.

"That's good," Beck responded without emotion. "Grace learned how to make a most delicious strudel and every year she makes it for Oktoberfest. You should ask her for the recipe, Miss Colby."

By evening's end, Beck had talked freely about growing up in Buenos Aires. And he discussed some of the values he had learned while attending military school in Argentina, emphasizing the importance of discipline and detail. Both attributes, he said, were very important in explaining his success first as an engineer and inventor and now as an innkeeper.

As the evening progressed, Beck grew increasingly ebullient. He spoke rapidly, gestured expansively with his hands. Clyde found herself almost charmed by this different side to Beck. He was delightful. She could see why Grace had been attracted to him and why Davy was so loyal. Horace regaled them with amusing stories about the funny things guests had done during the twenty-odd years he'd been at Far Horizons—the honeymooner who took the wrong door and locked himself, nude, in the corridor; the stars who had stayed at the resort—Bing Crosby, Sonny Bono, Frank Sinatra. About Lucille Ball who'd sent a private jet back to Beverly Hills to pick up the formula for her hair color; about Elvis Presley who'd ordered room service at 4:00 AM for a half-dozen fried peanut butter and banana sandwiches.

His laugh grew louder and Grace grew quieter as if by her reticence, she could calm him. Clyde also wondered if her dour mood had something to do with the possible sale of the resort she'd mentioned.

Afterward, on her way to her room, she paused in the doorway of the lounge for a moment to listen. Lila was at the piano bar and playing one of the local favorites, the Jim Croce classic *Time in a Bottle*. Clyde was standing in the shadow of an Areca palm humming, singing along under her breath when someone called her name. Startled, she glanced over and caught sight of Penny sitting on a barstool near Lila. He was wearing a dinner jacket and hoisting a brandy snifter. He gestured to the empty barstool next to him.

As she approached, he lofted the snifter. "Have a drink with me?"

She walked around and leaned against the piano, nodding a greeting to Lila who'd confessed to being an amateur chef in an earlier conversation. "I'd love to, Penny, but I have to get up at three-thirty in the morning. The TV business plays havoc with a person's social life." But she did want to talk to him, although this certainly wasn't the place. It was too public and too noisy. "I've got an idea," she said bending close so she could speak into his ear. "Remember when we were talking about tennis the other night and you said you knew how I could improve my serve?"

"I remember," he said, nodding and speaking louder so he could be heard over the sounds of the music, of people making cocktail chatter and the clinking of glasses.

"Let me take a raincheck on the drink," Clyde persisted. "But if you'll take some time with me on the tennis court tomorrow after we're finished shooting, I'll buy lunch."

He smiled and raised his brandy glass in a salute. "Delighted, my dear. What time? Ten? Ten-thirty? And I'll reserve the court."

"Let's make it ten-thirty. See you then, Penny."

Leaving, Clyde smiled and waved farewell to Lila. The piano player was an oasis of light and fire in the dark lobby. The soft spotlight focused on her hands on the keyboard making her diamond rings, her blonde hair and the sequins on her electric blue blouse shimmer and sparkle.

A scant half-hour later, as Clyde sat on the balcony of her

room, a light rain blew in from the west. The mist dampened her hair, but the air felt so good, so clean she couldn't bring herself to go back into her room. Every time she thought about Eli's beating, she wondered again why a person's religion should matter so much that someone would actually try to kill another human being. She wasn't a fool and certainly you didn't remain naïve long in the news business. Nonetheless, she was continually stunned by the cruelty of the human race.

Certainly she could understand killing in self-defense; although, if she were honest with herself, she wasn't sure she could do it. She supposed she could even understand killing accidentally in a dispute or for survival, but not religion. As long as the practice of that religion didn't harm anyone else.

During dinner, she hadn't had a chance to talk to Andy. However, after Beck and Grace had gone up to their suite, she'd had an opportunity to tell him about Eli's investigation, but decided against it. That could be counterproductive. He had enough on his mind with the show. He didn't need to be distracted or worried about her. And he would worry. Now, alone in the dark where she was prey to her fears, Clyde hoped with all her heart that she hadn't made a mistake by not telling Andy and that Penny could give her some tidbit of information about Sam that would enable her to trust him.

The rain intensified. Driven by the querulous, gusting wind, large droplets of water stung and soon she was drenched. She hurried through the French doors and the wind slammed them behind her so hard the glass rattled. Once inside, she headed for the bathroom where she toweled herself dry. It was early, not quite nine, but she donned her sweat shirt, resolutely put the chocolate—uneaten—on the nightstand, pulled back the spread and crawled between the sheets. At least she had a plan for the next day.

She closed her eyes. But sleep danced out of reach. Sam McKenzie's hurtful words echoed in her mind. What did he mean he knew about women like her who were leery of commitment? And why did he get so furious? Then she thought of Eli again and unwanted tears stung her eyes. She sat up in bed and turned the light on. She reached for the chocolate on the nightstand and consumed it in two quick bites. She took the key to the minibar out of the nightstand's drawer, opened it and took out a huge Hershey's chocolate bar, which she ate, square by square. Then she had a package of pistachio nuts, which she polished off with a small wine cooler. Her stomach rolled and rebelled, and guilt compounded her misery.

Finally, it might have been hours later, she fell asleep. Outside, the rain thundered into a squall. Winds whipped around the corners of the resort. Clyde tossed once or twice, burrowed deeper beneath the sheets, and soon sank into a heavy and dreamless slumber.

NINE

"NO, NO, BABE! You're still coming in too soon with that line," Andy said for the fourth time. "And Bern, fix that key light. You've got the top half of her face in shadow. Pete, I'm getting feedback. Check your mikes."

Clyde rubbed her arms. The kitchen would have been chilly except for the lights.

"And can you punch it up a little?" Andy was saying. "We need more energy and enthusiasm." Then his familiar smile lightened his bony face, mitigating the gravity of his expression. "Not a pinch. Not a dollop. Clyde, we need a soupçon more pizzazz."

That was still another reason she loved working with him. In addition to his sense of humor, he knew what to say. If he had to tone her down a little on camera, he said something serious, but not just anything—something he knew she could relate to, something that would help her adjust her emotional range naturally. She trusted him implicitly. He was ever the professional, but more than understanding production techniques, he had a sense of what was right, of what worked and what didn't.

"Henri Doucette," she said, smiling into the camera, forcing herself not to think about how sleepy she was, "has created his delicious Acapulco Lime Snapper." She gestured to the beautifully garnished fish on the platter the chef was holding toward the camera. "But don't go away. We have more tasty treats ahead for you. After these messages, we'll return with

Henri and watch, as—exclusively for Clyde's Gourmet Galley—Henri prepares his avocado en gelee."

"Works for me," Andy said, when she finished speaking. "You nailed it that time. Okay, you and Henri take a break while we get some pick-up shots for B-roll. Just to cover us." He gestured to Bernie. "Bern, bring those lights in."

For all practical purposes, that marked the end of the day's shooting for Clyde and she was glad. She headed for her room. She had time for a nap before she met Penny for tennis. Ordinarily she enjoyed every step of the process including researching the locations, writing the script, the actual shooting and the editing, she mused as she rode up in the elevator. Moreover, she loved the food. Every scrap and morsel, every scent, every texture. Never mind that she had to knock herself silly exercising to work off the unwanted pounds, she loved it all. But today her mind was focused on the meeting with Penny.

Once in her room, she smiled when she discovered a plate bearing two kiwi fruit tarts waiting for her on the table by the French doors. A note had been slipped beneath the lace paper doily the tarts rested on. It read, *"Bon ami, A sweet to aid your energy level."* It was signed, *"Henri."*

What a nice thing for him to do, Clyde thought. But then he was a very nice man. She nibbled at one of the tarts determined to take just a taste, but it was so delicious her resolve fled the scene and she consumed the entire tart, looking longingly at the second. But enough was enough and she was sleepy.

Shrugging out of her clothes, Clyde creamed her face to remove the heavy makeup, slipped nude between the sheets. She yawned and stretched out, but sleep eluded her and as the hours passed, all she could think about was her tennis date with Penny. It was urgent that she talk to Penny, vital she find out whether or not she could trust Sam. And, if she could, she'd have to figure a way to get past yesterday's quarrel. A little before ten, she gave up, got up and slipped into her tennis togs, grabbed her racquet, and headed downstairs.

"Tennis, Miss Colby?" Davy asked when she emerged into the lobby. Every time she saw him, she was struck by the resemblance between son and father. Their features were heavy and intensely masculine. And with his blonde hair and brilliant blue eyes, he was almost handsome. Horace Beck must have been every bit as handsome twenty years earlier. And yet, Grace had left her imprint, for Davy had one dimple in his left cheek. It flashed on the rare occasions when he smiled.

She nodded. "I'm meeting Mr. Dunn." She strode through the dining room to the tennis courts. She checked with the pro in the tennis shop. Penny had reserved the front court, but when she arrived, he was nowhere to be seen. She did a few stretching exercises, then sat down on one of the green benches that fringed the courts to wait.

The sun was rising toward its zenith and the air was muggy and heavy. Its rays glanced off the asphalt parking lot beyond. Waves of heat and the glare turned her vision into slashes of silver against black velvet. She rubbed her eyes and the back of her neck with the heavy Turkish towel the attendant in the pro shop had given her.

She tried to ignore a nagging sense that something was wrong. Penny had not struck her as inconsiderate. If something had come up, he'd have left a message. She waited a few more minutes then decided to leave. Something must have happened. She decided to call his room. As Clyde walked back toward the resort, Davy emerged from the dining room and waved at her.

"Miss Colby," he said, standing in the dining room's doorway, "maybe you'd better sit down a moment." He gestured toward the green bench.

"I'm not tired. I haven't played yet. I'm still waiting for Mr. Dunn, but I'm about to give up on him."

He lowered his eyes. "Yes, I know. Please won't you sit down? I have something to tell you..."

"Tell me what?" Since he apparently wasn't going to tell her anything while she was standing, she conceded and sat on the edge of the bench.

He shifted his weight uneasily, rocking back and forth on his heels then finally sat down beside her. "It's about Mr. Dunn."

"Well? Is he going to be late? Does he want to reschedule? What's the deal?"

Davy cleared his throat then said, "Mr. Dunn won't be meeting you this morning."

"So?" She waited then said, "Davy, you will drive me bananas if you don't tell me whatever it is you want to tell me."

He looked away toward the tennis courts. "Mr. Dunn is dead. He died last night."

"Died?" She sagged against the back of the bench, trying to comprehend what he had said. "Dead? Died last night?" The image of Penny singing along with Lila at the piano bar flashed in her mind. "But he was fine last night. I talked to him. At the piano bar in the lobby. What happened?"

"Heart. Possible aneurysm," Davy said. "Or a stroke. We're not sure." He rose, closing the subject with the terse explanation. "Can I get you anything? Help you into the lobby? Take you to your room?"

"No. I didn't know Penny that well. I mean I thought the world of him, but what about his family?" Clyde realized she wasn't making much sense, but she was having a tough time grasping what he'd said. Penny dead? Every instinct she possessed told her it couldn't be so.

"They've been notified, Miss Colby. Everything has been taken care of. His body was shipped to Kentucky about half an hour ago."

"So soon?" She felt a sense of loss. She thought of the fun they'd had playing Scrabble on Sam's boat, of how silly he'd looked as Nero. First Greg Lanken, now Penny. And Eli. Mustn't forget Eli.

Could there possibly be a connection between them?

"If I can't do anything for you," Davy was saying, "I'd better get back to the front desk."

He left her alone then and, after a few moments, she rose and started toward the lobby. She knew it was fanciful, but the day suddenly appeared gray. Dim. She pushed through the heavy glass doors into the dining room. The early lunch crowd was filing in. Most guests had grown accustomed to seeing her and the crew, and now several waved and smiled as she passed their tables. She did her best, but she could muster only a faint grimace she hoped they would interpret as a smile.

Clyde stopped at the desk to see if she had any messages. Her thoughts in turmoil, she was caught completely unaware when a hand landed on her shoulder. Whirling around, she confronted Sam and was immediately, desperately, illogically happy to see him. "Sam, I…"

He nodded. "Penny. I know. I just heard. Horace told me."

"What are you doing here?"

"I was supposed to have lunch with the two of you. He felt you were being unfair to me."

"I guess there's nothing we can do for Penny, is there?"

Sam didn't answer at first, sadness shading his dark eyes. "No. Horace told me all the arrangements are in progress. He's upstairs with a maid now supervising as she packs Penny's belongings. They'll be shipped to his family. But you and I still have to eat. We can have that lunch."

"I couldn't eat a thing."

Patiently, he took her hand and held it. "Clyde, you need to get away from here for a while. They serve great grouper fingers at the Rattlesnake's Den. The fish is so fresh you'd swear they'd just caught it out the back door. What do you say?"

She nodded. "I should change." She gestured toward her tennis shorts.

"You're fine. Come on. Let's get out of here."

She was completely disarmed. He was so considerate, so thoughtful of her feelings even though he had been closer to Penny than she had. Then the warning voice shrieked accusingly in her mind. *Have you forgotten, Dummy? You were having lunch with Penny to pry information about this man. But Penny thought you were being unfair. That must mean…but you have only Sam's word for that…*

The drive to the restaurant was a silent journey. Her thoughts returned again and again to the previous night when she'd seen Penny at the piano bar. He'd been in good spirits and seemed perfectly healthy. She still couldn't believe he was dead. At the

Rattlesnake's Den, they ordered the grouper fingers and the food was perfect. Crunchy on the outside with light, spicy batter. The fish was fresh and mild, but she hardly tasted it and could only manage a bite or two. She made small talk, determined not to discuss anything other than superficial issues until she had dealt with Penny's death. Sam followed her lead and they discussed her show, his sailing school, the stock market.

After lunch, because she didn't want to go back to the resort and she didn't want to go to the *Sanity*, he suggested giving her the grand tour of his sailing school. It was housed at the marina in a neat, two-room frame cottage that had once been someone's vacation retreat. In the front room, he'd hung posters displaying the different types of sails and knots along with photos of sailing vessels, his business license and his captain's papers. His office was furnished with a battered old desk topped with a calendar and a file box for three-by-five cards. At the side of the room, a long folding table with six collapsible chairs faced a blackboard.

He ushered her into the back room, which was comfortable and casual. It contained a card table, a plaid-upholstered sofa and chairs that encircled a potbellied wood stove. Navigational and hurricane charts were on the wall.

Without asking, Sam reached up into the cabinet and took down a glass canister that contained a package of *Café de Oro* from Honduras. He spooned out and measured the beans, ground them, put the coffee into the filter with a pinch of salt and made a pot using spring water from the cooler.

She watched his spare, no-moves-wasted procedure. "Penny was fine last night when I talked to him in the lobby," she said finally. "He looked as healthy as you do. And how quickly everything was handled. By the time Davy told me about it, Penny's body was already en route to Kentucky. Don't the Florida Statutes require an autopsy when the death is unattended? Don't bodies have to be released by the medical examiner? Of course, they do," she answered her own question. "My dad's a judge. We discussed this any number of times when I covered the police beat."

"You've got me there," Sam said. "I'm no lawyer."

His actions were so normal. Even the brewing of the coffee was so ordinary, so non-threatening she could hardly believe they were discussing something as insidious as the unexpected death and autopsy of a friend. He poured two cups, handed her one and sat down beside her on the sofa.

"It's almost as if he never existed. He's here and gone and that's it," she said.

Sam rose. He strode over the window and stared out at the marina. From where she sat, she could see the sun striking the water and the *Sanity* moored to the dock. Next to the *Sanity* was the 24-foot J boat he used for his students.

"I asked some questions," he said after a moment. "The medical examiner, Rudy Schroeder, was there within the hour. The body was released within two. That's damn good service even for a community as small as Rattlesnake Key."

"What are you saying?"

"I'm not sure. But it's very curious that every single detail could be handled so smoothly and so quickly. Almost as if…" His voice trailed away.

"As if what?"

"I don't know yet. When I do, I'll tell you."

"How involved in this are you, Sam?"

"I thought maybe Eli had told you."

"Never mentioned a word."

"Eli came to me with his suspicions about six months ago, although I was already concerned about it. The problem was that neither of us had complete, round-the-clock access to the resort. That's why Eli—against my advice and wishes—decided to bring you into it."

As the afternoon passed, Sam's forthrightness reassured her to the point where she felt comfortable asking him about the photo she'd seen on the *Sanity*.

"You don't have to answer, of course."

"No, Clyde. I want to tell you. I was married," he said and

even though his expression was controlled, his voice even, she sensed the pain it concealed. "Our daughter died in a car accident. That ended the marriage."

He sipped his coffee and put his feet up on the scarred coffee table cluttered with sailing magazines. "I'd been through some pretty bad stuff in Desert Storm, but it was nothing compared to Melanie's death."

"I'm so sorry," she said. "The idea of losing a child..." Remembering the photograph and the beautiful little girl and Penny, she had to repress her tears.

"Her mother almost cracked up," he said, continuing as if she hadn't spoken. "I wasn't in much better shape. At first, we were okay, but the months passed and we didn't talk about the accident and then we didn't talk about anything. When Melanie was gone, Linda wanted out. She didn't want to work through anything; she wanted to move on. And she did. "

"How awful for you to lose both of them."

He rose from the sofa and walked over to the window and stared out across the marina. "You were right," he said. "I don't give many lessons. I don't really need to. I was a very successful stockbroker in Baltimore. Cell phones. PDAs. Fax machines at home with dedicated lines. Internet access at home with a database linked directly into financial centers around the world. The works. The day my wife's divorce was final, I walked into the office and told my partners I was quitting. By the end of that day, I had cleaned out my office, sold the house to one of the partners and was on my way out of town."

He crossed the room again and sat down beside her. "And that's probably a lot more than you ever wanted to know about Sam McKenzie."

Clyde was silent. She couldn't think of a thing to say. Sitting so close to him on the lumpy couch, his pain was almost tangible. Their shoulders touched ever so lightly and she was very aware of him.

"I haven't talked about the past in a very long time, but I wanted you to understand."

The silence lengthened and Clyde stared straight ahead, her

thoughts in turmoil. Too much. There was too much to comprehend, too much to put together and make sense of Penny's death. Greg Lanken's death. Eli's beating. *What did it all mean?*

And now the twists and turns of this new involvement with Sam. Their relationship would never be the same after this afternoon. He had revealed too much. And he was not a man who shared or spoke of himself easily. At last, she felt she could trust him. If she had questions, she could just ask. And he would answer. Honestly. But his words about commitment had hurt. In part, because there was a measure of truth to what he had said. She didn't trust easily, didn't let anyone close—especially men. While she could commit and be loyal, she couldn't reveal. And self-revelation was an important part of any relationship.

"One thing I must know," she said after a long pause.

"Ask. Let's get the bullshit out of the way."

"What are you and that bartender at the Last Resort up to? Why are you always around? Why are you always aware of what's happening even before the authorities? Who are you?"

His lips stilled, his eyes reflected his shock at her barrage of questions. The corners turned up in the early stages of a smile. Then he threw his head back and laughed. "I should have known, Miss-Colby-like-the-cheese. Let a news hen ask one question and she bores in for the kill." He leaned back against the sofa, rubbed his eyes and pushed a lock of hair off his forehead before answering. "Now let's see. I'm who I told you I was. But, being perfectly honest with you, I'll confess that I do hang out at Far Horizons a lot and I do have a reason." He gathered his thoughts.

"When I first came to Rattlesnake Key, I wanted to leave every vestige of Baltimore behind, but every now and then, I'd run across an acquaintance or an old friend from my days in the business."

He rose, filled his cup again, and gesturing with the coffee pot, asked if she wanted a refill, which she didn't. He sat down again, this time a little farther from her as if he needed distance.

"Then about nine months ago," he continued, "I got a note from a close friend, another stockbroker—a partner in a huge Cincinnati firm—saying that he was going to be vacationing at Far Horizons for a couple weeks. He wanted us to get together. He'd been my best man so I couldn't turn him down and, besides, I thought it was time.

"Bob came down, we had a few drinks, went fishing, sailing and then he was dead. Just like Penny. And I had just as many questions as I do now. So I started sniffing around, as they say in the detective novels."

"That's it? The whole story?"

He nodded. "The whole story. I haven't had much luck although I have made a lot of friends on the island and they keep me posted on what's happening—as much as they know. The big problem is getting close to Horace. He's friendly, but never lets his guard down. Now with Penny's death and Eli's beating, I'm more convinced than ever that something's going on there, but I don't know what."

Clyde released the breath she hadn't realized she'd been holding. The sense of relief she felt was so strong she felt as if she'd lost ten pounds on the easiest diet she'd ever undertaken. She took his hand and met his eyes directly. "Then maybe we can help each other, Sam," she said. "I know how to check out news stories and you know the territory. What do you say?"

He clasped her hand and held it. "I think we'll make a dynamite team."

She nodded. A partnership formed. An alliance.

Very slowly, he leaned forward. The sunlight streaming through the window warmed the couch. The air was rife with the scent of salt water and fish. Outside, she could hear sea gulls screaming, cadging food. His face was so close now she could see the tiny worry lines around his eyes, the cleft in his chin, and the slight scrape on his neck where he must have cut himself shaving this morning. And his mouth as it neared hers was opening, softening, inviting her in, luring her with its promise of closeness, of intimacy.

She had a choice. She could say no. She could back away;

tell him to fuck off, that he'd misread her. "I'm just sorry you're so damned good-looking," she whispered as she bent in and met his mouth with her own.

The clocks of the world did not stop, she thought later. The sun didn't pause in its journey across the sky. Heat lightning didn't shatter the peace of the afternoon, but had any of these events taken place, she wouldn't have noticed. The way he surrounded her, the way his mouth gently consumed hers, Sam McKenzie was all she had thought he would be. Clyde was a little embarrassed by the urgency of her own response. He drew her to him so that she lay across his lap.

"Sam," she said, when she could get her breath, "I haven't told you everything."

"I'm sure," he said, kissing her again. "And there's time." His hands traced the outlines of her body, touching, arousing, creating a need, a demand.

She pulled her lips away from his. "It's hard to think straight."

"Haven't you heard," he said as he drew her closer again, "there are times when you aren't supposed to think?"

"No, we have to talk."

"Talk? For God's sake, Clyde, do you realize this is the first time almost since the night on the boat that we haven't been talking?" He pushed back his sleeve and studied his watch. "It's a little after three. Why can't we have this afternoon? Just this afternoon." Then he trailed his finger down her throat along the neck of her blouse, to the point where her breasts swelled. He bent to kiss the flesh there, but she sat up abruptly, swinging her legs around so that her feet were on the floor again.

Tucking her blouse back into her tennis shorts, she brushed her hair back from her face. Then she rose and moved across the room. "Too many things are happening too quickly."

"Not for me."

She forced herself to look away, to stare out the window until she could get a grip on what was happening here. "No," she said finally, "We've got to figure out what's going on with Eli and Penny and Greg Lanken. You and I have time. You said so yourself."

"Hey, you're using my own words against me. That's not fair." He paused. "But you're right."

"You give up too easily, McKenzie. You could have argued a little."

He rose in one sinuous movement and crossed the room. "Okay. Talking is your idea anyway," he said, taking her in his arms. "Besides, I must admit I'm a bit curious. I've never made love to a woman named Clyde before."

"Nope," she pulled back. "Sit down over there," she pointed to the sofa. "Please. We are going to stay a safe distance from one another and talk about all the strange things that have happened at Far Horizons in the past few days."

"More coffee?" Sam strode across the room to the coffee-maker.

"Thank you," she said formally, extending her mug. "Do you have any paper around here? When I'm trying to figure things out, I like to make lists."

He filled her cup, steadying it with one hand, and then put the pot back on the burner. In the front room, he rummaged through several desk drawers and returned with a sheet of letterhead and a ballpoint pen imprinted with Rattlesnake Key Sailing School. She pulled the chair up to the table and prepared to write.

"After we make the lists, we need to make a plan," she said. "That way we won't go off on tangents."

"Is that how you investigate news stories?"

"Well, that's part of it. You talk to a lot of people and ask a lot of questions. And check public records—depending on the story, of course. But if you were a stockbroker, you know how to do research."

"Different kind of research, but it doesn't sound too hard."

Before long it was twilight and they were stymied. Time and again they had gone over the facts as they knew them. "What can the deaths of your friend Bob Harrison, Greg Lanken and Penny Dunn have in common?"

"Other than the fact that they were all officers in large, profitable corporations, I don't have a clue."

"And Eli's beating. We can probably rule that out."

"Why do you say that?" he asked.

"Because it seems obvious, doesn't it? That there's no connection between the three deaths and the beating? Eli's beating is clearly motivated by anti-Semitism. The men who died weren't Jewish."

Sam took a swig of cold coffee and grimaced. "You buy Eli's beating as a coincidence? I don't. And I don't think we should draw any conclusions at this point. I think we should gather all the information we can, then figure out what we've got."

"Okay, let's get started." She swallowed the last of the lukewarm coffee in her cup.

"Are you hungry?"

"I'm always hungry," she said, then glanced at her watch. "Oh, damn. Is it that late already? I was supposed to meet Andy and the guys for dinner."

He took her cup. "They can figure out for themselves that you're not there. Now we've got to work on that note Eli sent you and his reference to *Kristallnacht*." He glanced at the clock on the wall of his office. It was mounted on a piece of oak cut in the shape of an anchor. "It's a little after seven. Library's open till nine. What do you say?"

"I say let the bookworms beware! But if you're going to deprive me of one of Henri Doucette's gourmet concoctions, you've got to buy dinner."

"I can handle that."

TEN

THEY STOPPED BY FAR HORIZONS long enough for Clyde to change and pick up her messages which included one from Palmetto Bay Junior College asking her to speak to the broadcast journalism class. That done, they headed across the causeway to Palmetto Bay and the library. Lillian Albritton wasn't on duty that evening, but the intense, bespectacled college intern on duty took her responsibilities very seriously. Her nametag identified her as Elsie Feldstein.

"Kristallnacht?" She cocked her head, brown eyes glittering, and led them upstairs to the same area where Lillian had taken her a few days earlier. *Was it really only two days?* Clyde marveled.

"Wait here," the young woman instructed and returned moments later with thick volumes of World War II history and a file folder crammed with clippings.

"You'll find no reference to it in your popular encyclopedias, but it's of special interest to Rabbi Meyers and the members of the synagogue. That's why we have so much material. They've been putting together some kind of exhibit. The Rabbi says we must never forget." She addressed Sam directly, making eye contact as often as possible.

"And all you said was hello," Clyde whispered as the young woman walked away.

"Elsie is overwhelmed by my charm and manly good looks," Sam retorted as he sat down across the desk from her. "Elsie appreciates me."

"Yeah, sure."

It took less than an hour, but by the end of that brief period of time, Clyde was appalled both by her own ignorance and the event itself. *Kristallnacht,* she learned, translated from German as "Crystal Night" or "Night of Glass." She read with horror of the night of November 9, 1938 when throughout Germany, the Nazis plundered 267 synagogues, wrecked 815 shops, arrested 30,000 Jews and murdered thirty-six. It started, she pointed out to Sam who by now was reading over her shoulder, two nights earlier when a German diplomat named Ernest von Rath had been murdered in Paris by Herschel Grynszpan as an act of protest against the deportation of Polish Jews from Germany.

Sitting there in the neat and tidy library, it was almost impossible to envision a world where such brutality could exist. She had rambled on so often about the importance of knowing what was going on in your community, of staying current, of being involved. She had seldom considered the importance of knowing what had gone on before so you could avoid its repetition.

"They were incredibly brave," Sam said, his dark eyes grave.

She nodded. "I can't believe how viciously they were brutalized. And that we did nothing."

"Got enough?"

She nodded, sick inside to think of the insane, all-consuming hatred those pages represented.

They returned the clippings file to the librarian and, walking silently, side by side, left the library. Once in the parking lot, she paused. "Let's stop by and see Eli."

Sam put his elbow under her arm and gently pulled her along. "We'll stop if you want to, but don't get your hopes up. I called earlier and Eli still hasn't regained consciousness." He brushed a lock of black hair off his forehead. "The longer he remains unconscious, the worse the odds are that he won't make it back even if he lives."

When they were in Sam's Lexus heading down Gulf Boulevard to the hospital, he said, "One thing we can't ignore."

"And that is?" She twisted in the front seat to see the expression on his face because he sounded so apprehensive.

"The date," he said. "It's only a few days till *Kristallnacht.*"

"I thought of that," Clyde said. "But I feel as though we're battling against spider webs. If, as Eli wrote, something is going to happen at *Kristallnacht,* we know it probably involves the synagogue, but how is Far Horizons involved? Or *is* Far Horizons even involved? And who? Horace, as Penny said, 'runs a tight ship' and is a strict taskmaster, but I can't believe he'd be involved in anything like this." She remembered how amusing he'd been the previous night. "He's good to his help, and he loves Grace and Davy."

"Your logic, Clyde, doesn't compute. Even Adolph Hitler loved animals and was good to his mother. Besides, I didn't think you were that fond of Horace."

"I wasn't. I'm not. But last night I saw a different, kinder, more appealing side to his personality. Of course, we both know people are not always what they seem. But it seems such a stretch to link anyone at Far Horizons to something so bestial. They all seem so normal."

They drove down Gulf Boulevard in silence. Christmas shoppers crowded the sidewalks, their cars clogging the streets like plaque clogging arteries. The streetlights were decorated with tinsel angels holding trumpets aloft. Window displays glittered and gleamed with holiday trappings.

At the hospital, Eliahu was in his usual place in Eli's room. He emerged from the shadowy corner as they entered. Eli lay motionless on the hospital bed. He seemed even paler, smaller than the previous night. The machines continued their incessant monitoring of his human life, pumping, blinking, bleeping, forcing the air into unwilling lungs, nourishment into a stomach to be processed by a body following by unconscious rote the rituals of mindless life.

"Nothing has changed," Eliahu said.

The old man seemed to have aged in only a day. His head quavered on his long, thin neck as if it were too heavy or as if he had lost control of the muscles. Today he wore the same black sweater and still looked as if he were cold, but from an internal chill rather than the weather. Sam insisted on getting the old gentleman a cup of hot tea from the cafeteria and she waited, sitting in the silent gloom, for his return. Eliahu was barely aware of her presence, but he brightened when Sam came back.

"Have you eaten?" Sam asked when he returned carrying the Styrofoam cup.

Eliahu nodded. "My friends from the condo, they force feed me." He managed a weak smile that touched only the corners of his pinched lips. "They threaten to push the food down my throat when I argue that I am not hungry. Besides, the doctor says I must be strong because Eli will need me. He says Eli will require months, years perhaps of physical therapy. If he makes it."

Clyde resisted the urge to hug him, but Eliahu possessed a stoic, innate dignity she didn't wish to assault. She thought again of what Eli had told her of Eliahu's horrible experiences in the concentration camps. And knew that somehow Eliahu would survive, regardless of what happened to Eli. But the pain… She ached for him.

"Can we do anything for either of you?" Sam asked.

The old man waved his hand in negation. "No, no. I wait now. That's all I can do for Eli. All anyone can do. That and pray."

"Then I think we'll call it a night," Sam said. "We haven't eaten yet." He took her hand. "Anyplace in particular you'd like to eat?" he asked as he led her to the door.

She shook her head.

Once inside the elevator, he said, "If you want to stop at the *Sanity,* I'll fix some scrambled eggs. I might even be able to whip up an omelet of some description. How does that sound?"

She hesitated, not wanting to hurt his feelings. Then, as they emerged from the elevator into the hospital lobby, she said finally, "Not tonight, Sam. I know I said you had to buy me dinner, but after everything that's happened, I'm just not hungry." She took his hand. "I want to be with you, but I need time to think."

"And tomorrow there's *Lifestyles of the Rich and the Hungry* to film."

"Was that a note of sarcasm in your voice? I grant you my TV show seems almost inconsequential in the face of Eli's tragedy, but I am here to work. And I have to stay focused. I can't afford to let myself be sidetracked or detoured."

Sam laughed. "Are you calling me a detour? I don't know whether to be complimented or insulted. I've been called a lot of things in my forty-odd years, but I've never been called a detour. All right, Sherlock, what's our next move?"

"I'm thinking," she said as he opened the car door for her. "Tomorrow as soon as I've finished shooting, I think we should drive into Palmetto Bay. Didn't you tell me that's the county seat?"

"Right."

"Well, then, let's go to the county courthouse and see if we can find the death certificates of any other people who died at Far Horizons. Check out the cause of death."

"Good thinking."

As they drove across the causeway, Sam kept glancing in the rearview mirror. "What's wrong?" she asked when he'd done it for the fourth time.

He paused before he answered peering into the black night behind them. "I keep seeing this tan station wagon. I've noticed it several times today. It's behind us now."

"You don't suppose it's the same car that followed Eli, do you?" She could hear the fear in her voice and it made her mad. She would not permit herself to be intimidated.

The remainder of the drive to the resort was tense. They spoke little, glanced often in the rearview mirror. The station wagon maintained a consistent distance, about six or eight car lengths behind. When they turned into the entrance of Far Horizons off Matecumbe Road, the wagon continued past and Clyde let out a gasp of relief. She didn't even realize she'd been holding her breath.

Sam insisted they stop in the dining room for something to eat. The room was deserted and while they couldn't order a regular meal, the short-order chef agreed to put together a platter of cold sandwiches. That suited Clyde fine. It was late and she was more tired than hungry. "Sam," she said later when she walked to the lobby with him, "would you do something for me?"

"What?"

"Call me when you get back to the *Sanity* so I won't worry all night."

It wasn't until much later, after she was in her room at Far Horizons and about to go to sleep, after he'd called to tell her he was okay, that she realized something unusual had happened. She had had to remind herself to stay focused on the show. So much for Josh's complaint that she was too driven. But then her ex-husband had never really known her. Or even tried to. And maybe, just maybe, the failure of their marriage hadn't been all her fault.

She sat up in bed. Was this a result of the newly developing relationship with Sam?

Or the mysterious things happening at Far Horizons?

And was it a good thing?

Maybe Josh hadn't been man enough for her. That's what her Dad had said all along. Maybe he was right. Now that was a thought! And a splendid one at that.

Then there was Sam.

But she didn't want to think about Sam or her sex life. Not now. Not with people suffering. Now was not the time. Actually, now wasn't a good time for any distractions.

She grabbed the remote off the nightstand and clicked on the television. That was the ticket. She lucked out and found an oldie but goodie late-night flick. The singsong voice of Roland Toler as Charlie Chan investigating a murder in *Shadows Over Chinatown* lulled her to sleep in no time.

ELEVEN

SHOOTING, THANK GOD, went well the next morning. Andy was in rare form. Despite the fact that Clyde had spent a very restless night, her makeup masked the dark circles under her eyes. Henri Doucette and his staff were very cooperative and within four hours, they had filmed the preparation of the Calabaza Flan, which Henri chose to serve flaming with rum. It made dramatic film and Andy was ecstatic.

They encountered a few problems—Bernie hadn't recharged one of the battery-operated lights and couldn't find an adapter so he could plug it into a wall socket. They had to track down the resort's maintenance man so they could borrow one of his. A whippoorwill perched on the branches of a Brazilian pepper tree outside the kitchen window persisted in breaking into his plaintive song just as Andy was ready to shoot. Finally, Pete went outside and flapped his arms to chase the bird away. Once the warbling fowl had been displaced, filming went smoothly.

It was still nearly 6:00 AM before Andy had what he needed and she was free to return to her room. Sam showed up as planned at eight-thirty and they put the next step of their plan into action.

CROWDED INTO A CUBICLE in the county clerk's office later that morning, Clyde rubbed her eyes. Not only were her eyes tired, she was getting a headache from staring at the constantly moving fine print of the microfilmed death certificates. And even her shoulders hurt from bending over the viewer. The certificates weren't cross-indexed by place of death, which meant that she and Sam had to go through every single death recorded in Everglades County. They had started with 1974, the year Beck had first reopened Far Horizons. But it was slow going. Five hours of work and she had only three names. Across the narrow aisle, she could see Sam's dark head. He, too, was staring intently at the microfilm viewer.

Time for a break. She grabbed her shoulder bag and crossed the few steps that separated them. "Any luck?" she asked, rubbing the back of his neck and shoulders.

"Not much."

"Want to get a cup of coffee?"

"Thought you'd never ask," he said. He removed the roll of microfilm he was viewing, replaced it in its cardboard carton and slipped it back into the empty slot in the standing file at the end of the aisle. "How'd you sleep last night? Did you have a guilty conscience?"

"A guilty conscience?" she echoed as they walked past the counter where the two clerks in the office were shuffling through and separating a huge stack of preprinted legal documents—mortgages, deeds, blue-backed divorce complaints. "Why should I have a guilty conscience?" she persisted as they pushed through the double glass doors and walked down the hall to the tiny snack bar. It consisted of a counter and three small tables positioned against a glass wall overlooking the street.

"Sending a poor man to bed alone and lonely."

"Hush," she said, blushing as the blind man who operated the stand for the State of Florida, followed the counter with his hand until he stopped in front of where they stood.

"Get us a table by the window. I'll get the coffee."

She did as Sam asked, still blushing because she knew that even though Sam had spoken in an undertone, the counterman had undoubtedly heard him.

She was grateful that the blind man gave no indication of having heard. He merely said, "Help you, sir?" He stared ahead stiffly, wiping his hands on his apron, which was slightly splotched with food stains.

"Two coffees," Sam said. "One black, one with cream."

The counterman carefully placed the coffee on the counter and two creamers out of his apron pocket. "Two sixty-five."

Sam left bills and change on the counter then carried the Styrofoam cups to the table, placing one cup and the creamers in front of Clyde.

As they sat there relaxing, Clyde looked out the window across the hibiscus hedge and glanced idly down the street. To the left where Gulf Boulevard intersected Lee Street, the street on which the courthouse was located, tourists wandered in and out of boutiques and art galleries. A trio of violinists, positioned in front of an old restored movie theatre, sat behind music stands with sheets of music flapping in the gentle breeze from the Bay. She couldn't hear the music, but watched as their upper bodies swayed and they tapped their feet. It was a pleasant moment and not for the first time, Clyde acknowledged that the changes the West Coast of Florida had experienced in the fall out from the opening of I-75 were not all bad. She liked the little boutiques and art galleries and the introduction of the different cuisines and the emphasis on the arts.

She thought about Sarasota, the town where she'd grown up. Residents were still struggling to accept the fact that it was no longer a sleepy small town that had once been a fishing village where the Ringling Brothers Barnum & Bailey Circus had its winter headquarters. The new Sarasotans, like many of the people who'd settled on the West Coast, were wealthy and cultured. And determined to protect their area from becoming an asphalt paving lot. She was still musing about the changes and sipping her coffee when she spotted it.

She sat erect. "Sam?"

He looked up from the notes he'd jotted on a legal pad. "What?"

"That station wagon. Over there. Next to the Ford Taurus." She pointed down Gulf to a tan station wagon parked beneath an oak tree.

"It looks like the one that followed us last night."

Hand shaking, she carefully placed the plastic cup on the table. "This is getting heavy," she said turning to face him. "Maybe we'd better tell someone what we're doing in case something happens to us." She picked up her cup again, forced her hand to be steady and took a long swallow. When she put the cup back down, she jerked her hand nervously and brown liquid sloshed over the cup's side. "Except what would we tell them?" she asked as she wiped up the spilled coffee with a napkin. "We don't know anything yet. And who would we tell? Andy has so much on his mind and he worries so. Eli said not to go to the police. He didn't strike me as paranoid. He must have had a reason for telling me that."

"Yeah," Sam said, doodling a spider's web on his legal pad. "Eli had found out something about the police department, but he didn't have a chance to tell me what it was."

"I'm glad I'm not in this on my own."

"I'm glad you're not, too, because you have a tendency to rush headlong into situations. And this one is dangerous." He cupped her hand in both of his.

"What makes you think I'm so rash?" she demanded.

"Take that cooking demo. You've never done one, but your first will be in front of a potential audience of four-hundred. And Andy's told me about some of the stuff you got into as a police reporter."

"Oh."

"And I'm determined to make sure nothing happens to you. That's why you should stay with me on the *Sanity.*"

"We have to be practical, Sam. Think what we would lose."

"What?"

"Someone on the scene. At least if something happens, I'll be right there."

Sam swallowed the last of his coffee. "That's precisely what worries me. Finish your coffee and let's wrap this up. My eyes are crossing and I don't want to do this so long that the condition becomes chronic."

By mid-afternoon, they had scanned twenty-eight years and

Clyde was feeling increasingly uncomfortable. The deaths at Far Horizons had started in 1992 and a pattern was emerging that helped her understand Lillian Albritton's offhand crack about Far Horizons being the last resort.

"Do you realize," she said to Sam, scanning the lists on their two legal pads as he drove back to far Horizons, "that at least two men have died at Far Horizons every year for the past decade?"

"That many?" he asked, looking behind him in the rearview mirror.

She ran her forefinger down the lists. "That many," she echoed. "Most died of heart attacks, cardiac arrest. A couple from allergies. A couple from breathing problems. Well, that'll do it. If you quit breathing, you die every time. And," she continued, "Did you notice the occupations listed on the death certificates? Every single one who died was a CEO, CFO or chairman of the board. Something like that. And some of them were from foreign corporations. What could that mean? Something? Nothing? Did they die because they were in high stress positions?"

Sam glanced at the rearview mirror. "Anyone following us?"

"No, I think you lost them in town."

"Were any of the people who died Jewish?"

"You're thinking of Eli, aren't you? Remember that he was just a reporter." She scanned the list again. "Three or four. Not enough to make a definite link to Eli's beating."

Sam shook his head thoughtfully, his eyes focused on the rearview mirror. "Knowing this area, Clyde, I can't believe we've got two major, simultaneous conspiracies. But I'm sure we're on to something. I'm willing to bet most resorts don't have two deaths a year. Not a-hundred-and-fifty-room resorts. Maybe some of the huge hotels with twelve-hundred rooms do, but not ones this small." He turned onto the causeway heading across the bay toward Rattlesnake Key. "You're very quiet," he said after a long silence. "Okay, I'll bite. What are you thinking about now?"

"About our next step. What we do now."

They were about halfway across the causeway. The atmosphere was still and the water was smooth as a mirror. The sky was clear, interrupted only by a few puffy, cotton ball clouds. Sam said nothing, but when they had exited the causeway, he turned left onto Matecumbe Road.

"Sam? Far Horizons is to the right."

"News flash, Clyde," he said. "I live here. I know where Far Horizons is."

"Well, where are we going then?"

"You'll see."

She said nothing more until he turned onto the sandy road that led to Rattlesnake Key Marina. The road twined along the shoreline. On their left, the waters of the Gulf of Mexico sparkled. The road twisted to the right, and for a time, red mangroves obscured their view of the water. On the left, scrub oaks, Royal palms, Australian pines and palmettos masked Matecumbe Road from view. Finally, Sam took a side road that broke through the brush. He brought the car to a halt on a knoll that overlooked the water. They were surrounded on three sides by oaks and palms and mangroves. Farther down the road lay the small building that housed his sailing school. Beyond was the dockmaster's building. Ahead was the planking of the marina, and beyond that, at one of the slips, rocking gently, waited the *Sanity*.

Sam got out of the car, came around, opened her door and led her down the dock to his boat.

"You can say no," he advised as they reached the slip where the *Sanity* was tied off.

"I know."

He took her hand. "Something very nice happened between us yesterday," he said. "It was special. At least to me." A smile played around the corners of his full mouth and within the span of a breath she remembered the way his mouth had felt and tasted and she had trouble getting her breath.

"We can't ignore it," he said. "I won't let you." He jumped down and looked up at her from the deck.

"But now—"

"Is not the best time," he finished for her. "I know. But there never seems to be time. You're either working on your show or we're trying to figure out what happened to Eli and what's going on at Far Horizons. I want us to have time. Time when I feel you're safe. And away from the unpleasantness and," he paused, "away from whatever might lie ahead. Because we don't know what that might be."

He waited.

After a minute or so when she had said nothing, understanding that he was giving her an opportunity to protest, he directed, "Untie that line."

She did as he instructed. Then she took the hand he offered and jumped down onto the deck.

A brisk wind had emerged from the east and soon they were sailing along the coast parallel to Rattlesnake Key.

"I like your boat," she said standing next to him at the helm.

He laughed and he was more relaxed than she had ever seen him. "And that, by God, is high praise coming from a woman who early on dubbed me an arrogant wind jockey."

She had the grace to blush. "Tell me about this boat. It means a lot to you, doesn't it?"

"What do you want to know?" He took his eyes from the horizon and stared at her as he said, "It's fifteen feet four inches at the beam, displaces 46,500 pounds. It carries 260 gallons of fuel and 450 gallons of water. And it's my version of your lighthouse."

"Now all you need is a good cat."

"A good cat?" He raised an eyebrow.

"Yes. At the end of the day, there's nothing like going home and being met by an animal that's delighted to see you. You don't have to walk cats, which makes them lower maintenance than dogs. And a cat never asks you what's wrong, never complains if you're a few minutes late, never questions your taste in friends and never complains you're extravagant."

Sam laughed. "Of course not. Cats just ignore you, don't they?"

"You've obviously never lived with a cat. They are every bit as affectionate as dogs—although, thank God, they don't lick you with big slurpy tongues."

"I'll think about it. Could be good luck, I suppose. I heard or read something about that."

They sailed in silence, neither feeling the need to make conversation. In fact, Clyde found the silence healing and refreshing. Thirty or forty minutes later, they sailed past the snake's head and then Clyde spotted the tiny island she'd thought looked like a snake's fang when she'd seen it on the map.

She discovered it was their destination and soon Sam tied up to an old, abandoned dock on the eastern side of the island facing away from Rattlesnake Key. The drop-off was steep and, on this side of the island, the water was so deep, they couldn't see the bottom. They faced the limitless blue-green waters of the Gulf of Mexico and Clyde found it easy to pretend Rattlesnake Key and Far Horizons didn't even exist.

The air was still and hot and smelled faintly of salt. Gulls circled overhead before flying to a small islet where they nested on the branches of the mangroves. Once the boat was secured, he told her to wait on deck while he went below and rummaged in the cabinets, taking out a blanket. Then he retrieved a bottle of chilled *Fume Blanc* and two glasses from the refrigerator in the galley. He climbed onto the dock, set the wine and blanket down, and then reached back for her. They strode cautiously down the rough, decaying planking onto a pristine white beach littered with driftwood. At one end, a scrub oak tree leaned at a seventy-degree angle, blown half over either in a storm or by time's erosion of the shore. Its huge roots were bared to the elements, but it was not dead. Its limbs were vital and green with tiny leaves. Farther down the beach, a strangler fig climbed the trunk of a Sabal palm.

As he ushered her up the meandering path that led inland, she noted that the island was much larger than it looked on the map that couldn't begin to do justice to its beauty. It was a tangled mass of shades of green and brown and beige, speckled by sun shadows. They ascended the gentle slope to a small hill just beyond the shore and followed a trail that wound upward between a dense stand of Australian pines and a copse of live oak trees. At the very top of the hill, Sam spread the blanket beneath the fronds of a Sabal palm. Before them stretched the glittering, shimmering Gulf. Its waters swept on beyond the horizon, endless and restless, displaying its fretfulness in short, and choppy waves.

"When I first retreated to Rattlesnake Key, I sailed out here day after day. Sometimes, if I stayed too late, I wrapped up in a blanket and slept right here. I did that for months. Gradually, I was able to forgive myself for being alive when my child wasn't. Gradually, I began spending more time in the village. I started getting acquainted with the people and I realized I was making my way back." He sank down on the coverlet and reached for her. "Listen," he whispered.

She knelt next to him and listened obediently. After a moment, she said, "But I don't hear anything. Nothing but the wind in the trees."

"Exactly." He twisted the corkscrew into the neck of the wine bottle, removed the cork and poured the wine into the two glasses. "No cars, no telephones or television sets. No chattering, inane conversation. Just us. To us." He paused and the expression on his face settled back into the lined geography of sadness and unrealized dreams. "And to Penny. I'll miss him."

"To us," she echoed. "And to Penny. Wherever you are, I hope you're okay."

She sipped the crisp white wine, leaned back against the trunk of the palm, and closed her eyes enjoying the sense of renewal the peace had brought. She luxuriated in the heat of the sun, the warmth of his body next to hers. She welcomed the strength of his arm encircling her waist and leaned back to look up at him. It was there, registered in his face, like his honesty and his humor. The caring. The sense of commitment. And she thought about his kindness to Eliahu. And to Penny whose last days had been much happier and more enjoyable because Sam had been his friend.

She closed her eyes again to bask in the sensations as he

lowered his mouth and consumed hers. His mouth was moist, tasting of the wine, but layered and enriched by his unique flavor. The pressure of his mouth on hers grew harder; more intense as she felt his fingers fumble with the tiny buttons of her blouse, felt the fresh air wafting gently across her flesh as he eased the constricting cloth from her shoulders.

"No," she whispered. "No," but she felt a desperate need to prove that she was not dead, that despite Josh and the others who had betrayed her by their shallowness and superficiality, she was emotionally alive and unafraid. She felt still another need almost as urgent as the first—the need to forget the ugliness and danger surrounding them for however long she could. But it was more. It was desire for this one man.

She heard his breath grow harsher, felt him draw back, and listened as he whispered, "Yes."

Clyde opened her eyes to study his face and could tell by his expression that he felt the same needs she did, the need to reassure himself and to create a distance, however brief, from the evil and hate corrupting their world. Her heart accelerated as he freed her breasts and cradled them in gentle hands. She lifted her arms and encircled his neck, drawing him closer, closer until he groaned. Sam pulled back and bent his head until his lips grazed her throat. She felt the welcome warmth of his breath and gasped as he traced with his mouth and lips the texture of her flesh from the hollows of her neck to her nipples, suckling them as carefully as if they were delicate, exotic fruit.

With urgent hands, he untied the belt of her wrap-around skirt and she lifted her hips, helping him to liberate her body from its final encumbrances. His belt stabbed the soft skin of her belly and she twisted away until he had worked free from his jeans, until she could feel the length of his sinewy body against hers.

"Clyde," he breathed. "Clyde. You could be a man with that name."

She kissed the laughter on his mouth, tracing the outline of his half-open lips with her tongue. "A man, huh?" she whispered in his ear, nibbling the lobe, thrusting her tongue.

"Oh, God, Clyde," he groaned. "I don't care what your name is." With urgent hands, he positioned her so that she lay sprawled on her back on the blanket. She arched her hips; he spread her thighs and slid effortlessly into her moist, welcoming body.

"Oh," she managed. "Oh!" And then she surrendered herself to the rhythms and sensations that crowded out all rational thought, all control.

When he was spent, she still didn't want him to leave her body and they lay so close she could feel his heart beating. They didn't talk. Words would have intruded upon the closeness they felt in that moment. When their breathing eased and their hearts slowed, she twisted within the shelter of his arms, put her hands on either side of his face and kissed him full and gently on the mouth. She was not trying to arouse him, merely to share, to communicate without words the myriad emotions washing over her, but she felt him growing hard against her and her heart and body responded to his once again.

Afterward, they lay on the blanket side by side, bodies barely touching, and he said, "I lied."

And she knew whatever he was talking about wasn't important so she didn't react. "So did I."

At that, he sat up. "You did? About what?"

"That whole thing we just did. Twice. I felt nothing," she said and laughed. "Could we try that again until you get it right?"

He chuckled. "But I was serious."

"All right, I'll play your game. What did you lie about?"

"I lied when I said I didn't care about your name. Why did your parents name you Clyde?"

She looked up at him and smiled in her best imitation of Mona Lisa. "Am I to believe," she asked, arching an eyebrow, "that you made love to me to get close enough to force me to reveal my deepest, darkest secrets? Did I ever tell you about the time I was attending a seminar at the University of South Florida in St. Petersburg and at lunch I went to one of my favorite restaurants— Peter's, it was called. French cuisine. They had divine desserts.

Did I tell you I love desserts? And instead of eating a normal lunch, I had three desserts—a puffy, light as air chocolate *éclair,* pineapple tart à la royale and crêpes Suzette—"

"Clyde, what the hell does that have to do with what we were talking about?"

"Nothing," she said in a very reasonable tone of voice. "I was trying to explain how I feel. At this moment, I am as satisfied as if I had eaten three of Peter's finest desserts."

"Why would anyone name a tiny baby girl Clyde?"

"Maybe," she said and paused thoughtfully, "maybe it's a nickname. On the other hand, did you know that people call my Dad Big Clyde and me Little Clyde? Maybe my parents wanted a boy? Oh, Sam, sometimes I can be so absentminded."

"That's ridiculous. I ask you again, what mother would name her child Clyde?"

A brisk breeze riffled the edges of the blanket and she reached for her blouse. "I don't know you well enough yet," she said, pulling the blouse around her shoulders so that she could put it on.

"You are a pain in the ass," he said. "And just for that I'm not cooking your dinner."

"Ever?"

"Ever."

BUT HE DID.

Because they didn't want to leave the island. Not yet. She couldn't bear to return to Far Horizons, to think about death and injury and prejudice. About Eli lying so still. And Penny whose body was probably just arriving to be taken to the funeral parlor. And so he built a fire and cooked steak, dangling it over the fire speared on a sharpened palmetto frond. He buried a can of asparagus in the coals and sliced thick slices of French bread to wrap the meat, capturing the juices.

"No dessert?" she complained, wiping the steak juice from her chin.

"I can come up with something," he said with a smile, "But it won't be Peaches Flambé or Crêpes Suzette."

She dreaded the moment when the sun dropped below the horizon and she knew they must return. He doused the fire and collected their trash. When he had finished, he said to her, "Come on."

She nodded and joined him on the dock. He tossed the blanket and trash aboard, dropped onto the deck then reached up for her. The trip back was peaceful. They stood together at the wheel, his arm wrapped around her. She felt warm and safe and cherished. She hated those moments when he wasn't physically touching her, even though common sense told her to step carefully, not to trust completely. After all, this might be a line. But he seemed like a good guy.

Once they were in the car and on their way back to the resort, when they were both silent, he said, "Clyde, regardless of what happens here, your show is going to be a wonderful success. Because you know what you're doing and you're good at what you're doing."

She looked across at him. "How did you know?"

"Know what? That you've been worried about the show making it? Because I am getting to know you." His face, more relaxed than she'd ever seen it, was filled with warmth. His eyes looked deep into hers, deeper into her heart and mind and for the moment she panicked, fearing he could read the unwritten record of every mistake, every lie, every thought she'd ever had. And worse, that he'd know how hard it was for her to trust. This wasn't right. She'd made a big mistake.

When they pulled into the parking lot at the resort, Sam broke the silence, gesturing to the two patrol units in the parking lot. "Something must be up," he commented as he helped her out of the car.

"I see what you mean. For Chief Westendorf to send both police cars out here, it has to be major."

Once they entered the resort, she wanted to get to her room as discreetly as possible, but Davy was on duty behind the desk and the moment he spotted her, he stopped what he was doing and called across the lobby, "Miss Colby?" His face froze into a mask of shock. He shook his head and continued. "My father wants to see you. He's in his office."

"I'm tired, Davy. I'll see him tomorrow."

"It's important. He needs to see you tonight." Davy's face was pale.

Sam said, "Might as well do what he says. And I'm going with you." He followed as she continued down the corridor, stopping and knocking when they reached the door to Horace's office.

"Come," a voice resounded from within.

Clyde was surprised when they entered the office. The small room was packed. Andy, Bernie and Pete were there along with Horace and Grace Beck, the police chief and two police officers. Andy was sitting in a chair at the far side of the room. He was holding his head in his hands. He looked terribly upset, more stressed than she could ever remember seeing him. Bernie and Pete were leaning against the wall, blank-eyed, staring as if they had suffered a death in the family.

The chief was on the telephone. "No, no word yet," he was saying. "But we've got volunteers posted—"

Grace rushed to her immediately, relief flooding her face. "Miss Colby, you're all right. I'm so glad."

"Of course, Grace. Why wouldn't I be?"

At the sound of her voice, Andy looked up. His eyes widened and he jumped up. He bounded over to the door and dragged her inside. He hugged her so hard she thought he'd break her ribs.

"Clyde, where the hell have you been?"

Confused, she looked at him. "I've been with Sam. Why? What's wrong? What happened?"

Bernie, his freckled face red with excitement, called out, "Clyde, are you okay? Really okay?"

"Of course. What's this all about?"

Chief Westendorf slammed down the receiver as he, too, recognized her. "Miss Colby?" he said, surprise tingeing his voice. "We've been searching for you. We've even had the Everglades County Sheriff's Department organizing roadblocks."

"But why?" Sam demanded, speaking for the first time.

"Because we got an anonymous report that Miss Colby was missing. Possibly kidnapped. We checked it out and none of her crew knew where she was. We even called her station. They didn't know anything either."

"And we hadn't seen or heard from you since early this morning," Andy interjected, a slight accusatory note creeping into his voice. "We didn't know where you were or who you were with."

Sam clutched her arm. "She was with me all the time and she was fine," he said defensively. "Who called you?"

Westendorf didn't respond to the question. Instead, he studied her with a cold, suspicious expression on his face. "There is one other possibility we considered."

"What's that?" Clyde demanded.

"That the whole thing was a publicity stunt. To get some attention for your show."

"You're kidding, I hope," she snapped. "Either that or you're insane." Clyde's fury sent her adrenaline soaring. Her mind told her she shouldn't, but she was so angry she disregarded her own advice, stepped directly into Westendorf's path and lifted her chin so that she could look him square in the eyes. "For your sake, I hope you haven't said anything like that outside this room!"

She paused, swallowing, choking back the rage. "Because if you even hint at anything like that," she continued in an icy tone, "my station and I will sue the shit out of you and the town of Rattlesnake Key. I've been in this business for fifteen years. I never have, and I never would, stoop to anything that dishonest. Nor would I put my friends through an ordeal like that. Come on guys," she said to her crew. "Let's get out of here. Sam?"

"I'll be there in a moment, Clyde. You go on ahead." Sam stepped back to open the door for her.

"Chief," Clyde said as she left, "I will be glad to cooperate with you as you investigate this false report. And I can assure you my station and I will press charges against the person or persons who spread this false information. And I regret any inconvenience this has caused you or the sheriff's department."

She enjoyed the sense of physical release as she slammed the door closed behind her.

TWELVE

THE FINAL SHOOTING went well. They filmed the serving of the meal in the dining room. Beck remained adamant that he would not appear on camera. However, Henri Doucette more than rose to the occasion. He donned a sparkling white chef's uniform with the ever-present Far Horizons logo emblazoned on the pocket. He was entertaining, knowledgeable and charming. Skillful editing and voiceovers would resolve any problems his accent presented.

For her part, Clyde was decked out in the black halter dress with the broad white satin lapels. She loved the simple, slimming, classic lines. Now she was in the lobby, doing the tag-out, the closer. Standing by the coral fireplace, she concluded with a preview of the next show. She waved and said, *"Ciao,"* adding after a beat as her trademark tag-out, "down."

Andy teased, reminding her she wouldn't count as a real pro until she could come up with as many readings for *"Ciao down"* as Scott Bakula had for "Oh, boy" in his TV series, *Quantum Leap* or Jane Pauley's "We're history," for her *Time and Time Again* series on MSNBC.

"That's a wrap, sweetheart," he said in his best imitation of the stereotypical Hollywood director.

The crew's work here was done and the realization that Andy and the guys would be returning to Miami had been in the forefront of her mind all morning. As she walked down the corridor to the elevator, she acknowledged that she would miss them. She felt safer knowing Andy, Bernie and Pete were on the grounds. Now she was vulnerable, but that was her fault. She'd be leaving with them if she hadn't promised to do that cooking demonstration for the Marching and Chowder Society and the talk before the broadcast journalism seniors at the Palmetto Bay Junior College.

On the other hand, she mused as she stepped into the cage, the extra time would give her an opportunity to figure out what was going on here. And it was going to be hard to leave Sam. At least this way, they'd have a little more time together.

As the elevator glided to her floor, she thought back over the events of the past evening. She couldn't quite buy into Sam's panic. Some crank, maybe even a misguided fan, had played a prank. That's all the false report of her kidnapping was. A joke. Sam insisted it was a warning to her and that it had something to do with the guy in the tan station wagon, but that was crazy. No one warned Penny or Greg. The killer, if it was the killer, wouldn't have warned her. Whoever it was would have snatched her and been done with it.

She'd finally shared with Andy everything she and Sam had found out—not that there was much yet. At first, Andy thought they were paranoid to suspect anything suspicious about Penny's death, but by the time she showed him the list of people who'd died at the resort he was convinced. He would have preferred that she leave with them, but Andy wasn't hyper. Andy thought that because she was a public figure, she wasn't in any real danger.

Besides, she didn't know anything that would make her a danger to anyone. Yet. All the guilty party or parties could know was that she was asking questions.

Clyde slipped the keycard into her door and was surprised at the sight of an unmade bed. The bathroom hadn't been cleaned either. Towels were strewn around and the bathroom was as messy as she'd left it earlier when she'd been in a hurry to get downstairs. Usually, Dawn was here by now, waiting for her even though it was still early. Especially since they'd had a chance to discuss her art career. She had mentioned Dawn to Rod the Clod, who really wasn't such a bad dude, and he was looking forward to receiving Dawn's portfolio. She'd also given Dawn the name of a friend in the University of Miami art department, a friend who could help her get a scholarship.

Clyde changed into her regular clothes—in this case a favorite raw silk, pink shirtwaist dress with matching flats and purse—and Dawn still hadn't arrived. She called downstairs and had a convoluted conversation with Davy who told her he'd send another maid. When she insisted she wanted Dawn, he finally admitted that Dawn hadn't shown up for work.

What now? she wondered, sitting on the edge of the rumpled bed. Dawn had had the sniffles yesterday morning, but otherwise seemed fine. Even with a cold, she'd have been at work or would at least have called because of the plans she and Clyde were making.

In response to a knock, Clyde opened the door to a maid who introduced herself as Dorris with two R's. The woman was sturdy of build and stood at least five-ten. She had a no-nonsense manner, short wavy black hair, a Jay Leno chin and a trace of a mustache on her upper lip. Dorris swept into the room and bustled about so efficiently and noisily she nearly drove Clyde out of her mind.

After Dorris had moved on to the next room, Clyde paced, restive and unsettled. The same instincts that had helped Clyde as a reporter kicked in. Those instincts told her something was terribly wrong, and she decided to ask Grace for Dawn's phone number and address.

Downstairs in the office, Grace went through the Rolodex of dog-eared cards where she kept the data on the housekeeping staff. She pulled out Dawn's card, studied it briefly then handed it over.

"It won't do any good to call, Miss Colby, although you are kind to be so concerned," Grace said. "I telephoned when Dawn didn't come to work. Her mother said Dawn didn't come home last night. She's very upset, but she doesn't know any more than we do."

"I don't wonder that she's upset," Clyde said, scribbling the phone number and address in her reporter's notebook. "Dawn strikes me as very responsible. And considerate. She wouldn't worry her mother. How do I get to her home? In case I need to."

Without comment, Grace scrawled the directions in pencil on the back of an outdated breakfast menu.

Once back in her room, Clyde dialed Dawn's phone number. No answer. She began work on her talk for the journalism class, but tried Dawn's number every half hour. No answer. The hours passed slowly and Clyde grew more and more agitated. By mid-afternoon, she could no longer stand around waiting, doing nothing. She had to talk to Dawn's mother and find out for herself what was going on.

Following Grace's directions, Clyde drove to a remote area of Rattlesnake Key, an area known as Safety Hill because, Grace had explained, it was higher than the rest of the island that had been prone to flooding during the 1920's. She took Garden Lane to a compound of modest, somewhat rundown homes. Grace had told her the cottages had been built to house workers brought in to take care of the gladiolus fields. The tired dirt no longer supported growth so the land around the homes was gray-black and barren and the houses reflected neglect and abandonment.

She found a dented gray metal mailbox with the name Hicks in faded black letters in front of a bungalow that had once been white. Now the paint was dingy, flaked and peeling.

The surroundings and the house explain a lot about Dawn's lack of confidence, Clyde thought. But talent could be found anywhere and background could be overcome. Confidence could be nourished and nurtured until it was strong. And Dawn was worth the effort. For now, the important thing was to find out what had happened. Three steps led to a screen porch. She climbed the steps and knocked on the screen door, which was secured only by a hook. The screens had been torn and patched with tiny squares of wire.

The tired, pale, drawn-looking woman who came to the door was probably only a few years Clyde's senior, but she looked a decade or more older. Clyde could see the resemblance to Dawn, the shape of the face, the high cheekbones, and the deep-set green eyes. A tall man, skin wrinkled and burned by the sun came to stand behind her. He placed his hands on her shoulders.

"Mrs. Hicks?"

"Yes, ma'am," the woman answered. She stood on a braided rug inside the porch but away from the door. "What can I do for you?"

"I'm Clyde Colby. Your daughter and I met at Far Horizons where we've been filming a cooking show. I'm looking for her."

The woman came closer to the door and now she could see how swollen the woman's distressed eyes were. "So am I, ma'am," the woman said nervously, wringing her work-reddened hands in her apron. "She worked late yesterday at Far Horizons, some banquet or something, and she was making extra money busing dishes. Well, ma'am, she just never came home. And that's not like my Dawn."

"She'll be okay, Darla," the tall man soothed.

Clyde felt a chill. "Did you report this to the police?"

"'Course, I did, ma'am. I went down this morning and filed a report and left a picture. But they say it's too early to look for her." Smiling timidly, the woman unhooked the latch and opened the door. "Would you like to come in? This is my husband Duane, Dawn's stepdad."

Clyde nodded in acknowledgement and stepped onto the porch. "Is there anything I can do to help?"

The woman's plain face brightened then grew sad again. "No, ma'am. Dawn talked about you all the time. About how you were trying to help her with her art. She was so excited."

Clyde took a business card from her purse and wrote Far Horizons' phone and her room numbers on the back. "Please call me if—*when* you hear something."

Mrs. Hicks nodded, her thin shoulders slumped. Duane put his arm around her. "The police will find her, honey. She'll be all right. You'll see."

"I'm sorry, Mrs. Hicks," Clyde said and patted the woman's shoulder. "I'm sorry."

The mother gestured with the card. "I'll call you." She dredged up a smile. "Or better yet, I'll have Dawn call you herself when she gets home."

"Fine, Mrs. Hicks." Clyde walked back to her car wishing there was something more she could say or do to be of help.

She should never have gotten involved in this. She should never have listened to Eli. She wasn't in the news business any more. She got too involved. She should drop this whole thing right now. The trip back to Far Horizons was laced with guilt-ridden "should haves" and "could haves."

When she arrived at Far Horizons, Andy was loading the tomato red WTBR van. It had a silver lightning bolt painted on the side of the van along with the station's call letters and logo. "I think we got a winner here, Clyde," he said referring to the boxes containing the rolls of tape he'd shot. He had packed them in a cardboard carton and stashed it on the floor of the front seat on the passenger's side. Bernie was loading the dismantled lights and Pete was carrying the sound equipment in its black trunk. Pete climbed into the back and Bernie handed the equipment up to him.

"Clyde," Andy said. "Can we talk?"

She forced a grin. "You and Joan Rivers. What about?"

"I've been thinking since we had that talk. There's too much funny stuff going on here. Cancel the PR shit, Clyde," he urged, putting his two hands on her shoulders. "You don't need to do the cooking demo here. Do it on the other coast where you'll draw a bigger audience. Come back with us."

It was tempting, but there were too many reasons to stay. "I can't, Andy. I need the experience doing these demos," she said slowly moving away. "If I'm going to screw up, it's better to do it in a place like Palmetto Bay where there are fewer people to see me do it," she said. "But I am certainly going to miss you and the guys."

Andy's eyes brightened. "I know. I'll call Rod and see if he'll let me film you doing the cooking demo. We can use it for B roll or something."

"Sure, Andy, and those dogs you bet on every Saturday

night at Calder Racetrack are going to sprout wings and fly and make you a sweet fortune. In fact," she said, "given how tight our budget is and how Rod the Clod feels about me, you've got a better chance of betting on a dog or a nag with wings than you do staying over to shoot my cooking demo."

"I hate it when you're right, but I'll tell you this much. If you aren't on the road in that blue Bronco of yours headed back to Miami as soon as that cooking demo's over, I'm coming back and drag you home." Andy pointed a finger at her face.

"All packed," Bernie interrupted. "See you back at the station, Clyde." His freckles looked even darker and she wondered idly if he'd been getting too much sun. He and Andy hugged her, Pete waved.

"Keep it on the road, Princess," Pete said. The three climbed into the van, Andy driving. He backed around so that they were heading out of the parking lot. Once they turned left onto Matecumbe Road and headed toward the causeway, they vanished from her sight and a sense of desolation settled over her.

Sam.

She'd be glad to see him, but she didn't expect him until early evening. He'd had a sailing lesson scheduled for the afternoon, one he couldn't cancel because his students were members of the alternative learning class from Rattlesnake Key Middle School.

She could check on the status of the search for Dawn. Westendorf seemed like a nice enough guy. Maybe he'd tell her something he wouldn't tell the mother. Maybe she could get him to waive the 24-hour stay before beginning an investigation.

Clyde climbed back into the Bronco and headed toward Rattlesnake Key. When she reached the police station, the chief's desk was empty. A short, stocky uniformed officer was the only person in the station except for the blonde secretary who was studying herself in her compact, dusting powder on her nose. She looked at Clyde and smiled, but the smile was devoid of interest or curiosity. The uniformed officer was at the water fountain. He turned as she entered.

"Morning, Miss Colby." He greeted her coolly, crossing from the water fountain to stand by the wooden railing that barred visitors from the rest of the room. "Something we can do for you?" She remembered him now. He'd been in Beck's office the previous night. She hadn't paid much attention then, but now she took a second look. Officer Bubba, she thought. The desk plate read Sgt. Stan Reeves.

"Yes. You can answer some questions," she said focusing her attention on him.

"Questions? About what? We still don't know who made that phony call," he said defensively.

"That's not why I'm here."

He moved forward and held open the wooden gate. "Come on back." She followed him and he gestured to the wooden barrel chair that sat next to his desk.

"Here?" she said, looking around the room. Anyone could walk in.

He shrugged. "You want privacy? We have the interrogation room."

As he led the way to a door in the back wall, Clyde thought that this was probably stupid. She knew the interrogation room would have a one-way mirror. Even in the sticks like Rattlesnake Key, they would have a one-way mirror. So she wouldn't have any more privacy than in the other room. Nonetheless, it was a minor victory and she followed as he opened the door and preceded her into a windowless chamber.

"Sit down," he said and kicked the chair away from the table and toward her with his foot.

She smiled politely and sat down. She'd done enough to make an enemy of him the night before when she'd threatened to sue his department. "What about Dawn Hicks's disappearance? Or Eli's beating? When you add those to the anonymous report that I was missing, it seems to me there are too many strange things happening in Rattlesnake Key for you to just be sitting here."

There was a long pause. The only sound in the room was the drone of the window unit.

He looked at her as if measuring how important she was, how much of a problem she'd create if he didn't answer her questions.

"We have absolutely no reason—not one—to believe there's any connection between the false report of your kidnapping and Miss Hicks not going home last night," he said finally and shook his head. "Doubt if we will, Miss. It was undoubtedly a joke. Your being famous and all."

"What about Dawn Hicks's disappearance?"

"Far as we know, Miss Colby, Miss Hicks' disappearance is nothing more than a girl who gets bored, walks off her job and leaves town. Or goes off with a boyfriend. Happens all the time."

"In Rattlesnake Key? You've got a lot of missing girls here?"

"Dammit, of course not. I meant in today's world. Around the state."

She leaned forward, ignoring the chair, and placed her hands on the table. "Something has happened to Dawn. I'm sure of that because Dawn has every reason not to disappear. I've been working to get her an internship at the station where I work and a possible art scholarship at the University of Miami. Dawn was too excited and happy. She had no reason to disappear without telling anyone." But Clyde could tell he wasn't impressed. She hoped he wouldn't let the apparent personal animosity he felt toward her prevent him from doing a thorough job. *If this were Miami,* she thought. Ruefully, she reminded herself this was far from Miami.

"We're doing everything we can. We've put out Dawn's description. We got it with every sheriff's department in South Florida plus the Florida Highway Patrol. And Chief's out talking to Mrs. Hicks right now. He's gonna check with the neighbors and her co-workers, too. We're doing everything we can."

"What about Eli's beating?"

"Chief's on top of that. We're a small department and we're doing the best we can."

She sat back, not satisfied, yet not sure what else she could do.

He splayed his hands on the desk in front of her. "Hope that answers your questions. I got other things to do. Like you say, I shouldn't be just sitting here." He came around the table and guided her to the door of the interrogation room.

She went without protest. She still didn't know why Eli hadn't wanted her to go to the police, but it was clear that Sgt. Stan Reeves wasn't going to be of any help.

"I understand your crew left this morning," he said as they re-entered the front office. "You must be almost finished here. I'll bet you'll be glad to get back to Miami. Where you'll be safer," he added with a smile.

She managed to smile, too, but felt a chill. Silenced by the dread that was swamping her, she stared at him, then turned and walked out of the station.

He'd smiled, but his words had sounded very much like a threat. Was he the reason Eli hadn't wanted her to talk to the police?

THIRTEEN

BACK AT FAR HORIZONS about a half an hour later, Clyde picked up a copy of the *Palmetto Bay Observer* from the rack by the front desk. Dawn always left a copy in the room for her, but Dorris with two R's wasn't that guest oriented. That lack of attention to detail would be reflected in the tip she'd leave when she checked out, Clyde thought. In the lifestyles section, she saw Eli's feature story and Kathleen Terpen's photos.

Scanning the article as she walked along the corridor, she was relieved. Rod the Clod would be ecstatic and wouldn't be nearly as upset that she'd stayed behind at the station's expense. Binky Beresford's lifestyles editor had given her the lead position on the section front and she'd gotten lots of ink. Two full columns plus two photos on 1D and a jump to page four with two more photos and three full columns. Almost a full page. And Eli's story was well done. The article was accurate, perceptive—at times revealing a little more than she might have preferred. But she would have to learn to cope with the media, as the person being interviewed not the interviewer.

The photos were okay. One shot, a candid, taken when she was looking down at the grill, revealed her ever-looming bit of a double chin, but overall, the pictures were okay. At least, she didn't look like a puff pastry.

Still engrossed in the paper, she inserted the keycard and opened the door. Once inside her room, she jumped at the sight of a body lying on her bed. Thank God she had the presence of mind not to scream because she realized at once it was Sam.

"How the hell did you get in? You scared the shit out of me, McKenzie."

"Glad to see you, too." When she'd calmed down, he said, "Dorris with two R's. And a wide green picture of General Grant. This shows what kind of security you have here. Damn, I'm glad to see you, Clyde. Even if you are testy. Now where have you been and what have you been up to?"

"I've got more bad news," she said, sinking down on the bed beside him, tossing her purse and makeup kit on the chair by the bed.

He grew serious, the lines around his generous mouth tightened. "What bad news?"

She told him about Dawn and her visit to the police station, but carefully refrained from sharing Sgt. Reeves's comment that she'd be safer in Miami.

"What about the tan station wagon?"

She went blank.

"Dammit." He slammed his fist on the nightstand. His face was twisted by quick anger. "You didn't even look, did you? You're not stupid. What do I have to do to get through to you?"

"I had a lot on my mind."

"We'll deal with that later. Now what else has been happening?"

She filled him in on her visit with Dawn Hicks's mother.

"The police department is probably operating on the theory that she ran off with a boyfriend, and she was afraid to tell her mother," he said. "That's par for these guys."

"But I explained about her career as an artist, and that I was helping—" Clyde started.

"You're not in Miami now, Clyde," he interrupted. "Many of these men are from the Stone Age. They believe women should be keeping the caves clean, the fire bright and having babies, not making pretty pictures. But you're not a dumb hick cop. There's no excuse for your carelessness."

"Enough of the lecture." She studied his unlined, tanned face, serious eyes. Even though she really didn't want to hear what he had to say and even though he really didn't have the right to say anything to her, she had a hunch he was right.

"Frankly, Sam, now that I've been here a while I can't imagine why you stay in Rattlesnake Key."

"Simple," he said as he sat up, supporting himself on his elbow. His anger was gone as quickly as it had appeared. "This is a great place to hang out and exorcise the ghosts. You're changing the subject," he accused.

She nodded. Rising, she walked over to the dresser and started removing her makeup with a tissue. She stared into the mirror. Without the makeup, she looked strained and tired. "Did you see Eli's article?"

He sat up on the side of the bed and reached over to the chair where the paper lay. He studied her photograph. "Yes, I think he did a good job. He seemed to see past that big-city façade you put up sometimes."

"Yeah, I liked it, too." She couldn't remember when she'd felt so drained.

"Sad to think it might be the last article he ever writes."

She hadn't considered that and it made her sad. Unbidden tears spilled down her cheeks. She lowered her head so Sam wouldn't see them, but she was too late. He rose quickly from the bed and came over to her, placing his arms around her waist.

He looked over her shoulder at their image in the mirror. "I'm sorry, honey. I spoke without thinking." He reached to pull a tissue from the box on the dresser and, turning her to face him, wiped away the tears. "For the moment, Eli is safe," he said quietly. "But I'm more than a little concerned about you, and I have an idea. Why don't you and Andy change rooms? I'd feel a lot better." He planted a light kiss on the corner of her mouth.

"Andy and the guys left this morning," she said quietly, bracing herself for the explosion of anger she feared would come next. But she was pleased when it didn't.

"Okay. Then you'll stay with me on the *Sanity*."

"Absolutely not. If we're going to find out what happened to Penny and Greg Lanken, I have to be right here. And we won't discuss it again." She paused, and then said, "I'm getting hungry. And what about Eli? Don't you think we should go by and see him?"

"First things first," he said sinking down on the bed and pulling her to him. "Eli would understand. In fact, he'd definitely approve."

THE RECEPTION AREA of the hospital was bedlam when they arrived a couple hours later. Glaring lights illuminated the lobby. Thick black extension cords snaked across the gleaming tile floor. Reporters and cinematographers from both local television stations along with newspaper reporters and their still photographers crowded the reception desk. Clyde knew from her media pals in Miami that federal authorities were investigating the rise of new Nazis and skinheads in South Florida, and that had drawn media from bureaus all around the state. She watched as the out-of-towners jostled regulars for the best positions—as she could remember having done that many times herself. Late afternoon visitors who stopped by on their way home from work were bottlenecked by media. A uniformed sheriff's deputy stood at the entrance to the main body of the hospital and she wondered if Westendorf had finally asked for help or if the sheriff had muscled in on the media exposure since it was an election year. So far, the deputy seemed to have the situation under control.

As they watched, a reporter separated himself from the crowd followed by his cinematographer who was attached by the umbilical cord of his microphone. The reporter positioned himself in front of the ward doors. "The vicious attack on a news man, coupled with the anti-Semitic nature of the assault, has drawn federal investigators to this remote island in South Florida," he was saying as his cameraman panned across the crowd. "And today the story took a bleaker turn."

Clyde felt a sense of despair build. The only thing that could have drawn so much media—unless there'd been a late—breaking story she'd heard nothing about-would be a change for the worse in Eli's condition. Clyde glanced at Sam. His face was a study in shut-down caution. The news could not be good. She reached for Sam's hand and they were silent as they forced their way through the crowd and down the hallway to Eli's room.

Eliahu stood outside the open door to Eli's room as they approached. From the doorway, she could see a nurse stripping and remaking Eli's bed with fresh linens. Another nurse, portly and dark-haired, was gathering Eli's belongings from the portable closet in the corner and placing them into a black plastic bag. She banged her hand on the closet door as she shut it. The tinny sound echoed in the all too quiet room. The nurse brought the wounded fingers to her mouth to suck out her pain. Eli was nowhere to be seen.

Eliahu stood erect in the doorway. His body trembled. His stark, vacant eyes were those of a man in shock. Sam crossed the corridor and patted his bony shoulder.

"Eliahu…"

"He's dead," the old man croaked, pulling away from Sam's touch. "My Eli, he's dead. It's not enough that I lose his mother and his father. Two beautiful young people. No, he——" Eliahu shook his fist at the ceiling. "That abomination has taken my Eli, too." He whirled and did a strange little jig, shifting his weight from one foot to the other, then back, raising and lowering his hands, twisting his hands in generous circles. He reminded Clyde of a hapless human scarecrow caught in a maelstrom. He made a keening sound and, as if on cue, his three friends drifted down the hall and surrounded him, shielding him while he launched into a rambling, often incoherent tirade. They led him into the hallway.

One of his friends, a stocky, broad-shouldered dark-haired man with a dour face shadowed by a dark beard came back to where they stood. "Mr. McKenzie, we know you are Eli's friend and Eliahu's. If you like, one of us will call you with information about the service."

"Please," Sam said, clasping the man's thin, milk-white hand. "We were both Eli's friends." He gestured toward Clyde standing next to him. "We want to know. And if there's anything we can do. Say, do you want us to run interference to get you through that herd of media in the lobby?"

The man shook his head. "No," he said, "the doctors have shown us how we can get out a back entrance without being seen." With a backward wave toward them, he hurried down the hallway to join Eliahu and his other companions.

Clyde steeled herself. She could not deny that Eli had been in a coma, but his vital signs were strong and improving. There was no reason why Eli should have died. But there was no reason he should have been beaten either. She felt a wave of depression followed almost immediately by a surge of energy as the adrenaline of rage kicked in. Now it was murder. Would Westendorf take it more seriously now? No drug addict had killed Eli Nussbaum, and she'd take it to the Attorney General in Tallahassee, and even to the Florida Department of Law Enforcement, if necessary. If the state authorities couldn't handle it, perhaps the feds could step in under the Hate Crimes Statute.

"Sam, I want to talk to that nurse," she said motioning toward the heavy-set brunette who was backing out of the room. Before he could comment, she strode hurriedly out of the room and down the hall in pursuit.

"Nurse! Nurse!" she called.

The woman halted and turned. "Me? You want to talk to me?" Her nostrils flared indignantly and Clyde realized she'd forgotten and used her "big city" voice. She'd learned this week that a softer approach worked much better in small towns.

"Yes," Clyde panted a little out of breath and using a much softer tone. "About your patient Mr. Nussbaum."

The nurse's small dark brown eyes turned deliberately blank. Her blood-red lips thinned. "I can't discuss Mr. Nussbaum. It's a murder case now." She fluffed her permed hair.

The nurse was already suffering from the self-importance syndrome. Clyde had seen it many times when she'd covered the police beat. Witnesses on the scene, next door neighbors, best friends. In the light of publicity, they became as important as the victim and the victim's family, many times enjoying their new if temporary status, turning arrogant and pompous.

"Let's go, Clyde," Sam said, emerging from Eli's room and catching up to take her elbow.

"But—" Clyde started to protest.

He smiled at the nurse. "You're absolutely right to be discreet, Nurse Powell. We're just upset about the death of our friend."

Nurse Powell brightened. "Mr. McKenzie, I didn't notice you. Tell you the truth, this nice young man's death has affected everybody on the floor. It's such a tragedy."

"Yes, it is." Sam motioned for Clyde to move back. She did, bristling, but standing out of the way by the nurses' station. "What happened to him?" Sam was asking. "When we saw Eli last night, he seemed to be getting stronger, gaining ground."

The nurse nodded. "We were talking about it on break. He seemed to be doing fine. There was no indication that he was regaining consciousness, but his body was healing. Rapidly. Faster than we had expected. The other nurses and I thought it was a good sign." She was holding on to the linen cart, getting ready to move on.

Casually, Sam placed his hand on the cart. "So what happened?"

"I was down at the nurses' station," she said rolling her shoulders as if in despair. "Nurse Chachen, she was getting ready to give him his meds, started yelling 'Code Blue.' And sure enough, the monitors at the nurses' station registered flat lines." She looked him in the eyes for the first time, tears forming in hers. "It was that sudden. Like he gave up. The cardiac arrest team worked for more than three quarters of an hour, but he never came back."

Sam glanced at Clyde, then back at Nurse Powell. "But you have no reason to suspect foul play? Here in the hospital, that is."

The nurse began to push the cart. "Of course not. There will be an autopsy, Mr. McKenzie. We've had instructions to release the body to Dr. Schroeder so you might check with him later."

"Do you have any idea when he'll do it?"

The nurse's eyes were expressionless once again as she said, "Probably first thing in the morning." She started to wheel the cart on down the hall then turned back. "One thing, Mr. McKenzie. I don't think he suffered."

Clyde watched the broad back of the nurse disappear down the hall, and then rejoined Sam. "I have an idea. You know Binky what's-his-name, don't you?" she asked.

"The editor of the *Observer?* Sure."

"What if we go talk to him? What if we ask him to let us see Eli's notes?"

"Why should he?"

"Because you're his friend and because Eli asked me to help. And because I'm staying at Far Horizons. If, as I suspect, there's no connection between the deaths at Far Horizons and Eli's beating death, Beresford still wins because I'm on the inside."

"Let's go," Sam said. "If I know Binky, he's at the office working on Eli's obituary. He wouldn't let anyone else do it."

FOURTEEN

TAKING A LEAD from Eliahu's friends, they exited the hospital through the same back entrance marked "Emergency Personnel Only." They made good time, but it was nearly eleven when Sam and Clyde pulled into the parking lot of the *Palmetto Bay Observer*. On impulse she had suggested they stop off to see Medical Examiner Rudy Schroeder first.

They could have called ahead if Clyde hadn't left her cellphone in her room, but that might not have helped because the feisty, pint-sized M.E. was downright rude. He'd been barely civil when Sam asked how soon he was going to perform Eli's autopsy. When Clyde asked why autopsies had not been conducted on the bodies of Penny and Greg Lanken, especially since their deaths were unattended, Schroeder erupted. He demanded she tell him where she had gotten that information. When she refused to tell him, the M.E. threatened to call and register a complaint with her station manager.

She didn't let him see her discomfort, but Clyde was painfully aware that she was walking a tightrope. She didn't need anyone complaining that she was nosing around a news story. Especially when she was supposed to be fostering good relations in the community. Surely there was someone, she mused as she got out of the car, surely there was some agency to whom she could report her suspicions about Schroeder.

The light in Binky Beresford's office shone like a beacon in the darkened newsroom. From where Clyde and Sam stood on the sidewalk peering through the glass doors of the *Observer* newsroom, the editor was distinctly visible. His office was separated from the rest of the newsroom by glass partitions and he was spotlighted in the light of his desk lamp.

Sam was figuring out the intercom system when a burly, white-haired, paunchy security guard rounded the corner of the building. He marched over to where they stood. His expression made it clear that, in his opinion, it was too late even for business calls.

"That your car, Mister?" he demanded, gesturing toward the Lexus.

Sam nodded.

"Got any ID?"

Sam obligingly dragged his wallet out of his hip pocket and presented his driver's license.

The guard looked at it and nodded. "Ordinarily I wouldn't bother you for your ID," he said in a friendlier tone, "but one of the reporters was beaten and management has tightened security."

"No problem," Sam said.

Pressing the intercom key imbedded in the pad next to the door, Sam identified himself. Beresford buzzed them in.

The newsroom was silent. Unnerved, Clyde shivered. She paused on the threshold. For her, the area was haunted with the images of Eli galloping through the newsroom, his long legs churning. She envisioned him the day they'd met, talking to her over his shoulder, full of excitement and enthusiasm. And life.

Eli. Penny. Greg Lanken. She pushed the victims out of her mind. *Got to stay focused.*

"Clyde. Clyde," Sam said. "Are you all right?"

She nodded, drawn back to the present.

"Then come on." He strode between the desks, stepping over piles of old newspapers, press kits and press releases, maneuvering between wastebaskets. In the sports department, he sidestepped a fishing rod and a tennis racquet one of the reporters had leaned against the support column. "Watch out," he said. The editor's office was behind the Sports Department. Beresford motioned for them to come in.

Sam opened the door and ushered her inside.

"Miss Colby," Beresford said. "Sam. Won't you have a seat?"

He waved his hand toward the two armchairs positioned in front of his massive desk. Clyde sat, taking the measure of the man as she did so.

Binky Beresford was a distinguished man of medium height and build, probably in his late forties. He had a mane of gray hair, wore gold-rimmed spectacles and a lived-in face with bags under intelligent, alert blue eyes. He was sitting in front of a computer terminal, glasses shoved to the crown of his head. He rubbed his eyes, fatigue in every line of his face. As they neared his desk, he closed the document he was working on.

"An editorial," he said. "What can I do for you?"

Clyde had learned from the conversation with Nurse Powell. She was in foreign territory so she sat back quietly and let Sam do the talking. As always, she admired Sam's easy way with people. He could be very direct, she knew that from their arguments, but Sam could also be so subtle and disarming that people would tell him things they didn't want or intend to reveal. The thought crossed her mind that Sam would make a good cop. Or reporter.

Beresford's desk was clear except for whatever he was working on and a nameplate which, instead of his name, read, "Eschew obfuscation." The condition of the editor's desk told her he was not only compulsively neat, but someone who kept his own counsel. A loner. Or very secretive. Behind the desk on the wall were photographs of a much younger Beresford with Presidents Jimmy Carter and Gerald Ford. And Raymond Burr, the actor.

That was interesting. Did that mean Binky Beresford was a fan of Perry Mason, the lawyer and the law? Or the actor? On the credenza was a studio portrait of an elegant, gray-haired woman with patrician features. Wife? Mother?

Now Sam relaxed, long legs crossed at the ankles. He made a steeple with his hands on his chest. If she hadn't known, she would have believed Sam was discussing the weather. A matter of murder. She studied the curly black hair on the backs of his strong, hands. The veins stood out as he pressed the hands together, the only signal of his tension.

"We're here about Eli," Sam said. "You lost a good man tonight." He briefed Beresford on their investigation ending with the request they had discussed in the car coming over.

"Eli's notes? That's highly irregular, Sam," Beresford said, pausing thoughtfully.

He pulled a pipe from the rack sitting on the credenza behind his desk and filled it with tobacco from a pouch he kept in his right-hand drawer. From his deliberateness, she could tell it was a ritual in both form and time from which he drew pleasure. Focusing intently as if these were the most important actions of his life, he tamped the contents of the bowl, lit a match and drew. The fragrance of sweet tobacco filled the room. When he was satisfied, he sat back and put his feet up on the desk.

"Now," he said taking a second deep draw on the pipe. "Let's go through this again. Sam says, Miss Colby, that Eli asked you, an outsider, to help with the investigation." His voice was laced with a tinge of skepticism. "Do I understand that correctly?"

"We both knew something wasn't right out there and the advantage was, of course, that I was on site," she said. "Eli told me you hadn't been able to get anyone out there under cover."

"And now you want access to his notes?"

"His notes and all the stories he's done in the past six months."

"What are you hoping to find?" He closed his eyes, resting them. "You know, I've already lost a good man. Why should I allow you to put yourself in jeopardy? The less you know the better."

She leaned forward and clasped her hands on his desk. "I'm already in jeopardy. And you forget that while I may be working in television as a cooking show host at the moment, I'm also a trained reporter. Why should you be the one to decide whether or not I'm going to put myself in additional jeopardy? That's *my* decision, and I choose to pick up where Eli left off. With or without your help."

He didn't seem to react or buy into her assertiveness, but she wasn't surprised. He dealt with aggressive, charged-up reporters every day. "I already have someone working on it," he said mildly.

"So? Is there anybody who can't use a little help? Especially when it's free. And no strings. The story's his. Or hers."

"But what are you looking for?"

She paused. "Maybe something about the men who died out there. Maybe something about the people who beat Eli. How will I know until I look?"

Sam gave her a look that said back off and she did. "Remember the story of the Colombian drug smugglers you got because of my contacts with the DEA in Baltimore?" he asked Beresford.

Beresford nodded without opening his eyes.

"And the Mariel gang who tried to move in?"

Beresford chuckled, dropped his feet to the floor and swung his body around. "And you're calling in your markers."

"That's right. You haven't turned Eli's stuff over to the police yet, have you?"

He sighed. "No. But I've put them away for safekeeping." Beresford put the pipe down, took a key ring out of his back pocket and bent down to unlock the bottom drawer of his desk. Removing a metal box, he unlocked it and retrieved a manila folder wrapped with rubber bands. The folder bulged with reporter's notebooks, scraps of paper, telephone messages.

"This is what I took from Eli's desk the night he was beaten." He reached back and flipped a switch on the wall behind his desk turning on the overhead light. He spread the contents of the folder across the top of his desk. "You can't take anything with you, but you're free to look at it here. I hope you can make something of this. I haven't been able to."

Clyde tried to calm the excitement building in her stomach. When she'd been on assignments, she'd sometimes gotten this feeling and nearly always it happened right when she was on the verge of a breakthrough. There was something here. She was sure of it. All she had to do was figure out what.

"Damn," Sam griped as he shuffled through some of Eli's papers, "do all reporters have such lousy handwriting?"

"It's called note taking," she said as she flipped through the pages. "And some of us do it deliberately. We don't want anyone else reading what we've got,"

It didn't take her long to decipher his system. He identified the people he interviewed or researched by their initials. He identified locations by the initials as well, but drew a tree to indicate a place. Thus, Far Horizons became FH followed by a stick tree, and Horace Beck would be HB. She found a number of references to both, and had to smile when she saw "Clyde" repeated over and over.

Unfortunately, the majority of the information was written in Gregg. It had been years since her one abortive semester at business school when she'd studied shorthand. She flipped through the pages again. Sam gave up, but she wasn't about to do that. She pushed, tracing the shorthand symbols with her finger, willing the memorized symbols to translate themselves to her.

"It's nearly 3:00 AM," Sam said finally. "Look." He pointed toward the editor.

She looked across the desk at Beresford. He was asleep, feet on the desk, arms folded across his chest.

"Just a few minutes more." She dug into the pile of notebooks and pulled another out. What made this one different? She stared. A plain reporter's notebook. Maybe three inches wide, six or seven inches long. Labeled *Reporter's Notebook*. No mystery.

Then it hit her. This one *was* different.

On the covers of all the others, Eli had written the dates he'd used them and the subject. Palmetto Bay City Council. PB Redevelopment Authority. Courtney trial. This one had nothing. The cover was blank. And yet it was filled with entries. "FH. HB. DB. 17. GL. LUNG PARALYSIS. SC. APD. $5 mil."

Over and over, Eli had doodled the number 17. He had surrounded it with arrows and question marks. He had written it in Roman numbers XVII, he had written it in the European style with the line drawn through the seven. He had spelled it out. But an address—1875 Calle Sarmiento—had been printed in the same erratic combination of capitals and lower case letters as the script. Could the seventeen have something to do with an address?

Down the side of another page, he had listed a series of initials: HB, DB, FW, GB, RS, IT. On another he had written, *"Warheit Macht Frei,"* followed by an equal sign then the words, "Work sets you free," and a final note, "Must tell Binky slavery has been abolished. Yuk yuk!"

"Sam, I don't know what I'm looking at yet, but I think this is important."

Sam jumped, startled by the sound of her voice, knocking a pile of notebooks onto the floor. "Clyde, it's late. You've been up almost twenty-four hours. So have I. Let's call it a night." He bent to pick up the tablets from the floor. "Work on it tomorrow after you've had some sleep."

"Mr. Beresford," she said, ignoring Sam for the moment. "Er, Binky. Binky?" She called in a slightly louder voice.

With a gentle snort that was half a snore, the newspaper editor came awake. He grimaced from stiffness as he put his feet on the floor and glanced at his wrist watch. "Damn! I've got to get home. Mrs. Beresford will have some exquisite torture planned. I was supposed to be home no later than midnight." He ran his fingers through his thick gray hair. "Find anything?"

"I don't know," she said honestly. "I think so, but I'm not sure. I know you want to keep the originals, but could I make a copy of some of the pages from this book?"

Still groggy from sleep, he nodded. "Sure. Copier's in the newsroom. Which one was it?" She showed him. He nodded again and picked his pipe out of the ashtray and tapped it against the side to remove the cold ashes while rummaging in his middle drawer. He pulled out a gray plastic square with a counter at one end. "Key to the machine. You'll need this."

Sam took the key and led her back into the empty newsroom. One reporter had left his terminal on and the gray screen stared like the eye of a vigilant monolith. Getting fanciful, Clyde, she chastised herself. No time for that now.

Sam leaned against the wall while the copy machine

warmed up and she realized how tired he was. And how exhausted she was, too, for that matter. The fluorescent green hands of the round clock on the wall pointed to a quarter till four. It seemed a lifetime since she'd gotten up in her room at Far Horizons and dressed for the morning shoot. Andy and the crew would have been home hours ago. She yawned. Sam was right. She needed sleep. She'd think better. And now, thanks to Eli and Binky Beresford, she had more to think about.

The machine clicked and clacked into life. She made the copies and removed the key. "All done. Let's go."

Beresford was shutting down his computer as Sam returned the key to the copier. They left together, the security guard half-saluting as Beresford climbed into his car. He waited and watched as they drove out of the parking lot before following.

She didn't argue as Sam turned left just past the causeway. The marina was much closer than Far Horizons and she was too tired to object. He parked and led her down the planking to the *Sanity*. The sky was paling, segueing into the gray of dawn as she followed him down the companionway into the cabin. She fell asleep in Sam's double bed lulled by the gentle rocking of the waves. Wrapped in his arms, she felt safe for the first time in days. Numbers and initials danced before her eyes until unconsciousness claimed her.

Only when the morning light turned peach and pearl did she stir, whimpering in her sleep. In her dreams, she and Dawn were being chased down shadowy streets and alleys by lumbering, faceless figures that loomed behind them. For weapons, the phantoms carried huge, glittering numbers—ones and sevens. The numbers had lethally sharp edges and were made of shiny metal.

FIFTEEN

THE WARMTH OF THE SUN awakened Clyde the next day. It blasted through the slats of the Venetian blinds and she rolled away to avoid a stray sunbeam.

Something was different.

Her bed was moving. Gently, but definitely, it was rocking. It took a moment for her to remember. She was on Sam's boat. Propping herself on her elbow, Clyde sat up and looked around the cabin. The beautiful teak walls, the brass appointments, the gentle rocking. But where was Sam? She yawned and stretched. From the galley, she heard sounds of pans rattling and smelled the welcome aroma of brewing coffee.

"You up yet?" Sam called.

"If I wasn't," she said with a smile, "I certainly am now. What time is it?"

"Eight-thirty."

"Oh, good God, Sam. I've got to get back to Far Horizons. What if someone tried to call me?" She scrambled around the cabin gathering her clothes. She'd take a shower once she got back. Damn, the silk dress she'd worn was a mess. How on earth could she walk through the lobby of Far Horizons looking like a transient? She cringed as she stepped into yesterday's lingerie.

Sam was standing in the entry, spatula in hand. "Calm down. If they called, they left a message. Andy wouldn't have gotten back until late yesterday afternoon. He wouldn't have even

started working on the stuff he shot until this morning. Relax."
He turned and walked away.

She knew he was right, but there was so much to do. And,
oh God, she had the cooking demonstration this afternoon.
And she needed to know about Dawn. Had the autopsy been
done on Eli? The familiar sadness descended as it always did
when she thought of Eli. What a loss. Such a waste.

"Clyde, I can hear the wheels grinding all the way out here.
Come have coffee and some breakfast. Then we'll hit the deck
running, pardon the sailing metaphor."

When she entered the galley, he was standing in front of the
stove scrambling eggs and frying bacon. The table was set for
two with a single red hibiscus in a vase. Two cups of steaming
coffee and dishes of colorful fresh fruit waited—diced pineapple, cantaloupe and watermelon.

"I'm starved," she said, then remembered. "No wonder. We
didn't eat dinner."

"So much was happening," Sam said, turning away from the
stove to look at her. "Considering everything you went through
yesterday, you look fine."

She winced. "Fine? This dress is so wrinkled it looks like I
slept in it. I don't know how I'm going to crawl through the
lobby without being seen."

He laughed. "Stick your chin up and walk through that
lobby as if your dress is supposed to be that wrinkled."

"A good bluff is a good defense," she said, sitting down at
the table. "Everything smells and looks wonderful."

He slid scrambled eggs onto the plates. "Pardon the fingers,"
he said picking up bacon slices and arranging them alongside
the eggs. Placing the plates on the table, he kissed her on the
cheek and said, "Good morning," before sitting across from her.

The food tasted delicious and she told him so. But there was
so much to do, she was restless.

"All right," he said at last.

"All right?"

"Yes, I'll hurry. You're the only woman I've ever known who
can rush me without saying a word."

"WHAT DO YOU HAVE to do today?" she said when they were in his car heading toward Far Horizons. The traffic on Matecumbe Road was heavy.

"Trying to get rid of me already, are you?" he teased. "I have some things to do at the school, but let me know if you go anywhere before I can get back"

She looked out the window at the passing scenery to mask her irritation. She hated it when men became overprotective and tried to keep track of her. Or tried to keep her from doing what she wanted to do. Sam should realize she wasn't stupid.

The business about the station wagon had frightened her. And Dawn's disappearance, too. Furthermore, it was not lost on her, although she wasn't about to mention it, that she and Dawn looked alike. If something had happened to Dawn, it could well be a case of mistaken identity. That she was the target. She wasn't about to take unnecessary chances.

"Well?" Sam interrupted her thoughts.

"I've got that cooking demo at two in Burdines."

He was quiet. "Can you wait until one-thirty to leave for the department store?"

"No way," she said, shaking her head. "I have to be there by noon. Twelve-thirty at the latest. We have to get everything set up."

"I'll catch up with you at Burdine's then. But you've got to keep your eyes open. Stay alert. I don't want to lose you. I'm getting used to having you around."

She flinched, hoping he hadn't noticed. There would be time later to straighten out any incorrect assumptions he might have about their relationship.

He pulled the Lexus into the parking lot at Far Horizons and stopped beneath one of the beautiful Royal Poinciana trees. He was preparing to get out of the car when she stopped him, putting a hand on his arm.

"I'll be fine."

"You sure?"

"Of course. It's broad daylight."

"All right," he said. "I'll see you at Burdine's. Be careful and make sure you keep your cell phone with you."

"Yes, yes." She opened the car door and edged out. "I've got to get going."

The trek through the lobby seemed endless. Although the majority of the guests were too polite to openly display their curiosity, she felt as if every eye was glued on her as she proceeded in her wrinkled dress to the elevator.

Once in her room, she took a quick, very hot shower, washed her hair and changed into jeans. The air was brisk so she put on a long-sleeved blouse with a pullover sweater.

She called Mrs. Hicks. No word on Dawn.

She called the police station. Chief Westendorf wasn't in, but the blonde secretary who answered the phone told her there were no new developments in the investigation of Dawn Hicks's disappearance.

Binky Beresford had had no word on the autopsy, he told her, but results were expected later in the afternoon. She listened politely while he explained that toxicology results would take weeks to get from the Florida Department of Law Enforcement lab.

And then she had a few moments so she removed the photocopied sheets of Eli's notebook from her purse. She spread them out on the bed and studied them. Same as last night. She knew there was something there. *But what?*

"1875 Calle Sarmiento," she read the address aloud from the sheath of photocopied notes. Using Spanish street names was quite common in South Florida. She could look up that address. See if it was local. When a cursory scan of the telephone book did not turn up the name, she called the library.

"No," Lillian Albritton's pleasant voice informed her, "there's no street by that name in either Palmetto Bay or Rattlesnake Key village. And I hope you haven't forgotten about this afternoon, have you?"

Clyde assured her she had not forgotten the cooking demonstration. "I'll be at Burdine's between twelve and twelve-thirty. That should give us enough time to prepare, don't you think?"

"That will be fine. We're really excited, Miss Colby," she said. "We usually have people who talk about local history or something like boating. We've never had a cooking demonstration before."

After she hung up, Clyde fell back on the bed and laughed out loud. They were even. She'd never done one either. The rest of the morning, she alternated between studying Eli's notes and preparing for the cooking demo. She'd decided she'd wear a red gabardine pants suit. Ordinarily she didn't like red; it was too bold, too noticeable. However, red was a power color or so the wardrobe consultant had told her in Miami. And she wanted to be in command of her audience. So red it was.

Sam called about twelve. "Anything happening?" When she had brought him up to date, he said, "Services for Eli will be held tomorrow afternoon at the synagogue in Palmetto Bay. I told Rabbi Meyers we'd be there."

"Fine." she agreed.

"When are you leaving for the cooking demonstration?"

"Quarter of an hour."

"I wish you would wait until one so I could take you."

"That would make me late."

She heard a sigh of resignation. "Okay, I'll be there as soon as I can, Clyde, but please be careful. And look out for—"

"I know. The tan station wagon."

"Anything, Clyde. Be on the look out for anything."

With those reassuring words echoing in her ears, she hung up and proceeded to get dressed. Truth be told, she was scared. She would have much preferred he drive her. But she would not be intimidated. Once fear got a stranglehold, it choked the vitality out of a person's life; it limited possibilities. She would not let fear take her prisoner.

She surveyed herself in the full-length mirror one last time. The red pants suit was the right choice. She looked strong. In control. And it gave her face a much needed jolt of color. She gave her image in the mirror a thumbs up, grabbed her purse and left.

Right on schedule, she drove out of the Far Horizons parking lot. She cruised along, windows open and the breeze playing with her hair. She stuck a BeeGees tape in the tape deck and tapped the song's rhythm—*Staying Alive,* her favorite from the *Saturday Night Fever* album—on the wheel. An oldie, but goodie. She liked the old songs. They weren't all jazzed up with synthesizers and computers that turned four musicians into the equivalent of a big band. Old music was more honest and pure somehow.

Turning left onto the causeway, she noticed the steering wheel seemed stiffer, less maneuverable than usual. Almost as if the steering wheel fought her. Since she managed to turn without a serious problem, she wasn't upset, remembering that the car was usually parked in a garage. The stiffness could be a result of the combination of parking in the open and the rather nippy November air.

A little further along the causeway, she pulled out to pass another car. Again the wheel was stiff and unresponsive and she barely managed to return to the proper lane of traffic in time to avoid oncoming vehicles. She tried to slow down, pumping the brake pedal, but the car slowed only slightly.

Then, for the first time, the possibility occurred to her that what was happening wasn't accidental. It was no coincidence that both the brakes and the power steering were giving her trouble.

Verging on panic, she focused on her driving, gripping the wheel even tighter. Despite her efforts, it became increasingly difficult to make even the smallest adjustments necessary to keep the car on the highway. The Bronco displayed a tendency to pull to the right and she had all she could do to keep from running into the concrete railing. She tried again to slow the vehicle, but the Bronco wouldn't respond. She stomped on the brake with her full weight. Nothing. She jerked the emergency brake. Nothing.

Clyde stared at the road, knuckles white from the strain, wrists stiff. She mustered all her strength, focused all her will on keeping the vehicle in its proper lane and headed straight. Once on the off ramp, she took a deep breath, but her relief was short lived. And premature. She had sailed onto Gulf Boulevard into the traffic. Desperate, she clutched the steering wheel, her mind spinning as she tried to figure out what to do next. She couldn't stop the damned thing and she couldn't steer it. She could shove it into first gear, but there was a chance she'd be rear-ended if she slowed down too quickly. And if the motor stalled, she'd be stuck in the middle of traffic with no way to avoid being struck.

A section of Gulf Boulevard ran parallel to the water. The shoulder was a strip of white sand maybe 30 feet wide. It couldn't be called a beach, but sometimes sunbathers or local fishermen used it. She prayed it was deserted.

Almost as the thought came into her mind, she spotted the mini beach ahead. She leaned on her horn, the blatting scattering sea gulls and shore birds. Bumping and jolting across two lanes of traffic onto the shoulder, the Bronco dropped down the slight incline and rolled onto the hard-packed sand.

Clyde twisted the wheel. The vehicle was in the water before she managed to slam her foot on the clutch and drag it into reverse gear. The Bronco jerked to a halt. The motor coughed and drowned.

For long minutes, she sat in the front seat, bent over the steering wheel, trembling. Tears of relief, anger, and frustration spilled down her cheeks. Fears she had been unable to acknowledge because of the urgency of the prior moments now flooded her mind. Visions of her face being destroyed so that she couldn't work in television. A collision in which she'd lost a leg or been paralyzed. Even, she shook harder, her death. Who would tell Iris Medea? She could hear her mother. "I told that child that being a TV reporter was dangerous." And her dad. He'd be furious.

Sitting in the front seat of her disabled Bronco with the waters of the Gulf washing past the vehicle, she faced facts. She took excellent care of her vehicles. This malfunction, whatever it was, couldn't be an accident. She acknowledged that someone was trying to kill her. Besides, the Bronco was only six months old. She conceded at last that this was more than she could handle. This was beyond her. She'd call Bill Trent in the Attorney General's office in Tallahassee. They'd once had a relationship, one that even her dad had approved. He would know what she should do. Let the professionals handle it.

She drew a deep breath. Then another. She gave herself some time. Time to catch her breath, to regain control. Get past the moment, she told herself fiercely. Focus on the future. What *was* next? The cooking demo. God, she couldn't do a cooking demonstration. She was shaking like a bowl of half-set gelatin. No way. Clyde opened the Bronco's door and looked down at the water swirling over the floorboard.

"If Clyde Colby can't hack the cooking show, dump her. It's just business." Rodney Delmont's words echoed in her mind.

The station was now paying her expenses at Far Horizons. She was shaken by this accident, but not hurt.

She'd been a reporter. She knew you stayed with your story, you finished it. She and Andy had been in a shoot-out once in Liberty City and they'd finished the story. She'd had her car tampered with when she'd reported on the grand jury investigation into the shooting death New Year's Eve at the sheriff's hunting camp. She'd done the story.

She was an experienced television journalist. For escape from the moment at hand, she did what she'd learned to do. She slipped into the Clyde Colby persona, the television professional.

Slipping off her red high heels, she rolled up her pants legs and jumped down. Her knees buckled and she sat flat on her rear end in the surf.

"Shit!"

Sopping wet, she struggled to her feet, grabbed her purse and slogged her way to the beach. Once on the sand, she looked back at her blue Bronco.

She loved that vehicle. It was the first one she'd bought all by herself. Her father had always had the last say on cars she'd bought before she married Josh. Then Josh had taken over. But this car was all hers. She'd picked it out on the dealer's lot, negotiated the loan shopping around at several banks for the best interest rate, and had made mincemeat of the car salesman who'd tried to tell her she had to have the extended warranty protection plan. Saved her more than a thousand bucks. Now there it sat, decorating the surf off Palmetto Bay. The damaged car was a personal affront.

She would think about it later. She pulled her cell phone out of her purse and tapped in the number of Sam's sailing school. Nothing. No dial tone. Of course, salt water wasn't good for cell phones or cars.

What now?

She waded through the sand, which shifted at her every step, made her way to the street and stuck out her thumb. A condiment salesman came by in an old black Honda. His backseat was filled with cardboard cartons labeled with different peppers and herbs. He was courteous and solicitous, accepting without question her explanation that she'd had an accident, making sure she wasn't hurt.

They passed a tan station wagon. A blonde-haired man in his thirties was at the wheel. He paid no attention to them.

She felt herself grow pale. The salesman asked if she was all right, if she needed a doctor.

She forced herself to smile. "No, no, I'm fine. Just drop me off at the Mall." It was only a little lie. Physically, she *was* fine. Emotionally, she barely had control.

Once he dropped her off at Inventors Mall, she walked to Burdine's, stepping gingerly because her wet shoes were gritty with sand. Riding the escalator to the second floor, she hoped no one would notice her torn hose, then chastised herself for her stupidity. She was in a department store. She asked directions to the ladies' department where she discovered that wet charge cards would work and bought dry lingerie and another pants suit. Next she went to the shoe department and finally to the hosiery department. Then she located the ladies restroom where she surprised herself by throwing up. She rested her head against the cool porcelain bowl then, thoroughly irritated with herself, got up, sponged off with paper towels, changed clothes and refreshed her makeup.

Hurrying down the aisles as she searched for the housewares department, Clyde caught sight of Lillian Albritton. The petite librarian, standing beside cookware display, was wearing a sheath with a cowl neck made of a shiny Paisley print. She was surrounded by a small group men and women.

"We were getting concerned, Miss Colby," the librarian said as she walked up. "It's a quarter after one. You have plenty of time, but you had said you would be here at noon."

"I had an accident. But I'm pretty much all right," she added hurriedly seeing the looks of concern on their faces. "And I'm here now."

"Have you reported it to the authorities?" the librarian asked.

"I'll do that as soon as we're through."

The librarian introduced her to the members of the committee, which was composed of the officers of the Palmetto Bay Marching and Chowder Society. Since key limes were abundant and available nearly year round, she had decided she'd build her demo around this fruit. She had selected recipes for lime nut bread with lime glaze, lime cookies and lime cream puffs.

At her direction, the committee members emptied paper bags filled with the key limes they'd brought from their yards. Dividing the duties, two squeezed the fruit and grated the rinds. Two others measured and separated the ingredients for the three recipes into three sections and prepared them, working on the pickled oak and white tile counter. One member, consulting her often, organized the utensils she'd need so that everything was ready. Even Sam, who'd arrived shortly after she had, pitched in. They didn't have a chance to talk, but she smiled her thanks. She was impressed as always by his taste. He wore a pale blue blazer that emphasized his tan and a crisp white shirt with stone-washed jeans that hugged his well-proportioned frame. A man to look up to, figuratively and literally, she thought.

It wasn't until 1:45 when the first members began trickling in, that the fact that she was doing her first cooking demo sank in and she was terrified. Visions of disaster plagued her. She could see herself dropping bowls filled with ingredients, scorching the cookies, the cream puffs turning out chewy. Her hands shook so badly, she either clenched them in front of her or hid them beneath the apron.

Fortunately, the people were very accepting. They enjoyed it even when she made a mistake such as holding up the baking powder and calling it lime zest. As each dish was finished, the audience tasted and approved and, at the end of the session, took away every copy of the recipes she'd brought.

"An unqualified success," Sam declared. Right behind him flocked the committee. The members were effusive with their thanks. It wasn't until she was alone with Sam that he realized something was wrong.

"What is it? Why are you so pale?"

"It's a long story," she said. "It's my car. I need to call the auto club and the sheriff. So, if you've not made other plans, I really could use a ride to a car rental agency."

He looked at her very solemnly. "What's going on? Why didn't you call me?"

"My cell phone got wet and wouldn't work."

"Your cell phone got wet? We're not leaving this store until we get you another one. I don't want you out of touch. And why do I have a hunch there's a lot more to this story than you're telling me?"

"A lot more. And I promise to tell you everything if you'll give me a ride. I'll even buy you a drink." Clyde grabbed her purse.

"Such an offer I can't refuse. Even if I end up paying."

After she had made the necessary calls from the office at Burdine's and purchased a new cell phone, he led her out of Inventors Mall into the parking lot. "You don't need to rent a car. I know you've got that talk at Palmetto Bay Junior College. I'll take you where you need to go."

She accepted, grateful for his company, and it would have seemed like any other normal afternoon except that they both kept looking at the rearview mirror. Practically every time they took a corner, Clyde flinched. She'd had her own version of a near-death experience and it would be a while before the im-

pact of that close call lessened. During the drive to the junior
college, she told Sam about the accident, her suspicions that it
wasn't an accident, and concluded with her decision to call Bill
Trent in the Attorney General's office. While she was ambiv-
alent about giving up, Sam's relief was evident.

"Hallelujah." He lifted both hands from the steering wheel
in a gesture of gratitude to the gods. "Now I can get a decent
night's sleep."

Sam waited patiently while Clyde talked to the journalism
class. She was relieved because it went well. She was pleased,
too, because their questions were thoughtful.

"Good job, honey," he said once they were in the car. "You
may not realize it yet, but you're a natural at this PR stuff."

"A natural? How do you figure that?"

"Simple. You're a natural because you are natural. And because you tell the truth. I predict great things in the future for
you." Then he laughed and reached across the front seat to draw
her closer to him. "The near future," he said. "Maybe even tonight."

Once back at Far Horizons, they had an early dinner. He insisted they stop in at the Surfriders Lounge for an after dinner
drink where he had a long talk with Sullivan. When she asked
him about it, he shrugged and changed the subject, telling her
she looked exhausted.

"I am. I'm about to fall asleep right here. My chin is going
to drop right into my vodka tonic." Clyde swiveled on the bar
stool. She picked up her purse from the counter. It was just after
ten and the bar was packed.

"I'm coming up with you," Sam insisted. "After that business with your car, we can't be too careful. You and I may know
you're giving up, but the bad guys don't."

"This time I won't argue," she said as she rubbed her neck,
which was beginning to stiffen. She gestured to the bartender
who brought their check. She signed it and couldn't resist. "I'll
write you off as a business expense."

"Tact," Sam said as he rose and helped her off the bar stool,
"is not your strong suit."

In her room a few minutes later, he checked thoroughly, but could find no signs of anyone suspicious having been there. "The smartest thing would be for me to stay," he offered, but she shook her head.

"No, I need my time. And space." But she stood on tiptoe to kiss him on the cheek. "Thank you."

He moved back from her and looked stern. "From now on, Clyde, you are going to take some basic precautions. Every time you leave the room," he instructed, "I want you to put a match between the door and the top of the jamb. Then before you re-enter the room, I want you to check. If that match is lying on the floor, don't go in. Call me. I don't care what time it is, call me. Use my cell phone."

Clyde nodded.

"And be sure to lock the door after me. And don't open it until you know who's there. And if there's anything suspicious, like room service when you haven't ordered, refuse to open the door and call me. And keep those French doors locked, too."

"Sam. *Sam.* I'll be all right. Don't worry."

"I wish I felt as sure of that as you do."

"What a thing for you to say, you ass. You should be reassuring me, not turning me into a bowl of jangled nerves."

He tamped his full lips into a severe line. "I want you so nervous that you think twice before you even go to the bathroom. I want you looking under the bed, in the rearview mirror. I want you questioning the intentions of every single person you meet."

"Thanks a lot," she said and almost pushed him out of her room.

Once he was gone, she glanced around the room. It seemed unfamiliar, violated. She no longer felt safe. It was, of course, only her perception that had changed, but the shadows seemed darker, unnatural. Outside, the trees dancing in the breeze cast warped images against the sheer curtains. Always before she'd watched the changing shadows and whimsically likened their twisting shapes to those of graceful Balinese dancers. Tonight,

the silhouettes were weird and unsettling. Tonight, she thought
sadly, fear was her roommate. She longed for morning and sunshine.

She took her shower, creamed her face and donned her
nightshirt. Then, before she slipped into bed, she retrieved her
briefcase from the bottom drawer of the bureau and took out
the photocopied pages from Eli's notebook. She carried them
to the bed and crawled between sheets, bracing her back against
the headboard. She decided to call Bill Trent in the morning
and fax him these notes. The only problem she could foresee
was that the ever present terrorist threats had everything in government stalled. Would he be able to get to this case in time?
Then she fretted about Eli. Could she have done something to
have prevented the beating? If she had agreed to help right
away, would that have made a difference?

Sitting up, she spread the notes against her knees. She loved
crossword puzzles, Scrabble, word games. That's what this
was. A word game. Think of it like that. Now what was she
overlooking? What didn't she see?

She studied the lists of initials. HB. Horace Beck, obviously.
DB. That would be Davy. And GB would be Grace. But what
about FW? And RS? Then there were the initials IT and EM,
followed by a series of exclamation points. Who could these
refer to? Obviously, people who lived in or near Rattlesnake
Key.

She yawned. It had been another in a series of long, endless
days and she was finally sleepy.

One last chore.

Clyde reached down and dragged the telephone book from
the bottom compartment of the nightstand. When in doubt, let
your fingers do the walking, she mused. She flipped the direct-
ory open to the blue pages of the phone book to the government section. She'd jot down the number of the Attorney
General's office in Tallahassee so she could call first thing in
the morning.

As she riffled through the blue pages, a page labeled "Rattlesnake Key, Village of" caught her eye. Without knowing

why, she ran her finger down the list of elected officials. As she did, a steel fist of disbelief and fear seized her chest so fiercely she could barely breathe.

She leaned back against the headboard. There it was. In black and white. And it proved that whatever Eli was onto, it was a truly major conspiracy.

IT. Rattlesnake Key Mayor Irwin Thompson.

FW. Rattlesnake Key Police Chief Frank Westendorf. And he seemed so nice.

RS. County Medical Examiner assigned to Rattlesnake Key, Rudy Schroeder.

GV. Assistant State Attorney Gus Vaughn.

That had to be it! There were too many matches to be coincidences. Instinctively, she reached for the telephone on the nightstand to call Sam.

But no.

Now she knew she couldn't trust the telephone. It would be too easy for the police chief to install a wiretap.

The cell phone. She dug it out of her purse and dialed his number. It rang, but he didn't pick up. Wasn't that just like a man? Any man. Even Sam. They would lead you to believe you could trust them, depend on them and then they would betray you. She glanced around the room nervously, slid out of bed and padded over to the French doors. She rattled the knobs to make sure they were locked, repeating the procedure at the door to the corridor.

Back in bed, she studied her watch.

2:00 AM.

Hours till dawn. Obviously she couldn't talk to Sam and tell him what she had figured out. Where was he and why wasn't he answering his cell phone? Another realization shoved all thoughts of Sam aside. Did she dare call Bill Trent? Not at this time of night. By the time she got through telling him such a wild story and so late at night, he'd be sure she was certifiably insane. Better to wait until daytime. If she did convince Bill Trent it was urgent, she reasoned, he'd tell her to call the police. And she'd tell him the police were involved. And he'd say

sure and write her off as a flake. No, she had to have proof. And
however urgent the matter, even in more normal times, it took
state agencies time to respond. It wasn't like calling the police

The hours stretched ahead as long as a lifetime. A chill sen
her scooting down beneath the covers. A lifetime. The words
were ominous.

Clyde gritted her teeth and sat up again. She would no
panic. She had four hours. The photocopies were lying strewn
around the bed covers. She collected them, formed them into
a neat stack and once again started studying Eli's notes.

Finally, just before dawn she dozed, head sunk forward on
her chest, every light in the room blazing. Her dreams would
have made a Jean Claude Van Damme movie seem introspec-
tive for in the landscape of her fantasy, she was in the water
buffeted by waves, going down and down, yanked out, rescued
at the last moment by a giant, disembodied fist. A fist clutch-
ing a spatula.

And then she was running down a narrow corridor with
walls that seemed to breathe. And sweat. Moisture oozed from
the walls. Where was she? Her destination was the room at the
end of the hall. Running. Running. There was the door, but it
was misshapen and uneven. And emblazoned with Gothic numerals that flashed red. The number was seventeen.

The revelation jarred Clyde awake. She sat erect, breathing
rapidly as if she'd been running. Her heart was pounding. Cold
sweat beaded her brow. Finally, she understood.

Seventeen was a room number.

SIXTEEN

NOVEMBER 8

THE MORNING WAS DRESSED in serene chiffon ribbons of peach, lilac and robin's egg blue, but Clyde felt far from placid. She dressed hurriedly, her hands fumbling with buttons and zippers. It took two tries to get her lipstick on straight. Taking a deep breath, she grabbed her purse and left the room. In the hallway, she looked both ways before proceeding to the elevator. It was deserted. At 6:15 no other guest was stirring. Her brain was in such a maelstrom, she was halfway out the lobby on her way to the parking lot before she remembered she had no car. Memories of her close call the day before flooded her consciousness. The Bronco was in the garage. And the shock had worn off. She was face-to-face with the reality that it was possible someone had tried to kill her. Sam. She had to call Sam.

Desperate, she surveyed the desolate lobby then headed for a corner out of sight, dialed Sam's cell phone number and waited. After two rings, she heard his voice, husky with sleep.

"Yeah," he said. "Clyde?"

"Oh, Sam," she breathed. "I called you last night. Where were you?" She was so glad to hear his voice she couldn't stay mad.

"What's wrong?" he demanded.

"I—" There was so much she couldn't begin to explain.

"Never mind. Where are you? In your room?"

"No. In the lobby."

"Relax, I'll be right there."

"How long—" she started to ask, but he'd hung up. She looked around the lobby, uncertain what she should do next.

It was unfair of him to leave her hanging like that. Didn't he understand she was frightened and upset? Where was he? And how long was it going to take him to get here? She wouldn't have left him up in the air this way. She drifted over to one of the leather sofas in front of the fireplace and was about to sit down when she saw him coming through the doorway leading from the dining room.

He was wrinkled and unshaven. A trace of a beard highlighted his prominent bone structure creating dark, sharp indentations. The shadows lent his face a primal even predatory look. He had never looked better to her. But how on earth had he gotten here so quickly?

"Sam?"

He grinned. "Don't ask. All I will tell you is that I am probably one of the few hobos Far Horizons has ever hosted with his own cellular phone." He stretched and groaned. "I don't recommend a palm tree as a backrest."

"You mean you were—"

"Your room was never out of my sight." He chucked her under the chin. "You're not the only one who can be stubborn, Mizz-Colby-like-the-cheese." Then he brushed the hair out of her eyes. "Didn't get much sleep, did you?"

"Sam, we've got to talk. I figured out—" She paused. "I called you last night and you didn't answer. Where were you?"

"Honey, I was right here. I left for just a few minutes. Went to the men's room. Why didn't you call back?"

She didn't know what to say. Why hadn't she? She felt stupid. And exhausted.

"Want some coffee?" He put his hand under her elbow to lead her into the dining room. "It's too early for Davy or Beck to enforce the dress code," he joked, indicating his wrinkled jacket and trousers.

"Not here."

"Where then?"

"Anywhere but here."

"Then let's head for the boat, honey. I could use a shower and some fresh clothes."

They walked out of the lobby and through the parking lot then turned left onto Matecumbe Road. About a quarter of a mile farther, she spotted the Lexus parked in front of a closed and shuttered restaurant with "For Sale" signs by the entrance. It wasn't until they were inside the vehicle headed toward the marina that Clyde took a deep breath and relaxed.

ON BOARD THE *SANITY,* Sam said, "Your turn to cook. You know where everything is. If you don't, hunt around until you find it." He vanished into the cabin, emerged with a towel wrapped around his middle and made for the head. Moments later as she made coffee, she heard the shower. Rather than cook, she scrounged in the refrigerator for orange juice. Then made toast, which she served with guava jelly. By the time she had everything on the table, Sam reappeared freshly shaven and neatly groomed.

While they ate, she explained about the initials and the room number. "But I don't have enough information. I need proof before I call Bill."

"Absolutely not," he said, his tone of voice indicating he would brook no discussion. "You are finished playing detective. Your investigation is concluded. You've got to return to Miami where you'll be safe."

She stared at him. "Oh, yes. I'll be safe there." Sarcasm laced her voice despite her best intentions. "They won't worry about what I know or what they think I know if I'm in Miami. Isn't there some sort of geographical statute of limitations?"

"Geographical statute of limitations? You lost me."

"Well, that means what I know about crime on Rattlesnake Key won't count as long as I'm in Miami. It's like that old adage if a tree falls in the forest and there's no one to hear the sound, it doesn't exist. In other words, if I'm not on the scene, the crime I know about doesn't exist."

He slammed his coffee cup into his saucer. "You are incredibly pigheaded."

"If you won't help me," she said, "at least I hope you won't get in my way."

He wasn't about to give up easily and he argued for a good half an hour before conceding. She knew enough not to show the quick elation she felt when at last he agreed to help.

"We've got to get into room seventeen," she concluded after explaining what she thought should be their plan of action. "But how?"

He shrugged. "Your friend Dorris with two R's? If I could get into your room with fifty bucks, I'll bet *two* General Grants would get us the use of her master key."

Everything in her wanted to beg Sam to untie the *Sanity* and head for a place that was safe, a place that was what it seemed to be. But the moment the thought lodged itself in her mind, it was brushed aside by a parade of familiar faces: Eli, Penny, Greg Lanken. Maybe Dawn. Where was Dawn?

"When are we going to do this?" she asked.

"How about now?"

"Works for me. Let's do it before I lose my nerve."

Sam reached across the table and cupped her chin in his hand. "That'll be the day," he said, kissing her lightly. He rose and started clearing the table. "Let's go and get it over with."

"Right." She got up to help, piling the dishes in the sink, starting to run water to wash them.

"Leave them," he said. "They'll be there when we get back."

That was the perfect thing to say, she reasoned later. Reminding her that this, too, would end. There would be time to do the dishes, time to worry about Clyde's Gourmet Galley, the normal chores and responsibilities from which was woven the fabric of one's life.

Back at Far Horizons, Sam proved once again he was a good judge of character. It was still early, not quite nine o'clock when they got back. As luck would have it, Dorris with the two R's was working on the second floor west hall where Clyde's room was located.

"Dorris," he said smiling. "Remember me?"

She nodded and smiled, but looked uneasily up and down the corridor.

"We're alone," he assured her. "Got a question for you."

"Yeah?"

"Could I look at your chart?" When she looked blank, he continued, "The one that shows which rooms you have to make up. The occupied rooms."

She shrugged and handed him the clipboard. Clyde read the list over his shoulder as he ran his forefinger down the columns of room numbers. They looked at one another as his finger stopped at seventeen. It was not marked.

"Vacant," she whispered.

"Bingo," he said. "Now Dorris…"

With the aid of three General Grants and the assurance they would protect her, Dorris was only too happy to temporarily relinquish her master key.

Downstairs in the hall, Sam made sure no one was coming before he slipped the keycard into the door. He ushered Clyde inside quickly. Once across the threshold, she stood in front of the closed door and surveyed the room. It was rectangular, a little narrower than average, but beautifully furnished with antiques from the Victorian period. It was undoubtedly a man's room. The furniture was rich mahogany, heavy and dark. The pieces were unusual including a bureau with bombé front and sides. In the corner was an umbrella stand. The walls were decorated with the mounted head of a glassy-eyed deer, a silver tarpon and paintings of hunting scenes—red-coated riders and foxhounds, hunters aiming at a flock of ducks overhead. It was unlike any of the other rooms she'd seen in the resort.

Perhaps it was the heaviness of the furnishings, perhaps the fact that the room was crowded with furniture. Whatever the reason, she felt unsettled and oppressed in this chamber crammed with antiques.

She crossed the room to the window, which overlooked the tennis courts. Glancing outside, the view reminded her of her first night at Far Horizons when she had been assigned to room number nineteen, right next door. The night her sleep had been disturbed. Twice. And Beck had told her the sounds she heard were from a nearby generator. But, she reasoned now, that couldn't have been the case. The supply closet was immedi-

ately adjacent to room seventeen and would have at least muffled if not completely masked the sound of a generator.

So, if the generator wasn't where the supply closet was,
where was it? And why would Beck tell her such a lie?

To her left was a king-sized bed covered by a heavy, striped
maroon and gold spread with a *fleur de lis* pattern. The draperies were of matching fabric. A panel in the wall behind the bed
had been framed in molding painted gold. The inset panel was
covered with matching fabric.

Sam was standing as impassively as she was. He, too, looked
thoughtful.

"See anything?" he asked finally.

She shrugged. "The furnishings are ornate, the room is a little smaller than the others, but that's all."

"Okay, let's check the closet and drawers. Maybe someone
left something here that would give us a clue."

Sam not only checked the contents of the drawers, which
were empty, he pulled them out and studied their backs and bottoms. In the closet, he tapped the walls, looked above and
below the luggage rack. Behind the mirrors. On his hands and
knees, he felt along the baseboards, tugged at the carpet to be
sure nothing could be hidden beneath it. While she watched,
he repeated the procedure in the bath. She was impressed by
his thoroughness.

Then they stood, motionless, in the middle of the bedroom.
Looking around. Trying to figure what to do next. She heard a
scratching sound and Sam literally picked her up and threw her
on the bed. He fell on top of her, pinning her like a wrestler,
kissing her, mussing her hair. The studs of his denim jacket
pressed into her face and she tried unsuccessfully to pull away.

"Sam," she mumbled, trying to complain, trying to tell him
she didn't like this rough stuff, that she wanted up. But she
could hardly breathe. Every time she managed to pull her
mouth free or squirm away, he clamped his lips down on hers
again. This was no fun. Panic overwhelmed reason and she
began to struggle.

"Ahem."

The sound, although not loud, carried. Abruptly, Sam freed her. She sat up. Beck stood inside the door, a keycard in one hand, a clipboard in the other and a strange expression fixed on his face.

She felt her face grow hot and blossom into tomato red.

"Miss Colby?" Beck said coldly, referring to the clipboard. "I believe this room is vacant. Has your room assignment been changed without my awareness?"

She simply didn't know what to say. She was absolutely humiliated. Even though they weren't doing what he thought. And she was paralyzed with fear. Beck was possibly a murderer. And certainly no fool. He would know why they were in room seventeen. Wouldn't he?

Usually her TV training saved her. She'd carried on when lights had fallen on the set behind her during a broadcast, when the teleprompter had broken and she could barely remember what the next word was. But this time her quick wit let her down.

Sam came to the rescue bridging the awful silence. She didn't know whether she was more relieved because he had a story for Beck or because she finally understood his mad behavior. She needed Sam, needed to be able to trust him.

"Ah, Beck," Sam was saying, a sheepish, embarrassed expression on his face, as he tucked his blue polo shirt into his waist. "It's all her fault." He grinned and she sent him a look that would have killed. Murder came to her mind. His murder. "I don't even know how to explain. We were in the hallway and we were, well, you know, kind of fooling around. And we were leaning against this door and it was unlocked. I guess someone left the door ajar. Anyway, we sort of fell in here and she…well, Ms. Colby just got carried away. I…" He ran his fingers beneath his collar to straighten it. "You know how aggressive women are today."

"Me?" she started, but Sam's warning glance silenced her.

Beck nodded. At first, he looked suspicious, but then he adopted one of those man-to-man expressions on his face. As a rule, Clyde hated that look. Around the station it always meant she was about to be excluded from a discussion of something they didn't want her to know or something they figured she wouldn't understand. But, she reminded herself, here it meant rescue.

"Miss Colby is a very lovely woman. But the room—"

"Of course," Sam said. "We'll get out right away."

"Wait a minute," Clyde said. "My earring." She walked around to the far side of the bed and looked down at the carpet between the bed and the window. Then she spied it, the gold lion's head earring. She bent to pick it up. Something shiny caught her eye.

Tracks. Like mini-railroad tracks.

Beneath the bed.

She caught her breath, stilled her face.

Focus, focus, focus.

That was the secret when you were on a TV set or a shoot and all hell was breaking around you. Focus.

Beck mustn't see any change in her facial expression. She mustn't think about what the tracks meant. She mustn't think about what would happen if Beck figured out what they were up to. She and Sam had been found in a romantic tryst. She had found her earring. An earring she valued. That's all there was to this whole situation.

Focus.

"Got it," she said, pasting a Clyde Colby cooking show host smile on her face, holding the earring aloft for both men to see. "Now if you fellows will excuse me," she said, "I've had enough excitement for one day." She glared at Sam. "You and I have to talk about your behavior!"

Sam looked at Beck and shrugged as if to ask what can you do with the little dears? Clyde gritted her teeth. Then the elation of her discovery carried her out of the room and down the hall. Sam followed, still making small talk with Beck. She played the game, striding ahead of both men.

Beck paused outside his office door.

"What gave us away?" Sam was asking. He was running his big ham of a hand nervously through his thick black hair.

"One of the maids told Grace she thought she'd seen someone enter seventeen and checked to see if it was to be made up."

"Can't get away with a thing," Sam chuckled, punching Beck on the shoulder. "Never could."

Sam caught up to her as she was striding out into the lobby. They hadn't talked about what they were going to do after they searched seventeen, but she didn't want to go back to her room to talk. She didn't feel safe at Far Horizons. Sam at her heels, she continued through the lobby into the parking lot, smiling at several of the guests who recognized her.

When she let him catch up to her in the parking lot, he asked, "What's up?"

A shiver of fear went through her. "Do you think Beck knows what we were doing?"

"I don't know. At the very least, he now suspects something," he said as he unlocked the car door. "Beck isn't dumb, but fortunately, he doesn't know you as well as I do. But when you waved that earring in the air, I knew you were on the trail of something."

She smiled, but it was more of a grimace. The sky was blue. The sunshine was warm. The palm trees were swaying. The Gulf of Mexico glittered behind them. A totally benign environment. And yet she felt completely surrounded by malignancy.

"Let's rephrase that last statement," she said gravely. "Let's say I'm on the track of something."

SEVENTEEN

NOVEMBER 8

STANDING JUST INSIDE THE SYNAGOGUE in the foyer, Clyde watched as the crowd left the synagogue following Eli's memorial service. Off to the side, she saw Eli's grandfather and his three friends from the condo as they left by a side exit. She spotted Binky Beresford leaving with a group of people she assumed were Eli's co-workers. A plumpish, but attractive young woman with thick red hair, a red nose and a huge handkerchief wept quietly as she passed where Clyde and Sam stood. She was obviously distraught and Clyde was surprised. Somehow she hadn't expected Eli to have a personal relationship other than his grandfather.

The building was air-conditioned and the blowers were blasting out refrigerated air. Despite the heat outside and the number of people in the room, Clyde was chilled. She hadn't known what to wear. Her wardrobe was limited because she hadn't expected to stay so long, but she'd settled on the navy blue suit with the slim skirt. The fabric was lightweight, and instead of a blouse, she'd added a ruffled white silk dickey and a slim gold link belt. However, the chill had more to do with the peril. Even here, where she should have felt safe among Eli's friends and in a house of worship, she could not relax. She found herself constantly looking around. Studying the people. Most were strangers, but she saw many from Rattlesnake Key. Mayor Randolph Thompson, Police Chief Westendorf, Sgt. Reeves, members of the city council.

Their rationale, Sam had told her after a conversation with

Horace, was that Eli had been killed on Rattlesnake Key and their appearance was their way of paying their respects. But she knew why they were there. They were spies, trying to find out what, if anything, the Jewish congregation had learned about Eli's beating.

For the hundredth time she wondered if it would have helped if she had immediately consented to help Eli. Was there something she could have done? Should she have agreed, and then insisted on having dinner with him and his grandfather that same evening? If she had, he would not have been in that parking lot and he would still be alive.

She waited a moment, unsure what to do, but gathered her nerve and approached the rabbi.

"I'm not Jewish," she said and he smiled.

"I would have guessed," Rabbi Benjamin Meyers said, but not unkindly.

"I have a question."

"Ask," he replied.

"Why is now a good time for the *golem?*" she asked.

"Where did you hear of the *golem?*" His dark eyes, rimmed by thick-lensed glasses, widened.

"I saw an old movie about it, and then one night at the hospital Eliahu was talking about the *golem* and…"

"And?"

She was puzzled as a memory filtered through the banks of her mind into full consciousness. "And the night I arrived at Far Horizons, Halloween it was, Davy Beck, the son of the owner, was wearing a *golem* costume."

"Davy?" A hint of a smile spread his lips. "Wait a moment after the others have gone and I will tell you the story of the *golem.*"

Sam, who'd been speaking to Binky Beresford, returned. "I thought you were in a hurry to leave," he said.

"I'm waiting to talk to the rabbi. He is going to tell us about the *golem.*"

As the others filed out of the synagogue, Clyde noticed the police chief standing with Sgt. Reeves. She could barely bring herself to nod at him let alone speak. What was he doing? Did he still believe Eli had been beaten by a drug addict? Did he *really* believe it was a drug addict? And where was Dawn?

When finally the synagogue was empty, the rabbi returned. "Will you come into my office?"

They followed him through a door on the side of the altar. The office was small and unbelievably cluttered. Books and papers and newspaper clippings were scattered everywhere. On the desk. On the floor beside the desk. On the chairs. He swept the papers off the sofa against the wall across from the desk and indicated they should sit. Clyde was impressed. Obviously the man was a scholar and she felt sure she would get some answers here.

"A glass of wine?" He reached behind him to a bookcase and removed an elegant lead glass decanter that seemed out of place in the masses of printed material.

"Thank you," Clyde said and Sam nodded.

He withdrew three matching lead glass goblets and poured the rich red fluid.

"L'chaim," he said and they toasted one another.

"So you want to know about the *golem,* Miss Colby?" He smiled at her look of surprise. "Oh, yes I know who you are. You're a local celebrity." He took a sip, appreciating the full body of the wine. "Eli and I were friends," he said after a pause. "He talked to me about you. Good things. He liked you."

She felt tears forming and wiped them away, but said nothing.

"I will tell you what you want to know, but I must know something, too. Are you sure Davy Beck wore the costume of a *golem?"*

She told him what the costume had looked like and about the word on the monster's forehead. "It was a foreign word. *Maeth."*

"You're sure the word was *Maeth?"*

She nodded. "I like words, I notice them."

"Ah, yes, that's part of the story, too," he said and settled back in his chair, a wooden barrel chair that looked as if it might have come from a Salvation Army Thrift Shop. "I know," he said. "This chair looks terrible, but it's so comfortable I can't throw it away. Mrs. Hoffmann makes me two new cushions every so often and the rest of the people in the synagogue put up with it. Now—" He adjusted a pillow in the small of his back and began.

"In February of 1872," he said, "the sexton—he officiated at burials sometimes even digging the graves—traveled to the rabbi's chamber in Altneu Synagogue in the Jewish quarter of Prague. He told the white-bearded rabbi that the people were frightened. Mordecai Levy's son had been beaten and blinded by a horde of Christians who screamed he had slain a Christian babe to use its blood for Passover Services. And Rachel Loew had been forced to take the communion wafer by order of the Monk Matteus. The Cardinal of Prague had ignored the pleas of our people." He settled himself more comfortably in the chair.

"The sexton told the rabbi he had to help and the rabbi responded that three nights past he posed a dream question to *Hashem* and God had graced him with an answer. When the sexton asked what the answer was, the rabbi said, 'We are to create a man of clay, a *golem*, and he shall wreak havoc on our enemies. He shall protect us from persecution.'"

"A man of clay," Clyde interrupted thoughtfully, shifting on the sofa to look at Sam. "That's exactly what Davy looked like Halloween night."

Rabbi Meyers nodded and continued his story. "The rabbi told the sexton to fetch the rabbi's assistant, and when the three were together in the rabbi's chamber, he explained they must spend the next three days in prayer and fasting for purification. Three days later, it was Sunday, the tenth day of *Adar* of the year 5352 after the world was created, the three met at the *Mikveh* where they bathed with reverence. Then the rabbi led them to the banks of the Moldau River."

Rabbi Meyers rose and stared out the window. The bright sun created a nimbus around his balding head. "Splinters of lightning cracked the dark sky over the city or so our legend goes," he continued, picking up the thread of the story. "Night breezes teased the flames of the candles the sexton held aloft. The rabbi intoned the stirring phrases of *Hazoth,* the midnight lamentation for Jerusalem. Then the assistant handed the rabbi the Book of Psalms from which he read the sacred words.

"The rabbi represented the element of air, the sexton represented water and the rabbi's assistant was fire. Kneeling on the riverbank, the rabbi placed the scroll and *Sefer Yezirath,* the Book of Creation, on the ground. The men plunged their hands into the moist earth and formed the image of a man. They formed a semicircle at the *golem's* feet, staring into its as yet sightless eyes. Its coarse mud features glistened in the candle flame. The air was hushed. The waters of the Moldau became as still as the folds in a corpse's shroud. Then, moving seven times east to west, they paced the perimeter of the effigy and the rabbi recited the secret *zirufim* or formula.

"As the trio stood at the *golem's* feet, tendrils of steam gushed from the mud, the *golem* began to glow until at last the entire mass was a fierce, angry red."

He paused, then rose and walked restlessly around and sat on the edge of his desk. He looked directly at Clyde as he said, "The rabbi spoke to the sexton imparting the sacred words of creation which he spoke aloud seven times. The air was filled with the sound of hissing and clouds of steam rose as the water doused the fire. Rivulets of water spouted from the body and as the men watched, the apertures through which the water flowed became skin pores. Hair began to grow. Nails formed and hardened on its fingers and toes. Wisps of static electricity crackled outlining the silhouette of his head. And the rabbi intoned the powerful words from Genesis, '…and the Lord God formed man of the dust of the ground, and breathed into his nostrils the breath of life; and man became a living soul.'"

Rabbi Meyers smiled. "In the days and weeks ahead, the *golem* did indeed wreak vengeance and justice for our people. The first, but not the last victim of the *golem* was the monk Matteus."

"Wow," Clyde breathed.

"No wonder Eliahu was talking about needing a *golem*," Sam said.

"But I wonder why Davy would wear the *golem* costume."

"You can be sure it was not a gesture of respect," Rabbi Meyers said. "That's why I asked you about the word on the golem's forehead."

"You've lost me again," Clyde admitted.

"When the three men made the *golem*, they wrote the word *aemaeth* on the creature's forehead. That word translated reads life. When they had no further use for the golem, they erased the a and the e so that the word became '*maeth*' or death and the golem dissolved back into a lump of clay. The fact that Davy had the word death on the *golem's* forehead I think is a twisted joke."

"But Davy doesn't seem the type—" Clyde started.

"I'm sure it wasn't Davy's idea. Horace is and always has been the brains behind anything that happens at Far Horizons." The Rabbi shook his head.

Forty-five minutes later as Clyde and Sam walked out of the office, Clyde felt as if her head were whirling on her shoulders. From what Rabbi Meyers had said, Horace Beck had never overtly taken a stand against the Jewish community in Palmetto Bay, but he had made it impossible for any Jew to live on Rattlesnake Key.

"But how could he do that?" Clyde had demanded as they stood in the doorway.

"He has powerful friends, Miss Colby," the rabbi had said. "When your business and golf partners are the mayor, the chief of police, the head of the zoning department, you can make it very uncomfortable for an enemy. Any of our people who bought property on Rattlesnake Key were subjected to organized harassment. Developers who wanted to build on Rattlesnake Key would find it extremely difficult to get the necessary permits from the building department. The environmental protection people would find continual violations. Young Jews who want to live on the island and work find it impossible to get jobs."

For all that he presented as a kind and benevolent facade to his guests, she, too, had glimpsed Horace Beck's dark side that night in the corridor when he had grabbed her arm so hard he had bruised it. Unconsciously, she fingered her upper arm. Loyal to his family to a fault, unfailingly courteous to women, what was Horace like when he was completely unguarded or in the company of people he trusted, Clyde wondered as she and Sam got into his car.

"All that new information about Horace," Sam said thoughtfully, inserting the key into the ignition, "puts a different light on things, doesn't it?"

Clyde nodded. "And yet, Sam, we still have no reason to link him to Eli's beating."

"Let's rephrase that. We have reason, but no evidence."

As they drove out of the synagogue's asphalt parking lot, Clyde luxuriated in the blooming Ixora with its tiny red-orange blossoms that fringed the blacktop. She heard a squawking and looked skyward to see a flock of parrots landing in a massive banyan tree. She'd heard about parrots, canaries and parakeets escaping from captivity and breeding in the wild, but she'd never seen them. The sky was alive with the sounds of fluttering brilliant blue and green wings, scarlet and yellow bodies.

"How beautiful," she said.

"Clyde, you cannot afford to forget your life is in danger. Not for a moment." He opened the car door.

"Dammit, Sam," she snapped, "I know I'm in danger. And I know you keep reminding me to be cautious because you think it's for my own good. But sometimes I get tired of looking at everyone and everything suspiciously. Or watching every vehicle on the road. I've gotten to the point where every tan station wagon sends me into a panic. It isn't fair." She stared angrily out the window.

Sam said nothing.

"I really need to check on my vehicle," Clyde said he turned onto Gulf Boulevard. "Do you know a place called BR's Auto Service?"

"Sure do. I told Tommy Thompson, the tow truck driver, to

take it there yesterday. I know BR personally and he's the only man in Palmetto Bay or Rattlesnake Key I'll trust with my car. It's not far."

BR's was tucked between a Popeye's Chicken stand and the Palmetto Bay Savings and Loan. It was not what Clyde would have expected. Sam drove into the driveway of a neat, frame home that was painted a pale violet and trimmed in purple. The yard was decorated with plastic purple flowers.

"BR lives there with his invalid mother," Sam explained. "She selected the colors for the house." He drove past the house and continued into the backyard. There, in the center of a clearing fringed with scrub oaks and Australian pines, she saw a small, square concrete building that served as an office. A modest wooden sign identified the building as BR's Garage. Attached to the office was a lean-to with two bays. A stubby, blond-haired man with a pronounced limp came toward them as Sam pulled into the yard.

"Sam," the man called, hobbling toward them.

"'Nam vet," Sam explained. "He came home to find his wife had run off with his best friend." He opened the window, leaned out and waved. "Bucky, hi."

Clyde spotted her blue Bronco. It was in neither of the bays, but parked to one side out in the open. She was encouraged. That must mean it was already fixed.

"Clyde Colby, meet Bucky Reese."

She leaned across to shake the hand he stuck through the window. "Friend of Sam's is a friend of mine," the man said.

"Clyde owns that blue Bronco," Sam explained, pointing to the vehicle. "We came to find out where you're at with it."

Bucky's gray eyes grew troubled. A frown wrinkled his forehead, lending his round, cheerful face a look of consternation. "Sam, can I talk to you a minute?"

"But it's my vehicle." Clyde protested.

"Let me find out what this is all about," Sam said. "I'll tell you everything."

Still irritated, she waited as Sam got out of the car and walked side by side with Bucky to the Bronco. The two heads, one so dark, tilted down toward the other so blonde looking upward, bobbing as they conversed. Bucky popped the hood. Their heads vanished, blocked from her sight by the blue hood. The two men bent over the motor. She could see Bucky's elbow flailing and she assumed he was showing Sam what the problem was. In a few minutes, the men stood back and Bucky slammed the hood closed. Bucky waited by the disabled Bronco as Sam returned to her. The expression on his face alarmed her. There was tightness to his jaw, a squint of barely repressed anger narrowing his eyes.

"Sam, what is it?"

"That accident?" His voice was rough and cold.

"What about it?"

"You were right. It was no accident. Somebody cut a power steering pressure hose. They hacked it almost all the way through. That way, after two or three turns the pressure would blow it out and it would be difficult to control. The brake lines and handbrake cable were also cut."

"Oh, God." The fear that had diminished that morning when Sam had appeared in the lobby of Far Horizons now returned with a vengeful power. Until now, there'd been a chance she'd over reacted. Now it was definite. Somebody was trying to kill her. Somebody wanted her dead.

She shuddered, thinking with sudden longing of her lighthouse and her cats. She even missed her mother. And Dad. She longed to be with him in the kitchen of his townhouse cooking some special dish. Clyde wanted her life back.

Sam reached in through the window of the vehicle and took her chin in his hand. "One thing to remember. You're not alone."

She nodded. Maybe this wasn't all bad. Maybe with proof of the tampering, she had enough. Maybe this would be enough to convince Bill Trent. She had Eli's notes. And there was that metal track under the bed in room seventeen. Why was it there? What was it for? There were too many unanswered questions. No, she decided, it was too soon to go to Bill.

"Sam," she said, managing a small, tight laugh, "Now give me the *bad* news. What about the Bronco?"

He shook his head. "The hose would be a simple matter to repair. A couple hours work. Brake lines could be replaced. But Bucky says the salt water did your Bronco in. Once the salt water gets into the electronic components, it's a wake for the wagon."

"What?"

"A very poor joke," Sam said. "Bucky says insurance companies automatically total cars that have been damaged by salt water."

Clyde sighed. For once, she couldn't think of a snappy retort. She felt a tremendous sense of loss. She loved that car. It was like losing a friend. Then she forced herself to make a reality check. It wasn't like losing a friend. Eli had been a friend. This was a mechanical creation, made of wires and plastic and steel and computer chips. No, it could be much, much worse. And maybe whoever it was didn't really mean to kill her. Maybe it was a warning.

As if he'd been reading her thoughts, Sam said, "Whoever did this was thorough. If you handled the brake failure, the power steering would finish the job."

"Finish the job," she repeated. "You mean finish me. Well," she said at last, "at least I'm fully insured."

EIGHTEEN

As THEY DROVE OUT of the yard, Bucky waved and limped to the violet house. Clyde watched in the rearview mirror as a tiny woman wearing an apron and her hair pulled back into a bun opened the screen door and emerged onto the porch. The expression on the woman's wizened face made it clear that she was not pleased. Holding clippers in one hand, she pointed to a leggy, scraggly, salmon-colored bougainvillea bush in the front yard. Bucky nodded dutifully and took the clippers. As Sam turned the corner, Bucky was heading toward the bush.

"I'll bet some days he thinks Vietnam wasn't so bad," Sam said. He glanced across at her. "This has been one hell of a day for you." His solemn eyes studied her face. "How about a drink?"

She nodded. "I'd love one. And your buddy, what's her name, at Rattlesnakes Den can go easy on the tonic, heavy on the vodka. But I also want to call the insurance company. I'm going to need wheels."

"With my connections, you can make your phone call to the insurance company from the Den."

Clyde forced a grin. "As long as I have a quarter, you mean."

"We can handle that, too," he said, turning left onto Gulf Boulevard and heading back toward the causeway and Rattlesnake Key.

As they drove down Matecumbe Road for yet another time, Clyde thought how familiar it had become. If it weren't for the death and despair, she could have found this a wonderful place. The people were kinder. They cared about each other and kept track of one another. However, she thought wryly, there was some truth to the statement that people came to Southwest Florida and died—10 or 20 years later their bodies followed suit.

A wave of anxiety followed by fatigue swept through her. It had been so long since she had slept soundly.

Gnawing at her was the idea that somebody had worked on her car, somebody she might even know. Somebody she might even think liked her. Someone she trusted. Grace? Nonsense. Max, the waiter she joked with every day at lunch? Davy? She thought about how nice he'd been the day he came out to tell her Penny had died. She'd never been a very good judge of character; she'd always been too trusting. Was that going to get her killed?

At the thought of Dawn her mind stilled. Dawn. Was it her fault Dawn was missing? Surely they couldn't be suspicious of a motel maid who dreamed of becoming an artist. Had the bad guys gotten so paranoid that it was dangerous even to be friendly with her? *Please, God, let Dawn be all right.*

"Sam, we've got to check with Chief Westendorf. Right away. There must be some news of Dawn by now. People don't just vanish on Rattlesnake Key. I'll bet by now her mother is hysterical. And, Sam, there's something I have to know."

"First let's get you that drink and some food." Sam took his big hand off the wheel and patted her hands, which she had clenched tightly in her lap. "What is it you *have* to know?"

"I want to know why you were late that day you said you'd take me to the hospital to see Eli."

There was a silence as he pulled into the restaurant parking lot. Then he looked at her and said, "I was in Miami. Trying to interest the FBI in what was going on in Rattlesnake Key. They said not to talk to anyone else about it."

"But what did they say about an investigation?"

He laughed. "The agent-in-charge said he'd get back to me. Satisfied?"

When they entered the Rattlesnake's Den a few minutes later, Avis was on duty behind the bar. She looked at Sam, he nodded and within minutes she placed a Chivas on the rocks and a vodka tonic on the table in front of them.

"Run a tab, Sam?"

"You got it," he said. "And keep us liquid."

"Right on, good buddy," she said. Broad hips rolling, Avis left them to themselves.

"Avis is a good bartender," Sam said. "She leaves you in peace. Now drink up." And he leaned against the booth's leatherette back and watched, mother-hen like, until she had taken several long swallows.

The alcohol warmed her stomach, creating a reassuring sense of euphoria. She knew it was false courage due in large part to the fact that she'd barely eaten all day and was drinking on an empty stomach, but it felt good to relax. Besides, she didn't have to work. Work. The world of TV cameras and kitchens seemed so far away.

"Where did you go?" Sam asked, leaning forward so that his too serious eyes were level with hers. "You certainly weren't here with me."

"Sorry." She felt around in the pocket of her suit jacket and rattled her change, feeling for quarters. "I think I'll make those phone calls now." But Sam had already jammed his hand in his pocket. He put two twenty-five-cent pieces on the table. "You never have the right change."

"Now how do you know that?"

Sam laughed. It was an open, relaxed laugh and listening to him made her feel better. "I pay attention. I'll bet you the next round of drinks that you don't have the right change. Without looking, put all the change in your pocket on the table."

She slapped her change down. Five pennies, three nickels. "All right, wise ass," she said, picking up the quarters. "Next round's on me. But," she added, "this time I won't put you on the expense account. This time you're personal business."

"Mizz-Colby-like-the-cheese, if you're not careful you're going to turn into a really nice human being." He squeezed her hand as she slid out of the booth. "Hurry back."

While she was at the telephone, he ordered grouper fingers and French fries for them.

"I AM NOT THE TYPE," he said as she slid back into the booth, "to take advantage of a woman who is drinking on an empty stomach. What news of Dawn?"

"None."

"At least by now they should have started a full-scale investigation. Westendorf and his men will find her."

"I can't tell you how relieved the idea of Westendorf and his men investigating does *not* make me feel. Of course, if they had listened to me or her mother..." Clyde rolled her eyes.

"Did they find out if she had a boyfriend?"

"No one serious. She'd been dating one guy very casually, but they checked and he hasn't seen her in more than a week."

"Did you get through to your insurance company?" Sam sipped his drink.

She nodded. "My coverage includes a rental car, but I'll have to pick it up on the mainland."

Sam shrugged. "I'll take you over when you're ready. In the meantime, don't worry about Dawn. She'll turn up. You'll see. It's a misunderstanding, a miscommunication of some kind."

She said after a moment, "I appreciate what you're trying to do. You're unbelievably kind. But something has happened to her. I've gotten to know Dawn. Dawn was—*is* ambitious. I understand ambitious women. Dawn has a dream and I want to help make it come true."

Avis appeared bearing two red plastic baskets containing crisp golden French fries and grouper fingers. She put them on the table and checked their drinks with a quick glance. Both glasses were still half full, so she left.

"Eat. You can't afford to get sick. You've got the world to save."

At that, she finally smiled and picked up her fork. The food was delicious and she found herself eating ravenously, but she couldn't get Dawn off her mind. How was she? Did she have food to eat? It was suddenly difficult hard to swallow because it almost felt as if she were eating for both of them. Somehow if she ate enough Dawn wouldn't go hungry. Or be hurt. Damn, if only there was something she could do.

"Dessert?" Avis appeared with a coffee pot and two white china mugs. "We've got some delicious key lime pie. Home-made."

"Clyde?" Sam raised an eyebrow.

She shuddered and pushed the basket away. "No way. I shouldn't have eaten those French fries. I've already got at least five pounds to work off before the next shoot."

"I know whatcha mean," Avis commiserated. "Coffee?"

Clyde nodded. "Black, of course." She managed a smile. "Thank you."

Avis was pouring Sam's coffee when the six o'clock news came on the television set Avis had behind the bar. Clyde stared at Sam, reacting as she heard the word *"Kristallnacht."*

Sam nodded. "Avis, turn that up. Quick!" He called and Avis did as he asked, although her thick, unplucked eyebrow rose in surprise at the urgency in his voice.

The news tease over, they suffered through four commercials and finally the local anchor came on screen. Behind him was black and white archival film footage of a European town, uniformed soldiers breaking glass windows and burning buildings while people scurried away.

"Rabbi Meyers and the members of Temple Beth-El Synagogue will hold a candlelight vigil tomorrow night to honor the memory of the victims of *Kristallnacht,*" the anchor read from the teleprompter. He segued smoothly into a reader. "On another sad note, a memorial service was held today at Temple Beth-El for Eli Nussbaum, *Palmetto Bay Observer* reporter found beaten last week."

"We've got to warn Rabbi Meyers," Clyde said, sipping her black coffee. The coffee burned her tongue and she stirred it so it would cool. "Of course," she said in a discouraged tone, "I don't know what we can warn him about since we don't know what's going to happen."

"You're right. If he knows something's going to happen, at least he can alert the Palmetto Bay Police Department to keep the Temple under surveillance."

"And maybe," she said slowly as the idea gelled, "if we go

back to Far Horizons maybe we can sneak into room seventeen again and find out why there are tracks beneath the bed. From what Rabbi Meyers told us today, I would be surprised if there isn't some tie between everything that's been happening and Horace Beck and Far Horizons."

He groaned. "I can't tell you what it's going to do for my peace of mind when either the FBI gets off its duff or you get enough to satisfy this jerk in the State Attorney General's office." He waved to Avis to bring the check.

"Bill Trent's a very nice man," she said, but he was silent. She had another idea, but waited until he had paid the check and they were in the car.

As Sam drove out of the Den's parking lot, Clyde said, "I have an idea."

"I can hardly wait."

"Let's go to the Surfriders for an after-dinner drink or two. My treat. I'll walk out into the lobby with you, say good night and then you'll take your position by your favorite palm tree on the beach outside my window."

"Not the palm tree."

"Yes. Then after everything's calmed down, I'll come down and open the fire exit on the second floor and let you in."

"I can't believe it. You're really going to let me stay in your room tonight?"

Clyde fixed him with her most businesslike stare. "Don't get your hopes up. I suspect that by the time we get to bed, you're going to be too tired to do anything but sleep."

Sam grinned.

The Sundowners were playing in the Surfriders when they arrived. Clyde liked their music as a rule, but tonight she couldn't relax enough to enjoy them. She kept wondering about room seventeen. Her paranoia was rampant and she looked at everyone as a suspect. Sullivan, the bartender. The waitress. The customers. She kept wondering who had sabotaged her Bronco. Who wanted her dead? Were these people really guests? Customers? Or were they hired assassins? And where was Dawn?

It didn't help matters when shortly before eleven o'clock, one of the visitors from the mainland who had left about half an hour earlier returned, complaining bitterly because the bridge on the causeway was stuck.

"If we had some decent elected city officials, this wouldn't happen," he groused. "This is the fourth time since July the bridge has got stuck. Second time in the past week. Somebody ought to bring those bastards in Tallahassee down here and let them get a good feeling for what it's like to have your whole life messed up. You think my wife's gonna believe the bridge was stuck? Oh sure, she will after the *Observer* prints it, but I'll be in deep shit until that happens."

The fact that they were trapped on Rattlesnake Key was unnerving, until she put it in perspective. Compared to everything else that had happened, a bridge that wouldn't open was petty stuff. At about eleven-thirty, she glanced at her watch and said, loudly enough for others at the bar to hear, "Sam, I have got to get some sleep."

And he played along. "Your place or mine?"

She pretended to be offended, but walked into the lobby with him and pecked him a good night kiss.

Heading for the elevator, Clyde paused when she saw Horace and Davy in the corridor off the office. She deliberately staggered slightly, then continued past the office to the terrace and stood out there, ostensibly breathing in the fresh air, enjoying the beauty of the beach by moonlight, a stunning scene spread before her. The beach was so gorgeous it was difficult to remember that insidious evil was alive and well and functioning in Rattlesnake Key. However, her vigilance paid off. She stood off to the side of the terrace under the sea grape tree and watched.

Before long, Davy emerged from the office. He was carrying three cardboard cartons stacked upon one another. Clyde had seen this type of carton in the TV station. It was the letter-sized carton used to store documents. At the station, they stored scripts in them. Within a few minutes, he was followed by Horace who carried two similar cartons.

What was going on?

She waited until they were gone and then hurried into the elevator. In her room, she changed into her favorite jeans, Reeboks and a tee shirt that listed the names of other cooking show hosts in tiny letters with lines drawn through them and Clyde Colby in huge type. While waiting until the hotel had quieted down so that she could admit Sam, she drew out Eli's list. Stretched out across her bed, she studied the numerals.

She'd figured out the initials. And the room number.

But what did the dollar figures represent?

She decided she'd take a nap, just an hour or so. She reached over, grabbed her travel alarm, set it for an hour, turned out the light and rolled over.

But she couldn't sleep for the finger of an idea had pried its way into her consciousness. Suppose—yet it was ludicrous. Horace Beck was running an extremely profitable resort business. He was making a ton of money.

No, the idea was ridiculous. Crazy. But the notion wouldn't let her rest.

A murder-for-hire scheme.

The victims were wealthy, powerful executives whose families or business partners had reasons to want them dead.

"You're demented, Clyde," she muttered aloud. "Time for a reality check." But then she remembered the night on board the *Sanity* when Penny had told her his board considered him a pain in the ass because he was holding up a major investment in a theme park in Japan. Well, she'd bet that investment wouldn't be held up much longer.

No. The idea of a murder-for-hire enterprise absolutely did not make sense.

Did it?

She was still arguing with herself when the travel alarm went off. In the dark, she reached over to shut it off.

She rose and, staying in the dark, slipped out her door and started down the hall. The corridor was brightly lit and she proceeded cautiously.

Sensing movement at the end of the hall, she ducked into a

doorway. Pressing herself against the door, she peeked around the doorjamb.

It was Grace and she was carrying suitcases.

What the hell is going on?

Had the sale of the hotel had gone through more quickly than they had planned? But if that were the case, why were they packing and leaving in the middle of the night?

NINETEEN

CLYDE DUCKED INTO the doorway and waited as Grace proceeded down the hall to the elevator. Only after Beck's wife was safely inside did Clyde emerge. Once the coast was clear, she hurried down the hall to the landing and opened the fire door. Sam was waiting on the landing and slipped inside. He wore black slacks and pullover and even black moccasins and socks.

"I didn't notice before, but you look like a jewel thief," she accused as she led him down the corridor to her room. Once they were inside the room, she asked, "How are we going to get into seventeen? Any bright ideas?"

Sam shrugged, dug into the pocket of his trousers and pulled out the master keycard. "We have a friend in Dorris. Actually, Dorris is saving to take her grandson to Disney World. Turns out the kid has leukemia."

"Oh, God, Sam. That poor woman. And I've been so mouthy to her."

"You can't solve the problems of the world, Clyde. We've got troubles of our own. And one of them is to keep you alive."

There it was again. Ever present. The threat. The warnings. Dorris with two R's might have her woes, but Sam was right. Clyde had her own problems as well as obligations to others. Dawn. Eli. Penny. The litany rolled unbidden into her mind. "I'm ready," she said.

"We'd better take the stairs," Sam said. "Elevator's too noisy this time of night."

Clyde nodded and cautiously they descended the stairs. Her mind whirled busily with questions, and she kept it occupied so she couldn't think of what would happen if they were caught. This time Sam couldn't claim they were overwhelmed by the passion of the moment.

She cringed as the desk clerk, who was reading a paperback novel, yawned and stretched. Before crossing the lobby, they hovered in the shadows, waiting for what seemed like forever until he went behind the key rack. Any noise this time of night seemed magnified. They walked casually down the hall, holding hands pretending to be lovers beginning or ending a late-night tryst.

While Sam proceeded on to room seventeen, Clyde remained in the alcove where the drink and ice machines were kept and functioned as a lookout. Glancing over her shoulder, she watched as Sam inserted the keycard. From where she stood pressed against the wall, she could see both up and down the hall and she observed that the lights in the office had been extinguished. Whatever task had so engrossed Davy and Horace, it was finished. For the time being.

"Got it," Sam whispered.

She hurried to join him as he slipped into the dark room. Once inside, Sam moved right to the windows and drew the draperies before turning on the nightstand light. It cast a small pale arc of light, but it was sufficient.

"Let me show you," she muttered and took his hand, pulling him away from the window to the side of the bed. She knelt. Drawing him down beside her, she pointed to the track. It barely glinted in the light, but Sam had a pocket flashlight, which he flicked on. They could see it clearly. The track was about three inches wide and screwed to the floor.

"Pretty heavy gauge steel," he said, rubbing his fingers along the smooth metal surface. "Must be an unusually heavy bed."

She moved quickly to the other side of the bed. "There's a track on this side as well."

Sam squat-walked backward to the foot of the bed. He gestured with the flashlight toward the foot. "It's securely fastened to the track on what looks like casters. Look," he pointed to a piece of metal which jutted up from the track right behind the foot. "That stabilizes and holds it steady so it won't roll." He tried to flash the light beneath the bed, but the bedstead was only a quarter inch off the floor.

"What's this contraption for?"

"You got me," Sam said. "Let's check the head of the bed."

There they found the same track and stabilizer. "Rollers. This bed moves. But why?"

She took the flashlight from his hand and clambered onto the bed. Running her hands against the wall at the headboard, she felt a break in the panel. "And this wall separates."

"Show me," Sam said, crawling upon the bed with her. She guided his hand, splaying it flat, and felt along the fabric paneling. After only a few seconds, Sam found it. A division in the wall. "Jesus," he whispered.

The division came right down a stripe so it was not discernible. The two sections were so tightly aligned that it was impossible to force it apart with their bare hands. Sam's penknife was ineffectual, too.

"If only we had some tools," Clyde said. She thought longingly of her tool kit in the Bronco, but she didn't have that either.

Sam turned off the flashlight and the lamp on the nightstand. They huddled side by side in the dark in the middle of the bed. What was this, Clyde wondered. Why was the bed on a track? What was behind this wall? And how could they get in there?

She scrambled off the bed. "Let's check the switches. There must be a way to get into that other room from here."

"My thoughts exactly," Sam said. His voice was steady, solid. In this room in the dark, the sound of another human voice was incredibly reassuring.

Within a few minutes, they had looked for anything that might be used as a turn-on mechanism, flipped every switch in the room. None were other than what they seemed—standard light switches.

She slumped in the chair by the desk. "Now what?"

"Do you want to go back to your room?" he asked.

"Of course I want to go back to my room." She twisted around in the chair so that she faced him. In the dark, she could barely see his face. "I want to go back to a time when I wasn't scared to death I was going to be killed. But I can't do that. We can't give up. Now," she said, "if you're through asking dumb questions, let's figure out what we're going to do next."

"Dumb questions? Dumb because I give a damn about what happens to you? Maybe you're right. Dumb and tired. Tired of your being so damned defensive."

Chagrin, an uncomfortably familiar emotion, returned. "Okay. Okay. I'm sorry I'm so shrewish."

Focus, she drilled herself. *Focus. Think. You're a smart woman, Clyde, she encouraged herself. You figured out the room number and the initials. You can do this.* But the uncertainties crept back. If she'd really been smart, it wouldn't have taken her so long. Maybe a lot of good people would be alive. If she were so damned smart...

From Sam's side of the bed there was only an uncomfortable silence. After a long moment, he whispered, "Clyde, I apologize for snapping, I—"

"Forget it. Help me think."

Time. Silent time measured only by the internal synapses of formed thoughts and unspoken words, heartbeats and breaths to meter the passage of the moments.

Sometimes when Clyde worked on a script and was searching for the right word, she deliberately shifted mental gears. She would think about something else and just when she was about to give up, the right word or phrase would sneak into her brain as if it had been there all along. She would try that now.

And so she went back to the beginning, back to her arrival that rainy night step by step. There'd been the confusion about her reservations. Horace had straightened that out. Then Davy had taken her right by room seventeen to room nineteen.

And then what? Nothing. That's what. This wasn't working. Try something else.

Wait a minute. Davy had checked the available rooms then taken her down the hall. They'd made one stop. For towels? Yes, and soap. *The closet.*

"The closet, Sam," she said thoughtfully. "There's a supply

closet on the other side of this room. I remember because that first night when I was staying in the room next door, Davy stopped to get towels and soap for me."

"Good thinking. Let's check it out."

They straightened the bedspread, checked to make sure everything was as it had been when they entered. Sam edged the door open and checked the corridor before gesturing for her to follow him as they left the relative safety of the room. The supply closet, an unmarked door, was immediately adjacent to room seventeen.

The door was wood, probably dating back to when the resort had been built in the heydays of the 1920's. It was, of course, locked. Furthermore, this door required a key rather than a keycard.

He rattled the doorknob. "I've always wanted to see if this works," he said as he pulled out his billfold. He pulled out a charge card and inserted it between the door and the jamb below the lock. He jiggled the card and pulled on the knob.

No luck.

"I've got an idea that's at least worth a try," Clyde said and stretched on her tiptoes, reaching along the top of the doorjamb with her fingers. A key dropped onto the carpet, glinting in the light.

"That's what always impresses me," Sam said wryly. "Good, old-fashioned detective work."

"I'm always losing keys," Clyde explained. "I've learned to stash them in different places so I don't have to search. I figured Grace might have done the same thing because I've seen her as forgetful as I get."

While she was speaking, Sam pushed the key into the lock and turned it. The door angled open. He stepped in and Clyde followed almost bumping into him. From the ambient light in the corridor, she could see that they had entered a square room maybe eight feet wide by ten feet deep.

She eased the door half shut behind her. They were in semi-darkness for a moment. She felt along the wall but found no switch. Then Sam reached up, batting the air until his hand ran into something. He pulled a string dangling from the ceiling and turned on the bare fixture with its single light bulb. She closed the door.

Although her first impression was of chaos, there was order. The floor was stacked with vacuum sweepers, mops and brooms. Drums of cleaning supplies had been rolled against one wall next to linen carts. Against the other wall was a wooden strip of coat hooks. Aprons and uniforms were dangling from it.

She followed Sam as he warily picked his way through the maze. They stepped over buckets to reach the back wall, which housed a set of metal shelves. The top shelves contained cartons of individual-sized guest soaps and small bottles of shampoos and body lotions. On the middle shelves were stored neat rows of peach-colored face, bath and hand towels. On the bottom shelf were bath mats and paper supplies—peach-colored face tissues and toilet paper. Stacked boxes contained glass bud vases, paper doilies and table candles for the bar.

In the very back of one shelf were four cans of Slim Fast and Clyde grimaced. She'd have to go back on a diet to get rid of the extra pounds she'd picked up. She looked at Sam as they stood in front of the shelved supplies. "You're very quiet. What are you thinking?"

"That," he said, gesturing to the left, "must be the common wall. But have you noticed, Clyde, this closet doesn't seem as deep as the bedroom."

"Yes," she said, facing the rear wall squarely. "I see that."

He grasped the shelving. "We've got to move these." Ever so carefully, they angled the metal shelf partly away from the wall.

Sam tapped the partition with his penknife. "It's hollow," he murmured. A note of excitement crept into his usually controlled voice.

"What do you suppose is back there?"

"I don't know, but the bad news is we can't get there from here. Not without breaking through the wall. Tell me again," he said staring at its blank, smooth surface "about the night you stayed in room nineteen."

Vigilant, the hotel quiet around them, she stood near in the supply closet and, almost whispering, told him once more of the strange sounds she'd heard the night she checked in, sounds which seemed to be coming from the direction of room seventeen. The grinding machinations of a motor, followed by the silence and the recurrence of the same sound about a half an hour later. And then she thought to tell him what she'd figured out about the murder-for-hire scheme. He didn't laugh.

"It makes sense," he said, eyeing the wall. "But it raises as many questions as it answers. Why would Horace do it? How did he pick these men? How did he kill them so that year after year, they all appeared to have died naturally?" He rubbed his open palm against the wall. "What is so lethal about room seventeen?"

"Maybe it's not what's in room seventeen," Clyde said slowly. "We checked it thoroughly."

"Help me pull this shelf all the way from the wall," Sam said.

They lifted and shoved. It wasn't easy because the shelves were heavily weighted with the supplies. The shelf legs grated and rasped as they dragged them across the bare concrete floor. Each time they made a noise, Clyde flinched, sure they were going to be discovered. And each time as no one came barging into the closet, she breathed a little easier. At last, the shelf stood free and Sam directed the beam from his flashlight into the dark corner previously hidden from view.

"Clyde," he said and the note of discovery in his voice drew her attention immediately. "There." He pointed with the light and Clyde saw what appeared to be a ventilation duct. Small, square, only about thirty inches to a side. "Looks like some kind of air intake. But sealed shut from this side. I might be able to get the grate off, but damn, we could never fit through that."

Clyde took a deep breath. "Wrong, Sam. You couldn't, but I can. It'll be a tight squeeze, and even with a few extra pounds, I can do it."

He grasped her by her upper arms. "Dammit, Clyde. That's the guy's job. Besides I don't want to see you get hurt." He touched her cheek.

They stood in the supply closet, hidden behind the shelf, surrounded by shadows. She looked up at him. In the course of all the things that had happened, she'd lost track of Sam the man. She'd thought of him as her partner in this investigation and as her friend, but not as a man with pride.

"Sam," she said softly, "I care about you, too, but I can't and won't make your decisions and you can't make mine. So here's the deal. Don't look."

Without another word, Sam used his knife and with the blade he jimmied the intake cover from the duct widening the access, and revealing about a three to four inch drywall boarder to cosmetically accommodate the size of the metal intake cover. Clyde kissed him quickly and then before she could lose her nerve, she dropped to her knees and pushed her head and shoulders through the opening.

She shivered. The air in the chamber was musty and cold. Really cold. It must have been forty degrees. An air conditioning unit in the wall was keeping this room almost frigid. And it was so black, totally without light except for the pale light that entered through the vent they'd broken through. She crawled through on her stomach and sat with her back against the wall. She couldn't see an inch in front of her face even after her eyes had adjusted.

"Are you alright?"

Sam's voice was a beacon of sanity and she hung on to it. "So far so good, Sam. But pass me the flashlight. It's darker than the inside of my station manager's heart in here."

He chuckled and it was a wonderfully normal sound.

She heard the sound of his sleeves brushing against the side of the duct and clasped the flashlight as he passed it through. She rose, keeping her back to the wall and flashed the light around the area. It was about the same size of the closet, but the walls were a dull gray unfinished concrete.

She directed the beam toward the far wall and saw that it was windowless, but then spotted the air conditioner. She flashed the light to her left where she saw clearly the separation in the wall they'd discovered in room seventeen. She lowered the shaft of light to the concrete floor. The track glittered in the illumination and she saw that the steel looked to be the same gauge as in the other room. It extended back into this room the length of the bed.

So the bed somehow rolled back into this room on those tracks. And then what? She flashed the light to the ceiling and was amazed to see a window about four feet square in the ceiling alongside what looked like a covered vent.

"What's going on? What do you see?" Sam demanded, his voice laced with curiosity and concern.

She described what she had learned and, in the process, lowered the light, which sliced through the darkness like a sharp knife through aspic...to a bundle of rags in the corner. She caught a glimpse of curly, dark hair trapped in the light. She dropped the flashlight.

Her heart stilled in her chest. Her knees buckled and she slid to floor, her back against the wall. She didn't realize she had screamed, but she must have for Sam was going wild on the other side of the wall.

"Clyde. Dammit, Clyde, what's going on in there? Are you all right? Clyde?"

But she couldn't answer. She was only vaguely aware of the sound of a series of thuds and bangs inside the air duct. And then there was an implosion as the drywall façade on the other side of the concrete wall bordering the duct gave way and Sam was down on his knees in front of her.

All she could do was point. In the dark, of course, he couldn't see what had distressed her. Not until he had scrounged around on the floor and retrieved the flashlight. He turned the light on her and, for the first time saw where she was pointing.

The corpse lay crumpled in a heap.

In the beam of the flashlight, Clyde saw the forest green pullover with two cats wearing boxing gloves. It was the sweater she had given Dawn because the girl also loved cats.

Dawn Hicks was no longer missing.

TWENTY

"SHIT," SAM WHISPERED.

For maybe ten seconds, she didn't know what to say then she said, "Let's get out of here. Right now."

"What about her?" Inadvertently, he flicked the light toward the inert body as he gestured.

"Dawn. She has a name. Dawn."

"Sorry, babe."

Clyde had seen corpses before. You didn't last long in the news business these days without seeing a traffic fatality or a murder scene. But this was so eerie. She was sitting there in a cold, windowless, concrete chamber with the body of a murdered acquaintance. She could feel the panic rising and she was desperately afraid she was going to throw up.

Sam had walked across the chamber to the body and she huddled in the thick darkness brightened only by the thin streak from his flashlight. She watched as he knelt, checked for a pulse, gently turned the head. She flinched as she caught a glimpse of the sightless eyes.

He closed the lids. "She didn't suffer. She was garroted. Quick and clean."

"And we both know why she was killed, don't we? She was wearing a shirt I gave her. And we look alike. That night of the anonymous report that I was missing. Whoever did this got Dawn by mistake."

Sam was very, very quiet. Then he said, "One other thing, those tracks under the bed? They led back into this room. The whole bed must roll into this room."

"That's what I figured, too."

He grunted. "Poor kid. Now let's get the hell out of here."

He helped her through the gaping hole in the wall he'd created around the duct back in the supply closet. Once he'd emerged from the chamber he said, "We've got to put this place back in order so Horace won't know we've been here. And we've got to notify the authorities. You've certainly got enough for your guy Bill in Tallahassee."

It was easier to be logical now that she was out of that cell. "That might take too long," she said after taking a breath. "Anyway, murder should be reported to local authorities. But," she said and paused, "I don't trust the locals. They have to be involved. Because of the autopsies. Or lack of autopsies rather. Not even the sheriff's department. Westendorf's involved and the sheriff's department could be compromised as well."

"I've got some connections, Clyde, but with the bridge stuck, it could take hours for them to get here."

She paled. She'd forgotten about the bridge. Then she remembered the man in Surfriders whose wife was going to be furious because he was going to be home late. That seemed like such an insignificant problem compared with what they were facing. They were trapped on Rattlesnake Key. Studying Sam, she was reassured by his calm control. She pushed the hair out of her eyes and stood erect, shoulders back. "What next?"

"Next we straighten up."

It took maybe half an hour, but they worked silently, hurriedly. They pushed the shelves back against the wall. Sam swept the debris from the wall out of sight. Clyde restacked boxes and supplies on the shelves to mask the gaping fissure.

"That buys us a little time, babe," he said surveying their work. "Now let's get back to your room. We'll hole up and call in the troops."

She felt an incredible sense of relief when Sam finally shut and locked the closet door behind them, but as they walked down the hall toward the elevator, Clyde pulled on his arm and he halted. "I've got a better idea."

"What?"

"Call from the *Sanity*. I'd feel safer there anyway."

He sighed. "Why didn't I think of that? Okay. The car's parked down the road. In front of the Island Inn."

Displaying a confidence she didn't feel, she followed Sam as he strode quietly through the lobby out into the night. A sliver of a moon had made about three-fourths of its journey across the night sky. The air was chill and damp. A light fog had rolled in off the water, which blurred the sharp images of the huge Royal Poinciana trees in the parking lot. As before, they turned east on Matecumbe Road. They walked steadily for about ten minutes, but as they neared the roadside restaurant, Sam quickened his pace. The Lexus was angle parked in front of The Island Inn.

Sam was standing on the driver's side, digging into his pocket for the car keys when a car careened into the parking lot and stopped horizontally behind the Lexus, blocking their exit. The now familiar logo of a coiled rattlesnake gleamed in the rays of the security light mounted on a pole in the restaurant parking lot. A police car.

The door to the cruiser opened and Sgt. Reeves, Officer Bubba, emerged. The badge on his uniform shirt glittered ominously.

"Help you folks?" Reeves stood with his hands on his hips. His biceps looked as though they would burst through the sleeves of his pale blue uniform. His hand eased toward his wide gun belt.

Sam glanced at her. Even in the moonlight, she could see tension tightening the muscles in his face. "We're fine, Officer," he said.

"This your car?" The officer demanded, nodding toward the vehicle.

"Sgt. Reeves," Sam said a note of patient cordiality in his voice. "You know this is my car." Before he could take the car keys out of his pocket, the officer had withdrawn his gun.

"Take your hand out of your pocket very slowly."

"Wait a minute," Sam protested, but the cop was implacable.

When Sam had removed his hand from his pocket, Reeves

clasped Sam by the upper arm and said, "Just come with me, sir. We'll straighten this out." The barrel of the gun glinted as he pointed it first at Sam and then waved it at her. He led them to the patrol car and opened the back door.

"Sgt. Reeves," Clyde interjected. "This is crazy. I'm Clyde Colby. And this is Sam McKenzie. We're not criminals," she said. Adopting a calm, logical tone of voice while backing away from the gun, she continued, "He has the sailing school here. I have a cooking show on television. You know who we are. Let Sam show you his driver's license and the whole thing will be straightened out."

The policeman moved forward, but said nothing, gesturing for them to climb into the patrol car's backseat behind the grill. When they didn't move at once, he said, "Don't make me use this." He lofted the gun. It was a .357 magnum and she knew from the shootings she'd covered in Miami that if he fired, it would make one hell of a hole in her gut both coming and going. And the tone of his voice was so final, so cold, Clyde knew he wouldn't hesitate. She turned to climb into the vehicle.

Intense disappointment followed by panic swamped her. She had looked forward to being on board the *Sanity*. But the *Sanity* was moored at the Rattlesnake Key Marina, a good twenty miles away. Behind her, she heard Sam stumble and looked back to see him almost felled by a blow from the officer's gun.

"That's not necessary, you asshole. We were going to the police station with you. We weren't resisting," Clyde snapped.

"Clyde," Sam said quietly, holding his head. "Chill until we can figure this out."

The cop grinned as he slammed the door behind them. "We're not going to the police station, Ms. Colby."

"Then just where the hell are you taking us? We have a right to know."

The cop slid into the front seat and looked over his shoulder through the grill at them, but said nothing.

"Westendorf is behind this," Sam said.

Nodding, the officer explained. "When Chief saw your car parked off the road in front of a restaurant that's been closed for nearly four months, he figured something was up," Reeves slid the key into the ignition. "Chief said to keep an eye on it. If you showed up," he continued as pulled back onto Matecumbe Road, "Chief said I should bring you in. Possible breaking and entering."

As soon as he turned the patrol car south, Clyde realized the cop was taking them back to the resort rather than the police station in downtown Rattlesnake Key. A wave of apprehension heightened her panic. Still there was a measure of hope. It was obvious Sgt. Reeves meant them no good. They must get away from him. It might be easier to escape at Far Horizons where she knew the territory rather than the jail. Perhaps this wasn't such a bad break after all.

"Don't think about escaping," Reeves said over his shoulder in a rough, arrogant voice. "We have more people working with us than you know. More than enough to handle you two."

By the time they reached the resort a few minutes later, the fog had grown dense and they had difficulty seeing the entrance. Against the backdrop of the inn's façade, a few golden lights beaming from guest rooms penetrated the fog, but most of the building was dark.

The cop hustled them out of the car and through the lobby. Grace was behind the desk and she looked worried as the policeman stopped.

"Where's Horace?" the cop demanded.

"On the dock," Grace answered. Her china blue eyes had a desperate glaze that was as frightening to Clyde as Reeves's .357.

"Grace," Clyde pleaded. "You have to help us, please!"

Grace stared down at the lacquered cypress counter and fiddled with the pad containing the registration form and the sign-in pen. Fingers trembling, she obliviously straightened the pad and positioned the pen at a different angle.

The cop herded them down the corridor past the darkened office onto the terrace. Once outside, he shoved them toward the dock. Clyde stumbled, and Sam took her elbow. A trickle of blood slid down the side of his face. It was drying black in the moonlight.

As they reached the end of the terrace nearest the dock, the officer nudged her in the back with his gun. "This is far enough," he said.

In the pallid light at the far end of the dock, she recognized Horace, Davy, Max, Todd, Raymond, Westendorf and the other male employees of Far Horizons. Max, the waiter she had liked, was hurrying down the pier carrying a cardboard carton about two-feet square and a coil of something that looked like a slim rope. The other men, their identities cloaked by darkness, stood facing the mainland with their backs toward Reeves.

The launch's motor was idling. Horace was at the wheel.

"Chief," the officer hailed, but the men were already boarding the launch. "Over here," Reeves called. "Chief?"

But Westendorf, engrossed in untying the lines, didn't hear. He tossed them to Max on board the boat and jumped into the boat as Horace gunned the boat's powerful motor. The speedboat made a wide arc in the water and headed north in the direction of Palmetto Bay.

The scene on the dock was surreal. Clyde shivered. Now what, she wondered as they waited, standing in the shadow of the sea grape tree, a cop prodding them in the back with a gun that felt as big as a cannon.

"Now what?" Sam asked.

Reeves paused for only a moment. "Back inside. Now."

Once inside, Reeves paused only a moment at the desk. "I'm taking them up to your place to wait for Horace and the chief. Gimme the key."

Her blue eyes lowered, Grace didn't speak as she reached below the counter and handed over a keycard.

"Where are they going?" Sam asked Reeves a few minutes later when they were in the elevator.

Reeves shoved the Magnum into his back. "Not that you need to know, but they're going to the mainland. It's a religious observation." He laughed at his own joke.

Clyde looked at Sam and whispered, *"Kristallnacht."*

He frowned and rubbed a hand soiled with dust and grime from the closet through his thick, black hair. Then he sighed. "And time is running out."

"Enough talking," Reeves said.

The elevator ground to a halt, the doors opened and they stepped out into the hall. He nudged them to the right. "Keep going," he urged until they reached to the end of the hall. Once there, they paused in front of a door with a name card reading simply "Beck" enclosed in a metal bracket. Sam glanced at Clyde. His expression told her he had a plan, but what? The only thing she could do was keep her eyes open, stay focused.

Holding the gun in his left hand, Reeves inserted the key-card into the slot with his right. The green light on the lock mechanism went off and he opened the door. He shoved them through. As they entered, Sam pretended to stumble, and then supporting himself on the doorjamb, he locked his right foot behind Reeves's leg and tugged, pulling Reeves off balance.

Reeves fell heavily to the floor. Sam grabbed him from behind his neck, banged his head against the doorjamb several times until the cop's head drooped indicating he was unconscious. Sam grunted. "I haven't forgotten everything I learned in the Persian Gulf." He dragged the inert cop inside the room. "Find something to tie him up with," Sam said.

Clyde paused just inside the threshold surveying the room with surprise. A kitchenette extended off the sitting room. She hurried into the kitchen and found half-packed boxes of china on the floor. A coil of twine rested on the table.

She grabbed it up and hurried back into the sitting room. "This isn't very sturdy," she said worried. "Will it do?"

Sam smiled reassuringly. "With the right knot and two or three wraparounds, it'll do fine."

"I'll call for help," she started, but Sam interrupted.

"Forget it. With the bridge closed and Grace on the desk, we're screwed. Besides, who are you going to call?" He rolled Reeves into the apartment. "We've got a little time. Let's see what we can find to tie Beck and Westendorf to the murders."

While Sam checked Reeves's bonds, Clyde looked around. Two doors led off the sitting room, one to the right, one to the left. The sitting room was beautifully decorated with antiques and she was struck with the similarity between this room and room seventeen. The furniture was polished and well cared for. She walked across the Oriental rug to stand before an antique mahogany china closet filled with elegant china and crystal.

On the wall was an intricate hand-carved clock and Clyde recognized it as coming from the Black Forest in Germany. Two large suitcases lay half open on the floor. Clothes were strewn over the chairs and across the Victorian sofa.

A large cardboard box sitting on a footstool in front of a well-worn recliner drew her attention. Intrigued, she knelt to study the stack of books on the floor beside the footstool. It was half filled with volumes from a mahogany bookcase against the wall. Out of curiosity, she read some of the titles and was intrigued to discover that many were textbooks and scientific treatises dealing with genetics and DNA and RNA.

"Clyde," Sam called. "Come help me. We've got to find a place to hide him."

She opened the door to the left. It was a very feminine bedroom, done in shades of pink. She walked in and glanced around. Women's clothes were strewn about. On the pink-skirted dressing table, cosmetics and personal items, a razor, a manicure kit, a blower dryer had been neatly lined up. A small leather case sat on the floor by the table. She opened another door and it led into a walk-in closet.

"Coming," she said, then returned to the sitting room. Working together, they dragged the still unconscious officer into the closet. Sam used the belt from a terry cloth robe that hung on a hook as a gag.

"Okay, now we've got to figure this thing out. I don't know how much time we have, how much time before Horace and his cohorts return," Sam said, "and we can't afford to make any mistakes."

"Of course," Clyde almost shouted. "Binky Beresford," she said over her shoulder. "If we can't trust the authorities, Beres-

ford must have some contacts." She hurried to the phone and
dialed.

"Good thinking."

She turned her attention back to the phone as the editor's
sleepy voice on the other end of the line said, "Hello. This better be good."

Speaking quickly, she told him about finding Dawn's body
and about room seventeen and the strange metal tracks. "We're
stranded out here, Mr. Beresford. We need help."

Binky's voice came cross the phone strong and steady. "And
you'll have it. As soon as I get off this phone, I'll contact the
authorities."

"No," Clyde said. "Don't you know anyone in the FBI?"

There was silence then Binky said, "Sure, but this is a local
issue."

"Not the local authorities. The FBI. Please. We have our
reasons."

Binky grunted and she switched off. "He's sending help,"
Clyde assured Sam. "Right away." She felt giddy from relief.
She could almost breathe again.

Sam grunted. "Good. Now let's get out of here."

"Get out of here?" she persisted. "We can't leave until we've
checked Horace's room. We've got to find out why they were
headed to Palmetto Bay. It must have something to do with
Kristallnacht and we've got to find out what."

"Yeah, okay," Sam said, slowly turning and walking back
into the sitting room. "I just wish I knew how long we have before Horace and the others get back. Or that this room was on
the other side of the building so we could see or hear the launch
returning."

Clyde determined there was nothing in the living room. She
opened the door to what she assumed was the second bedroom,
looked in and gasped. This room—she'd been right, it was the
second bedroom—was also in disorder. A flag stand with the
silver emblem of the SS lay on the floor. Draped across the bed
was a Nazi flag. The black Swastika on the white background
against the blood-red flag looked virulent and out of place

among the graceful antique furniture. A huge trunk was open, its shelves half-packed. It was to this that she was drawn first.

On the shallow, top shelf laid several books. The first she picked up was *Mein Kampf* by Adolph Hitler. On the flyleaf, there was an inscription and while she couldn't translate it from the German, she could tell it was directed to Wilhelm Beck and signed A. Hitler. She flipped to the title page and saw that it had been published in Munich in 1927.

"Look at this," she murmured and handed it to Sam. A paperbound treatise entitled "The Final Solution" rested on the shelf alongside *Mein Kampf*. It was printed in English and a quick scan of the table of contents revealed it dealt with cleansing the Aryan race and the systematic extermination of mental defectives, congenital abnormalities, the Gypsies and the Jews. She felt as if her hands were dirty. She replaced it and picked up the second, hardbound book, which was entitled *In the Shelter with Hitler* by Gerhardt Boldt. It, too, was autographed by the author and inscribed to Wilhelm Beck. But Beck had penned his own name and address inside the book. The address was 1875 Calle Sarmiento, Buenos Aires.

Sam walked over to a stunning Italian fruitwood roll top desk. He half opened the top and pulled out a ledger. He lowered himself into the golden-oak desk chair. Ornately hand-carved, the chair was decorated with oak leaves intertwined with Swastikas. He riffled through the pages, stopping near the back of the book.

"Look at this," he said pointing. "We've got proof of the murder-for-hire scheme!" He paused, and then said in a very quiet voice, "Those boxes. Remember the boxes they were loading on the launch?"

Clyde nodded.

"I'll bet those boxes contain explosives. And we know that whatever the reason Horace went to the mainland, it had something to do with *Kristallnacht*. Now what is the one place he could blow up that would make a statement and do the most damage? The synagogue." He answered his own question, his voice half an octave higher in pitch, tinged with frustration.

At the same time, she looked where he was pointing. On the page was written a list of men's names. Opposite each were a date and a figure.

She gasped as she comprehended what she was seeing. She recognized many of the names. They were the names of the men who had died at Far Horizons, the names she and Sam had painstakingly researched at the courthouse. The amounts opposite the names began at $250,000, which was printed next to the earliest date.

The two most recent entries made her flinch. The sum of $1.75 million was penned opposite Greg Lanken. She swallowed hard as she read the final entry and wiped a tear from her eye. The name was A. P. Dunn. The date was November 3. The sum was $5 million.

"It *is* a murder-for-hire scheme," she said. "Murder a la carte."

"What are you talking about?" Sam demanded.

"Think about it, Sam. Each murder was planned and carried out to order. Each murder was individually priced. Murder a la carte."

Sam shook his head. A sad expression darkened his face and she knew he was thinking about his friends Bob, Greg Lanken and Penny.

He handed her the ledger and reached into one of the desk's sections where he pulled out a rolled-up magazine for mercenaries entitled *Warriors of Destiny*. When he unrolled it on the desktop, she saw that it was open to the classified section. A boxed ad read simply, "Business Problems? Seeking a permanent solution?" And it listed a mailbox on Rattlesnake Key.

"I'll bet if we check, we'll find Horace and his crew rent that box," he said, adding thoughtfully, "And that's how they recruit their customers," Sam said. "Very clever."

"But why would the executives of large corporations read *Warriors of Destiny*? That doesn't make sense."

Sam looked at her sagely. "The executives wouldn't on a regular basis, but when they had a need they might. Besides, their bodyguards and security people would. Did you notice how many of these ads were for surveillance equipment and weapons? Anything in the trunk?"

Clyde shrugged. "So far, mostly personal memorabilia."

"I've finished the desk, I'm going to check out the closet," he said pointing to the corner of the bedroom. "Hold on to that ledger and the magazine. We'll need them."

"Right," she said putting them on the end of the bed. She returned to the trunk where she knelt and as she lifted the top tray, she heard Sam whisper, "Jesus." His voice was so distressed Clyde knew immediately something dreadful was wrong. She dropped the tray and hurried to his side.

From the top shelf in the closet, he had lifted down a box, a small white box about six by two inches bearing the date 7/5/43. He had the lid in his left hand, but he was staring down at what looked to be fifty or sixty gold fillings. Some were loose; others were trapped in yellowing teeth.

She clapped her hands across her mouth to keep from throwing up. She had thought she was distressed before, but the sight before her and the human suffering it represented was truly appalling. She backed away.

Focus, Clyde. Focus. Don't think about the people, the human beings those teeth represented. They've been dead at least sixty years. But it was just the remnants of the Nazi's victims. Clyde marveled that someone could live with as much hate bottled up inside as Beck must. It would color everything. No wonder he didn't appreciate his wife and son.

Sam's face was pale. She saw beads of sweat on his forehead. He looked at her and she realized he was as upset as she was. She wanted to do something to help, but couldn't think what. He kept his eyes focused on hers and, without looking down, replaced the lid. He put the box back where it had been, took a deep breath and wiped his forehead with the back of his hand leaving a faint streak of dirt. "I wonder what Zyklon B is?" he said, his voice rough with strain.

She looked where he pointed and saw two metal canisters.

"Whatever it is, it must be lethal because it's got that skull and bones." She read the label. A white band straddled the canister. On the top line, black lettering read, *"Giftgasi."* The skull and bones decorated the middle. The bottom line was comprised simply of the word "Zyklon B." She shuddered. Beneath the canister, she found a pamphlet written in German with the rough sketch of an insect. And the date 2002.

"Pesticide. And they're still making it." She shuddered. "Let's get out of here. We've got the ledger, we've got the ad." Clyde sighed. "I don't think there's a question that Horace and Davy were involved in Eli's beating given all this Nazi paraphernalia and I think Binky can get somebody in here to investigate and wrap this thing up. But let's get done and get out of here. I want to take a shower for hours to see if I can ever feel clean again."

"Clyde, you're one hell of a woman."

She laughed. "And that's one hell of a *non sequitur* if I ever heard one." She returned to the trunk. A small leather box drew her attention and she picked it up and opened it. A man's ring rested on blue velvet. She placed the heavy, silver ring in the palm of her hand.

In the center, a skull had been soldered onto a bed of oak leaves. The massive ring was decorated on one side with a Swastika in a tilted square. On the other, a rune looked like a backward N in a triangle. Inside the band were engraved a date 11/9/39, the words *S.lb Beck* and the signature *H. Himmler.*

"Take it if you want to, but let's get out of here," Sam urged.

"One minute, Sam." She picked up a packet of photographs wrapped around with a rubber band and sheathed in clear plastic. She removed the plastic, then the rubber band. She stared at the photos. She felt her face grow pale, felt her stomach roil.

"What's wrong?" Sam said and took the photos from her hands. "Jesus." Together they stared at the Polaroid of Binky Beresford. He was nude and he was not alone in the photo. He was twisted into an erotic position with a young boy.

"Mr. McKenzie, Miss Colby, I will take those."

Clyde wheeled around so rapidly she would have lost her balance except for Sam's stolid frame behind her. He reached out and steadied her.

Horace Beck stood in the doorway of his bedroom. He was smiling. Behind him to his right stood Davy. On the other side to the left was Binky Beresford. Beyond them in the sitting room, Clyde saw that Frank Westendorf, now out of uniform, was standing with Grace who was quietly crying. Her left eye was red and swelling shut. Her mouth was bruised and swollen and black and blue marks were forming on her upper arms.

"Actually, this was very considerate of you both," Beck said calmly. "Oh, I'll take the ring, Miss Colby," he said approaching and plucking it from her hand. "We would have found you, but it would have taken time. You, Miss Colby, have proven to be unexpectedly ingenious. I knew Mr. McKenzie would prove to be a worthy adversary, but you surprised me."

Clyde was silent, but thought back to the evening they'd had dinner together in the dining room with Andy and the crew. In contrast to his almost manic behavior that evening, Horace was now very calm, very controlled.

TWENTY-ONE

Max used the same cord Sam had used on Reeves who was rousing now. He tied them, Sam first. The twine, which she discovered the hard way was unexpectedly strong, burned her wrists. Behind her, she felt Sam's body. Strong. Warm. Alive. His heart was beating a pulse of life and strength.

She stood captive in the room that housed Horace Beck's barbarous trophies and felt rage growing in her gut. Frozen into immobility, she was stunned by the sudden, personal awareness that it wasn't enough to be right and motivated by a belief in and a desire for justice. Good people died every day. She and Sam could die. No, she refused to accept that. They'd come too far to have it end like this.

Sam struggled, but Davy and Westendorf who stood to one side held guns that looked immense to Clyde. Westendorf stood so near she could read the word Luger engraved in an oval on the frame. The huge guns were impressive and Sam was smart enough not to take unnecessary chances. Nonetheless, at Horace's direction, Davy approached Sam. Even though he wasn't struggling, Davy struck him on the side of the head, knocking him unconscious.

He sagged against her and she supported him as best she could while he slumped to the floor.

"You fucking bastard!" she snapped. "I hope you rot in hell."

He ignored her. "Help the others," Horace instructed Westendorf. "Free him first," he pointed toward Reeves, who was dazed but recovering. "When you're done with that, we can handle this. Take Reeves and go with them."

Westendorf nodded and slipped into the next room where Grace was shoving linens and towels into a carton.

In the room where she and Sam were being held, Davy and Horace were packing his books and memorabilia. While their attention was diverted, Clyde scouted the room for something, anything she could use for a weapon. The flagpole. With its sharp, pointed top. She sidled, back against the wall, quietly, carefully toward the ornate flagpole, but it was heavy and cumbersome and Max moved so quickly that almost before she knew what was happening, he was wrapping cords from the Venetian blinds around her ankles to hobble her.

He lowered her to the floor, rather gently she thought, and the crazy idea wandered through her mind that perhaps it was because she was a good tipper. He wasn't as gentle with Sam who was now lying beside her, slowly regaining consciousness, his eyes glassy with pain.

Binky Beresford, who'd been standing by quietly stepped forward, hand extended. "Horace," he said and his voice was hoarse and raspy. "Give me my pictures."

Beck merely smiled. "Later," he responded, but his tone was amused.

"No. Now." His mane of thick gray hair, which was usually neatly combed back, hung around his face making him look disheveled and distraught. His elegant hands with their long, conical fingers were shaking. "Those pictures can ruin me, Horace, and you know it." His voice was strident, desperate. "My wife—she mustn't—give me those pictures." He stumbled forward and shook his fist in Beck's face. "Now, dammit. I've done everything you asked. You promised."

"But," Beck replied, turning his back on the frenzied editor, settling calmly into the chair in front of the roll-top desk, "even though Grace and Davy and I will be in Germany, we will need friends in America. We have certain investments here. How can I be sure you will continue to cooperate?"

"You motherfucker," Beresford shrilled. "That wasn't part of our bargain." Lunging across the room, he attacked Beck knocking him backward in his chair so that the stunned hotelier sprawled on the floor.

Davy hurried into the room from the sitting room where he'd

gone to help Grace pack. Beresford had his hands around
Beck's throat and was banging his head against the floor. Davy
held a gun in his hand, but waved it about ineffectually, too surprised to act.

"Give me the photos," Beresford ordered and slammed
Beck's head against the floor.

Beck, his face red, his blue eyes distended as he gasped for
air, looked past Beresford to his son. "Shoot," he ordered.

From behind Davy, Frank Westendorf reappeared. Without
the slightest hesitation, he lowered his Luger, its barrel bulky
with a tubular silencer, and shot Binky Beresford three times
in the back. The odor of cordite corrupted the fresh air. Blood
and bits of tissue sprayed the wall and floor, spattering Beck's
clean white shirt.

The editor groaned and slumped to one side, then sprawled
on the floor. A pool of blood unfurled beneath his body like a
mammoth red blossom. Beck eased out from beneath Beresford and, supporting himself on the arm of the desk chair, stood
erect. He looked at Davy, disappointment naked in his eyes, and
said, "Get rid of this." He kicked the dying man with the toe
of his shoe. A final sigh escaped the editor's lips. His body
lurched in one last paroxysm.

Clyde felt her stomach roil in shock. The murder, the taking of a human life had been done so dispassionately and it had
happened so quickly she could barely comprehend what had
happened.

"I'll take care of it," Westendorf volunteered and, after wrapping the body in a blanket to control the blood, he and Max left
the room dragging the editor's body between them. Copious
gouts of blood left a wide, red trail on the floor.

Once Westendorf and Max had left, Beck returned his attention to her and Sam. He seemed in no hurry. In fact, his
mood, while not as charming, was reminiscent of the evening
he'd brought the wine to her table. "I'm very sorry you had to
be exposed to such unpleasantness."

Grace, at Beck's order, had moved into the room. Wide-
eyed and trembling, she busied herself with the packing, snif-

fling quietly. Although they were obviously in a hurry, Horace smiled, savoring the moment. He straightened the handsome golden oak desk chair and sat down again.

"That ring you were holding, Miss Colby," he said, brandishing the silver band. "It was my father's. It is very special, the *Totenkopfring* or what you would call a Death's Head Ring. It was given within the SS to recognize personal achievement, devotion to duty and loyalty to Hitler. This Sig-rune," he pointed to the backward N, "represents the recipient's membership in the SS." He gestured to Grace.

At Beck's direction, she retrieved the jewelry box from the top shelf of the trunk where Clyde had left it. She handed it to Beck who replaced the ring and snapped the top shut. "My father received his ring for his service to *der Fuhrer* at Auschwitz."

"Auschwitz?" The sound of Sam's voice surprised her and she looked quickly to her left where Sam, arms tied behind his back like hers, was pushing himself up, and supporting himself against the wall as she had.

Beck nodded, his clear blue eyes distracted. "My father was a hero, but he spent his last days in hiding. We moved constantly because always those swine," and he spoke the word as if it were a curse, "Always they were looking for him." Even looking back from the space of decades, Beck's anger and outrage were evident.

"Auschwitz?" Sam repeated and Beck smiled.

It was a smile that literally made Clyde shiver. It touched his red mouth where the corners curved upward ever so slightly. It pushed up the flesh of his cheeks, giving him a slightly cherubic look. But the eyes. She thought back to the first time she had come to believe evil really existed. It was while she had been interviewing a man who had raped and murdered three young boys. The void in that man's eyes, the absence of soul had chilled her then as Beck's eyes did now for they, too, were vacant, soulless.

"Auschwitz was the scene of my father's greatest success, even though Rudolf Hess took the credit," he was saying. "My father was a doctor at Auschwitz, a member of the *Sanitatsdienstgrade* charged with the euthanasia of the Jews and other undesirables and the supervision of the *Desinfektoren* or disinfectors."

"But Eli," Clyde interjected, "why Eli? The war is over. Why did you kill Eli?"

He looked at her sternly. "He was getting too close. But pinning the Star of David to Nussbaum's coat was a mistake. It was too soon. Officer Reeves, the officer responsible for that assignment, was disciplined. He jeopardized our group. But only by exceeding his orders in his zeal because the Jews are the eternal enemies of the Aryan race."

Clyde started to reply.

"Now please, Miss Colby. No more interruptions," he scolded as if she were a schoolgirl. "My father," he continued, his voice laced with pride, "was confronted with what seemed to be an insurmountable sanitary problem, that of exterminating hundreds of these undesirables in an economical and efficient manner. I don't need to tell you this was a tremendous difficulty. And it was my father solving it. It was my father, Wilhelm Beck, who advised using the Zyklon B."

Clyde shifted her glance to the closet, thinking of the canisters Sam had found only moments earlier.

"Yes, Miss Colby," he said, following the direction of her gaze. "I have the Zyklon B, too." Beck chuckled. "It was appropriate to use pesticide to exterminate human pests. But I digress. I, too, have made good use of the substance."

An unfocused expression glossed his eyes for a brief moment. She glimpsed the crags and craters of the man's inner landscape and realized that Horace Beck was completely mad. He was charming and delightful to the public—especially to his guests, and he masked his lack of emotional balance brilliantly. Well, most of the time.

"My father would finally be proud of me," he was saying. "I have often thought it would be so good to be able to talk about my killing chamber with him."

Grace, who'd been packing the trunk, slammed the lid.

"This is ready," she said, addressing Beck who rose and neatly closed the roll top of the desk.

"Killing chamber?" Sam questioned and she marveled at his calm.

"Yes," Beck responded. "You have been in my killing chamber."

"Room seventeen," Clyde breathed.

"Yes, Miss Colby."

"The bed. The bed, on which you stupidly thought I believed you were pleasuring yourselves, is on rollers. I designed the mechanism myself. My father always said I had superior mechanical aptitude."

Clyde looked away. She wasn't sure why, but she knew it was important not to let him know that she and Sam had uncovered his secret behind the supply closet.

Beck swiveled at the sound of Max and Westendorf returning. The two men appeared in the doorway. Max whispered something to Davy who turned pale. Standing next to Westendorf, he brushed sweat from his forehead. Westendorf had a strange expression on his face that Clyde couldn't decipher. It was obvious something was wrong.

"Father—" Davy began but paused, apparently unable to continue.

"What? What?" Beck demanded and Westendorf moved further into the room.

"The synagogue, Horace. Somebody tipped the sheriff's department and they found and disarmed the bombs."

Beck was quiet for a long moment. His bushy eyebrows straightened into a rigid line. Clyde felt a surge of joy. Thank God they'd called from the Rattlesnake's Den. Beck looked at Grace for a long moment, then asked, "The men?"

Westendorf took a deep breath. "Captured."

The lines around Horace's full mouth hardened, looking as if they were trapped in concrete. "Our men will not betray us. They will die first." His eyes grew even colder.

"Grace," he growled. The expression on his face, his bushy white eyebrows had soared, his mouth had tightened. "You have work to do. You are not yourself packed and we have much to do and not much time."

Wordless, she nodded and backed out of the bedroom.

"As I was saying," he continued smoothly, "the bed is on tracks. It is transported into my killing chamber. I will show you." He went to the corner of the room and pulled back a corner of the carpet, then removed a square of wood.

"Frank, Max, bring them over here," he instructed the waiter and the police chief. They did as they were told.

Clyde, shoved by Westendorf, walked unwillingly to where Beck stood. Sam by her side, she stared at the floor, following Beck's pointing finger.

At first, she didn't understand what she was seeing. The floor beneath the carpet was wood. Pine. But beneath the section of wood Beck had removed, she saw what looked like a piece of dark glass about four feet square. Next to the glass, a square of metal was imbedded in the floor. In the center of the metal square was a hinged door.

"I don't understand," she said.

He knelt beside them and lifted the hinged top. "Into this, I drop the Zyklon B pellets. They fall through the vent into the room below and as soon as the crystallized Prussic acid is exposed to air, it becomes the gas. It works quickly, although the speed depends on, among other factors, the amount of humidity in the atmosphere. It paralyzes the lungs. Sometimes my victims, who are lying on the bed, never even wake up. At least, not until a few moments before they die."

"And this," Sam said, "is how you killed the business executives."

"Exactly. I am so pleased you comprehend."

"You took a terrible chance killing Mr. Lanken and Penny so close together," Clyde said. The bonds were tight and her wrists were stinging, pain was singing up the nerves of her arms, but she focused on her question. "Why did you kill two men so soon? Always before there were only one or two deaths a year."

"We received an extremely generous offer for Mr. Dunn. It came at the last moment. And we knew we were leaving."

"But why did you need so much money?" Sam asked. "You've turned Far Horizons into a very profitable enterprise. And you've got other investments around town. Plus royalties from your inventions."

Beck nodded. "But I did not raise the money for myself. Or for my family." He left them in the corner and joined Davy who was taking the clothes from the closet and putting them in suitcases. "Not even for Davy, who is the future." It was obvious he had already forgotten Davy's earlier failure to shoot Binky Beresford.

Davy looked around and smiled at his father. The love he felt for his father was so obvious, but Clyde couldn't help but wonder how he could love such a madman.

"No," Beck said, patting his son on the shoulder before turning back to Sam and Clyde, "this money is going back to Germany. Now that the reunification of Germany has been accomplished, we can return and resume our work. Pick up where my father and the party left off. And this money, this $25 million, will be put to good uses.

"Returning to the homeland, it will be wonderful. Davy can marry a good German girl and have a real life." Then, as if caught by a long-suppressed need to boast, he added a final layer of horror. "We are part of a worldwide group. We are the sons and the grandsons of the heroes of the Third Reich. The world has not heard the last of us."

"But your *Kristallnacht* plot—"

"Was foiled. And we shall take care of the traitor." He glanced toward Grace who was packing dishes and crystal from the china closet in the sitting room. "But that," Beck said with a pleasant smile, "will be none of your concern."

His face hardened as he realized what Grace was packing. "No, no. You idiot!" he yelled. "Not those ridiculous dishes! We will buy new. These are too heavy. They break so easy. I told you!"

Grace, tears in her eyes, re-entered Beck's bedroom. Sweat

had created a pattern on her white blouse with its familiar sunset logo. "But Mr. Beck, we've had them since we were married," she began.

"I told you no," he said decisively and turned to Frank Westendorf. "We are finished in here. Bring them." Beck's expression changed only slightly, but his eyes were vicious, soulless. "Now Miss Colby, Mr. McKenzie."

Clyde had been lulled in part by Beck's explanation and by what she now realized was the unrealistic hope that Beck meant them no harm, that he would escape to Germany and leave them alive. Now she stared at the canister of Zyklon B, which Davy, in cleaning out the closet earlier, had left on the floor. With a deadly sureness, she knew precisely what Beck had in mind for them. The image of Dawn's lifeless body in the room below flashed before her eyes. They would be joining Dawn and, if Beck were successful, soon they would gasp for breath, their lungs would be paralyzed and they would choke for oxygen. She felt her mouth rearrange itself into a maw of dread.

"You always surprise me, Miss Colby," Beck said. "Your perception. You are very quick. Especially for a woman."

Next to her, she could feel Sam struggling with his bonds. "Tell me, too, Horace," he demanded.

Beck smiled. "Ask Miss Colby, she understands."

Sam looked at Clyde and she nodded toward the canister.

Sam said slowly, "It won't work, Horace." Speaking more rapidly, he added, "You'll be caught and brought back. We have friends. And Miss Colby is a well-known television personality. Questions will be asked."

"I know," Beck said, his amusement barely suppressed. "Even as we speak, the sheriff's deputies or FBI or the DEA are speeding to your rescue. Correct?"

"Believe it," Sam said in a strong, convincing voice.

"FBI?" Clyde said. "DEA?" Where did that come from she wondered. Then she understood and had to give Sam credit for trying. A bluff. And a good one, at least from the standpoint of the conviction in Sam's deep, self-possessed voice.

Grace was standing on the threshold, scanning the room with grief-filled eyes. "Mr. Beck," she murmured. "Davy."

"Clyde!" Sam yelled, looking toward her. Beck and Davy followed the direction of his eyes and their attention was diverted. Sam launched himself at Beck, knocking him to the floor. "Run, Clyde."

And she tried, hobbling awkwardly, but Westendorf was too quick and Davy balled his fist and, as if to make amends to his father for not killing Beresford, he slugged Sam again and again. In the stomach. In the kidneys. He drew his fist back once more, but Beck called out, "No, Davy. He must be conscious."

Grace looked at Davy with tears in her eyes then came forward. She put her left arm behind Clyde's waist and grasped Clyde's right forearm in a fierce grip. "I will take Miss Colby down, Mr. Beck."

Clyde struggled away as something sharp pierced her hip.

"Get away from her, Grace. Frank. Max. Take them down. Grace, get out of here. You know what you have to do. Do it. You have made arrangements for a car on the mainland?" He barked orders and Clyde could just imagine the man his father had been.

Grace nodded. "Yes, Mr. Beck, a rental car will be waiting for us at the city pier."

Struggling, Clyde and Sam were hustled out into the corridor. She dragged her feet, desperate to delay their captors, but they pulled her along as if she were weightless. Westendorf's Luger was firmly ensconced in Sam's ribs and she cringed at the thought it might accidentally go off.

"Miss Colby, if you or Mr. McKenzie make any noise," Westendorf said, "I will not hesitate to shoot Mr. McKenzie." He removed a silencer from his pocket and screwed it into the Luger's barrel, all the while speaking in such an emotionless voice she had no doubt he would do it. Sam looked at her with such regret she wanted to cry. Except that she didn't have time. She had to think. There must be something they could do, but what?

As they proceeded down the hall toward the elevators, she

was cheered by the fact that Beck did not accompany them, but stood watching in the open door. The odds were better. Once they reached the lift, Beck retreated back into his suite. The sound of his door closing echoed down the corridor toward them.

Their pace continued steady, inexorable. Their destination loomed with such finality, Clyde dared not think of what lay ahead. Did this death hurt? Did it take long? She remembered the half hour between the sounds of the motor she'd heard that first night. Did that mean it took a half hour to die?

In the ride down to the first floor, Clyde went over everything that had happened in Beck's killing chamber. She searched her memory for whatever she could remember of its dimensions.

The details.

Anything about the tracks.

The bed.

Room seventeen.

Surely there must be a way to escape. But despite her attempts, she had no moment of sudden revelation. In fact, the more she thought about it, the more obvious it became that their only chance lay in escaping either in the corridor or once they were in room seventeen. If Westendorf and Max ever got them into the chamber where Dawn's body was, they were as good as dead, too.

They were at the door now. Davy let go of her arm as he turned away and inserted the keycard in the slot. He bent slightly at the waist and a flicker of hope was born. This was her chance. With her eyes on Sam's, she sagged to the floor and kicked upward with her hobbled feet. She struck between Max's legs with as much force as she could muster. He howled with pain and dropped the keycard, but instead of letting go, he grabbed her by the hair, pulling her up so that he could grab her by the throat.

Sam twisted his body, drew back his right foot and kicked Frank in the shin. With a curse, Westendorf released his hold. Using his body as a battering ram, Sam threw himself against

Max trying to free her. The attempt was futile for even though tears of pain were streaming down Max's cheeks, he clutched her neck in a death grip.

She saw Frank ball his fist. She saw the fist coming and realized too late it was directed toward her. She tried to duck, but without success. She heard the thud of bone striking bone, but before she could feel the pain, Clyde dropped off the edge of the world into a black void.

TWENTY-TWO

THE PAIN RETURNED FIRST. After that, awareness surged back by degrees. Clyde realized it was her jaw that ached. After isolating the pain in her jaw, she realized her wrists and her shoulders hurt as well. She opened her eyes. She was lying on her side, wrists bound behind her, on a bed next to Sam who was also lying on his side, his back to her. He struggled with his ropes, which were connected to hers, preventing them from rolling away from each other toward either edge of the bed. She glanced around.

Where were they?

The antique furniture, the dead game on the walls, the hunting prints swam into view as her vision cleared.

Room seventeen. And they were alone.

Now she became aware of another pain. This one wasn't as hurtful as the others, but it was new. She had something sharp in her jeans pocket, something digging into the flesh of her buttocks.

"Sam," she said softly, not sure whether or not the room was bugged.

"Hi, honey," he whispered in weary pain. A fresh cut on his forehead was bleeding. His jaw was swelling. His black shirt was ripped. "You okay?"

She tried to smile, but her jaw was so sensitive, it hurt when she moved her mouth. Instead, she nodded and even that small movement caused a twinge.

"We're in big trouble," Sam said. "But I'm working on getting these knots loose. If only we have time—"

"There's something sharp poking in my back pocket. If I roll toward you, could you get it out?"

"You don't know what it is?" He didn't wait for her answer. "Let's try it."

Head throbbing, shoulders stiff and cramped, Clyde maneuvered herself closer while Sam reached back. She felt his hands fumbling in her hip pocket.

"It feels like a pair of small scissors. Manicure scissors maybe. Lie still." His voice was hushed.

"Grace," she whispered.

"What?"

"Grace must have put them there. When we were in Horace's room."

As she lay in the room where death was such a frequent guest, the sound of an engine cut the stillness. The bed they were lying on shuddered. The tremor was slight, but Clyde knew what it signaled. The grinding sound of the motor was the noise she had heard that first night. She heard a whishing sound and twisted her neck around. The wall behind the bed was parting.

The bed jerked, and began sliding backward. "Oh, God, Sam," she urged, "hurry."

"I am," he said and she could feel him sawing with the scissors against her ropes.

The bed slid smoothly on the tracks.

"Sam!" she screamed, no longer worried about whether they were being monitored.

"Twist your wrists."

The bed ground to a halt and the two sections of the wall slid together behind them. They lay in the dark. She moved her wrists, trying to help. Her ropes frayed, separated and she was free. She didn't know whether to laugh or cry.

"You did it."

She felt the bed shift as Sam was now able to roll away from her. Even in the dark, she quickly found his hands, took the scissors from them and hacked at the twine. She paused, losing precious seconds when a ray of light from above penetrated the darkness. She looked up and saw Beck's face framed in the window in the ceiling.

"Sam." She knew fear underscored her voice.

"Never mind. Get me loose."

Focus, she told herself. *Focus.*

She continued her efforts, but the manicure scissors were small and the rope was at least a half-inch thick. She almost burst into tears when the scissors broke. But she took one of the blades and continued hacking until at last the rope parted. Sam ripped the rest of the bonds from his wrists and rubbed them.

And then a sound, a tiny sound she would never forget if she lived reverberated throughout the killing chamber.

The sound of pebbles striking concrete. And she knew the falling objects weren't pebbles.

They were pellets of Zyklon B.

And, in a matter of minutes, those pellets would be transformed into gaseous prussic acid.

"Clyde." Sam's voice was calm. If he could be calm, she could, too. "On your side is the supply closet wall. Find where I broke through earlier tonight. Push over the shelves on the other side. Get out."

"What about you?"

His voice was muffled when he answered. It came from somewhere below. *On the floor,* she wondered.

"When I checked out Dawn's body, I saw a piece of loose track." He rolled over.

She heard the strident, screeching noise of a piece of metal being ripped from the floor.

A new and alien sound invaded their space. She froze.

A hissing.

With a frantic cry, she felt along the wall until she found the rough edges of the torn duct. She reached through and pushed against the shelf on the other side.

No luck.

Was this what Penny had experienced? And Greg Lanken? Were they awake when they died?

She shoved again.

The hissing was louder. How much time did they have?

She met resistance on the other side and the hissing was quieter as if the transformation from pellet to lethal gas was closer to completion.

Desperation and determination vied for her energy. They would not die like this. Not here. And not now.

She felt Sam on the bed beside her.

"Got it," he said, waving the section of steel track. "A weapon. We need something. Together, Clyde. Got to do this together," he instructed. "One, two—"

Before he could say three, she heard the shattering of the glass in the ceiling and a shot. The bullet whined and ricocheted off the concrete wall in front of them. Above them she heard a muffled curse and saw Davy trip in reaction to the recoil of the gun. Then he was hurtling through the window.

Sam shifted his arm and the shard of track penetrated Davy's solar plexus as he landed. The impalement was so complete the steel glittered as it emerged from Davy's back and the young German collapsed on the bed.

Above, Clyde heard a soul-piercing cry of agony. "My son, my son. You killed my son." It was Beck's voice, but unrecognizable in its anger and grief.

Focus, Clyde. Focus.

She drew back and kicked with both feet against the shelving. But this time, finally, she heard the incredibly beautiful thuds and thumps of bottles and boxes striking the bare concrete floor on the other side of the wall.

Air suddenly flooded in. And light.

"Sam," she called, gulping in huge breaths of air.

But he didn't respond. She whirled and looked back through the vent. To her amazement, he was standing on the bed struggling with Beck, whose face was a mask of rage and madness.

Beck was trying to aim the cumbersome Luger he held in his hand. Sam drew back his fist and struck Beck square on the right side of the jaw. Beck's eyes rolled up in his head. He fell onto the bed and rolled into the corner next to Dawn's body. Next to the pellets.

Beck choked, gasped for air.

"Don't come over here, Clyde," Sam said.

But it was too late.

She had hurried to his side to help, but she stopped. For there, in the shadow-ridden light illuminating the killing chamber, she saw Davy's violated body. A shard of steel, bloody now, jutted from his mid-section. Great gouts of blood spurted, spreading along the concrete in grotesque patterns.

Davy wasn't quite dead. His chest was moving, but weakly, barely rising and falling. He stared at them, recognition and pain mirrored in his eyes. Then the eyes glazed and the head slumped forward.

Sam reached over and pulled her head against his shoulder, blocking the sight. "Let's go," he said. "We're not out of this yet."

In the corner, Beck gasped and choked.

They squirmed through the duct and scrambled out of the chamber into the comparative safety of the supply closet. Hurriedly, they piled boxes and rags to block the ragged aperture of the air-intake duct.

Sam grabbed her arm. "Good enough. Let's get out of here."

As he pushed her ahead of him toward the door, they heard a strange rattle from within the chamber. Then silence. She knew without looking that both Beck and his son were dead.

Sam shoved the door open, looked up and down the hall then, seeing no one, reached back and grabbed her arm. He half dragged her down the corridor. On the far side of the office, he hesitated. To the left lay the lobby and beyond that the parking lot, to the right was the beach.

"Come on," he said turning right. "We've got to get to the launch. Westendorf brought the launch back."

They emerged onto the terrace, turned right, and headed for the dock where the resort's launch rocked in the tide, a white ghostlike silhouette in the graying light and fog of dawn. But as they hurried toward the boat, Clyde saw the running lights of another launch approaching rapidly. "Oh, my God, Sam. Beck's men. They escaped."

"Quick," Sam said. He ducked beneath the dock and she followed suit.

Standing there in chill water up to her ankles, huddled next to Sam for warmth, Clyde despaired. She knew the shock, the cold water, the biting air and fear were a deadly mixture, and even as the heat of Sam's body warmed her, her teeth chattered. The sound seemed outrageously loud. She was sure it could be heard by the men who were clambering out of the boat and jogging along the wooden dock over her head toward the resort.

One man stationed himself above them. She heard a crackling sound and then he said, "Yes sir, I've directed the men to secure the exits, sir."

"Sullivan?" Sam yelled. "Sullivan, is that you?"

"McKenzie? Where the hell are you?"

"Sullivan? What are you doing here?"

"FBI, man. Come out and I'll show you my badge."

Sam grabbed her in an embrace so fierce, she almost fell into the surf. "We're safe. We're really safe, Clyde."

He took her hand and dragged her out from under the pier. They staggered up the hard-packed sand to the pier. The burly bartender was descending the steps. "Bring me up to speed, Sam."

Sam briefed him on Westendorf, then the deaths of Beck and Davy. "Stay here until we get the place secured," Sullivan ordered and they waited.

As they walked up the beach toward the resort accompanied by six other agents wearing black windbreakers with FBI stenciled on the backs, Clyde asked, "The FBI? Then you weren't bluffing back there?"

Sullivan chuckled. "I've been investigating reports of neo-Nazi activity on Rattlesnake Key for several months. We got a tip from the Sheriff's Department after the attempted bombing of the synagogue, but I have to admit I wasn't sure we would make it in time. Wait here." He disappeared into the resort. Lights were appearing in different windows and she wondered what the guests must think.

Clyde was numb. It would take time to absorb the fact that it was truly over and they were safe. It would take time to grieve for Penny and Eli and Dawn, time to deal with the corruption

and evil. Time to worry about the show, the television career
that had been in the shadow for days.

For now, she felt nothing. Then it hit her. She was starved.
She desperately wanted a cheeseburger. And French fries. And
a double chocolate milkshake. Yet in the next moment, she was
overwhelmed by bone-numbing exhaustion.

It seemed to take hours, but by her watch it was only twenty
minutes before the agents, Sullivan in the lead, returned to
their launch. Two agents escorted Westendorf whose hand-
cuffs glittered in the illumination from the security light. Grace
followed, head down, also escorted by agents, also handcuffed.

"I need you to come with us to the office," Sullivan said.
"We need to get your statements."

They boarded the launch. Clyde tried to thank Grace, but
the woman was completely unresponsive.

"Shock," Sullivan said. "We'll take her to the hospital on the
mainland."

The waters of Palmetto Bay were choppy, but Clyde didn't
mind. Sullivan wrapped a blanket around her and Sam kept his
arm around her until they reached the yacht basin. Once they
reached the sheriff's department, they were taken to a temporary office on loan to the FBI agents because there was no local
bureau. Sullivan insisted they both swallow hot coffee laced
with brandy. Fortified and finally warm, Clyde managed to
focus while dictating her statement. Sam briefed Sullivan completely, telling him where they'd find the rest of the men and
the evidence of the Neo-Nazi plot and the murder-for-hire
scheme. Clyde explained about Eli's notes and room seventeen
and the killing chamber.

And Dawn.

WHEN THEY WERE FREE to leave, they emerged into bright sunlight. Sullivan directed one of the agents to give them a lift to the
Rattlesnake Key Marina. The causeway was open again, and the
trip back to the island was much shorter than their journey earlier
that night. As they walked down the wooden pier, Clyde mused
that the pervious night all seemed like a dream—or a nightmare.

Safely on board the *Sanity* in the clean morning light, after a long shower and several belts of Sam's Glenlivet, Clyde finally fell asleep in the cabin. When she awoke, the sun was low in the sky and Sam was next to her. His arms were wrapped securely around her.

She yawned and stretched and went back to sleep.

The next time she awoke, the sky was dark. A glance at her wristwatch told her it was about 8:00 PM. She was alone in bed. When she called Sam, he answered, telling her to join him on the deck.

She slipped on one of his shirts and padded, barefoot, to join him. The lights of Palmetto Bay glittered low on the horizon and she was reminded of the night, only days ago, when she and Penny had been sitting here. This time, although the grief was still there, she felt a sense of peace because Penny would be avenged. The information they had uncovered would be helpful in halting the activities of Neo-Nazi groups in a number of cities around the United States.

Beck's men were in custody. And the bombs had been found and deactivated. The *Kristallnacht* observation at the synagogue had been held without incident.

As she leaned against the *Sanity's* railing, Clyde thought of Grace. Her son was dead. And her husband. And she was in the hospital for the moment. Even worse, according to Sullivan, Grace would probably have to do jail time. Clyde was determined to help her. There were mitigating circumstances. Grace deserved to get a break because she'd saved their lives. Clyde hated to think where she and Sam would be if Grace hadn't slipped those manicure scissors into her jeans pocket.

Sam handed her his glass and she took a sip. "I'll fix you one if you want it, honey," he said and she shook her head.

"Dinner would be good," she said.

"Already in the works, just waiting for you to get up. By the way, Andy called. He wants you to call. My cell phone is on the bureau."

"Later," she said. "I'm starved."

This time, Sam got it right. The table was nicely if informally appointed, reminiscent of a country kitchen in France. Red and white napkins and tablecloth. The meal was simple, a hearty beef stew Sam had cooked all afternoon in a crock pot. Crunchy French bread. A rich Burgundy wine. Crisp garden salad with a vinaigrette dressing. Fresh strawberries and a nice Brie for dessert.

After two helpings of stew and chunks of the bread not to mention two glasses of wine, Clyde felt wonderful. She helped Sam with the dishes.

"I've got a great idea," Sam said as he dried the last wine goblet. "Why don't we take a long weekend and go gunkholing?"

"Gunkholing?"

"Yeah. Gunkholing. Just sail down the coast and drop anchor wherever it looks good to us."

She sighed. "That sounds wonderful. I'll have to call Dad to ask him to take care of the cats for a few more days. That will depend on how well he and Tyler are getting along. And I'll have to call the station because I'm supposed to be back first thing in the morning. "

He held her at arm's length. "So listen, Clyde, after what we've been through together, I've got a right to know what your real name is."

"I'll make a deal with you."

"A deal?"

"Yes. You tell me what your bet with Penny was and I'll tell you my name."

"You first," he said.

She cringed, but nodded in agreement. "Clytemnestra," she confessed after a moment.

"I beg your pardon?"

"That's my name. Clytemnestra. But don't use it. Ever. I'm officially Clyde."

"What kind of mother would even think to name her offspring Clytemnestra?"

She laughed. "One of Greek descent who was both mad at her husband and her offspring. From what I've been told, and too many times to count, I might add, I gave Mother Iris nine months of absolute hell. And her labor was no picnic either. By the time of their divorce, I was so close to my Dad everybody called us Big Clyde and Little Clyde." She slapped him playfully, gently. "Hey, what about that bet?"

"Bet?"

"Yeah, the one you and Penny had."

"Penny," he said, putting his dishcloth carefully over the drawer handle to dry and taking her face in his big hands, "bet me I couldn't get you to tell me your real name." He bent and kissed her.

"And the prize?"

He laughed. "You are the prize."

The cell phone rang. He cursed, answered, listened and handed it to her.

"Clyde," Andy's voice resounded in her ear. "You've got to get back to Miami. Pronto."

"Can't do it. I've made plans."

"Well unmake them. You've made network news and Rod wants you back here no later than 8:00 AM. Rested. Looking good. The story about the Neo-Nazis is going to break nationwide with you as some kind of pop heroine, and he figures your involvement will give the cooking show a great kick-off. We've already had calls from GMA and the Today Show."

"Damn, Andy, Sam and I were going to—"

"Clyde, you've got to get back here. On the double. This exposure will get our show up and running much sooner than we had hoped. I'll see you first thing in the morning. Do you want me to pick you up at the lighthouse?"

"No," she said slowly, "I'll meet you at the station."

Sam had come to stand behind her. He had his arms around her waist. She disconnected and turned to Sam. "I've got good news and bad news. Which do you want first?" She twisted in his arms to look up at him.

Sam looked down at her; his chocolate brown eyes were warm and inviting. "I don't want *any* news, Clytemnestra." He kissed her again, fitting his mouth against hers, leeching her will.

Much later, when the moon was riding high against a black

velvet sky, after they had packed her belongings in her room at Far Horizons and loaded them into a rental car, she kissed him goodbye. The hard part was no longer learning to trust Sam. Now she had to work on revealing herself to him, letting him into her world.

"What are you doing for Thanksgiving?" she asked. "It's only two weeks away."

"Cooking," he said. "With you."

"Splendid," she responded feeling an incredible sense of relief that he would still want to see her, even though she was leaving, and grateful that he could understand how much her career and the show meant to her. "You can meet Big Clyde and the fearsome foursome. The cats. We'll see if they approve of you. And I have this great recipe for stuffing. Instead of chestnuts, you use swamp cabbage."

"Classy Florida crackers," he chided as he closed the door on the driver's side of her rental, "call it hearts of palm."

She pulled out of the parking lot onto Matecumbe Road. But a few miles later, as she turned onto the causeway, she was thinking that she had to tell Eli's story. And Horace Beck's. She owed it to Eli and Eliahu to do the best she could to be sure Americans knew the Nazi fascist threat had not really ended in 1945, that it was alive, and called for constant vigilance.

Her cell phone rang. Andy again. More instructions. As she disconnected, she made a mental note to stop off at a supermarket on the way home. She'd have to pick up some cucumbers. They were great eye fresheners. She couldn't have dark circles under her eyes when she reported to the station in the morning. And she was going to need tons of ice for her swollen jaw and tons of makeup to conceal the bruises.

And she'd have to be sure to pick up some Scotch for her dad or he'd never baby-sit the cats again. Tyler. Humdinger. Homer Sue. Pearl. It would be great to see the brat cats. Even if she had to put up with being totally ignored until they decided to forgive her for abandoning them.

From her over-sized purse on the passenger's seat, she pulled out her tape recorder and began making notes for the show.

APPENDIX

Chef Henri Doucette, of The Far Horizons Resort, is pleased to share with Clyde's readers some of his favorite recipes including those featured in Clyde Colby's Gourmet Galley TV show.

CHEF HENRI DOUCETTE'S RECIPE FOR GASPARILLA PAPAYA SOUP

INGREDIENTS
2-1/2 cups papaya*, chopped fine
3 cups chicken bouillon or stock
6 cloves garlic
1 cup cream
Salt and pepper to taste
1 teaspoon thyme
1 teaspoon parsley
1/2 cup chopped celery greens

DIRECTIONS
Boil bouillon, papaya and garlic
Add cream
Simmer gently
Add spices
Puree all in food processor or blender. Adjust thickness with more bouillon, if needed. Stir in celery greens for color and flavor.

Yield: 5 servings.

*An herb with melonlike fruit, the papaya grows as a plant. When ripe, the meat is bright orange to red in color with shiny, grayish black seeds.

CHEF DOUCETTE'S RECIPE FOR
AVOCADO* EN GELEE

INGREDIENTS
1-1/8 teaspoon unflavored gelatin
1-1/2 cup cold water
1-1/2 to 2 cups mashed avocado
1/4 cup lemon juice
1 stalk celery, sliced very thin
1/2 cup peeled and chopped tomato
2 green onions, chopped
1 tablespoon chopped chilies
1 teaspoon salt
1/4 teaspoon red pepper sauce
Salad greens for serving bed
Ripe olives
Tomato wedges or cherry tomatoes

DIRECTIONS
Sprinkle gelatin on 1/2 cup of the cold water in saucepan. Stir over low heat until dissolved. Stir in rest of cold water. Refrigerate until slightly thickened (Approximately 40 minutes). Mix avocado and lemon juice in large bowl. Stir in gelatin mixture, celery, tomato, onions, chilies, salt and pepper.

Pour into 4 cup mold. Refrigerate until firm, approximately 3 to 4 hours. Prior to serving, unmold on bed of greens and garnish with olives, tomatoes and whatever you select to make a nice presentation.

Yield: 6 to 8 servings.

*The avocado is also called the alligator pear by Florida crackers because the fruit is pear shaped and the skin has a thick, rough texture similar to the hide of an alligator. The skin is dark green to purple in color. Grows on trees seldom taller than 30 feet. The flesh is a pale or yellowish-green when ripe.

CHEF HENRI DOUCETTE'S RECIPE FOR
ACAPULCO KEY LIME SNAPPER

INGREDIENTS
1/4 cup chopped green onion
2 tablespoons unsalted butter
2 tomatoes, chopped
3 tablespoons fresh Key lime* juice
2 tablespoons chopped fresh green chilies
1 tablespoon chopped fresh parsley
1/8 teaspoon salt
1/8 teaspoon garlic salt
Dash pepper
1 pound red snapper
Lime wedges

DIRECTIONS:
Sauté onion in unsalted butter until tender. Add remaining ingredients except fish and Key lime wedges. Bring to boil, reduce heat and simmer 10 minutes. Place snapper in skillet, spoon sauce over fish, cover, simmer 10 minutes or until fish flakes easily when tested with fork. Serve with Key lime wedges.

Makes 4 servings.

*Key limes are wonderfully juicy. The trees bear almost year round. The fruit is deep green turning yellow when ripe.

CHEF HENRI DOUCETTE'S RECIPE FOR
CALABAZA FLAN

INGREDIENTS:
1-2/3 cups sugar
3 cups thin cream
2 cups strained calabaza*
1 teaspoon salt
1/2 cup Jamaican rum
6 eggs

DIRECTIONS:
Put a cup of granulated sugar into a round, deep, ovenproof dish and allow it to melt over low heat, stirring constantly. When it is an even, deep amber, remove from the heat and tip quickly in all directions so the sides and the bottom of the dish will be coated.

In the meantime, scald cream; add calabaza, salt, remaining 2/3 cup sugar, rum and eggs, slightly beaten.

Pour this mixture into the dish, place it in a pan of water and bake at 350 degrees for one hour or until a knife inserted into the center comes out shining clean.

Allow to cool, then invert onto a round serving tray. The bottom will be shiny brown.

Serve chilled or warm, flaming with rum.

Serves 6-8.

*Calabaza is a squash. Its size, shape and skin coloring may vary, but it has firm yellow flesh with a delicate flavor like Hubbard or Butternut Squash. May weigh 20 pounds or more.

CHEF HENRI DOUCETTE'S RECIPE FOR
CONCH FRITTERS

INGREDIENTS:
1 cup ground conch* (about 10 ounces)
1 medium onion, chopped fine
1 stalk celery, chopped fine
3 tablespoons Worcestershire sauce
1 tablespoon tomato paste
1 cup flour
1 egg, slightly beaten
1-1/2 teaspoons baking powder
Vegetable oil for frying
Seafood cocktail sauce

DIRECTIONS:
Thoroughly blend conch, onion, celery, Worcestershire sauce,
tomato paste, flour, egg and baking powder.
Heat oil to 375 degrees. Drop batter by rounded teaspoons into
oil. Fry until deeply browned, about 4 minutes. Serve with
cocktail sauce.

Yield: about 16.

* The conch is a mollusk with white meat. Its name is derived
from the Greek word meaning shell.

CHEF HENRI DOUCETTE'S RECIPE FOR CONCH SALAD

INGREDIENTS:
2-1/2 pounds of fresh conch

MARINADE:
1 cup Key lime juice
1/2 cup white vinegar
1/2 cup vegetable oil
1 tablespoon Worcestershire sauce

SALAD:
2 cups coarsely chopped red onions
2 cups coarsely chopped green peppers
2 cups chopped celery
2 cups coarsely chopped tomatoes

DIRECTIONS:
Chop conch. Combine marinade ingredients and marinate conch in refrigerator for 24 hours. Toss conch with salad ingredients. Refrigerate until ready to serve. Serve on a bed of lettuce.

Serves 12.

CHEF HENRI DOUCETTE'S RECIPE FOR
GUAVA CHUTNEY

INGREDIENTS:
1 stick cinnamon, broken
6 whole cloves
4 whole allspice
4 whole cardamom pods
3 cups peeled, coarsely chopped ripe guavas*
1 cup chopped onion
1/2 cup firmly packed brown sugar
1/3 cup golden raisins
1/2 cup cider vinegar
1/2 cup unsweetened apple juice
1 teaspoon mustard seeds
1 teaspoon peeled, grated ginger root
1 clove garlic, minced

DIRECTIONS:
Place first four ingredients on a cheesecloth square. Bring
edges of cheesecloth together at top; tie securely. Combine
guava, spice bag and remaining ingredients in a medium pan.
Bring to a boil. Cover. Reduce heat. Simmer until tender. Un-
cover and cook 10 minutes until thickened. Spoon into bowl.
Cool. Remove spice bag. Cover and chill.

Yield: 3 cups.

* The guava is a tropical fruit that grows on trees. Fruits are
spherical, about an inch in diameter. Some varieties have a thin
yellow skin. The pulp is pink to dark red and good to eat as
picked.

CHEF HENRI DOUCETTE'S RECIPE FOR
KIWI TARTS

NUT CRUST:
16 ounces walnuts, chopped medium fine
2 sticks unsalted butter
1/3 cup sugar
3 cups flour
1 large egg, slightly beaten
1 teaspoon grated lemon rind
1-1/2 teaspoons vanilla

KIWI FILLING:
10 ripe kiwi* fruits, peeled and sliced crosswise in 1/8 inch slices
1/2 cup apricot glaze (recipe follows)

TART SHELL:
Preheat oven to 350 degrees. In electric mixer, cream butter with sugar. Add flour, walnuts, egg, flavorings. Mix well so dough holds together. Divide dough in half. Lightly butter two 9-inch quiche pans with removable bottoms. Press nut mixture evenly into bottom and sides of pans. Bake 10 to 12 minutes. Crust can be frozen for future use.

APRICOT GLAZE:
Soften 1/2 package of gelatin in 3 tablespoons Cognac or Grand Marnier. Add to jam and heat over low flame until smooth and clear. Cool slightly.

FILLING:
BRUSH TART SHELL WITH APRICOT GLAZE.
Arrange slices of kiwi fruit in shell. Brush with glaze.
Chill tart until ready to serve.

* The kiwi fruit is ovoid in shape, roughly two to three inches in length and two inches in diameter. The skin is brown; the meat is green with many black seeds. To eat, cut in half and scoop fruit with spoon.

CHEF HENRI DOUCETTE'S RECIPE FOR PINK GRAPEFRUIT SORBET

INGREDIENTS:
3/4 cup sugar
2 1/4 cups pink grapefruit sections
1 cup fresh grapefruit juice
2 tablespoons grenadine
1 egg white

DIRECTIONS:
Place sugar in food processor or blender for about 30 seconds on high; remove and set to one side. Puree grapefruit sections in food processor; remove and set to one side. In saucepan, combine sugar, juice and grenadine; bring to a boil, stir until sugar is dissolved. Cool. Blend in grapefruit puree.

Pour into shallow baking dish and freeze until solid. Remove from freezer and let stand until slightly soft. Spoon into processor and mix until smooth. Add egg white and mix until mixture has a sheen. Pour into individual serving dishes, return to freezer until firm, at least 3 hours. Let stand to soften several minutes before serving.

Serves 6.

CHEF HENRI DOUCETTE'S RECIPE FOR
SEA GRAPE* MARMALADE

DIRECTIONS:

Pick fruit. Wash. Place in a large saucepan with water to cover. Boil until fruit is soft; strain through a colander. Save juice to make jelly.

Press fruit through colander. Measure; for each cup of strained fruit, add one cup of sugar, 1/4 cup lemon, lime or sour orange juice. Stir and cook until thick. Pour into sterilized jars. Seal.

* The sea grape grows wild near the seashore above salt water flood level. It has medium to large leaves that are thick and stiff, nearly round and marked with red veins. The sea grapes grow in clusters, 20 fruit per cluster. The grapes are 1/2 to 3/4 inch in diameter, creamy white to reddish purple.

CHEF HENRI DOUCETTE'S RECIPE FOR
TROPICAL SHRIMP SALAD

INGREDIENTS:
1/2 cup dairy sour cream
1/4 cup dovyalis* jelly
2 tablespoons bottled red wine vinegar and oil dressing
1 tablespoon soy sauce
1 teaspoon prepared mustard
1/4 teaspoon cinnamon
1 pound peeled, deveined shrimp, cooked and chilled
1 avocado, seeded, peeled and sliced
1 red sweet pepper, cut into thin strips
4 cherry tomatoes, halved
Lettuce leaves
1 papaya

DRESSING:
Stir together sour cream, dovyalis* jelly, dressing, soy sauce,
mustard and cinnamon. Cover and chill until serving time.

SERVING:
Line a large platter or dinner plates with lettuce. Peel papaya;
cut in half. Remove seeds; discard. Slice papaya. Arrange
shrimp, papaya, avocado and pepper strips atop lettuce. Garnish with tomatoes. When serving, spoon dressing on top of
salad.

Makes 4 to 6 main-dish servings.

DOVYALIS JELLY
2 cups dovyalis juice
3-1/2 cups sugar
1/4 cup liquid pectin
Bring juice to boil. Add sugar and pectin. Bring to rolling boil,
stirring constantly. Cook to jelly point. Remove from heat;
skim and pour into jelly glasses.

* The dovyalis is also known as the tropical apricot. Large shrub has small greenish-yellow flowers which appear September to January. The fruit's season is December to May. The fruit is round, reddish-purple with fuzz. The color of the flesh is apricot.

CHEF HENRI DOUCETTE'S RECIPE FOR SHARK WITH DILLED HOLLANDAISE

INGREDIENTS:
6 shark filets, about 8 ounces each, preferably black tip
2 tablespoons melted butter

DILLED HOLLANDAISE SAUCE:
6 egg yolks
1/4 cup fresh lemon juice
1/2 teaspoon salt
1/4 teaspoon paprika
1 teaspoon dried dill weed
1 cup butter, melted and sizzling hot
Parsley for garnish

DIRECTIONS:
Grill shark filets 3 to 4 minutes on each side, basting with melted butter. Transfer to heated platter. Combine egg yolks, lemon juice, salt, paprika and dill weed in food processor or blender. With blender running, add melted butter slowly but in a steady stream. Pour a small amount of sauce over each filet; garnish with parsley and serve. Put remaining sauce in a separate bowl to serve on the side.

HARLEQUIN®
INTRIGUE®

WE'LL LEAVE YOU BREATHLESS!

If you've been looking for thrilling tales of
contemporary passion and sensuous love stories
with taut, edge-of-the-seat suspense—then
you'll love Harlequin Intrigue!

Every month, you'll meet six new heroes
who are guaranteed to make your spine tingle
and your pulse pound. With them you'll enter
into the exciting world of Harlequin Intrigue—
where your life is on the line
and so is your heart!

THAT'S INTRIGUE—
ROMANTIC SUSPENSE
AT ITS BEST!

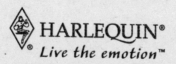